MW01244287

All the Ways We're Wrong

Thunderstruck, Book Three

Amelia Elliot

Acid Squirrel Media

ALL RIGHTS ARE RESERVED. No part of this book may be reproduced or transmitted in any form or by any means, electronic or mechanical, including photocopying and recording, or by any information storage and retrieval system, without prior permission in writing from both the publisher, Fitz & Ferd Ltd., and the author, Amelia Elliot, except in the case of brief quotations embodied in critical articles and reviews.

Warning: the unauthorized reproduction or distribution of this copyrighted work is illegal. Criminal copyright infringement, including infringement without monetary gain, is investigated by the FBI and is punishable by up to five years in prison and a fine of $250,000.

For more information, email copyright@ameliaelliot.com

Published by Fitz & Ferd Ltd. The names "Fitz & Ferd" and "Acid Squirrel Media" and their logos are trademarks of Fitz & Ferd Ltd.

Print ISBN: 979-8-9883734-5-2

Ebook ISBN: 979-8-9883734-4-5

Copyright © 2023 Amelia Elliot

https://ameliaelliot.com

This novel's story and characters are fictitious. Certain long-standing institutions, agencies, public offices, and well-known places and persons are mentioned, but the characters involved are wholly imaginary. The opinions expressed by the characters are those of the characters and should not be confused with the author or any real person, business, or agency.

Contents

For my sister.

This book contains mentions of rape (not shown) and Military Sexual Trauma, PTSD, child abuse (not shown), emotional abuse, and Attachment Disorder, explicit sex scenes, adult language, and the Oxford comma.

Playlist

Ava

Hard Out Here - Lily Allen

Gravity Is a B**ch - Miranda Lambert

Evacuate the Dancefloor - Cascada

Spice Up Your Life - Spice Girls

Perfect - Alanis Morissette

Party in the USA - Miley Cyrus

Circus - Britney Spears

Can't Get You Out of My Head - Kylie Minogue

Hands to Myself - Selena Gomez

God is a Woman - Ariana Grande

Red Blooded Woman - Kylie Minogue

Cake By the Ocean - DNCE

Shivers - Ed Sheeran

Your Love Is My Drug - Kesha

Love On The Brain - Rihanna

The Man - Taylor Swift

Hollaback Girl - Gwen Stefani

Confident - Demi Lovato

I Believe in You - Kylie Minogue

Killian

Old Time Rock & Roll - Bob Seger & The Silver Bullet Band

La Grange - ZZ Top

When the Levee Breaks - Led Zeppelin

Black Dog - Led Zeppelin

Going to California - Led Zeppelin

Stairway to Heaven - Led Zeppelin

Long Train Runnin' - The Doobie Brothers

Ramblin' Man - The Allman Brothers Band

Like a Rolling Stone - Bob Dylan

Hotel California - Eagles

Wish You Were Here - Pink Floyd

Foxey Lady - The Jimi Hendrix Experience

Hot Blooded - Foreigner

Born to Run - Bruce Springsteen

Sweet Emotion - Aerosmith

Heart of Gold - Neil Young

Hello Sunshine - Bruce Springsteen

Sunshine of Your Love - Cream

Lay, Lady, Lay - Bob Dylan

You can find links for this Playlist at
https://linktr.ee/ameliaelliot

You Can't Spell Amelia Without Email

Do you like fun stories, giveaways, and author confessionals? Want to know when Amelia's publishing her next book or how to get signed copies? Join her email list.

Don't worry, she won't spam you with a bunch of sales links. Amelia's emails will be the most fun you can have with your clothes on (besides her novels).

Follow the link (scan or click) to join in on the fun.

Chapter 1

K illian was relieved to see the hillside across the road staying put.

He leaned against the door frame of his one-room cabin, watching the hammering rain. It was pitch black, except for the illumination of the violent lightning. The flashes gave him brief glimpses of the rivulets rushing down the slope across the road.

He had been studying the mountain's rapid erosion for months. Wildfires had ravaged much of the area over the past two years, leaving the blackened ground soft and loose.

He stood under the eaves of the roof, getting splashed with mud from the force of the downpour. But he was too focused on his worries to move inside. There'd been an unseasonable amount of rain this year. Even though it'd been hot and sunny for the past two weeks, the water table was high, and the earth couldn't absorb this latest drenching.

Turning his head with the next lightning flash, he surveyed the campground. It was a Friday night in June, but the place was empty. For the past two months, a movie crew had occupied every cabin, tent space, and trailer hookup. But they had thankfully wrapped earlier that week, and as of that morning, they had all cleared out.

All except one. The star of the movie, a famous actress who looked like a blonde Jessica Rabbit come-to-life, had stayed. Ava Blum. He didn't know why she was still there. But her continued presence was adding to his anxiety about the water-logged mountainside.

Killian tried to reassure himself. This wasn't nearly as much rain as what he'd seen all winter and spring. While the inch of water that fell like a curtain was more than double what he would expect for all of June, it was a fraction of what had come down in May.

He hadn't worried in May. Although that was because he hadn't done the calculations yet. Since then, he'd taken measurements and confirmed that the ground alongside the road was unstable.

The road meandered past the cabins and doubled back, ending in a parking lot and scenic lookout on the crest above the campground. He thought about getting Little Miss Sex-on-a-Stick and driving her down to the motel along the highway. But he doubted he could convince her to get into a total stranger's truck. She would probably think he was a threat and give him hell.

For that matter, she might not be aware that he was even here at the campground. For the month that she'd stayed in a cabin a hundred feet from him, even though he'd been outside plenty of times, she hadn't so much as acknowledged his presence or glanced in his direction. Just another Hollywood snob.

The wind whipped around, driving the rain sideways into the mountain. He didn't want a dead movie star on his conscience. With a resigned sigh, he shrugged into his jacket and grabbed his keys off the table. He'd get his truck from the parking lot above the camp, and then he'd try to persuade her to leave till the storm passed.

Just as Killian stepped into the rain, a loud rumbling cut through the din of the downpour. In the next flash of lightning, he saw part of the hillside above the camp, the ridge next to the parking lot, give way. Mud rushed toward the cabins—right toward Ava Blum's cabin.

The lightning crashes were less frequent now as the storm moved east, making it impossible to see the campground in the moonless, cloud-covered night. He didn't know what the mudslide had hit, but the sound of crunching timber was unmistakable. The slide had taken out structures or trees or both.

Killian let out a string of expletives as he grabbed his ditch bag of emergency supplies and his axe. Squinting through the rain, aided by a well-timed flash of lightning, he looked up the hill for more flowing mud. He didn't want to be buried alive. As he couldn't see anything for more than a split second, but the rumbling had quieted, he took his chances.

Fishing out a flashlight from his bag so that he could at least see the ground he trod upon, he ran toward Ava's cabin as fast as he could. The wet, tree-filled terrain and low light hampered him, the mud alternately sucking at or sliding under his boots. Miraculously, he stayed upright and made it to his destination without injury a minute or two later.

More accurately, he made it to where Ava's cabin *used to be*. In front of him were long slicks of mud and debris. Sweeping the flashlight around, he located the remains of her cabin. It hadn't moved far.

The avalanche of muck had knocked it off its foundation, and the walls and roof had folded on themselves like a house of cards. Fortunately, the impact of the slide hadn't reduced the cabin to matchsticks. Some of the structure remained intact. She might still be alive.

"Ava!" he shouted, picking his way slowly through the slick toward the collapsed cabin. He didn't think she could hear him through the weather, *if* she was still alive, but he kept trying. "Ava!"

Arriving at the front door, ankle deep in muck, he steadied his stance. The door was intact in its frame, but now it slanted forty-five degrees to the right toward the ground, as did the rest of the front wall. He gingerly pressed on the wood to test its stability. It didn't budge. He pushed harder. Same result. "Ava!" he shouted again.

This time, she heard him. "Help! I'm trapped!"

"Can you move? Are you trapped under anything?"

"I can move. Please, just get me out of here!"

"OK, stay back from the door. I'm gonna make a hole." Bracing his legs more firmly, Killian hacked into the wood with his axe. After he'd splintered the wood, he sunk the axe's handle into the ground for balance, and kicked a hole in the door.

Shining his flashlight into the crawl space under the slumped walls and roof, he reached in. Ava's pale, terrified face appeared, and she grasped his hand. Together, with him pulling and her clawing and scrambling, they freed her from her prison.

"Oh my God!" Ava climbed up his body to stand. She clung to his shoulders and buried her face in his chest. "I thought I was going to die!" She trembled like a puppy during fireworks.

Although such a thing was foreign to him, he hugged her to comfort her, but only for a moment. They couldn't stay there. He removed her arms from his waist and ran his hands roughly over her body.

"What are you doing?" Even though she was right next to him, she had to shout through the loud storm.

"I'm checking to see if you're hurt. You might not feel it if you're in shock." He completed his pat-down. Satisfied that nothing was broken, profusely bleeding, or severely swollen, he stepped back from her. "Can you run?"

He barely saw Ava nod in the dark. "I can run."

"Good." He swept his flashlight around the camp. "We can't stay here. There could be more mudslides." He flashed his light toward the road. "The road to the parking lot washed out so we can't get to our cars. I'm not even sure that the parking lot is still there." He swung the flashlight again, toward higher ground. "The safest bet is to head to the mature tree line where the ground is stable. We need to get there as quickly as possible."

Wasting no time, he hooked the axe on his pack, slung it across his back, and snaked an arm around Ava's waist. Pulling her along, he jogged to the part of the forest that was untouched by fire.

It was about a mile away. Ava stumbled in the dark as they ran, even though he was using his flashlight to illuminate the ground in front of them. He tightened his arm around her, to keep her upright as they ran.

Twenty minutes later, they stood under a row of trees, catching their breaths. They were both soaked. He studied Ava for a minute. Her hair clung to the sides of her face, and she had mud streaked on her cheeks. Her eyes were enormous and shining with fear.

Ava wore tiny pajamas, though "pajamas" was a generous term for the scraps of fabric now clinging to her like a second skin. They were more of a suggestion of pajamas—barely-there shorts and a silky peach camisole the rain had made transparent. He could see all of her, every inch, even in the dark.

Ava hadn't dressed for a survival situation. But at least she was wearing shoes—hiking boots, mercifully—but no socks. "I'm glad you've got boots on," he said, his breathing having returned to normal.

"I put them on while you were breaking the door down." She shivered so violently that her shoulders jerked.

"That was smart." He shrugged out of his coat. It was still dry on the inside and warm from his exertions. He wrapped it around her shoulders.

She slipped her arms into the sleeves, zipped it up, and hugged it tight to her. It swallowed her. But at least she was no longer naked in all but name. "Thank you," she said.

He reached into his coat pocket on her hip and pulled out his phone. "I doubt we'll get a signal up here." No bars. Not even a whisper of a bar. The storm probably wasn't helping. Making a mental note to upgrade to the newer satellite-capable model, he dropped his phone into his rucksack.

None of this was ideal. Killian was the type of man who did things on a schedule, preferably early, so that he had time to deal with the unexpected. He kept to a routine, minimized the amount of stuff he had to take care of, and used lists to order his life. Prioritizing his responsibilities and avoiding complications was how he survived a chaotic childhood. It was how he made sure he succeeded when all the odds were stacked against him.

As he'd done many times, he relied upon his ability to stay calm in stressful situations. He took a mental inventory of their supplies. Having been the one to put it together, he knew exactly what was in the pack; he checked it every month, on the fifth.

Supplies:
Axe, check
Backpack, check
Life Straw, check
Redundant Life Straw, check
Swiss Army Knife, check
Rope, check
Wire, check
Compass, check
Thermal blanket, check
Phone, check
Phone solar charger, check
Emergency ration bars, enough for one person for four days, check
First aid kit, check

Bear mace, check

Matches in a waterproof matchbox, check

Lighter, check

Flashlight, check

Flares, check

Coat, check

Keys, though probably useless, check

Wallet, shit, nope

Liabilities:

Wet clothes, check

Nearly naked, terrified movie star, check

Killian evaluated their options for survival and rescue. "Well," he said after long consideration, "this isn't good."

He wiped the rain from his eyes. Without his coat, it soaked through his clothes. "The mudslide washed out the road, and even if we could get to our cars, we can't use them to get down the mountain or for shelter because the ground under the parking lot is unstable. That's where the slide came from.

"It's supposed to rain through the night. The ground is unstable above the cabins. We can't shelter in them and wait it out. We don't have any way to call for rescue, and they likely wouldn't be able to get to us for days, anyway."

Ava listened to him intently, not saying a word.

"My pack has water filters, so we won't die of thirst. I have emergency rations, but it won't be enough to feed us for more than a couple of days. I have a thermal blanket, but we won't be able to make much of a camp.

We're both soaking wet, so I'm worried about us staying warm. It'll be impossible to start a fire in this rain.

"It's roughly ten miles straight down the mountainside in this direction"—he pointed through the trees—"to get to the highway. From there, we can get to the motel in another couple of miles. I know it's a hike, but I think it's our best bet. Can you do that?"

"Y-yes," Ava replied through chattering teeth. "L-let's k-keep going. It's too c-cold. W-walking will warm u-us up."

He nodded. He shone his flashlight ahead of them, and they picked their way gingerly through the muddy forest floor.

An hour later, they'd made little progress. He couldn't see well enough to feel confident about their direction, so he kept stopping. And Ava kept slipping and tripping, requiring him to hold on to her. She was going to get hurt.

Killian sat down on a tree root. "Take a load off," he instructed, patting the root next to him. Perched awkwardly on the gnarled wood, she shivered with violent jerks of her shoulders.

"Let's wait until the sun is up. It's too dark right now, and we're just asking for an injury or to get lost." He moved to crouch in front of her, roughly rubbing his hands up and down her legs to generate some friction. "You need to warm up."

Ava sniffled, her face crumpled in misery. "I'm so cold. I don't think I've ever been so scared. The cabin fell down around my ears. It was terrifying." She swiped at her eyes and nose.

Killian didn't know what to do with crying women. He wasn't great with emotions in any situation, much less something as extreme as this. Growing up in the foster system, he knew how to survive, and he knew how to read people. But actually dealing with emotions? They were complications—problems that he couldn't solve with good planning and rational thinking.

He stared at her for a few seconds, watching her tears intermingle with the rain sluicing down her cheeks. Obviously, she was feeling the stress of her brush with death and needed more comforting. Heaving a sigh, Killian stood up and pulled her into a hug. "Hey, come on now, don't cry. It's going to be OK."

Sagging into him, she cried harder, making him frown. "A hike down the mountain in the rain isn't my favorite way to spend a Friday night, either. But we'll be there before you know it." He squeezed her gently to reassure her.

She hiccupped. "I'm sorry. I've always been a crier." Tilting her head to look up at him, she smiled weakly. "Thank you for saving my life."

"I was worried about the stability of that hillside," he confessed. "This is an unusual amount of rain—record-breaking for June. In hindsight, I wish you'd left with everyone else."

Stepping back from him, Ava covered her face with her hands and bawled. "I'm sorry I troubled you," she choked out.

He didn't know what to say as she stood there sobbing, and hugging her didn't seem to cure it earlier. Leaving her to her tears, he turned his attention to finding a suitable spot to camp. He dropped his pack on a patch of muddy grass and dug out the thermal blanket.

After Ava's crying quieted some, he requested she join him, trying again to calm her. "We can spend the rest of the night here. We only have a couple of hours till dawn. Then, at first light, we'll get off this mountain."

Heaving a large, shuddering breath, Ava walked over. Before he could do anything else, she launched herself into his chest again, clinging to him tightly. "Promise me you'll keep me safe," she said into his shirt.

As he searched in vain for the right thing to say, she looked up at him, pale-faced. She slowed her crying and schooled her features into a mask of serenity. She took a deep breath.

"You must be cold," she said, tilting her head back more to scrutinize him. She unzipped his coat, which she was still wearing, and pressed herself against him. Scooping her arms around him, she tried to wrap the open coat around them both. It wasn't big enough to get much past his forearms.

As much as he didn't like strangers touching him, he had to admit that the warmth of her body felt better than the chilly rain. She was tall, although he was even taller, so the top of her head tucked in under his chin in a perfect fit.

She sighed into his neck, and her shivering slowly subsided. They stood like that, warming each other in silence, for a long time.

"What's your name?" she eventually asked.

Chapter 2

Since she was holding onto him more tightly than she'd held any man since her divorce, Ava figured she ought to know his name.

"Killian," he answered.

She was still crying softly into this strange man's neck. It was making him uncomfortable, and she should stop. Then again, she'd been buried alive and was freezing to death on a mountain, in a storm, with a stranger.

Taking a deep breath to stem her tears, she shifted her focus to her companion. She recognized him. She'd seen him around the campground while they were there filming. He'd been staying in the cabin next to hers, but he didn't seem like a tourist. He seemed to be some kind of forest ranger.

Or maybe he was a lumberjack. He was broad-shouldered and very tall—burly even, with a dark, full beard. Every time she saw him, including this time, he wore a plaid flannel shirt, jeans, and heavy boots. Tonight he'd added a beanie.

She didn't suppose she'd ever met a lumberjack before. "Killian." She rolled his name around in her mouth like a sample of Bordeaux wine from her vineyard in France. It was a beautiful, uncommon name; she liked it. "I'd have never guessed that."

She tucked her nose into the spot where his throat met his shoulder. Noticing his scent, she inhaled. Sandalwood and cedar and pine and musk—it was exactly how she expected a lumberjack to smell. It'd been a long time since she'd enjoyed the warm, spicy notes of a man's soap. The earthy aroma made her feel safe, calm.

She could hear his voice in his throat and feel his Adam's apple bob when he spoke. "Why?"

"Killian doesn't seem like a lumberjack's name," she murmured into his neck, closing her eyes and relaxing. The warm smell of his skin was as good as any aromatherapy she'd had at expensive spas.

"I'm not a lumberjack. I'm a civil engineer."

She arched her back to look up at his face. "Are you sure? You're wearing flannel and a beanie, you're burly and you have a beard, you smell like trees, and you rescued me with an axe." She tried smiling at him, but unfortunately for her, he was a humorless sort.

"I'm sure I know what I do for a living." He stepped away from her again. He didn't seem to enjoy being touched that much—he'd stiffened each time, even when he was the one to hug her. Apparently, he'd had enough now that she'd finally stopped crying.

He sat down on the grass. Missing his warmth, she followed. The ground was frigid, and the cold pierced through her pajama bottoms. Not that they would protect her from anything more than a soft summer breeze. She drew her knees to her stomach and zipped his coat up around them.

They only had one blanket, so Killian tented it over the top of them to shelter them from the continuing rain. It was pitch black under the blanket, but she could feel his nearness, even though they weren't touching.

Despite the blanket over their heads keeping the heat in, and balled as she was into his coat, the hard ground sapped all of her warmth. No longer pressed against him, she shivered again. Damp leached into her bones, making her joints ache.

Killian had more clothes on than her, but the rain had soaked him through. He had to be freezing. If they didn't do something, they both wouldn't make it till dawn without becoming hypothermic.

"Killian?"

"Hmm?" he grunted. He was a grunter. This didn't surprise her in the slightest. Lumberjacks seemed like they would grunt.

"I'm cold."

He sighed. "I know."

"Aren't you cold?"

"Yes."

"We should cuddle."

"What?"

"Cuddle. Like, I should get on top of you, and we can share body heat."

"No."

His answer surprised Ava. They were strangers, but it was a sensible idea. This was a life-or-death situation, and he seemed to know about survival. "What? Why not?"

"Because."

"Because what?"

"Because I don't want you on top of me."

"Why not? Has the cold numbed your brain? I'm no survivalist, but even I know we should share body heat to avoid hypothermia."

"Because I don't like being touched by strangers."

She snorted. "I'm not losing fingers and toes to frostbite because you weren't hugged enough as a child."

He didn't respond.

After a few more minutes of miserable shivering, she decided she wasn't going to let either of them freeze to death. She unzipped his coat again and groped around until she found his lap. Straddling him awkwardly, she pressed her chest to his. He flinched.

"What are you doing? I said no." He rolled her onto her back and pinned her with his body weight.

"Hey!" She flattened her palms on his chest and pushed, but he didn't budge. He was a big man and solid as a tree trunk. She wasn't getting up till he decided it.

Frustrated, she growled, "I'm so cold, I feel like my nipples are going to snap off. You seriously won't share body heat with me?" At least he was making her front side warm, even if the grass was cold under the backs of her legs.

Suddenly, she realized she was getting exactly what she requested, even if he didn't intend it. She stopped pushing at him and pulled him closer instead. Clinging to his shoulders, she dug her fingers into his back and arched, pressing as much of her chest to his as possible. She hitched her legs on his hips to get them off the ground. She wriggled, creating friction to warm them.

"Stop that." His voice took on a pained edge.

She squirmed harder and rubbed her legs up and down his flanks, warming her knees and calves.

"I said, stop it, Ava."

"Why? It's making me warmer. Isn't it warming you too?"

"No."

"Maybe that's because your shirt is too wet." She plucked at the sodden fabric on his back.

Instead of answering, he tried to lift off of her, but she clung to him like a baby chimp. She shifted so that her arms were around his neck, forcing him to take her with him as he sat up. The blanket slipped off them and fell to the side, so they were getting rained on again.

A moment later, she was on his lap with her legs around his waist. He enveloped her with his massive biceps, anchoring her to his chest, forcing her to stay still. "Stop. You're practically naked and rubbing against me. I don't know you, and it's weird."

She stiffened, horror flooding through her. That had been the furthest thing from her mind. The last thing she would ever do was be sexually aggressive with someone who wasn't consenting. The very thought turned her stomach. "Oh. I'm so sorry, I didn't mean… It's just—" she stammered.

She forcibly calmed herself and tried again. "The thing is, I don't know any other way to stay warm. You don't want to freeze to death any more than I do. Can we just survive tonight, and then pretend like this never happened?"

After a moment, she felt him nod on top of her head. "OK, yes, we should keep each other warm. We should also minimize how much heat we lose into the ground. Get off me a sec. I need to readjust the blanket."

"OK." It took her a few seconds to stand because her legs were stiff from the cold. Picking up the blanket, he shook the beaded water off and walked over to a tree. Sitting down with his back to it, he drew his knees up and then motioned to her. "Come here. Sit on my lap, facing me."

She did as he asked, straddling him and using his thighs as a backrest. She carefully pressed her inner knees and calves along his sides, with her feet flat on the ground on each side of his hips, grateful that her frequent yoga classes had kept her flexible.

He draped the blanket over their heads, anchoring it between his back and the tree truck. They both stayed silent in the pitch black again, ignoring the fact that there was less than a foot of space between their faces.

"Thank you," she said at last. "This is better."

"The ground and tree are cold, but I'm warmer with you on top of me."
He paused a moment before adding, "You were right."

"I was... right?" She smirked, although it was too dark for him to see her
face. "I don't think I heard you properly. Say it again."

"No."

She laughed lightly, but felt him shivering between her knees. "You're
still cold because your shirt got soaked by the rain."

"That's why I was wearing a jacket," he responded dryly.

"Oh." She twisted her mouth. "I appreciate you letting me borrow it.
Thank you."

"Yeah, well, I couldn't let you run through the woods naked," he grumbled. "What I don't get is, why wear pajamas at all if that's what you're
going to wear?"

"The silk feels nice on my skin," she said with a sniff.

"But it's completely impractical. You were in a cabin in mountains, not
the Ritz-Carlton. There are wild animals and insects around. It's cold at
night."

Given that they were unsheltered in a forest, she shoved the thought of
wild animals and insects out of her mind. "I had plenty of blankets. I wasn't
planning on getting hit by a mudslide when I went to bed." She relaxed a
little against his knees. "And it's good for vaginal health to wear something
loose while you sleep."

He grunted again. "You don't have any boundaries, do you?"

She scoffed. "What? I have boundaries."

"So we just haven't found them yet?"

"There's nothing wrong with me wanting to have a healthy vagina."

"Wanting it is fine, but you don't need to tell me about it. It doesn't
concern me."

"Healthy vaginas concern everyone."

He surprised her by chuckling. After that, the conversation died. Not much of a talker, that one.

Her front side was chilly. Either she needed to zip up the coat again, or she needed to press against him. Worried that he was still too cold, as he continued to shiver, she opted to wrap her legs around his waist and fold forward. His damp shirt was frigid against her breasts.

She cupped his cheeks, then moved her hands around his face, checking the temperature of his skin. Her hands were icy, but his cheeks were icier. So were his forehead, nose, and the parts of his ears not covered by his beanie.

"What are you doing?"

"You're too cold."

"I'm fine."

"No, you're not."

She lifted herself until she was level with his face. Then she fisted her hand around his nose and blew hot air onto the tip. "I need you to get warm. You're my guide to the bottom of this wretched mountain, so you have to stay alive."

She blew on his nose again before moving her warmed hands to his cheeks. "I used to do this for my daughters when they were little and we went to play in the snow. I'm sure your mom did this when you were little. Every mom does this." She rubbed her hands together to warm them again and then placed them on his ears like earmuffs.

"I didn't have a mom," he replied, his voice betraying no emotion. "Well, technically, I have one. I don't know her. I grew up in foster homes."

Ava's heart wrenched in her chest, but she didn't know the right thing to say to that. She couldn't imagine not being a mother to her daughters. They mattered to her more than any other humans on the planet.

She rubbed her hands together vigorously again and placed them on his brow. Wet hair peeked out from under his beanie and clung to his forehead. Working her fingers under his cap, she checked whether the wet had permeated the fabric. Fortunately, his hair was dry. It was also soft and warm, soothing her aching fingers, and so she lingered.

"You can stop," he mumbled after a moment. "I told you, I'm fine."

Ignoring him, she ran through her routine once more: nose, cheeks, ears, forehead. And he let her, although she could feel his cheeks pulling into a frown when she framed his face between her palms.

Settling in his lap again, leaning forward, she tucked her cold nose into his neck, warming it, and surreptitiously breathing his woodsy scent. She patted his cheeks. "I know it's not enough, but hopefully that helped a little."

Instead of answering, Killian slipped his hands under the jacket, warming them on her lower back. Together, they formed a tight ball, sheltering from the storm.

Although she was considerably warmer wrapped up in him as she was, she could still feel him shivering. "Take off your shirt. It's evaporating the heat away." His shoulder muffled her voice.

He didn't answer her, so, leaning back, she took matters into her own hands. She made quick work of unbuttoning it and pushing it off his shoulders.

"Ava—" he protested as she jerked the fabric open, exposing his chest and abdomen.

"Don't be a prude. You need to get warm."

After quickly shrugging out of his jacket, she pulled her camisole off over her head and dropped it in her lap. Shuddering at the cold, she pulled the sleeves of his coat on again, and then pressed herself against him. She ignored how his chest hair tickled her peaked nipples.

"No one has ever accused me of being a prude before," he said, warming his hands again on her back under the jacket.

"Well, what's your problem now? Of all the times to be modest, this isn't one of them." She ran her hands over his clavicle and up his shoulders to warm him up, only noticing a little that he was solid and sinewy.

"I already told you, it's weird to be half-naked with a complete stranger. I don't like people I don't know touching me." He moved his now-warm hands down to the small of her back where the cold air had wafted up under the coat, protecting her from the draft. It felt so nice that her breath caught.

"You need to get over it." She vigorously rubbed his shoulders. "You're freezing. You don't need to be so stoic about it."

The skin of his torso warmed beneath her hands, and he stopped shivering. Since he wasn't resisting her, she carried on by skimming her fingers down the solid, ridged wall that was his abdomen. Then she skated her fingertips toward his jeans.

"Ava..." he said warily when she toyed with the button on his pants.

She stilled her fingers just under his waistband. "OK, hear me out. Your pants are soaked. You should take them off and get dry. For survival. I'm not trying, uh, you know, to seduce you or anything. That's the furthest thing from my mind. Despite my public persona, I'm not that way. I haven't slept with anyone since my divorce." She popped open the button.

"No chance."

"We're kind of in an emergency situation here. We shouldn't be stupid for modesty's sake. Everyone knows you're not supposed to wear wet clothes when lost in the wild. I've seen survival shows. They always get naked when their clothes are wet."

"I'm not getting naked with you, Ava."

"But I want you to be warm." She reached for his zipper, but he caught her wrist and moved her hand away from his pants.

"You've already done enough. My core is warm. Just relax." He captured her second wrist and placed her hands back on his shoulders. Then he wrapped his arms around her, underneath his coat, squeezing her tightly to him. His biceps were like vices, preventing her from going for his pants again.

Giving up, she sighed and sagged against his chest. At least they were sharing body heat now. She was significantly warmer. After several minutes, he relaxed his arms a little and began rubbing her back again, stroking her in lazy circles.

"You're skinny," he said suddenly.

She was somewhat offended at that. "Most men like my body."

"Your body is fine," he replied matter-of-factly. "I meant, we don't have much food. We're already using a ton of calories just trying to stay warm. And we still have a long hike down. I don't want you getting weak because you have so little body fat to burn."

"Fine? My body is more than fine," she protested, sounding petulant. She worked hard to maintain her figure. And she got paid millions of dollars because of her body, thank you very much.

"*That's* the part you heard?" He shook his head, grazing his chin across her hair.

She rolled her eyes. "I probably have more fat on me than you do." Groping his chest again, she confirmed he was indeed lean. "I can go without food for a day. I fast regularly. It's anti-aging."

"You don't eat on purpose? No wonder you're so skinny."

"I'm a healthy weight," she shot back. "I also exercise and can handle a hike. You believe we can do it, right? Hopefully in one day?"

"Yes," he drawled. "I was just going through contingency plans in my mind. I like to be prepared."

"Oh." She didn't want to think about the possibility of wandering in the mountains for days. But he wasn't talking again, causing her to worry. To quell her anxiety, she tried light conversation. "You seem to know your way around. Do you live on the mountain?"

"Yes."

"Why?"

"I told you, I'm a civil engineer."

Ava debated with herself before admitting, "I don't know what a civil engineer does." He probably thought she was a vapid Hollywood twit who couldn't think because she starved herself.

"I'm surveying the road and hillsides for erosion after all the wildfires for safety and stabilization."

"Oh." She racked her brain to come up with a something to say that didn't lead them to a discussion about the mudslide. "Uh, how long have you been a civil engineer?"

"About ten years," he said. "Do you always talk nonstop?"

"Are you always so rude?" she retorted. "We don't have to talk. I just thought, maybe it wouldn't be so weird, you know, how we're pressed together, half-naked, if we were a little better acquainted."

He took a deep breath. "I'm sorry. I need to think. Just relax and try to rest. We have to get going once the sun is up, and it's almost dawn."

"Yeah, sure." The dawn couldn't come fast enough, as far as she was concerned. The sooner she got back to civilization, the better.

Chapter 3

K illian wasn't able to concentrate on making contingency plans. Instead, he created a new mental list.

<u>Why It's Wrong to Lust After Nearly Naked, Terrified Movie Star:</u>
1. She'd just survived being buried alive in a mudslide
2. They're busy trying to survive the wilderness
3. She's vulnerable, and he's not a creep
4. She's an impractical Hollywood snob
5. She cries a lot
6. She talks a lot
7. She has no boundaries
8. She's a famous movie star
9. She hasn't slept with anyone since her ex-husband
10. She's complicated

She *was* a little skinny. He could feel the ridges of her spine and the angles of her shoulder blades under his hands as she hunched against him. But he'd have to be dead to not notice Ava Blum. And he wasn't planning on dying on this mountain.

He remembered once when he was a teenager he'd seen her on a magazine cover wearing little more than a smile, and he'd been... inspired. Every boy's—and man's—fantasy, she drew comparisons to Marilyn Monroe, with her sultry pout, platinum blonde hair, and bright blue eyes. But she was taller, leggier. And now she was here in the flesh, nearly naked, clinging to him, unbuttoning his pants.

She was softer than he'd imagined, and sweeter. When she warmed him with her hands, he was so surprised that he couldn't stop her. And he didn't want to, even when she worked her way down to his jeans. By then, he'd been thinking about ways he could warm them both.

It was an incredibly stupid train of thought. So he didn't let her take his pants off, even though his inner teenager was *not* happy about it. He was already taking liberties by rubbing her bare back and enjoying the feel of her breasts pressing against his chest.

She didn't give him long to ruminate on her sex appeal, however, because she started talking again. He ought to be glad for the distraction. But he was also exhausted and would have preferred the quiet. When she talked, she was... chirpy.

"So about those wild animals and insects..." she began. "What exactly are we talking?"

"Mostly deer and squirrels. There are also coyotes, mountain lions, and bears."

"Are there snakes?"

"Yes."

"Spiders?"

"Yes."

"I really don't like spiders," she offered after a too-short pause.

"I don't know many people who do."

"Yeah, but I *really* don't like them. Hopefully, you will never have to see what I mean."

"Ava..."

"Hmm?"

"Don't worry about spiders. Rest."

She was quiet for, perhaps, thirty seconds. "Killian?"

"What?" Five-year-olds talked less than this woman did.

"Are there really mountain lions?"

"Yes."

"Do they attack people?"

"Yes."

"Should we be worried?"

He stopped rubbing her back and then chuckled softly. "No, we don't need to be worried."

"Are you sure?"

"Yes, I'm sure. Mountain lions don't prefer to attack humans. When they do, they prefer solitary prey. Just by traveling together, we're deterring attacks."

"But what if we come across one?"

"We probably won't."

"But what if we do?"

"We won't."

"You can't be sure. I need to know what to do, so that I'm prepared, just in case."

He sighed. "Alright. If you see a mountain lion, do *not* run. Running triggers predators to chase. You want to make noise, make yourself big, and throw things toward it, but not directly at it, to scare it away. If you attack it directly, it'll fight back."

"Is that what you do when you see a coyote?"

"No, just leave coyotes alone. They don't attack people."

"Never? I once heard about a coyote jumping through my neighbor's window and eating her cat."

"Coyotes attack cats, not humans. You're more likely to be killed by an errant golf ball than to get bitten by a coyote."

"Really? Are you just making that up?"

"No, that's a true statistic."

"Oh, well, that's good." She snuggled into him and took a calming breath.

He rubbed her back again, soothing her. Her muscles relaxed under his touch. As she was being quiet, he thought she might sleep. Alas—

She jerked upright suddenly. "What about bears?"

He grimaced in the dark. "What about them?"

"Are there any around here?"

"Yes."

"Should we be worried?"

"No."

"Why not? I don't want to be eaten by a bear." She shuddered.

"Bears attack humans if they get startled, or they get cut off from their cubs. They don't hunt humans. The best way to avoid a bear attack is to make noise as we travel and to give them plenty of space." Smirking to himself, he added, "Making lots of noise shouldn't be a problem for you."

"Hey!" She tapped him lightly on the shoulder in protest. "It's called conversation. You know, what normal people do when they're together."

"At this hour, normal people sleep." He pressed her against him again, disliking the cold air filling the space between them.

Finally taking the hint, she didn't respond. Instead, she settled into him with a soft sigh. Killian closed his eyes. He let his mind wander. But it never wandered far from the woman he now cradled in his arms.

His juvenile lust aside, she was the opposite of his type. That was reason eleven for his list. He always went for petite brunettes who loved the outdoors and weren't afraid to get dirty; unassuming, down-to-earth women who didn't care for fashion and never wore makeup; breezy, easygoing types who wanted nothing more than a bit of fun and never overstayed their welcome.

For the past six months, he had exactly that kind of thing going with the motel owner's daughter. They hooked up every couple of weeks, usually at his place. Their nights typically included greasy takeout, kung fu movies, beer, light conversation, and casual sex. She was up front about seeing other people, and he was perfectly fine with that; in fact, he preferred it. Best of all, she never, ever stayed the night.

He didn't go for women like Ava Blum. She oozed wealth and privilege. Probably every item of clothing that she wore cost more than his entire wardrobe. There was nothing breezy or easygoing or casual about her.

"Tell me about your childhood," she said, out of the blue, case in point.

"I thought you were asleep," he said, feeling a tad mournful that she wasn't.

"I've got too much adrenaline to sleep. And since you're not asleep either, tell me about your childhood."

"Why?"

"Because," she huffed, "I'm trying to get to know you."

"Yeah, well, there's nothing to tell."

"Sure there is," she insisted.

"No, not really." He left no room for argument.

"OK, fine, Mr. Grumpy McGrumperson. Keep your secrets."

"I'm not grumpy. I just don't want to spill my guts to you five minutes after meeting you."

"I didn't ask you to. You don't have to go deep. But you could tell me *something*. Tell me why you became a civil engineer. I think you're the first one I've ever met. Do all civil engineers work in the mountains, posing as lumberjacks?"

"I'm not a lumberjack. Why do you insist on that?"

"Because." She ran her hands across his shoulders and down his biceps. "That."

"I'm missing something."

"You're built like you chop wood every day."

"I do chop wood every day."

"Why would you chop wood every day if you're not a lumberjack?"

"To heat my cabin."

"So practical." She laughed lightly. "You should embrace lumberjack-hood. Some women are really into them. Think they're sexy. It's a thing."

"But that would be dishonest because, as I've told you twice already, I'm a civil engineer, not a lumberjack."

"A pity." She squeezed his bicep again. "You're missing out on an obvious branding opportunity." She shrugged. "Doesn't matter to me, though. Lumberjacks aren't my jam."

"Then why would you keep bringing it up?"

"Just trying to be helpful. You could get lots of women."

"What makes you think I don't?"

"You live by yourself in a remote cabin in the woods."

"It's not *that* remote. Other people are a twenty-minute drive away."

"If you say so." She laid her head on his shoulder, nestling her nose in his neck. "I'm just saying, if you wanted, you could clean up with the ladies by really leaning into your natural lumberjackness."

"This is a ridiculous conversation."

"Do you want to talk about something else?"

"Yes."

"Then answer my questions, Paul Bunyan. Do all civil engineers work up in the mountains? How did you decide to do this for a living?" She was speaking into his neck, and her breath tickled.

"Don't call me Paul Bunyan. Civil engineers work on man-made infrastructure, which is more likely to be in cities than mountains."

"Then how'd you end up here?" She'd moved her roaming hands to his flanks. "Wood-chopping agrees with you. I'm not into lumberjacks, but I've always appreciated a well-muscled man."

"We still haven't come across anything even remotely resembling a boundary for you."

"That was a compliment. I mean, I can't see you in the dark, but your body feels like it's attractive."

He swallowed a chuckle. "Are you expecting me to thank you?"

"It's customary to thank someone when they compliment you." But she didn't wait for his response before barreling on. "Do you have any tattoos? You feel like a guy who would have tattoos."

"You can't feel tattoos."

"I know. But am I right? Are you inked?"

"Yes."

"I knew it! How many? What are they, and where are they located?"

"Calm down, Helen Keller." He fought a smile. Talkative people annoyed him, yet her sunniness in circumstances that would break most people struck him as admirable.

She groped him again. "Tell me about your tats. Or are they somewhere embarrassing? Do you have a kitten on your butt? Please say you do."

This time, he couldn't suppress his laughter. "Sorry. Nothing's inked on my butt. On my right bicep, I have a yin-yang symbol with a sun and a moon, inside a compass, inside a Celtic cross, with a dragon wrapped around the cross and my arm."

"Ooh, sounds deep." She trailed a finger up his right arm, over the tattoo he'd just described.

"It seemed deep to a twenty-year-old. It seems confused to me now. But it's on there, so all I could do was add to it. A few months ago, I got a portrait of my dog, Lola, on my right shoulder, shortly after she died."

Ava brushed her palm over his shoulder. "She must've been special."

"She was."

"Tell me about her."

"What do you want to know? I found her the year after I graduated from college, and she was with me everywhere I went for ten years."

"Everywhere?"

"Yup. She moved across the country with me a half dozen times. She went with me to work every day, rode along on errands, and loved to camp and kayak."

"Wow. I didn't know dogs could do that. But I've never had a dog. I've always assumed that I wouldn't like them. But so many people love dogs—my daughters included, they just got a dog at their father's—that I was thinking maybe I should reassess my lifelong anti-dog stance."

"You don't like dogs? Did you get bitten as a child or something?"

"No, I've just never had one. I've never had any pets—well, I had a rabbit once, but that was short-lived. My parents aren't pet people. They always said that pets were a lot of work and expense for very little in return."

Reason twelve for his list: she didn't like dogs. "I don't know that I can trust a person who doesn't like dogs." He was joking. Mostly.

"Then explain the appeal to me. What do you like about dogs?"

He thought about it for a moment. "Dogs are always happy. They are excited to wake up in the morning, excited to go for a walk, excited to see you, even if you were only gone for five minutes. They are pure, in-the-moment joy.

"What you get out of a dog, in exchange for taking care of it, is sharing in their happiness, entertainment, and unconditional loyalty. A dog will sacrifice its life for you. Dogs love you in ways that people can't."

She drummed her fingers on his shoulders as she evaluated what he told her. "What about Lola? What did you like about her? Why was she special?"

He smiled at her memory. "She had the cutest ears. They half-flopped over, but she could make them stand up when she wanted to. You always knew what she was feeling by how she moved them. And she was up for anything. She loved being outdoors."

"Is that why you took a job in the mountains? Because you like the outdoors, and camping and kayaking, just like Lola?"

"That's part of it. I also like the quiet. I'm not a big fan of people."

She lifted her head up. She was probably trying to see his face in the dark. He could practically feel her eyes boring holes into him. "Why don't you like people?"

Clearly, she wouldn't stop asking him things until he told her his life story. And since there was no way he could sleep with his back against a tree, in the freezing rain, with a nearly naked A-list actress clinging to him like a koala bear, he should just give in.

He sighed heavily. "OK."

"OK?"

"OK, I will tell you about my childhood. I will have a conversation with you. But this is a one-time thing. Don't expect more of this chitchat on the hike down the mountain."

"I almost hate to tell you this, but we've been having a conversation for a while." Ava's light laugh was low and throaty, sexy. "I do want to hear about your childhood, though. But wait a minute. I have to move my legs. They're getting stiff." She slid off of his lap and pulled her legs out from around his waist.

Spinning around, she shrugged out of his jacket. Then she sat back on his lap, this time with her warmed back pressed against his chest and her legs flanking his. She grabbed his arms and looped them around her stomach, her breasts resting on his forearms. Then she spread his jacket across their legs like a blanket.

Leaning her head back against his shoulder, she snuggled in. "OK, spill the tea, Kill."

"Don't call me Kill."

"I can't call you Kill. I can't call you Paul Bunyan. What am I supposed to call you?"

"My name is Killian. You can call me that."

"But that's too long," she whined.

"It's no longer than Paul Bunyan," he pointed out.

"But it's not as funny."

"Paul Bunyan isn't funny."

"That's because you don't have a sense of humor. What happened in your childhood to make you this way? I need to know."

He snorted. "Stop talking, and I'll tell you."

He waited a few moments to see if she would talk again. When she stayed silent, he realized he was going to have to keep his end of the bargain. "Alright, what do you want to know?"

"Hmm, where did you grow up?"

"New Jersey."

"Ew."

"Yeah, I know." He chuckled. "What else?"

"Did you ever know your mother or father?"

"No."

"Do you know who they are?"

"I know their names. They're on my birth records, but I've never tried to find them."

"Aren't you curious?" Her question instantly darkened his mood. She had abso-fucking-lutely no boundaries.

"No."

"Why? I wanted to know everything about where I came from. I took a bunch of DNA tests and researched my family tree going back ten generations."

After a couple of hours with her, the fact that she excitedly researched her family tree didn't surprise him. "Because the state terminated their parental rights to me by the time I was three. As far as I can tell, they didn't fight it. I don't waste my time on people who don't want me."

Sucking in a sharp breath, she reached up and placed a hand on his cheek. "I'm sorry, Kill."

"Don't be. And don't call me Kill. What else do you want to know?"

"Sidebar. Don't be mad, but my breasts are cold." She grabbed his hands and placed them over her bosom. She was more than a handful. "I would consider you holding my boobs to be an act of chivalry."

He squeezed her breasts—he couldn't help it—and smiled like a loon when she giggled. "You could just put on the jacket," he said, dousing them both with much-needed practicality.

He held the coat up so that she could put it on backward, slipping her arms into the sleeves. While quickly reviewing his mental list again, he tucked the collar around her shoulders and the waistband over her knees. Then he snaked his arms under the coat, looping them around her belly again.

She curled in on herself. "Oh my God, that's so embarrassing. I can't believe I didn't just think of putting the coat back on, and instead, my instinct was..." she trailed off.

"I'm surprised you're capable of being embarrassed," he mused.

"That's because you don't know me," she pointed out, her voice small. "Speaking of, we were talking about your childhood so I could get to know you."

He grimaced. "I don't want to talk about my childhood. Growing up in group homes isn't fun. Let's talk about something else."

Weak morning sunlight peeked under the blanket, and he could just make out her silhouette. Her head was leaning against his shoulder, chin tipped up to look at him. His eyes traced the contours of her profile, the lines of her jaw, the swell of her lower lip.

Rustling and snorting a few feet from where they sat interrupted their conversation and broke his stare.

Ava jerked and clutched his forearms. "Killian," she whispered urgently. "Do you think it's a bear? Should I make a lot of noise?"

Tugging the thermal blanket free, he peeked out before popping his head back under it. "It's a couple of deer. Have a look. It stopped raining."

He pushed the blanket down again, exposing both their heads. The deer lazily poked their noses through bushes next to them in the filtered morning light.

"Deer at dawn," she breathed. "That's got to be a good omen for my birthday."

"Your birthday?"

Ava craned her head back to give him a weak smile. "Yeah. Today is my birthday."

Chapter 4

Ava hadn't meant to tell Killian that it was her birthday. Sometimes she didn't think before she spoke. She may be older, but she wasn't wiser.

Killian looked a little surprised. "Happy birthday. I'm sorry you have to spend it hiking down a mountain with me instead of whatever you had planned."

"Funny enough, I had hiking planned. Although I intended to be by myself. But everything is more fun when you've got company, so it worked out for the best." She tugged lightly on his beard before rolling off of his lap.

Ava picked up her wadded, damp camisole off the ground and shook it. Gritting her teeth and squeezing her eyes shut, she took off his coat and threw the camisole over her head. The cold cloth brushing her nipples made her flinch. Exhaling the breath she'd been holding, she hurriedly wrapped herself in his warm coat again, putting it on the right way around and zipping it up.

Now that it was light out, Ava studied her companion. Killian folded up the blanket and carefully repacked it. Shrugging off his shirt, he fastened it to his backpack using built-in elastic cords so that it could dry. Then he hoisted the pack onto his back; she watched his obliques flex as he twisted. He looked as good as he felt in the dark.

She didn't feel guilty about enjoying the view. It *was* her birthday, after all. And it had been ages since she'd seen a man with his shirt off, outside of a movie set. But she didn't want him to catch her ogling. So she pulled her gaze away and fussed with the hem of his coat. "Are you, um— Do you need your jacket? It's pretty chilly."

He shook his head slightly. "You need it more than I do. Come on, let's go. We'll warm up once we get moving."

The deer were still grazing a few feet away, paying them no mind. "They aren't afraid of us?" she asked as he walked past them. She followed him.

"Deer have become accustomed to humans."

She thought they looked really sweet and docile. "Does that mean they're tame? Can you pet them?"

He looked back over his shoulder at her, his eyes telegraphing that he thought that was a stupid question. "Are you a Disney princess?"

"What? Of course not."

"Then no, don't pet the forest animals. Wild animals have parasites and diseases. There's a risk of rabies, and they might attack you."

She crossed her arms in front of her chest. "Don't talk to me like I'm stupid. Not all of us live out in the bush, Crocodile Dundee."

Killian rolled his eyes at her before turning away and picking up the pace. "I realize you live in Hollywood, but 'don't touch wild animals' is common sense, Ava."

She glared at his back, but her eyes dipped to his ass. The tight ass of an uptight ass. "I don't live in Hollywood. I live in Bel Air." She cringed internally at her childish comeback.

"What's the difference?"

"Hollywood isn't, uh, nice. It's mainly tourist traps with a lot of crime and a homelessness problem. You'd never find a celebrity there, except for red carpet events."

"And you live in a mansion in a swanky part of town, away from the dirty poor." It wasn't a question.

"You sound judgy," she sniped.

He didn't respond. Frowning at his grumpy mood, she followed along in silence. The ground of the forest was soft and sometimes sludgy. Mud sucked at her shoes and made her slip and slide. This was going to be a slow trek.

As they wandered, so did her mind.

Her fortieth birthday—the undisputed worst birthday of all birthdays for women. Today she was *forty*.

Divorced. Single mother. Middle-aged.

She tried to put a positive spin on it. It was a new decade and a new era: the era of the mature actress, focused on her craft. She could be the next Meryl Streep.

Yes! She would age like a fine wine. Then she remembered that expensive wine got bought by rich old men, stuck in a cellar, and ignored until it was time to show it off to other rich old men. Her positivity deflated like an old woman's breasts.

Forty. She hated the word. She said it over and over in her head until it had no meaning and sounded bizarre.

Was she a MILF now? She had three kids. She had the scars and stretch marks to prove it. Although, to be honest, she paid a very skilled, very expensive plastic surgeon to minimize those. Not to mention the grueling hours she spent with her personal trainer. Her tummy was flat and her skin taut.

But even with all the work she put into making her body the perfect specimen for the male gaze, no one seemed that interested in the F part of MILF. She hadn't slept with a man in the nearly three years since her divorce.

Not that she'd been looking. Given her sexpot persona, it would shock the world if people knew the truth. Namely, her ex-husband, Jack, was the only man she'd ever had sex with, if you didn't count... which she didn't.

The thought of being intimate with a new man terrified her. She liked sex, but she needed to feel comfortable—safe—with a man before she could sleep with him. So she'd been a one-man woman her entire life.

And that man was Jack. Until last Christmas, she'd thought they'd eventually work things out. That didn't happen. And now she knew it never would.

Without Jack as her future, Ava felt lonely, hopeless, and afraid. But fear was nothing new to her. She'd spent most of her life feeling afraid.

Usually she avoided things that scared her. Like, for example, spending time with men where sex could be a possibility. Or spending time with people who didn't approve of her. Or telling people *how old* she actually was.

This situation was especially terrifying. Not because sex was a possibility; it wasn't. Or because Killian didn't approve of her; although he probably didn't. Or because he knew how old she was; she hadn't said.

No, it was terrifying because she'd been buried alive, which was a wholly unpleasant experience. Now she was wandering a forest, possibly lost, with no real survival skills. It took all of her willpower to keep her anxiety under control and her tears at bay.

Ava's life depended completely on Killian. So she'd placed her trust in a grumpy, if nicely put together, stranger. Not that she had any choice. She'd been following him blindly through the forest since last night, giving him her complete faith from the moment he kicked open the door to her cabin and pulled her to safety.

Granted, that heroic act had earned him a good measure of her confidence. Reminding herself repeatedly that he was her hero, and a competent one at that, kept her panic relegated to the corners of her mind.

Slipping on the mud, she lurched forward and grabbed onto his waistband instinctively to keep from falling. Her pulse surged from the sensation of losing her balance. Without a word, he stopped and reached for her, steadying her, like he'd done a dozen times since last night.

Standing tall and letting go of his jeans, she took a deep breath. *Inhale courage. Exhale fear.* "Thank you."

Staying silent, he gently clasped her elbow and led her forward through the woods. And at that moment, she knew she could rely on him. They were going to make it off this mountain because he would make sure of it. She felt grateful for his steadying presence.

Still, she wanted information about how to survive in the wild. Information helped her control her panic better than breathing exercises and mantras. She cleared her throat. "How do you know which way to go?"

Killian grunted. "I knew you were going to insist on chitchat."

"Do you have something better to do than talk to me?" she snapped, her warm feelings toward him evaporating. "It's going to be a long walk. I'm trying to learn so that I'm not useless out here."

He held up a circular object. "I use a compass, obviously."

"Well, I didn't know you had a compass."

"It wouldn't be much of a survival kit if it didn't include a compass."

Ava did not care for Killian's tone, her hero or no. "Why are you being an asshole this morning?"

He was silent for a moment. "I haven't had coffee?" he offered with a lame shrug and a crooked smile.

Ava laughed, warming toward him again. She liked her coffee too.

They continued walking in companionable silence. When the ground leveled up a little, and she was no longer slipping in the mud, Killian dropped her arm. The sun was fully up, and she felt warm for the first time since escaping her collapsed cabin. There wasn't a single cloud in the pale blue sky.

Growing hot, she unzipped his coat. Her camisole had dried and was no longer see-through. Shrugging out of the coat's sleeves, she tied it around her waist.

With the jacket wrapping her pelvis in its heavy material, she was still too hot. As she walked, the sleeves kept loosening and slipping down her hips, pulling her pajama bottoms with it. She barely kept her pants on, no matter how hard she tugged on the knot to keep it fastened.

Navel-gazing, she failed to notice that Killian had stopped and was scrutinizing her. She crashed into a wall of sweaty man-chest, nearly losing her shorts altogether when her arms flailed in surprise.

Strong hands steadied her as she bounced. Snatching the silk pajama bottoms back up her hips, she looked up and saw his beard move when he spoke.

"Give me the coat."

She lingered against him for a moment before stepping back and untying the sleeves. Once in his hands, he rolled the jacket like a saddle blanket and strapped it to the bottom of his pack.

They resumed walking. The trees were less dense now and they could walk side-by-side.

"How old are you?" Killian asked, breaking the silence.

She blinked at the unexpected question before remembering that he was asking because it was her birthday. "Look at you, making conversation. I'm proud of you." She smiled sweetly at him. "I'm twenty-one."

Killian gave her a hard look. "Come on, Blondie, you can do better than that."

She affected a sultry pout. "Fine. I'm twenty-five. I'm getting old!" She heaved a dramatic sigh and threw the back of her hand across her forehead.

"Try again."

"Twenty-nine. That's my final offer."

Killian rolled his eyes at her. "Why can't you be honest about your age? Has Hollywood made you that vain?"

Ava gasped. "Wow. That was cutting." She chewed her lip for a moment. It wasn't like he was going to deny her a role because he knew how old she was. Maybe it would feel good to confess the awful truth to someone she'd never see again after today. She wrinkled her nose. "Forty." She cringed hearing the number out loud.

"Happy fortieth birthday."

"Thank you." She glanced at him walking next to her. "OK, I've confessed my shame. Your turn. How old are you?"

A sly grin spread across his face. "Guess."

Ava groaned. "Just tell me. You made me tell you my real age."

"You didn't ask me to guess. I would've guessed thirty-five, by the way."

"Ooh, you really are my hero." She batted her eyelashes playfully. "OK, I'll guess. You're somewhere between twenty-five and forty-five."

"That's true. But can you narrow it down more?"

She studied his face in the bright sunshine. He had strong bone structure, with a straight nose and a square jaw that his beard couldn't hide. He'd taken his beanie off an hour ago. Thick hair curled lightly onto his forehead. His hair and hooded eyes were so dark that they looked almost black.

"Hmm. Well, you have some crinkles in the corners of your eyes when you smile. But you also work outdoors, so they don't actually tell me much.

You don't have any obvious gray hair, but you could hide that easily with color. Beards make a man look older, but they can also hide laugh lines and jowls."

"I've never colored my beard or my hair."

"That sounds boring. I've been coloring my hair since I was a teenager."

"You're not a natural blonde?"

"No, I am. I just, you know, spruce it up a bit, change the shade here and there to match a look, or whenever I get bored." She tapped her chin, still studying him. "You're obviously in good shape and have all your hair. But I have no way of knowing how, uh, virile you are."

"I'm plenty virile, Sherlock."

"All men say that." She gave him a smirk.

"But in this case, it's true."

"I have no way of fact-checking, so I can't count it."

He grunted. "Do you give up?"

"I didn't say that." Picking up his hand, she rubbed her thumb over the callouses on his palm. "I assume these are from all that wood-chopping." She flipped his hand over. "You don't show signs of aging."

Releasing him, she chewed on her lip. "So probably not forty-five, but I don't think you're twenty-five either. You said you'd been an engineer for a while, so unless you're Doogie Howser, you're at least thirty..."

"Do you want a clue?"

"OK."

"My true age is less than the median of the range you gave."

Ava gave him the stink-eye. "A math clue. That's cruel. I've been out of school longer than I was in it."

"The pretty actress doesn't need to know eighth-grade math?" he teased.

Ava swung an elbow at his ribs, which he easily dodged. "Don't be mean, Kill. Not everyone is an engineer. I took math through calculus, I'll have you know. The median is thirty-five, meaning that you're younger than that, and now I'm jealous."

"Calculus? Really?"

"Don't sound so surprised. I'm not as dumb as my blonde hair makes me look." She stuck out her lower lip. "I'm not sure I want to know the answer to this, but how much younger are you than thirty-five? You're at least thirty, right?"

"I'm thirty-three."

Ava groaned. "I remember thirty-three. It's a distant memory. A time before cell phones, the internet, or even automobiles. We rode horses everywhere, wrote on parchment, and relied on torches for light. We lived in caves. Dinosaurs still roamed the earth. It was before the meteor, you see..."

"You better check your math there, Archimedes."

"Archimedes? I taught *him* math, I'm so old."

"Forty's not *that* old."

"You say that because you're a man. It's different for women. At forty, I'm no longer fuckable." Ava was only half-joking. "It's hard out here for a bitch," she sang.

"You look pretty fuckable to me."

Ava stopped singing at the unexpected, blunt compliment. Was it a compliment? He'd said it so matter-of-factly. "Thanks."

They walked in silence again. She listened to the crunching of the vegetation under their feet. The terrain was uneven, so she kept her eyes on the ground to watch her footing.

"I thought I had a gray hair once," Killian said, restarting the conversation. "It turns out that I had gotten Wite-out in my beard."

Ava laughed. "Honey child, I'm surprised you even know what Wite-out is."

"Did you just call me 'honey child'?" he asked incredulously.

"I did."

"Why?"

"Would you rather I call you Paul Bunyan or Kill?" she countered.

He shook his head. "I honestly don't know. Why can't you just call me by my name?"

"And miss out on annoying you? Where's the fun in that?" She raised a single eyebrow. "OK, so how do you know what Wite-out is?"

"Some stations I work at still have logbooks you write in. If you make a mistake, you use Wite-out."

"Ah."

"Have you ever had any gray hairs not caused by Wite-out?" he asked.

"That's a bold question to ask a woman." She worked her mouth for a few seconds. "Not on the top of my head," she replied carefully.

It didn't get past him. "Your answer implies you've had a gray hair elsewhere."

"Maybe, one time, in a different place. And it was extremely upsetting. I did *not* react well."

"You mean"—he pointed at the ground—"down there?"

"I really can't say. All I can tell you is that I scorched the earth and salted the fields so that nothing will grow back."

"What does that mean?"

"It means that I have a permanent Brazilian, thanks to the miracle of lasers, and I regret nothing."

He took a beat before responding. "See, no boundaries."

"You asked." She normally wouldn't be so brazen. But she was stressed, and a little punchy. Anyway, if he looked, it would be obvious. Her shorts barely covered her, and she wasn't wearing any underwear. She felt like she was on *Naked and Afraid*.

His face became inscrutable, and he kept his gaze locked on his footing. She wondered whether he was now picturing her naked, and she hid a smile in self-satisfaction.

Maybe she was still at least a *little* fuckable.

"You should've heard me when I found that gray hair. I hollered so loud, you'd've thought I found a dead body." Ava redid her ponytail as they marched. Now that her hair was dry, the loose wisps were tickling her brow. "They say you're supposed to age gracefully. Fuck that nonsense. I will *not* go quietly into that good night. Nope. More like kicking and screaming."

Killian looked at her, raising his eyebrows. "I'm glad I didn't hear that. You're plenty loud as it is." His lips tipped in a mocking half-smile.

She arched an eyebrow. "I'm a great screamer. Professional-grade. Not that you'll ever know." She gave him her patented, half-lidded, lips parted, sultry look—the one that usually got her compared to Marilyn Monroe.

He glanced away immediately, making her laugh silently. That expression, which she could summon at will, never failed her. It was a fun party trick. But it wasn't a natural, spontaneous expression; she'd perfected it in a mirror when she was nineteen.

He cleared his throat and changed the subject. "Why were you planning to spend your birthday hiking alone?"

"I don't want to talk about it," she grumbled, her playful mood evaporating.

"And I didn't want to talk about my childhood," he replied, poking her gently on the shoulder.

She frowned. "I *really* don't want to talk about it, Kill."

"Turnabout's fair play, Av."

She gave him a dirty look, but he had a point. She'd pressed him more than once in the few hours she'd known him. Anyway, he'd asked an innocent question. "I'm turning over a new leaf for a new decade. I thought that self-reflection, alone in nature, would be a good start."

"What was wrong with the old leaf?"

She glanced up and caught his eyes for a moment. He thought she didn't have any boundaries. But that wasn't true. She wore a mask and stayed shallow with most people, firmly in control of what they saw. Her feelings leaked out of her eyes too often, but not typically around strangers.

When she didn't answer him for a long time, he patted her on the shoulder. "It's OK. You don't have to answer. It's none of my business."

"Uh-huh." She kicked a rock, feeling like a sullen child.

He didn't push the subject any further. Somehow, that made her feel bolder about being unguarded with him. So she took a deep breath and answered him candidly.

"I got divorced almost three years ago. Even though I was the one who filed for divorce, I didn't want the marriage to be over. So when he moved on, I got jealous, and I realized I'd made a huge mistake."

"Why would you file for divorce if you didn't want the marriage to be over?" He tilted his head like a dog trying to understand English.

"Because I felt neglected. I thought that maybe, being deprived of his wife and kids for a bit, he might miss us and, you know, pay better attention."

Killian's brow remained furrowed. "Did you tell him you needed more attention, and he refused to give it?"

"No." She twisted her mouth. "Actually, he didn't know. I thought the divorce was a huge hint, but he didn't pick up on it."

"Why didn't you just tell him?"

"I don't know. Actually, that's not true; I do know. I was afraid. It was really stupid." She blinked back hot tears. "All I did was provoke him until he was angry with me, and then he went and met someone else. Now he's remarried.

"I can't even be mad about it because I was the one who pushed him away. And she's *great*." Ava's voice lilted emphatically. "She makes him happy. My daughters love her. Even I like her. So I fucked up my whole life because I'm a coward and an idiot, not realizing I was replaceable."

She scrubbed a hand across her eyes to wipe the tears away before he could see them. "I always do the wrong thing, say the wrong thing, feel the wrong thing. My parents say I'm too dramatic, too emotional."

Her voice became thick, and a weight settled on her chest. "I thought, after I'd had a successful career and a successful marriage for a while, that I was finally a better person, a proper adult. But it turns out, I'm not. I'm the same stupid girl I always was."

She stopped walking and covered her face with her hands. The panicky feeling that she'd been barely keeping at bay flooded her. Stress and fear overwhelmed her. She couldn't stop the tears, and they gushed. She began to ugly-cry, wishing fleetingly that the mud had swallowed her forever.

Wordlessly, Killian put his arm around her shoulders and gave her a light squeeze, no doubt trying to stop her from crying. Humiliation crept up her neck as she realized she was once again dumping her emotions on him. She was again making him uncomfortable. But she seemed incapable of stopping.

She attempted a lighthearted laugh, but it came out as a choked cough from all her self-loathing. "The failure of my marriage was my fault. At first, I blamed him, of course, but things are always my fault. I didn't communicate what I needed. I don't even know what that is half the time."

She took a deep, shuddering breath. "And now I'm forty. My career is stalling because I'm aging and I took a lot of time off to have kids. I'm divorced, a single mom, and too old to start over. I thought maybe staring at trees could tell me what to do."

Ducking out from under his arm, Ava scrubbed her eyes and put away her tears. She forced her face into a mask of serenity and regained her control.

He watched her composing herself, his eyebrows and mouth frowning slightly. "I do that too, when I need some clarity—stare at trees," he offered after a bit.

Ava stayed quiet while she regained trust in her shaky voice. "What do they tell you, the trees?"

He shrugged. "Nothing. They're trees."

"Then it doesn't work." She sighed, defeated.

He smiled softly at her. "No, it works. Walking in the forest reminds me that the world is beautiful. It reminds me to live in the moment and be content. That's about all you can do sometimes."

Chapter 5

K illian stopped to survey the horizon and check the time on his phone. It was a little after ten. They had been walking for four and a half hours. He still had no signal, so he couldn't be sure how far they'd gone, or how far they had left to go. But it'd been slow going.

At least the weather had cleared up. The sun shone, and things were drying. The low morning light and frequent tree shade meant that they didn't have to worry about sunburn yet, but he was already kicking himself for not including sunscreen in his emergency pack. Next time.

He glanced at Survivor Barbie standing next to him. Flushed from exercise, she wiped her brow with the back of her hand, streaking dirt across her skin. She had mud splatters up her legs. Wisps of hair escaped her ponytail, curling in a light-catching halo around her face.

Messiness didn't diminish her sex appeal one iota. Thankfully, her pajamas had dried and were no longer clinging to her like a second skin, although they were still transparent in the sunlight. He watched a bead of sweat roll between her breasts before training his eyes on the compass in his hand.

"I have to confess something," she said, looking bashful as she refastened her hair into her ponytail.

"What's that?"

"I have to pee, and I'm not sure what to do."

He gave her an exasperated look. "Didn't you ever go camping as a kid?"

"No."

Of course she hadn't. She probably had some perfect Norman Rockwell upbringing with pony rides at her birthday parties.

"Just go pee. There's no trick to it. Avoid poison oak."

"Poison what now?"

He facepalmed mentally. "Poison oak. It'll give you a nasty rash if it touches your skin."

"How do I know what's poison oak?" Her eyes widened.

He took her by the hand and led her to a suitable spot by a tree, like she was a three-year-old. "Here. There's no poison oak in this spot."

"Thanks."

He turned to walk away.

"Wait!" she shouted in a panic, even though he hadn't walked even three steps. "What do I use as toilet paper?"

He turned back to face her. "Do you need toilet paper to pee?"

"It's different for girls." She gave him a look that telegraphed that she thought he should know that already.

He gestured around him. "The world is your oyster. Leaves, grass, rocks, twigs, whatever looks comfortable." He paused for a minute. "On second thought, skip it because there could be bugs. Men shake. Women can too, more or less." He'd never thought he would talk about peeing in the woods with the glamorous Ava Blum.

He started to walk away again. "Will you shout at me when you are far enough away?" she called after him. "I don't want you to hear me."

"Whatever you want, princess. Just go. I don't want to be here all day."

"OK."

He walked back to the viewpoint where they'd been standing a minute before and waited.

Other men might find Ava Blum in the woods, wearing next to nothing, relying on them like some kind of damsel in distress, to be a fantasy come true. But not him. She chattered and cried and told him a lot about her divorce, even though he barely knew her. Because the woman had no boundaries.

Her lack of boundaries somehow induced him to say stupid, inappropriate things. Things like she looked fuckable to him. In his defense, moments before, he'd been staring at her tiny silk pajama bottoms sliding down her hips.

After that, she told him about her Brazilian. Then there were those smoldering looks she gave, seemingly unaware of the promises her heavy-lidded eyes and parted lips made. She was... unreal.

And she was affecting him, inappropriately, despite their circumstances. It wasn't right.

He mentally reviewed the reasons on his list why it was wrong to lust after Ava Blum.

She didn't like dogs.

She wasn't his type.

She was a movie star.

Her ex-husband was one of the biggest movie stars in the world. How is it that two people who have everything couldn't make a marriage work? Her explanation about how she was too afraid to say certain things had made little sense to him. Probably because she was complicated—another reason on his list.

If he had any doubt that she was vulnerable after the mudslide, they were gone after she sobbed behind her hands while confessing why her birthday was distressing her. She seemed broken, and that might've been since before the mudslide.

For many reasons, the main one being that he wasn't a creep who used women, she was off-limits. He needed to concentrate on making sure they survived their trek down the mountain. Because, let's be honest, she was also a woman who needed modern plumbing.

Speaking of, what was taking her so long?

She yelled at him, cutting into his thoughts. "Hey! Are you far away? I didn't hear you shout."

"You haven't gone yet?"

"No, I was waiting for you to tell me you couldn't hear me. I have stage fright."

He raised his eyes to the sky. "Just go already."

Changing the channel in his mind away from Marilyn 2.0 and back to their predicament, he studied the landscape. Despite his best efforts, he couldn't figure with any reasonable accuracy how far they'd gone or how far they had left to go. Generally, they were heading downhill, and would eventually end up in civilization. But he couldn't see the highway yet, or any trails or man-made structures.

A few minutes later, Ava trudged up behind him. "That was gross." She wrinkled her nose.

"Do you really have stage fright? That seems odd for an actress."

"Only when it comes to bodily functions. They tend to ruin the fantasy. I'm just fine on an actual stage."

He shrugged the pack off his back and dug inside. "Are you hungry?"

She nodded. "Thirsty too. I don't suppose you have a coffee maker in there? My love language is Starbucks." She got a wistful look. "What I would give for a sugar-free vanilla oat milk latte right now."

There wasn't a Starbucks within fifty miles of this mountain. "I don't even have instant coffee in this pack. I've got water straws and emergency rations bars."

She frowned slightly. "Any idea how far we've gone already?"

"Not really. We've been walking for four and a half hours. But we're going pretty slow because of the terrain. I also don't know how far we have to go, and we aren't taking a straight line there either."

She pursed her lips thoughtfully. "How many calories is each ration bar?"

"Five hundred."

"How many do we have?"

"Eight thousand calories' worth."

"So we have two days' worth of food, ignoring that we are probably burning well over two thousand calories in a day."

"Correct."

"And we don't have any other food?"

"Not unless you want me to hunt and kill something."

"Could you do that?"

"With what we have, not easily. If things got dire enough, I could set up rabbit snares. But that would require us staying in one spot, and rabbits won't feed us for very long."

She made a disgusted face. "I'd prefer to not eat rabbits. Can we forage?"

"Let's hope it doesn't come to that. I'd rather we keep moving than stop to look for vegetation to chew on."

She frowned again. "OK, you should have all the food. You need the energy."

His eyes bored into her at the ridiculous suggestion. There was no way he was going to agree to that. "What about you?"

"You need the calories more than I do. You're a lot bigger than me, and with all that muscle, you're burning a lot more energy than I am. You have less body fat than me, too. Anyway, I fast all the time, and I know I'll be fine even if I have to go for a week without food. I don't need it. But you do."

"No chance. I'm not eating all the food. I'm not carrying you down this mountain when you faint from lack of sustenance."

Her eyebrows pinched in stubbornness. "We need to be smart about this. I'm worrying about *you* fainting. We both need to walk off this mountain together. I'm not strong enough to drag you." She eyeballed the two bars he pulled out of the pack. "I'd honestly rather not eat."

"No way, Gandhi. You're eating. Have just one bar to start. We can reconsider things later in the day. Keep your strength up. Last night was exhausting as it is." He handed her a bar.

She made a stubborn face and opened her mouth.

He held up a hand. "Stop. Don't argue with me. Just eat it."

She closed her mouth and nodded. "OK. Thank you."

"Let's get going. We can eat and walk at the same time."

After another half an hour of walking in silence, their calorie-dense bars devoured, Ava spoke again. "The shadows are in a different direction to us now than they were earlier. Have we changed directions?"

He was briefly surprised by her astute observation. "Yes."

"I thought so. Why?"

"We can't go directly down the mountain. It's too steep. We have to take it in switchbacks."

"Oh. That makes sense." She picked up a large stick and began using it as a walking pole. "How do you know where to go? I mean, beside the compass."

"I don't know exactly where we're going. It's not like we're following a trail. I'm just using visual cues, my sense of direction, my familiarity with the area, and, of course, the compass. But when in doubt, we should walk downhill."

"Walk downhill... I've heard that before. That the probability of finding other people if you walk downhill long enough is pretty high."

"Exactly."

"When you figured that this would be a day's hike, did you figure the switchbacks into the mileage earlier?

"Yes, but only roughly. Ten miles was the straight distance down the mountain from the camp. We will obviously walk a greater distance than that. I don't know how many miles we will have to walk or how long it will take. Any estimate would be a wild guess because I don't know our path well enough to calculate it."

She nodded. "So we might end up walking more than a day."

He nodded. "Unfortunately."

"Thanks for being honest. I'm not some shrinking violet who can't handle things, you know."

"I never said you were." He didn't tell her he'd assumed it, though. But he was already learning that many of the things he'd assumed about Ava Blum weren't correct.

"Yeah, well, most people underestimate me. I'm tougher than I look."

"I believe it." And, to his surprise, he did.

A few minutes later, they walked into a clearing. Killian tipped his face up to the sun to enjoy its warmth for just a minute. Even though it was hot out, it was such an improvement to their cold, rain-soaked night.

"Killian! Stop! Don't move!" Ava shouted.

He froze. "What?"

"You're about to step on a snake."

He looked down. In front of him was a black, red, and yellow snake, about three feet long. He looked back at Ava. She was half crouched, clutching a rock, arm raised and ready to throw.

Killian quickly hid his amused smile. "Put the rock down, killer. You don't need to fight it."

"But it could bite you."

"It won't. And even if it did, it's not poisonous. It's a garter snake."

She lowered her arm, but still eyeballed the snake distrustfully.

"There you go," Killian coaxed. "Nothing to be afraid of. I'm glad we saw it, in fact."

"Why?"

"Because they live near streams, and I'm thirsty." The snake slithered off, and he began walking again.

Ava dropped the rock and picked up her walking stick before catching up with him. "So that's one rescue for me, although I think your rescue is worth at least five snake rescues, so we aren't even yet."

"Huh?"

"I just rescued you from stepping on a snake. That's not equal to rescuing me from a mudslide and taking me down a mountain, but it's not nothing. Maybe we'll be even by the time we get to the motel."

"I hope not." She was ridiculous.

"You don't want me to make things even?" she asked incredulously.

He side-eyed her. "Setting aside that the snake was harmless, I hope I won't need any rescuing, especially rescuing equal to pulling you from a mudslide and escorting you down a mountain. I'd prefer this be a smooth, rescue-free hike."

"Oh." She chewed on her lip. "I suppose that would be better." She matched his stride, and they strolled easily together. "So, tell me, how do we find this stream? I'm parched."

He'd been scanning their surroundings for signs of running fresh water, but had seen nothing promising yet. "We could try dowsing."

"What's dowsing?"

"We find a forked stick, kind of the shape of a Y. Then you hold it out and walk around. It will rotate and point you toward water when you walk by it."

She punched him in the arm. "Shut up. That's not a thing."

"Ow. You hit hard." He rubbed his arm, even though she hadn't actually hit him hard enough for it to hurt.

"Sorry. I didn't mean to hit hard. I take Krav Maga."

"You do Krav Maga?"

"Uh-huh. I just got my blue belt. I wish I had more time to train, honestly. It's taking me forever to progress."

"How'd you get into martial arts?"

"I take it for self-defense. I might not know how to deal with bears, but in LA, I'm more likely going to need to protect myself from, uh, men." She stammered her words a little.

Killian decided not to open that door any wider. "Well, anyway, dowsing is a real thing."

"How could a stick possibly locate water? It doesn't seem like it would work." She furrowed her brow, thinking way too hard about it.

"It doesn't. It's superstitious nonsense." He tugged lightly on her ponytail, watching her too serious face relax into a playful smile.

She swatted his hand away from her hair. "OK, so what's our Plan B? I hope something more science-based and less magic-based. Despite the blonde ponytail, I'm not a genie, and tugging on it won't do anything."

"You're not a genie?" He feigned shock. "Why did I rescue you, then? I already had my three wishes planned."

"Ha. Ha. Such a funny guy." She made a face at him. "Come on, what's the plan?"

"We look around. We could fan out, zigzag around a little more, but it'll slow us down. So I vote that we just keep walking as we are, and hope we get lucky and see water soon."

"Zigzagging sounds pretty haphazard." She grimaced. "I don't want to spend all day looking for water. More than anything, I want to sink into a motel bed. I don't care how lumpy it is. I don't care if the sheets are made of burlap and tears. I don't care if there's a dead hooker in the box spring. The thought of falling into a motel bed and sleeping for a dog's age is what's keeping me going right now." She smiled wistfully.

"Your bar for motels is pretty low," he deadpanned.

"I draw the line at bed bugs. A girl's got to have standards." She skipped a few steps in sudden impatience. "Come on. Let's just keep going. I'm sure we will come across some water. It rained buckets. There has to be water somewhere on the way."

But two hours later, it was nearly one, and they had found no water. It was hot, and the air was steamy from the evaporating remnants of the storm. They were again walking under a canopy of trees, at least, so they were avoiding direct sun.

"My mouth feels like cotton," Ava complained. "Dehydration isn't doing my skin any favors, either."

Her dewy complexion was the least of their worries. They needed to take in some fluids before they got heatstroke.

Killian stopped next to a large puddle at the root of a tree. He swung his pack off, unzipped it, and pulled out two blue tubes. She strolled up beside him and leaned against the tree, looking exhausted.

"We can't go any longer without some hydration," he said, handing her one of the blue tubes. He pointed at the muddy ground. "I tried to avoid it, but we're going to have to drink out of a puddle."

Ava looked at him like he'd grown a second head. "You want to drink mud?"

He nodded. "This is a Life Straw. It's a specialized filter that allows you to drink contaminated water safely. It'll filter out the dirt and bacteria and microbes."

"No. Negative. No way." Ava vigorously shook her head. "Not happening."

Killian gave her an exasperated look. "I can't have you getting heat-stroke. You've had no water. You need to drink. This is our best source." He pointed at the puddle again. "It's fresh from the rainstorm, so it shouldn't be that bad."

Ava wrinkled her nose in disgust. "You want me to drink alongside all the flies and dead squirrels? That has to be dangerous. I'm gagging just thinking about it." She dramatically retched.

He looked around. "I don't see any animal carcasses."

"Well, maybe there aren't any *right now*. But there probably were some."

He shook his head. Dropping onto his belly in the mud, he blew through the straw and placed it in the puddle. "I'll go first to demonstrate."

It took a few hard draws on the straw before the liquid came through. He was thirsty, so he drank from the puddle for more than a minute. It had a bit of a plastic taste because the straw was new, but he was so parched that it didn't bother him. Then he blew back through the straw to clear the mud from the filter.

Sitting up, he looked at Ava. "See, perfectly safe. Your turn."

Her face was frozen in horror. "There is no way—no way!—I'm doing that. My stomach turned just watching you. And now I'm afraid you're going to die of dysentery halfway down the mountain."

"Ava." His tone held a warning. "Drink."

"No." She challenged him with her eyes. "You can't make me."

He glared at her, silently considering what to do. She was right; he couldn't make her. And she didn't seem amenable to reason.

"Besides," she said, waving her arm at him, "now you're all muddy. I'm not rolling around in the mud, much less drinking it." Dark brown muck covered his abs, chest, and forearms from the ground where he had laid on his belly.

"You—you don't want to get dirty? That's what you're worried about?" Impatience and irritation knotted in his chest.

She put her hands on her hips. "No, I do not. I'm gross enough as it is."

Of all the asinine... He grabbed a handful of mud and flung it straight at her chest. Direct hit. It splattered over her breasts and splashed her chin and neck.

"What?" Ava gasped. "What in the actual fuck, Killian?"

"Get down here and drink!"

"No!"

Before she could dodge it, he threw another mud ball at her and got her squarely in her stomach. Then he threw another. It hit her shoulder and splattered her cheek.

"Stop it!" she yelled.

"Drink some water!" he yelled back.

"No!" She bent down, grabbed a handful of mud, and lunged to shove it in Killian's face.

He dodged. Missing him, she slipped and flailed. She landed in the mud on her knees before tipping backward. Suddenly supine, her breath left her in a whoosh. The force of her fall caused her to fling the mud in her hand into the air. It went straight up, then down, and hit her between the eyes.

When her breath returned, she screamed at the sky. Then she rolled onto her side to glare at him. "Ow, Killian, that hurt."

"Sorry. I didn't mean to hurt you. But now that you're down here, covered in mud, drink some water." Standing up, he retrieved her blue straw, which she had dropped in the melee, and handed it to her.

Snatching the straw from his hand, she looked at him with murder in her eyes. But then she rolled over and sucked muddy water from the puddle.

After drinking her fill, Ava stood and plucked at her camisole, a frown marring her features. Mud caked her, front and back, top to bottom. It was in her hair and smeared across her face.

Killian watched her with his arms crossed. "How was the water, Jackie Chan?"

"Not too bad." She craned her neck and twisted to look at her muddy backside. Then she smoothed her hands over her ponytail. "Is it in my hair?"

He nodded. "It's everywhere."

She frowned. "I don't think there's anything I can do to get clean."

"Nope."

She let out a frustrated groan.

"On the upside, mud is an effective sunscreen. So you might as well take advantage of it."

"Really?"

"Why do you think pigs and elephants wallow in mud? They are protecting themselves from the sun."

"I guess I never thought about it." She twirled. "Can you tell me whether there is any exposed skin?"

"You missed a spot." He grabbed another handful of mud and threw it at her. He got her right on the ass.

"Hey!"

He burst out laughing.

She scooped up two handfuls and rapid-fired them at his chest. Momentarily surprised, he stopped laughing.

"What?" she taunted. "Don't like a taste of your own medicine?" She grabbed two more handfuls and charged him.

He was still faster and stronger than her. But instead of dodging her this time, he lunged to grab her. She ducked under his grasp and shoulder-barged him right in the stomach, bringing her handfuls of mud around and smashing them into his butt.

"Oof!" he grunted from the force of her body into his midsection.

"Ha! Gotcha," she cheered, partially muffled into his stomach.

But she had also knocked him off balance. Tipping backward, he slipped and landed with a thud on his back. Last minute, he grabbed her and took her down with him. She crashed on top of him, knocking the wind out of him.

While he was still catching his breath, Ava got up and straddled him. She grabbed two more handfuls and went for his face again. He shoved her off and her mud balls went flying. They landed on his shoulders with a plop.

Killian quickly pinned Ava with his legs and then rolled on top of her, bearing his weight down on her shoulders with his hands so that she couldn't move.

"Get off me, you big lug. You're heavy."

He smirked. "Whatcha gonna do now, huh?"

She jerked a knee towards his crotch. "I'm not stopping until you are as muddy as I am!" she bellowed.

He evaded her knee by rolling onto his back. "Wow, Ava, you fight dirty."

She was already back on top of him, straddling his waist. "All's fair in mud wrestling!" She lurched forward to scoop up more mud.

He knocked her off of him. But she was fast, and she had some Krav Maga skills. They grappled, rolling around in the mud, until he was on his back again, letting her straddle him. He laughed. "Alright, alright, uncle."

"I accept your surrender," she gloated. She folded at the waist until she was lying with her cheek pressed onto his chest. Reaching up as she panted, she slid her mud-slicked hands down his face. "There. Now you're as muddy as I am."

"Jesus, Ava. When you commit to something, you really commit."

"My word is my bond," she said with a breathy laugh.

They rested on the ground for a couple of minutes before Ava rolled off Killian and offered him her hand. "We should probably get going."

"Yeah, we should." He stood and looked around for their supplies.

"Wait a sec," she said. She grabbed more mud and smeared it across the top of his shoulders and up the nape of his neck. "I don't want you to burn."

"Thanks." He fetched the backpack and dropped the Life Straws in a side pocket for easy access.

Ava studied the mud covering her hands as they resumed their journey down the mountain. "The two of us are a sight. I can't imagine what reception is going to think of us when we stroll into the motel looking like this."

"We'll just tell everyone it was the mudslide. Play the sympathy card. They don't have to know the truth."

"Good plan," she concurred. "I still can't believe you made me drink mud. No one is going to believe it."

"I'm just glad you drank. If you got heatstroke, I'd struggle to carry you the rest of the way, but I'm not leaving you behind."

Ava frowned slightly. She reached for his hand. "I'm sorry. I didn't think. From now on, I'll drink mud whenever you ask." Her tone was earnest. Then she laughed abruptly. "I can honestly say you are the only person I've ever promised that to."

He didn't respond. But he left his hand in hers as they walked.

Chapter 6

They'd been walking in comfortable silence for a while—at least thirty minutes. The mud had dried and flaked off, leaving them both covered with a soft brown, dusty powder. They were both thirsty again, but they still hadn't found any fresh water.

Killian scanned the landscape in front of them, hoping for a stream. He stopped abruptly. To his right, about twenty feet ahead, stood a bear cub—a bear cub without its mother. It didn't see them, as it was busy digging for ants in a log.

He reached for Ava, pulling her to a halt against his side, his arm across her back and his hand gripping her waist. Before she said anything, he held his finger to his lips in the universal shushing gesture. She looked at him quizzically.

Leaning down to her ear, he said in a low voice, "There's a bear cub ahead. Look around for the mother and slowly back up."

Her eyes widened. He could feel her short, shallow breaths under his arm. She was frightened, but kept herself under control and followed his instructions. They both stepped backward, carefully putting more distance between them and the cub.

Ava jerked her head to the left. "Killian, over there, the mom," she whispered. The mother bear was looking at them. She watched them, not moving. They were between her and her cub, but she didn't charge.

"Keep backing up slowly. We don't want her to think we're a threat. We don't want to trigger her chase instinct. If we can get far enough away without provoking her, we can wait for her and her cub to leave." He kept his voice low and calm.

Tucked into his side, Ava's arm slid around his waist and her fingers dug into his skin. She pressed herself into him.

"Take it easy, princess. We're going to be fine."

She nodded.

They moved together, their steps in sync. After they backed another twenty feet away, he guided Ava so that they were moving at an oblique angle to the mother, which the bear would find less threatening, especially now that they were no longer between her and her cub.

The bear still watched them. Then she stood on her hind legs and began to snort and stomp. He stopped moving backward. Time to stand his ground.

Instinctively, he maneuvered Ava behind him. "There's some bear mace in the bag," he told her, his voice now full volume. He spoke louder, but he kept his tone modulated, calm, for the bear's—and Ava's—benefit. "Try to find it and get ready to protect yourself. Hand me my axe."

"Your axe? What are you going to do with that?" Her fingers curled into the waistband of his jeans.

"Hopefully nothing. Just hand it to me, please."

She let go of his pants and worked on his pack. A moment later, she handed him the axe.

He raised his arms and made himself appear as big as possible. "Hey bear," he said loudly, but still calmly. "We're no threat to you. Go get your cub. We just want to get by and go back to where people belong. We're not here to bother you. Fuck off, bear. Get."

The bear dropped on all fours and ambled forward. It took a couple of steps toward them. He could feel Ava still rummaging through the pack.

"Come on, bear," he shouted, maintaining a steady voice. "Don't be an asshole. We've had a really long day, and you're standing between us and a hot shower. Take your cub and move along."

Ava stepped out from behind him and raised her arms, mimicking him. "From one mama bear to another," she shouted in monotone, "you're standing between me and my kids. I have bear mace, and I'm not afraid to use it. So you should probably just skedaddle. I take self-defense classes."

Killian gave her side-eye. Even confronting bears, she was ridiculous. "You heard the lady," he added. "She'll go straight for the knee to the crotch. Trust me, you don't want to provoke her."

Ava giggled. "You easily dodged me."

He waved his arms overhead again. That seemed to do the trick because the bear turned and moseyed over to her cub. Killian and Ava watched with bated breath as the mama and baby bear wandered away.

Dropping his arms, he turned to Ava. "I don't think Krav Maga works on bears. I certainly wouldn't want to be the one to test it."

"Probably not." She smiled softly. "I started going when my daughters got old enough to go with me. When they were born, I vowed they would never be victims and they'd learn how to protect themselves from an attacker. They're getting pretty good too. Last Halloween, a man in a gorilla suit jumped out at us, and my daughter Ingrid—she's the middle one—kicked him right in the goonies. I was so proud of her."

"Like mother, like daughter."

She rolled her eyes, although her smile broadened. Slipping the bear mace's tether around her wrist, she said, "I think I'll keep this on me for the rest of the hike, if you don't mind."

"Be my guest." He strapped the axe to his pack before slinging it on his back. "We shouldn't walk in silence anymore. That way, we don't unintentionally sneak up on another bear."

"Lucky for you, I'm an excellent conversationalist." Ava looked in the direction the bears had gone. "Do you think it's safe for us to keep going now?"

"Yeah, let's go." He led her down the gentle slope of the hill in front of them.

"Was that a grizzly bear?" she asked.

"Black bear."

"But it was brown."

He gave her an amused look. "Yeah, so?"

"Black bears are black. It's in the name."

"Some black bears are black. Some are brown."

She looked unconvinced.

Without thinking, he took her hand as they walked. "In the western part of the country, more than half of the black bears are actually brown. The lighter hair is adaptive to the hot weather. They are more likely to be black in the northern and eastern parts of the country."

"So how do you know it was a brown black bear and not a grizzly bear?" She stepped closer to him so that they were nearly rubbing shoulders as they walked along, their clasped hands swinging between them.

"Black bears have flatter faces and bigger ears. Grizzly bears have a hump on their backs, and black bears don't. Plus, we've hunted grizzlies to near extinction. They're only just returning. You are much, much more likely to encounter a black bear than a grizzly. Which, for you, my little city mouse, is a good thing. Black bears are surprisingly timid and known to run from house cats."

"Listening to you is like watching *Animal Planet*. How do you know all this stuff?"

"I work for the National Parks Service. It's part of my job to know the basics about the local wildlife. And I don't like being cooped up inside. When I'm not working, I'm usually doing something outside or reading."

"Well, I admit, it comes in handy. I probably would've tried climbing a tree. But you didn't tell me to do that, so I assume that's the wrong thing."

"Never do that. Bears can climb trees. Black bears climb trees especially well, and really fast." He gave her a stern look. "If you remember nothing else I've told you, remember that you don't want to trigger a predator's chase instinct. Most animals run faster than humans."

"See, this is why you're my Yoda. Guide me, wise mountain man." She bumped her shoulder into his arm.

He regarded her with amusement as a spring came into her step, and she broke into song. She improvised lyrics to the tune of "Evacuate the Dance-floor," although she was slightly off beat: "Evacuate the mountain! It's got unstable ground. Stop, this mud is killing me. Hey mister mountain man, don't let mud take me underground."

"A little morbid," he observed. "But it's impressive how you just made that up."

"My kids like it when I improvise lyrics to songs. It makes them laugh." Her face clouded over. "I miss them. I want to hear their voices. Even when they're at their dad's, no matter where I'm at in the world, we talk every day. They're probably worried since I didn't call them this morning."

Killian didn't know how to respond. Failing at conversation, he instead listened to Ava sing. She was now singing something about wanting a warm room with an exaggerated cockney accent.

"What are you singing?" he finally asked.

"It's from *My Fair Lady*."

"That's a musical, right? I haven't seen it."

She gasped. "You've never seen *My Fair Lady*? Audrey Hepburn and Rex Harrison—Julie Andrews sings. It's a classic."

He laughed. "Yeah, definitely not my speed."

"It's worth watching. Although I never really liked the story. But I love the music, and Audrey Hepburn's divine. That's who I named my first daughter after, Audrey Hepburn. Anyway, Professor Higgins—he's played exceptionally well by Rex Harrison—is actually a sexist, abusive jerk to Eliza Doolittle—that's Audrey Hepburn. He never gets better or seems to learn anything. But she goes for him anyway. I don't understand how that's romantic, even though I love the movie."

"I have no thoughts on this, being that I've never seen it." Killian wondered how she could both breathe and speak so many words at once.

"No, I suppose you wouldn't."

They walked along a ledge where the mountainside was steeper. Ava fell in step behind him. The trees were sparser here. The mud gave them some protection from the sun, but not enough. It beat down on them.

"How many kids do you have?" Killian asked, as she'd mentioned her daughter's name.

"Three."

"How old are they?"

"Audrey is fourteen. Ingrid is eleven. Bette is eight."

"Do you like being a mother?"

"Yeah, I do. I mean, it's really hard sometimes, and I sacrifice a lot for them. They're worth it, though. They're the coolest, funniest, nicest people I know. When I was in the collapsed cabin, the thing I was scared the most about was never seeing them grow up." She worked her mouth, trying to turn her deepening frown upside down.

"They gave me a pendant necklace for my birthday that said 'Mom' on it and had three diamonds in the colors of their birthstones. I was planning to wear it today, but I lost it." She rubbed at her eyes with the back of her hand.

The soil was loose and dotted with dried brush. It was too steep to head straight down, so they were cutting across the mountain again, adding miles to their already long hike. Picking their way through the loose ground and rocks, he was grateful that Ava had drunk from that puddle. He couldn't have dragged her down this part of the mountain if she'd gotten heatstroke. The terrain was too rough.

She began singing again, "to scare away the bears," she claimed. "La la la," she sang loudly. "Spice up your life!"

"Is that the Spice Girls?"

"Uh-huh."

"I was in elementary school when they were popular."

She stopped singing long enough to shoot him a dirty look. Then she started up again. "Shake it! Shake it! Shake it!" She shimmied her shoulders. Her voice was, admittedly, pretty good. And she made up for any wobbles with pure enthusiasm.

Killian's initial assumptions about Ava Blum were wrong—at least somewhat. She was full of energy and sunshine, sugar and spice. Resilient. Even though she'd nearly died, she sang club song parodies about it. And once she got dirty, she rolled around in the mud with childlike abandon.

It was foolish, wrestling in the mud like that; they didn't have excess energy to burn. Yet, he couldn't regret having had fun with her. It must be the stress of the situation. They'd needed the release.

It surprised him to realize that it felt like they'd been friends for years, even though he'd known her for less than a day. It must be because people bond in life-or-death circumstances. High arousal, it was called. An apt description.

Being around her was both arousing and distracting. He was struggling to focus on his mission: get her safely to the motel. Once there, he was going to shake her hand, wish her a happy life, and never see her again.

She'd finished her song and fell silent for a moment. Wanting to do his part in keeping the bears away, he searched for a conversation starter. He landed on, "Tell me about your childhood."

Killian immediately regretted the question. Hearing about someone's happy family—or worse, hearing them complain about their happy family—typically made him resentful.

"You want to know about my childhood?" Her voice lilted in surprise. "What do you want to know?"

"Where did you grow up?" he asked, parroting her question from when they were sheltering from the rain.

"All over. Army brat. I was born in Germany and lived there during my early childhood. I'm a dual citizen. My first language was German, but I rarely have a need for it now."

"But your parents were American?"

"My father is German. My mother was the one in the Army. She met him shortly after being stationed there. The Army moved us back to America when I was in second grade, and we moved to different states every few years."

"Mmm," he rumbled. He knew what it was like to feel unstable, to move constantly, to not belong anywhere. He wondered if that is what it was like for her, too. "Was it hard moving around like that?"

"I got used to it."

He couldn't see her because she was walking behind him, but he could tell by her clipped tone that she didn't want to talk about it anymore, so he didn't press. Anyway, his mood darkened thinking about that common aspect of their childhoods.

"What else do you want to know?" she asked, a minute or two later.

"I don't know. Nothing. We don't have to talk," he muttered.

"Yes, we do. Because of the bears, remember?" She poked him in his lower back. "Why are you grumpy suddenly?"

He shrugged. "I'm tired. I'm hungry, thirsty, hot. I want a shower..."

"Me too. But you don't see me acting like a little bitch about it." She poked him again.

He snorted a laugh despite himself. "Why do you keep touching me?"

"You don't like it?" Her voiced dripped with honey.

"No."

"I'll stop, but you have to stop being grumpy in return."

"OK," he said. "I'll try. Tell me something else. What was it like growing up on army bases?"

She hummed as she thought about her answer. "Other than the moving around, I guess it was probably not that different. I went to the local schools, did the normal kid things, you know. Hold on a sec."

He turned to see her bent over, tying her shoe. Her camisole fell forward, giving him an unfettered view of her breasts. He jerked back around.

What were those twelve reasons again?

She was vulnerable, and he wasn't a creep. That should be the only reason he needed.

"OK, I'm ready." She resumed walking. "My childhood was so different from my daughters', but that's because my and Jack's fame creates a lot of issues. My kids live in a bubble for their mental and physical protection. We try to give them as normal of a childhood as possible, but it's a challenge."

"You don't like being famous?" He'd assumed that she thrived on it, given how extroverted she seemed. He couldn't understand it, himself; he'd never want to be famous. Too people-y.

"It has its downsides, for sure. I like it for myself. I don't like it for my kids. Last year, I took Audrey to the Emmys. She was thirteen, so I thought it would be fun and that she was old enough. A bunch of creeps posted about her appearance online, and now more people recognize her on the street. It made her self-conscious and compromised her safety. Jack was furious. I won't make that mistake again."

He made a disgusted face. "Nothing sounds more terrible to me than dealing with strangers constantly. I live in a cabin in the woods on purpose."

"Most people wouldn't like being famous. My ex-husband sure doesn't. If he could wave a magic wand and undo it, he would. It's ironic that he's more famous than me."

"At least he makes pretty good movies." Jack Bullard usually made action movies, like a franchise where he played a Navy SEAL that had a bit of a James Bond flare to it.

Ava sniffed indignantly behind him. "My movies are pretty good too, you know."

His mouth twitched. "I don't think I've ever seen any of your movies."

"Seriously?" She sounded slightly strangled.

"Seriously."

"Why not?"

"Because you make chick flicks, and I'm a guy." He said it like he'd explained that the sky was blue.

"Men watch romantic movies," she shot back.

He kind of enjoyed ruffling her feathers. "Not by choice. They only go to make their women happy."

"First off, that's not true. Plenty of men enjoy romantic comedies or a good love story. Love, sex, and romance don't matter only to women. Second, haven't you ever wanted to have a sexy date night with a girlfriend? Wait, you're not gay, are you? I didn't mean to assume. Lumberjacks can be gay."

"I'm not a lumberjack," he reminded her. "Although it's irrelevant to my sexual orientation. Both engineers and lumberjacks can be gay. But I'm not."

"Oh," she said from behind him. "I didn't know. I thought maybe, because..."

"Because what?"

"You don't react to me how other men do."

That wasn't true, but he was glad he'd been hiding it well. He couldn't help provoking her, however. "Ego much?"

"Don't be mean." She kicked a rock past him. "I was just wondering if it's because I'm forty now. Although, after I told you about my Brazilian, there was a moment where I thought you might've been picturing me naked."

He had been, but he wasn't about to admit it. "You're really taking your birthday hard."

"Yeah, well... I'm not looking forward to becoming invisible to men, and it seems to be happening already. I know I shouldn't care, but I do, which is one of the many things wrong with me."

Killian regretted pushing her buttons. He tried to backpedal. "Princess, I can assure you, you have nothing to worry about. I'm just focused on our survival. In normal circumstances, you wouldn't even notice me, much less worry about my reaction to you. In fact, you didn't notice me the entire month you were filming, even though I lived one cabin over. What I think, or what any random guy thinks, about you doesn't matter."

Naturally, she missed the point. "I noticed you."

He grunted.

"Are you sure you're not a lumberjack? You grunt a lot."

"What kind of logic is that?"

She chuckled softly. "So getting back to your utter lack of cinematic culture, haven't you ever wanted to watch a romantic movie with a girl-friend?"

He stopped to check the compass and the time. Four o'clock. He worried they wouldn't make it to the highway before sunset. Scanning the horizon, he squinted. There was a stream not too far from where they stood. Finally.

"No woman has ever driven me to that level of madness, no." He tucked the compass back into the side pocket of his pack. "And God willing, no woman ever will. Not watching rom-coms is one of the many advantages of staying single."

Surveying the land, he picked out a slightly steeper path than what they'd been following, focusing on getting to the water as directly as possible. Pointing toward it, he said, "There's a stream. Let's go. We need to hydrate."

He tested the loose soil of the slope, his boots scooting down the hill. He skidded a few feet before coming to a stop. Once he was certain he was steady, he held his hand out for Ava to help her down.

"I feel sad for you," she said, looking at her feet. She stepped gingerly, using him for balance.

"Not necessary. I'm perfectly happy."

She stumbled and slid, smacking straight into his chest. He grabbed on to her, preventing her from falling.

"Thank you."

"You're welcome. How did we go from talking about your childhood to you judging my love life?"

"My childhood?" She concentrated on regaining her balance, her hands lingering on his chest for a moment. "Oh yes. I was an army brat."

"Yeah, we covered that. Are you going to tell me anything else about it?" Having found their footing, they headed toward the stream. She walked in front of him. He kept close, ready to catch her if she stumbled again.

She shot him an annoyed look over her shoulder. "Shut up and listen, Pig-Pen. I was just concentrating on not falling for a moment."

"Pig-Pen?"

"You literally have dirt swirling around you right now."

"Like you don't, Survivor Barbie."

She stopped, twirling to face him, and put her hands on her hips. "Did you just call me 'Survivor Barbie'?"

"Sure did." He crossed his arms, bracing for whatever mood she was about to hurl his way.

But he wasn't prepared for how she threw her head back and laughed.

Chapter 7

Ava laughed so hard that her sides hurt. It shouldn't have struck her as so funny, but the whole situation was both terrible and absurd. She could scarcely believe that she was in the wilderness with a growly, sexy, heroic man, feeling giddy at the prospect of drinking ground water. How was this real life and not one of her movies?

"You must hate every minute of this." She wiped away tears. "You won't watch one of my movies. But this whole scenario"—she twirled with her arms wide like she was in *Sound of Music*—"is the plot of a rom-com."

His brow crinkled. "I don't hate every minute, but I'll be glad when we get back to civilization. I also don't see how this would make for a funny movie."

"You don't? Look at me. I'm nearly naked, covered in mud, a fish-out-of-water. You're all grumpy and muscle-y. We're oil and water, but we're forced together. It's a perfect setup."

"You've lost me, princess. But if you're done laughing, then I'd like to get to that stream. I'm worried you're losing brain function."

She stuck her tongue out at him. "My brain is working fine. I *am* thirsty, however, so let's go."

They started walking again. "Princess. Survivor Barbie. I think you've called me half a dozen things by now. I'm going to have to up my game."

"What are you talking about?"

"Nicknames. You're making Paul Bunyan sound lame. I'll have to do better."

"I'm not making it sound lame. It's objectively lame."

"I'm ignoring that." She slowed down to manage steeper terrain. "What's your last name? I need to know what I'm working with here."

"Kelly."

"Your name is Killian Kelly?"

"Yes. You don't approve?" She detected a hint of sarcasm.

"Would you care if I didn't?"

"Obviously not."

"Yeah, well, I was just wondering. What's your middle name? Does it also start with a K? I hope not. That would make your initials very unfortunate. It's not Kieran, is it?"

"It's not Kieran. Don't worry. It doesn't start with a K."

"Thank goodness. So what is it?"

"I'm not saying."

"Why?"

"It's not something you need to know."

"Ooh, it must be something embarrassing." She clapped her palms together. "Now you have to say. You can't just leave me hanging here. I'll die of curiosity."

"Nah, I think you'll live."

"I definitely *will not*. You're killing me, Kill."

"Don't call me Kill."

"Then tell me your middle name."

"No."

"Then I'll guess."

"Suit yourself." He clamped a hand around her upper arm when she slipped. Her legs were turning into jelly, making it harder for her to keep her balance on the loose, dusty hillside.

"Hmm, it's probably something Irish. Liam?

"No."

"Sean? Seamus? Patrick? Declan?"

"No, no, no, no."

"Brian? Connor? Aiden? Tomas? Finley?

"None of those."

"C'mon, Killian, I need to know your middle name," she whined. "Mine is Hildegard. See, it's not that hard to share. I went first, and I didn't die."

"Your middle name is Hildegard? Your name is Ava Hildegard Blum?"

"Yes. I'm named after my grandmother Hilde. Your middle name couldn't be any worse than mine. Out with it."

He sighed. "It's Paul."

"Paul?"

"Yup."

"As in, Paul Bunyan?"

"As in Paul."

Ava cackled. "I knew you were secretly a lumberjack."

"If you're going to call me Paul Bunyan, then I'm going to call you Babe," Killian countered after a brief silence.

"Why?"

"Babe is his traveling companion."

"Aww."

"Babe is a big blue ox."

Ava laughed. "I forgot that. So you're comparing me to an ox?"

"No. An ox would be more useful on this mountain."

She scoffed. "No way. I'm better company than some big, dumb, smelly animal. I'm funny. Could an ox sing to you with made up lyrics? Could an ox tell you jokes? I don't think so."

"When have you told me any jokes?"

"Hmm," she thought for a moment. "Fair point. I'll tell you one right now." She cleared her throat. "Why can't Miss Piggy count to seventy?"

"Why?"

"Because every time she gets to sixty-nine, she gets a frog in her throat."

He chuckled. "That's a bad joke."

"You laughed. But I've got another one. Why isn't there a pregnant Barbie?"

"I don't know. Toxic beauty standards?"

"No, because Ken comes in a different box."

He laughed again. "That's even worse. Do you only know dirty jokes about dolls?"

"I know dirty jokes about fairy tale princesses."

"Alright, let's hear one."

"What did Cinderella do when she got to the ball?"

"What?"

"She gagged."

"Groan."

"That's what Prince Charming did." Ava snickered. She stopped thinking about jokes and slowed her walking to a crawl because she felt very unsure of the ground beneath her feet.

"Tell me more about your childhood. I bet you were a cheerleader in high school," Killian said, his voice close behind her.

"Nope. I wanted to try out, but my father told me I wasn't good enough and insisted I join cross-country instead. He said I needed to run so that I wouldn't get fat. Honestly, I think he just didn't want to pay for the uniform, and running shoes were cheaper. Well, he also worried a lot about me getting fat, so two birds, one stone."

The ground gave way under her feet. She slid, but Killian grabbed her arm again and stopped her. He moved in front of her, taking the lead. She gripped his forearm as they toddled down the slope.

"My childhood, in a nutshell, was strict," she continued. "My parents kept a firm schedule with chores and academics. They regularly inspected my room and expected that I would speak only when spoken to."

"You seem to have outgrown that habit," Killian remarked dryly.

"Hey! I should slap you for that. But lucky for you, I'm non-violent."

"Unless you're mud wrestling or fighting bears."

"The exceptions that prove the rule."

He laughed. Given the number of times she'd made him laugh today, Ava no longer considered him entirely humorless, merely susceptible to grumpiness.

"As I was saying," Ava continued, "my upbringing was strict. I was expected to please and would be punished when I didn't. It sounds harsh, but my parents thought they were doing the right thing. Now that I'm a mom, I can see how some things they did were damaging. Jack once tried to convince me to stop talking to them because he thinks they're abusive, but they're *my parents*."

Killian didn't respond to her little confession. Probably she over-shared. A familiar feeling of shame rose in her throat, silencing her. She shouldn't be talking disrespectfully about her parents. Nor should she be heaping her negativity and ingratitude on a stranger. What was wrong with her?

Ava concentrated on her footing and briefly dropped Killian's arm. Which was fortunate because, a second later, he slipped and tumbled down the hill by several yards. Since she had let go, he didn't take her with him.

Surprised, she called, "Are you alright?"

"I'm fine." He got to his feet and dusted himself off, looking annoyed.

Ava made it down to him a moment later. "You're bleeding." She grabbed his wrist. There was a long gash on his forearm that was dripping blood. She could see dirt and small rocks in the wound and frowned.

Killian adjusted the straps to his backpack on his shoulders as they'd gone askew when he fell. "I have a first aid kit, but we should get to the stream first or it'll be hard to clean."

She nodded, lifting his arm to elevate the cut above his heart. "At least we're at the bottom of the hill. It's pretty flat finally."

They reached the creek less than five minutes later and immediately dropped onto the muddy banks to drink. She didn't need any coaxing this time. She was really thirsty, and the rushing stream of crystal-clear water looked amazing.

Killian drank, too, and then submerged his arm in the cold water to remove grit from the cut. Ava worried about contaminants getting into the open wound and watched him with her mouth twisted.

She walked over to where he set the pack down on the bank and dug out the first aid kit. Crouching next to him, she grabbed his arm and peered at his injury again. She frowned at the angry red gash. "Does it hurt?"

"It's fine." He tried to pull his arm from her grasp, but she held fast.

"Let me. It'll be easier for me to do it." She ripped open some gauze and gave him a stern look. She applied light pressure to the skin around the wound, forcing blood to wash it out. Then she blotted it with the gauze.

"I'm a thirty-three-year-old man. I do not need you to mother me," he grumbled while she opened the iodine.

"Of course you don't." She poured iodine into the cut and rubbed it with a swab.

"Ow."

"I'm sorry. We have to kill anything that got into the cut so you don't get a blood infection." Twisting the cap off a tube of ointment, she dabbed it onto his skin. "It probably needs stitches. I'll bandage it as tightly as I can to keep it closed." She wrapped more gauze around his forearm, and then covered it with an ACE bandage, tying it off at his wrist.

He watched her work. "How do you know how to do this?"

"Try to keep the bandages dry." She smiled and patted his hand. "I have three kids. This isn't the first time I've had to field-dress a cut from a tumble."

"Thank you," he said while she returned the first aid kit to his pack.

"That's two." She handed his backpack to him. "Here you go, Mr. Grumpy McGrumperson."

"Two?"

"The snake and now your arm. I'm two to your one mega-rescue." She settled on the ground next to him and bumped his shoulder with hers.

Opening his backpack again, he removed most of its contents. Locating the emergency ration bars, he handed her one. "We both need to eat. I don't know about you, but I'm exhausted. We haven't slept in a day and a half, and we've been walking for ten hours."

Feeling ravenous, she took a bar without argument and scarfed one down. It tasted like cinnamon. "My legs are jelly. Any idea how far we have left to go?"

"No. Actually, I was thinking we should stop for the night. I don't know whether we can get to the road before sunset. I also don't think it's a good idea to walk down a narrow mountain highway in the dark."

"Yeah, let's rest." She unlaced her boots and pulled them off. "I'm getting blisters." She scooted to the stream and stuck her feet in. The icy water soothed her aching, hot skin. "Oh my God, I'm going to need the world's longest pedicure when I get home."

"Eat more." Killian stood up and handed her another bar.

She took it, looking up at him. "Thank you. The water feels good. You should try it." She ate the second bar at a more civilized pace, but still quickly.

He stood next to her, eating and looking at the water. When he finished, he nudged her arm with his knee. "I'm going to gather some wood for a fire. Will you be OK here?"

She nodded. "I'm going to wash in the stream really quickly so I can dry off while it's still warm out."

"Good idea. Just don't go too deep. You'd be surprised how strong the water can be, even in just a small creek. Be careful while I'm gone."

She watched him head off before wading in, still dressed in her silk pajamas. The water swirled around her mid-thighs, the current surprisingly strong, just as Killian had warned her.

Ava crouched low, submerging herself up to her breasts, and rubbed vigorously to remove the mud from her skin and clothes. Then she bent over and dipped the top of her head into the water, scrubbing mud out of her hair and scalp.

While bent over, something sharp struck her shoulder blade. She swiped at it awkwardly. It was a stick that had caught on the strap of her camisole. Crooking her arm behind her, she snatched at the stick and pushed it away. Then she stood up, whipping her hair back to get it out of her eyes.

Upon standing, the right side of her top fell down, exposing her breast. Her strap had ripped out of the material in the back when she'd removed the stick. "Goddammit." She frowned. "How in the hell am I going to fix that?"

Muttering to herself in dismay, she combed her fingers through her hair. It was a knotted mess. Dirt streaked her skin, and she imagined her hair was even worse. At least her sore muscles were soothed by the icy water, but she was freezing. Giving up, she waded out of the stream.

She stood on the shore, squeezing water from her hair, when Killian returned. She crossed her arms to cover her bare right breast. "Oh good, you're back. I need your help, please. I ripped my top."

He dropped a pile of wood on the ground. "What do you need me to do?"

Her left hand still covering her breast, she held up the strap in her right hand. Can you tie this to the other strap behind my neck so that my top will stay up?"

He walked over to her, and she presented her back, holding the strap over her shoulder for him. He took it from her and tugged. "I'm not sure it's long enough."

"Please try. Otherwise, I'm going to be flashing my breast at you for the rest of the walk."

He tugged again on both straps, the camisole lifting to expose her midriff. "I hate to break it to you, princess, but I've been able to see your breasts this entire time."

"What? How? My top has been dry since this morning."

"I can see through it when you're in the sun and down it when you bend over. Although I tried not to look."

"Why didn't you tell me sooner?"

"What good would that have done? It would've just made things awkward, and there was nothing you could do about it." He tugged on her straps again. "I think I got it."

"Thank you." She turned to him. "I'm sorry I've been flashing you this whole time. I hope I wasn't making you uncomfortable."

"Don't worry about it. I didn't mind the view."

Ignoring the heat rising in her face, Ava opted to change the subject. "You found some wood? It won't be too wet to start a fire?"

Killian walked over to where he had dropped it in a pile. He arranged it to make a fire. "Hopefully, we won't have any trouble. This is pine, which doesn't soak up the moisture as much because of its sap. I pulled dead branches off the trees, rather than picking them up off the ground, because they're more likely to be dry that way."

Ava watched him work. "Oh, that's clever."

He nodded toward his backpack. "The matchbox is sitting on the thermal blanket. Can you bring them both to me, please?" He selected a piece of tinder to light.

A little while later, she was lounging on the blanket, which he'd laid out for her, warming herself by a fledgling fire.

Chapter 8

The ground was hard, with sharp bits poking up through the space blanket into her backside. Ava was so exhausted, though, that she didn't bother to get up. Instead, she laid flat on her back, staring at the pale blue sky.

The fire wasn't big enough yet to warm her much. Her damp, tangled hair, wet clothes, and bare feet didn't help matters. Goosebumps broke out over her skin. She rubbed her hands briskly over her arms.

Killian dropped his coat on top of her like a blanket. "You'll need this tonight. The temperatures will drop soon."

Startled, she looked up at him as he stood over her, blocking out the sky. "Thank you."

He sat down on the blanket next to her and removed his boots. "How are you feeling?"

She rose onto her elbows. "Exhausted, dirty, sore. The cold water helped, but my hair is a lost cause."

"Going into the creek was a good idea. I'm going to do the same. It's too bad I don't have any soap. I'm adding that to the list."

"The list?"

"I have a list of items I keep in my ditch bag. I'm adding sunscreen and soap to it."

"Are you always this organized?"

"Mm-hmm. I like to keep track of things." He stood up and cleared his throat, squinting down at her. "I need to take my jeans off."

She blinked at him before she understood what he meant. "Oh." She covered her eyes with her hands to give him privacy. "Go ahead."

She heard the rustling of fabric and then the sound of him walking away. Peeking through her fingers, she watched him wade into the stream in nothing but his boxer briefs and ogled his muscular, powerful thighs. Lumberjack thighs because engineers weren't built like Khal Drogo. He must toss around logs or something.

She watched him crouch into the water to wash. "Hey," she shouted, jumping up and dropping his jacket. She ran to the bank of the creek. "Don't get your arm wet!"

He didn't see or hear her. Bracing for the cold water, she hurriedly waded in after him. Not paying enough attention to her footing, she stepped on something sharp.

"Ow!" Instinctively, she jerked her foot up. Losing her balance on the slippery rocks, she pitched forward. And then she was underwater. The cold shocked her. She launched back onto her feet and sucked in a sharp breath.

Killian's hand was on her upper arm a moment later, keeping her upright. "Easy there, killer."

"Your bandage," Ava stammered, her mind whirling. "You got it wet. I was trying to stop you. Now I'll have to change it."

"That's why you ran into the water?" Amusement crept into his voice.

"Yup." She looked down at the sharp pain coming from her foot. A cloud of red swirled in the crystal-clear water. "Damn it. I stepped on something sharp, and now I'm bleeding." She lifted her foot out of the water and stood like a flamingo.

With apparent ease, Killian scooped her into his arms, bridal style, and carried her out of the stream. Gently placing her onto the blanket, he gripped her ankle to check the damage. "Any idea what you stepped on?"

"No. Maybe a stick or a sharp rock. It doesn't hurt that much anymore."

"It doesn't look that bad. It's already stopped bleeding. I'll grab the first aid kit."

After he helped her clean and bandage her foot, and she changed the bandage on his arm, they got dressed and sat close together by the fire, watching the sunset. As the temperature dipped, she was grateful for his thick, downy coat. He had put his shirt, jeans, boots, and beanie back on.

"Everything looks purple," Ava observed, staring at the darkening sky and distant mountains. Wildflowers dotted the valley where the trees were sparse. "It's pretty. Purple is my favorite color."

Killian glanced at her and gave her a hint of a smile.

"What's your favorite color?" she asked.

"I don't really have one. White, maybe. I like white walls in a house."

"White? That's not a color."

"Yes, it is."

"I think, technically, on the light spectrum, white is the combination of all colors."

He chuckled. "It is. It's called polychromatic light. But white can still be my favorite paint color for walls."

"I guess you can like whatever you want. But why white? White walls are boring. You aren't boring. You know things like what 'polychromatic light' is." The shadows took over the hillside, and she stared at the fire, mesmerized by the dancing flames.

"White is simple and orderly."

"How you like your life, am I right? That's why you keep lists and live on a mountain in a tiny cabin." She glanced at his face. He was looking into the fire, just as she had been.

He nodded.

"Why? A little chaos makes life fun."

He kept his gaze on the fire as he answered. "When I was a kid, it was important for me to keep track of everything I owned. I never knew when I would get something new, or how I would get it, and I moved a lot, usually without advanced warning. If I lost something, I would have to live without. And a lot of the other kids were thieves. So I made a list of everything I owned and everything had its place in my suitcase. I kept track of when I would need new items and requested them early. The habit expanded from there."

"You kept all your things in a suitcase?" A lump formed in Ava's throat, imagining him as a little boy carefully guarding a handful of meager possessions.

He nodded again. "I could lock it and chain it to my bed."

Overwhelmed by the desire to hold him, her heart aching for his boyhood, she scooted over and laid her head on his shoulder. "Well, I'm glad you make lists and have an emergency bag. It's been handy."

He looked down at her. "We should get some rest, now that it's dark. Are you going to be OK sleeping under the stars, Hollywood?"

"I could sleep anywhere right now, I'm so exhausted." She crawled to the top of the blanket and positioned his pack for their pillow. It was going to be an uncomfortable night, but her eyes were already heavy. "I know it's not raining and we have a fire, but we should still sleep close to keep warm. We can share the pillow."

This time, Killian didn't argue. He scooted onto his back and stretched out his arm for her. Preferring his shoulder to the rucksack for her weary head, Ava snuggled into his side. She hitched her thigh onto his hip as though he was her custom-made body pillow and rested her knee on his leg. His arm pressed into her back and fastened her to him.

Within minutes, sleep settled heavily on her body like a weighted blanket. She barely had time to appreciate the unimpeded view of the star-speckled night sky before her eyes closed on their own. But as she drifted off, her stomach growled—loudly—snatching her from the gentle embrace of slumber.

"Are you hungry? Do you want another bar?" Killian asked sleepily.

"No, I'm fine." Ava yawned. "I'm fantasizing about the first thing I'll eat when I get home. The ration bars are surprisingly good, but they aren't the same as a hot meal. I was dreaming about a grilled steak, rare, on a bed of arugula with a raspberry vinaigrette."

His hand skimmed under the hem of the coat to brush the dip of her waist. "If we don't make it to the road tomorrow, I'll set up some rabbit snares."

"I don't eat rabbit," she responded reflexively, already drifting off again.

"It probably won't taste that great, but you won't care if it means not starving." His voice was a little stronger now, as though he'd woken up more fully.

She blinked, feeling vaguely bad about sounding ungrateful for everything he was doing to take care of her. "Oh, I just meant that I don't like to eat rabbit because I had a pet rabbit as a kid and..." She bit her tongue.

"And what?"

"And I talk too much. You don't want to hear my stories. I'll be quiet so you can sleep."

He tightened his grip on her. "You can tell me. I want to know."

She pursed her lips. "Are you sure?"

"I'm sure. With a cliffhanger like that, I'm curious."

"Uh, OK. Well, when I was eleven, I babysat the other kids on base. After an entire summer, I'd saved all my money and was looking for something to spend it on. A little girl I watched, Jenny, had a pregnant rabbit and offered to give me a kit. So I took the money I saved, rode my bike into town, and bought everything I needed—materials to build a cage, bedding, water bottle, pellets, and the like."

She squeezed her eyes shut, forcing the feelings that rose in her throat like bile back into the pit of her gut. "Jenny gave me a tiny, snow-white bunny with a perfect pink nose. I named her Edelweiss. She was so soft. I loved her instantly." Feeling foolish, Ava stopped mid-story.

"What happened to Edelweiss?" Killian prompted after a minute of silence.

"It was my fault, really. I didn't ask my parents' permission. I knew they would say no, but I did it anyway. So, I hid her in my closet. Of course, after a few days, my mother caught me, and my father was furious. He made me put her cage outside, and I wasn't allowed to bring her in because, 'Rabbits are dirty rodents.'" She lowered her voice in mimicry of her father.

"Rabbits aren't rodents," Killian observed.

"I know. But that was beside the point. He thought she was dirty, so out she went. For the next two months, I spent every afternoon in the backyard playing with her. By October, I was worried about winter because we were in Colorado. I begged my father to let me bring Edelweiss inside, or at least into the garage at night. He refused, saying that the only reason people should keep animals is for food and pelts, and livestock belongs outside."

"I was a sensitive child, and my parents were always trying to toughen me up. For weeks, my father told me that one day he was going to, uh, cook Edelweiss for dinner and use her fur to make my mother a hat. He was just joking, of course; he would say it, and my mother would laugh."

"Did you think it was funny?" Killian asked.

"No." She shrugged a single shoulder. "One day in November, I stayed late at school to work on a group project, so I didn't get to play with Edelweiss. When I came home, my mother served strange meat for dinner and ordered me to eat it, no questions asked. After I'd eaten, my father told me I'd just eaten rabbit, and that it was Edelweiss. I screamed hysterically and ran outside. But Edelweiss was in her cage."

"Are you serious? Your parents told you they'd fed you your pet for dinner?"

"Yeah. They were just joking, though. When I wouldn't calm down, even after seeing her in her cage, I got sent to my room and grounded for a month. The next day, I gave Edelweiss back to Jenny so that I knew she'd be safe. Then I refused to eat meat for about two weeks until my parents wouldn't let me eat anything else. So I ate nothing at all for two or three days before I broke and ate some chicken. I cried the whole time. This is why my parents say I'm overdramatic." She forced out a little laugh.

Silence sat heavily between them until Killian finally spoke. "You do realize how messed up that is, right? That your parents were being sadistic and cruel?"

Ava didn't answer him.

"Did they treat you like that all the time?" he pressed.

She shook her head on his shoulder. "No. Edelweiss was my first and last pet, so... Anyway, like I said, I'm overdramatic. I haven't eaten rabbit since that day. I should just let it go. Anyway, you don't have to worry about it. I won't refuse to eat rabbit if we need to for survival. I really shouldn't have brought it up."

"I'm not confident in my ability to catch rabbits, anyway. So let's get to the motel tomorrow, and then it won't be an issue."

"Ah, the motel." She sighed wistfully. "I think I'm most looking forward to a hot shower. But a bed may just edge it out. There's a rock jabbing into my hip."

He reached across his body, clasped her thigh, and pulled her higher on top of him, relieving the pressure on her hipbone.

"Thank you," she murmured. His body was hard, too, but infinitely more pleasant to lie on than the cold, rocky ground.

She listened to his breathing and the chirping of crickets. Feeling secure in his grip, she drifted off to sleep.

Something tickled Ava's forehead, rousing her. She was lying on her back. Mumbling softly, incoherently, she brushed at her hairline.

Something tickled Ava's hand. Her eyes fluttered open. Moonlight filtered into her consciousness. She remembered she was sleeping on the side of a mountain. The occasional rustling of the trees was the only sound.

It was so much more peaceful here than Los Angeles, with its bright lights and road noise. Even her luxury home, tucked into the gated community of Bel Air, suffered from the ever-present sound and glare of humanity. But she was cold, and the ground was hard and pointy, and she missed her bed. Her body ached, and it was too early. Ava sighed, closed her eyes, and drifted back to sleep.

Then she felt the whisper of something on her chin. Her eyes popped open and the night's peace shattered. Because what Ava saw made her scream.

As far as screams went, hers were professional. Her first movie was a horror film where she learned the art of blood-curdling, full-throated, lung-popping shrieks. Her voice reverberated throughout the quiet forest surrounding her.

Her assailant stood on her chest, utterly frozen. It was dark brown and hairy. A tarantula. And it was huge, at least the size of a dinner plate. OK, maybe more like the diameter of a saucer. OK, a coffee cup—a small coffee cup. Nonetheless, terrifying.

Still groggy and disoriented, focused only on the tarantula inches from her nose, Ava screamed again. The spider jumped impressively high and ran like the dickens. It was gone, but before she could register that fact, a man was on top of her. A big man.

A hand clamped over her mouth.

"Why are you screaming?" he demanded gruffly.

She stopped seeing what was in front of her as a flashback tore through her mind's eye. She couldn't move because she was being held down. She was overpowered. She was eighteen and innocent. But she wasn't innocent anymore. Not anymore.

"Stop! Please! Get off me!" she begged against his hand. Tears leaked out of the corners of her eyes.

She had asked for it. She was a tease who wanted attention. Isn't that what everyone told her? She was too emotional, too dramatic, too desperate for love and approval. She manipulated men with her looks and her tears. She deserved this.

She wanted to hide her shame. But she couldn't stop screaming. And now they'd come to her door. They were going to come in and see her like this. Then they were going to take her and examine her and question her. They would put her in jail. And everyone would know.

This can't be happening. Not again. Tears ran hot down her face, constricting her throat and choking her into silence.

Then something unexpected happened. He got off of her. He didn't hurt her. No one rushed in and pulled her out of the room. No one poked her or accused her or threatened her.

She wasn't even in a room.

Where was she?

He pulled her into his lap and rocked her like a small child. "Ava, what's wrong?"

Her vision cleared, and she recognized him. "Killian?" Peering at his face, she tried to control her quaking body so that he wouldn't notice how terrified she was. But, of course, there was no hiding it. She shuddered violently against his chest.

"Why were you screaming?" he asked again, gently.

"Why were you on top of me?" she countered.

"Because you woke me up with your screaming. I thought you were being attacked, and my instinct was to cover you, to protect you from whatever was attacking you. Sorry, I wasn't quite awake yet."

"Oh." She took a deep breath. "That's kinda sweet." She gave him a tremulous smile. "I *was* being attacked. By a tarantula. It was on my face, and then my chest." Ava was glad that it was dark because she flushed from her breasts to her ears at how overwrought she sounded over a little spider.

"You were screaming like that because of a spider?"

OK, yes, at first she was screaming because of the spider. But then Killian jumped on top of her, and she had a flashback to the worst night of her life. It had been quite a while—years—since she'd done that. Her mind was still reeling.

She tilted her chin defensively and spoke with a confidence that she didn't feel. "It was giant. Huge. Like the size of a volleyball. It was on my face." She shuddered dramatically.

"A giant spider?"

"Yes." She held her hands apart like she was estimating the size of a fish she'd just caught. "A massive, terrifying tarantula. All hairy and stuff. On. My. Face."

"Do you have arachnophobia?"

"No."

"Are you sure? You seem pretty terrified. You're shaking like a leaf."

"It was huge and aggressive. You didn't see it, so you don't know."

"Tarantulas are docile and not poisonous to humans. And they aren't the size of a volleyball. Not even close. They're two and a half inches."

She crawled out of his lap and settled back on the blanket, taking a deep breath. "I told you that you wouldn't want to hear how I scream at spiders."

"Well, you were right. Good grief, Ava." After poking the fire back to life, he laid down next to her and held his arm out for her to press into his side again.

Relaxing, she scoffed in mock offense. "It was on my face. I'd like to see how you'd react to a spider on your face."

"I wouldn't scream like I was being murdered. I can tell you that much."

She snorted. "I'm going to find a spider and throw it at you just to prove you wrong."

"I'd bet my life's savings you wouldn't be able to stop screaming long enough to pick up a spider, much less throw it at me."

She scoffed again. "I'm not some shrinking violet."

"Yes, yes, you know Krav Maga and you fight bears." He chuckled. "Do you think you can go back to sleep? It's still a couple of hours before dawn."

"Mm-hmm." But she didn't think she could. Her PTSD episodes gave her anxiety hangovers that lasted hours, sometimes days. Her veins buzzed with it. Instead, she stayed silent, letting him sleep.

She watched the moon fade into the starry sky as the sun rose, focusing on her breath. *Inhale courage. Exhale fear.*

She was safe with Killian. And to her surprise, somewhere deep inside of her, that felt true.

Chapter 9

Killian woke with a start. Ava wasn't on the blanket next to him.

The sun barely peeked over the mountains. The shadows were long, and it was still pretty dark. He rolled over and scanned the stream, but didn't see her. "Ava?"

There was a rustling behind a tree a few feet from him. Ava stepped out. "I'm sorry. I didn't mean to wake you. But since you're up, what does poison oak look like?"

"Why?"

"It was dark, and I wasn't thinking, and I grabbed some leaves to wipe with." She held up a cluster of three leaves on a stem.

He jumped to his feet. "Drop that! Get into the water right now. You need to wash it off." Of all the plants for her to grab randomly... This woman was going to be the death of him. He ushered her to the stream.

"Wait, I need to take off my shoes and coat." She tossed the coat at him and kicked off her hiking boots hastily.

"Take off your shorts, too. I won't look."

"What? Why?"

"Where did the leaves touch your skin? Did you use it on—to wipe? You'll need to take off your shorts to wash the oils off your skin and clothing."

"I didn't use it. I caught myself first. It's just on my hands and my calves because I stepped in it."

"That's good. That would've been... uncomfortable." He watched her wade into the stream and rub at her ankles and calves vigorously, wishing once again that he'd brought soap. "Not everyone reacts to the oil on the plant and gets a rash. If you wash it off right away, you might not react to it at all. Use alcohol wipes wherever the poison oak touched your skin. We've got some in the first aid kit."

He left her to scrubbing and walked back to the blanket. He pulled out the first aid kit and some food bars. He was repacking the blanket when she hobbled over, shoes in hand. She plopped down on his jacket. "I need to change my bandage now." She frowned.

He handed her the alcohol wipes, then crouched to replace the bandage on her foot. "At this rate, we're going to run out of gauze. You're very accident-prone."

She snorted. "You're the one who fell down the hill and used half of our bandaging." She put on her shoes and stood up.

He handed her a bar and a Life Straw. "Breakfast, and then let's get going. It's time to get you back to civilization, princess."

Fifteen minutes later, they were following the stream downhill. "I'm not such a princess, you know," Ava said grumpily.

He glanced at her. She was an atrocious mess, streaked with dirt and her hair knotted around her ponytail band. He raised his eyebrows.

"Shut up." She stuck her tongue out at him. "I'm tougher than I look."

"Because you've got the bear mace?" He was teasing her, but he thought she'd already proven that she was more than she appeared.

"No. Because I'm not just some prissy, emotional diva. I was in the Army; I've been through boot camp."

He stumbled through a step. "You were in the Army? Really? OK, princess, I have to admit, that surprises me."

"Yup." She crossed her arms and gave him a smirk.

"How long were you in the Army? Was that before you became an actress?"

Ava chewed her lip. "It was a long time ago, when I was eighteen. It's a long story. We don't need to talk about it."

He gave her a quizzical look. "You brought it up."

"Yeah, well, all you need to know is that I'm not just some silly, rich, Real Housewife of Wherever."

"I didn't think you were. Except when it comes to spiders."

She scoffed. "I woke up with a *tarantula* on my face. Screaming is a perfectly normal reaction to that."

He glanced at her again. Her normally sunny disposition had clouded over, but he couldn't figure out why. "I can't imagine you in the Army. You don't seem like the type to take orders and blend in. That's why I didn't join after high school. All that conforming would've made me miserable. I need my freedom."

She grimaced. "It wasn't what I wanted. I wanted to go to college and major in theater. My parents thought the military would be good for me because I'm too sensitive. On my eighteenth birthday, they told me I had to move out and join the Army. They wouldn't pay for a useless liberal arts degree. The Army was good enough for my mother, it was good enough for me, and I would be safe there until I got smarter."

Killian said nothing. He could sympathize, however, with adulthood coming at you fast. He, too, was kicked out of the group home the minute he turned eighteen.

"Anyway, joke's on them," she said, a tinge of bitterness in her voice.

"Why? Because you became an actress, anyway?"

She didn't seem to hear him. "When he—you know—I fought him. I scratched and slapped him. I even bit him. But he was too strong. So I started screaming. He put his hand over my mouth, but the watch heard me. The next thing I know, the Army police burst in and caught us, uh, in the act."

"Did he go to jail?"

"See, that's the thing. He told them it was consensual. He told them I was screaming and fighting because I like it rough." She gulped hard. "And they, the police, they believed him." Her voice got quiet.

"I was so young," she whispered. "I didn't even know what rough sex was, much less preferred it. But, you know, the way I look, and my personality, it's easy to believe that I'm..." Ava took a deep, shuddering breath. "The police brought me to medical, and I did a rape kit. Then they grilled me for hours. My command threatened to prosecute me for fraternization. I had to get a lawyer."

"The prosecutor thought I was telling the truth and wanted to bring the rape case. Around that time, the prevalence of sexual assault in the military was getting attention in Congress. The commanding officer thought I was a liability, an embarrassment to his career. So he found some excuse and administratively discharged me. He ordered the prosecutor to drop it. My rapist was never punished—not even for the fraternization. He stayed in the Army, and they kicked me out."

Killian was already a man of few words. And, growing up in the places he did, the terrible things people did rarely shocked him. Still, he didn't know the right way to respond. All he could muster was, "Jesus, Ava, that's—I'm sorry."

"Yeah, so you can see why I don't talk about it. It's not like the Army is going to tell anyone I was there or why I left." She shrugged lightly. "They gave me a one-way plane ticket to any place in the country. Just threw me out in the world as a traumatized eighteen-year-old without money or a place to go. Since I wanted to be an actress, I chose LA."

"Did you know anyone in LA when you moved there?"

Ava shook her head. "No. But I didn't know anyone, anywhere. My parents told me I couldn't come home. They were ashamed—blamed me for the whole thing. They thought I was lying, and using it as an excuse to get out of the Army. We didn't speak for a couple of years after that. Not until I got engaged to Jack. Now they're mad at me for screwing that up, but they love their grandkids." Her lips tilted with a sad, sweet smile that didn't touch her eyes.

She scooted out from under his arm and picked up the pace. "So now you know why I'm off this morning. It's been a while since I've had a flashback like that. I think the stress of the situation has my nervous system all keyed up. I'm sorry. I'm trying to be better."

He stopped short. "Wait." When she turned toward him, he grabbed both of her shoulders and looked at her hard. "Don't apologize. Don't apologize for things that aren't your fault. You did nothing wrong."

She blinked at him and gulped. "Oh. OK."

He dropped his arms. "Did talking about it help?"

"Yeah. Thanks for listening."

"Thanks for telling me." They resumed walking, side by side.

They strolled at an easy pace for a while, maintaining a comfortable silence, with his arm around her shoulders and her arm around his waist. How that happened, he didn't know. But she fit perfectly. She was exactly the right height and right shape, and leaning on each other seemed to make the walk easier. He couldn't think of any time he'd ever experienced such companionable silence with a woman.

"Can I tell you something else? I think talking about this stuff is helping me feel less anxious," she asked quite a while later.

"Sure, go ahead."

"You don't mind? I didn't think you enjoyed talking that much."

"Normally, I don't. But you're good company. Anyway, like you said, what else are we going to do?" Although, he could think of a few things—*inappropriate* things. But he was getting good at squelching those thoughts the moment they popped into his mind. Not that easy because, not only was she the sexiest woman he'd ever seen—even disheveled and filthy, he *liked* her. He'd not expected to like her.

"OK, here goes," she began, full confessional. "One reason I'm so upset about my birthday is because I'm divorced now, and I'm afraid that I'll be alone forever."

He sighed. "Forty isn't that old, Ava. If you don't want to be single, you don't have to be."

She shook her head. "You don't understand. After I left the Army, I wanted nothing to do with sex. I had to get treatment for my PTSD first. Jack went with me to therapy, and we learned how to deal with my attacks. I didn't have sex until we got engaged. I've dated no one since we divorced because I'm scared to try. What if I never feel safe enough with anyone again?"

Although he didn't show it outwardly, Killian grimaced inwardly. He'd been having fleeting, dirty thoughts about her, and now he felt like a lecherous asshole.

"It's ironic," Ava continued, "because my career is all about my sex appeal. Whenever I put on a show as the sultry, confident, glamorous actress, I feel like a fraud. It's all pretend. People think they know me, but they don't."

She stepped away from him before jostling him with her elbow. "I can't believe I've told you all this. I guess near-death and exhaustion really have removed all my boundaries." She heaved a deep breath. "Thanks, though. I feel lighter."

She stepped away to remove his coat as it was getting warm out. He was glad for the space. As he rolled the coat up and reattached it to his pack, he decided he needed to review his list again.

Why It's Wrong to Lust After Nearly Naked, Terrified Movie Star:

1. She'd just survived being buried alive in a mud slide
2. They're busy trying to survive the wilderness

The first two reasons hadn't changed.

3. She's vulnerable, and he wasn't a creep

At least, he liked to think he wasn't a creep. He might need to try harder.

4. ~~She's an impractical Hollywood snob~~

He scratched that one, now that he knew her a little better.

5. ~~She cries a lot~~
6. ~~She talks a lot~~
7. ~~She has no boundaries~~

These things hadn't changed, but he didn't mind so much anymore. He didn't know why, but they were getting struck.

8. She's a famous movie star

One hundred percent out of his league. Thinking about her curvy, lithe, tight—nope, he wasn't thinking about her body again—it was a waste of brainpower.

9. She hasn't slept with anyone since her ex-husband

10. She's complicated

11. She's the opposite of his type

All still true.

12. ~~She doesn't like dogs~~

Considering the pet rabbit story, she had good reason to not be a pet person. Struck.

Five struck and seven remaining. He needed to add another reason, however: She'd been sexually assaulted and had PTSD. Casual sex wasn't her thing, and that's all he did.

She was strictly, firmly *off-limits*.

Confident that he'd gotten his mind right on this, he focused again on their survival. With the hills rising all around him, he felt certain that they were nearing the road.

Chapter 10

Having unburdened herself, Ava felt the stress of her PTSD episode dissolving from her body. But Killian had gone muted.

She filled the silence with soft renditions of Broadway show tunes, working her way through *Chicago*, *Wicked*, and *Phantom of the Opera*—all plays she'd starred in at amateur theaters before she'd broken into movies.

They passed a fork in the stream that broadened it into—well, it wasn't quite a river yet, but it wasn't a shallow creek anymore, either. It babbled and rushed over rocks in little, swirling rapids. In any other scenario, it would've been relaxing.

She was halfway through "The Point of No Return" when Killian halted abruptly. "Look." He pointed.

Ava's head swiveled, but she didn't see anything. "What?"

"A trail marker." He leaned close and pointed again. "Across the river. See the post?"

Relief flooded her. "Oh my God!" She squealed and bounced on her toes. "Let's go!" Bending over, she tugged on her laces to take off her shoes so that she could wade across the stream.

"Hold on there, Speed Racer." Killian grabbed her wrist, halting her movements. "The water is deeper than you think, and moving pretty fast towards those rapids." He jerked his head downstream toward rocks that broke through the surface in a swirl of white foam.

"It can't be more than waist-deep," she argued, impatient to get to something man made.

"A waist-deep river can still exert hundreds of pounds of force, even if it looks calm."

"Oh. I didn't know that." She trusted he did, though. "So, how do we get to the trail?"

He studied the stream for a moment. "This looks to be an OK spot to ford across. We obviously don't want to cross at the rapids, and it looks like the trail veers away from the river, so I don't want to walk too far downstream and risk losing it. There were rapids upriver, too, so no point in backtracking."

"OK, so we cross here." She took off her shoes.

"Yeah." He held his hand out for them and tied the laces to a strap on his pack. "We don't want to fight the current. We will cross starting over here and go diagonally to the other side. Avoid eddies."

"What are those?"

"It's that circular movement, like a whirlpool. There's something underwater causing it to move like that." He pointed at a spot on the bank where a log disappeared under the surface and the water swirled.

He took off his boots and tied them to his pack. "I want you to hold on to my forearms, like this"—he demonstrated—"and face upstream. Keep your stance wide and stable, like you would in martial arts. We're going to cross in a slow circular motion so you don't fall, OK?"

She nodded. Squinting at the small rapids with sudden trepidation, she asked, "What if I slip?"

"If you fall, don't stand up. You could get injured that way. Float on your back with your feet in front of you, so you can push off rocks. Just ride it out until I come get you. These aren't big rapids." He held his hand out for her. "Try not to fall, though."

"You're not gonna take your jeans off?" She asked as he stepped into the water.

He shook his head, holding a hand out for her.

She took it. "But they'll get wet."

"That's OK. It's not cold, and they'll dry. Clothes are protective." He unlatched the waist strap on his pack.

"Why'd you do that?"

"Full of questions again." He locked his hands on her forearms near her elbows.

"I'm curious. You have a reason for it, I'm sure. I want to know."

They moved slowly into deeper water. He kept her facing upstream as they waded in past their knees, shielding the force of the current against her with his body. "If we fall, I don't want the pack catching and pulling me under. This way, I can easily get free of it. The important things inside it are in dry bags, so we could ditch it and pick it up downstream."

"That makes sense." The cold water stole her breath as it swirled against her lower abdomen. The ground was rocky under her feet and her cut throbbed. She couldn't believe how strongly the water pushed against her legs; he'd been right about the force.

"You doing OK, princess?"

She nodded.

"This is the hardest part, but we only have about ten feet like this. Just go with the flow."

She followed his lead. They'd made it more than halfway across the river when something sharp gouged the cut on her foot in just the right spot, shooting pain up her leg. "Ow!"

She jerked, lifting her foot off the ground and letting go of Killian to reach for it. It was an instinctive movement, and she immediately regretted it. The water was too strong for her one leg and she flailed.

Killian grabbed her, his fists bunching the material of her camisole. The frayed straps broke. Her arms went up, her body went down, and her top stayed in Killian's hands, deblousing her.

She went underwater, all confusion and shock and tumbling limbs. Feeling the ground bumping her hip, and a log brushing her arm, she grabbed at it and shot to the surface, standing up. She was three quarters of the way into a full stand when she felt another sharp pain up her leg. This time, it came from her ankle.

Ava froze. She wasn't supposed to stand up. Grasping the log with both arms, she stayed in a half squat. "Killian! Help! I caught my foot on something." Panic rose in her throat for the hundredth time in two days.

"I'm coming," he called from behind her. "Hold on."

A minute later, he was next to her, untangling her from the log and freeing her ankle. "Good news," he said, picking her up into his arms. "We're on the other side of the river."

She clung to him. "I'm sorry. I didn't mean to stand up. I wasn't thinking."

"It's OK. The first time I went white-water kayaking, I did the same thing and sprained my ankle." He carried her up the bank and set her down on a patch of grass. "The bad news is your top is beyond repair." He handed her the shredded fabric that was now more brown than its original peach.

She held it up in dismay. The straps were both broken. There was no way she could wear it now. Remembering that she was topless, she hastily crossed her arms across her breasts. "Goddammit. It's not like I have a change of clothes. Can I wear your jacket?"

Dropping the backpack onto the grass next to her, he unbuttoned his shirt. "It's too hot." He handed his shirt to her. "Here. Put this on." He dug out the first aid kit.

Rising onto her knees to put on his shirt, her shorts slipped. They would've fallen off her had she not snatched them to her body. She held them against her pelvic bone; they sagged on her hips. "Shit, the elastic broke." Frustrated tears stung her eyes. She hoped his shirt was long enough to cover her bits.

He looked at her for a long moment, his gaze burning into her skin. "Hand me your hairband." He moved behind her and crouched down.

She wrestled her wet hair free and handed the circular elastic to him. She broke more than a few strands, causing her to wince. No doubt she would have to cut it short now after all this damage.

Killian bunched her shorts and secured the extra material with her hair tie so that it stayed tight around her waist. "You're banned from the outdoors, Hollywood. Too accident-prone," he teased. "There you go."

She let go of her shorts and was relieved that they stayed up. "Oh, that was clever. Thank you." She finished putting on his shirt. It was wet from him picking her up and carrying her out of the stream. But it covered her up at least, falling to her mid-thigh.

He came back around to face her. "Let's see that ankle."

She sat down and stretched her legs out on the grass. Her cut was bleeding through the soggy bandage. Her ankle was tender to the touch, the skin scraped, and the top of her foot was already turning purple. He pressed on it, causing her to draw in a sharp breath.

"Can you put weight on it?" he asked.

"I don't know." She carefully stood up and tested it out. "Yeah. I'll be OK. It'll hurt in my shoe a little, but I can walk. I think it's just bruised."

He helped her clean her cuts and replace her bandage again. When he was done, she poked at the gauze wrapped around his arm. "Shoot, your bandage got wet again. I'm sorry. You would've stayed dry if I hadn't fallen. And we don't have enough fresh bandages to replace it."

"You don't need to apologize. You didn't fall on purpose." He carefully removed his bandage. "We're almost there, remember? I can put this back on after it dries if I need to, but I think we'll be at the motel before you know it."

"I hope so."

Putting away the first aid kit, he teased, "At this rate, you're never going to catch up to my save tally. You'd have to pull me unconscious from a burning building or wrestle an alligator before we're even."

"Or water land a plane or fight a lion. I may just owe you forever." She put on her shoes and walked over to the trail marker. It had "3 MI" etched on the post, filled in with yellow paint. "Does that mean we have three miles to go until the end of the trail?"

"Yup. It's still early. Probably around nine or ten. Hopefully, we will be at the motel before noon."

A big, stupid smile plastered itself on Ava's face as they started down the path. Finding a well-groomed trail gave her an enormous sense of optimism. They were going to make it to safety soon. It was wide and easy to hike.

Killian's mood also seemed lighter. He picked up the pace, his long legs eating up the ground. Pretty soon, she was out of breath and had to ask him to slow down, as she was near-jogging.

"Sorry, princess. I'm just really looking forward to that motel." He eased up and fell into step next to her.

"Me too. I've been fantasizing about what I'm going to do first. I haven't decided. Probably coffee. Then a shower, and maybe something to eat.

And then I'm going to use the fuck out of that bed. I'm going to sleep the longest, deepest, hardest sleep ever. Oh yeah, it's going to be amazing." She moaned in anticipatory pleasure. "What are you going to do first?"

"I'm torn between something to drink and a shower. Maybe both at the same time. Then food. Then I'm also going to sleep like the dead."

"Oh my God, yes. I cannot wait to crawl between fresh sheets in nothing but my squeaky-clean skin. I'm gonna tear those sheets up. Ooh, I've never been so excited about a bed in my entire life. Not even on my wedding night." She chuckled. "Don't tell Jack I said that."

He gave her a funny look. "I can't imagine I'll ever have the chance to."

"Oh. Yeah." Suddenly, it hit Ava squarely between the eyes that, once they got to the motel, she'd never see Killian again. Somehow, it seemed unimaginable that he wasn't a part of her real life.

Biting the inside of her cheek, turning her head slowly his way, she snuck another glance at him. Her time to ogle him surreptitiously was coming to a quick close. Shirtless, sweat creating a light sheen across his torso, he looked good. She licked her lips.

She wanted to study his tattoos up close, maybe trace the lines and colors with her fingers. Her gaze slid from his inked shoulder to the dark chest hair that tapered down the planes of his stomach and disappeared under his jeans. She swallowed a lump that'd formed in her throat and forced her eyes straight ahead.

It'd been so long since she'd lusted after a man. But Killian was damn fine, with that powerful physique and sexy beard. Apparently, she liked beards? She hadn't been aware of that before.

She thought about the motel bed—the one she'd just been fantasizing about to near orgasm. She imagined him in it with her, holding her as she drifted to sleep, like he'd done the night before. Then she imagined sleeping alone, and suddenly that motel bed didn't appeal as much.

He'd held her for two nights in a row, making her warm and safe.

Safe. He made her feel *safe*.

She thought about all the things that'd happened over the last two days. How he'd come for her after the mudslide, risking himself in the storm for a stranger. How he pulled her to freedom and led her down the mountain. How he'd picked her up and carried her when she'd fallen—twice.

She thought about how he made her drink water and eat food and how he'd built her a fire. He'd steadied her while they walked and taught her about survival. He'd shielded her when he thought she was in danger of an animal attack—twice. He'd doctored her wounds and literally gave her the shirt off his back. *And* he'd listened to her and didn't judge her when she told him her deepest, darkest secrets.

Her chest constricted. In that moment, her mind exploded with the idea that he might be the most extraordinary man she'd ever met. At least her life would never be the same now. Because he'd made sure she lived when she might not have otherwise.

She sucked in a breath. How did you thank someone for saving your life?

After five long minutes, she tried. She took his hand and cleared her throat. "Friday night was a terrible night with a cabin literally falling on my head. But it wasn't the worst night of my life. And that's all thanks to you."

They kept walking, but Killian slowed down and looked at her, his face unreadable. "It was nothing, Blondie."

"Nothing?" She nearly shouted at him. "Are you fucking kidding me? You literally saved my life. And that was just the beginning. You're my hero—my actual hero. Words can't do justice to the debt I owe you. I'd have to stop you from stepping on a thousand snakes to repay you."

Killian didn't respond. Instead, he stopped, craning his neck and cocking his head, his eyes focused in the distance. "Do you hear that?"

"Hear what?"

"Cars. I think we're close to the road."

Then she heard it too: the unmistakably familiar sound of tires whooshing across asphalt. "Yes! I hear it. Come on!" She jogged down the trail, pulling him along by the hand.

They rounded the corner, and the end of the trail came into view. A post marked where the path opened into a small, empty parking lot. The highway was only a hundred yards away.

Ava jumped in excitement. Then, twirling to face Killian, she grabbed his face with both hands and gave him a hard kiss on the mouth. "You saved us."

Chapter 11

Ava had never been so excited to see asphalt. She bent over and feigned kissing the road. Then she checked her laces while she squatted down.

Killian pulled his cell phone out of his pack. "Still no signal." He put the phone in his pocket. "I'll let you know when my phone is working."

"Do you know which direction the motel is in? I assume you weren't going to rely on your maps app." She finished tying her boots.

He checked the compass. "I'm pretty sure it's to the left, which is south down the mountain. I'll know for sure when I see the next mile marker or sign. If we head the wrong way, it won't be by more than a half mile."

"OK." Ava heard a rustling in the bushes next to the trailhead. Turning toward the sound, she saw a pair of blue eyes staring at her. "Oh!" She jumped back.

"What?"

She pointed at a gray nose poking out from under the bush. Then she saw a rope attached to the post that led toward the nose. "It looks like... a dog?"

Killian squatted down next to her. He held his hand out. The dog crept low toward him. It sniffed his knuckles, before rolling over and showing him her belly. "Someone abandoned her out here."

"Oh, that's awful." She crouched down and timidly rubbed the dog's chest, mimicking Killian's approach. "Why are her face and ears so red?"

"She's sunburnt. She's been here for more than a day. We can't leave her tied to this post; she'll die without water."

Ava watched Killian untie the dog and coax her to stand and follow him. He was saving another life without a second thought. "What kind of dog is that?" she asked. "A bulldog? I didn't know they came in gray. She looks like she's smiling at you."

"Pit bull. That's probably why she's been abandoned. Her owners decided they didn't want her and most shelters have so many that they won't accept more." He started walking toward the road, leading the dog by the rope. "She's leash-trained, it seems."

"I thought pit bulls were dangerous." The dog looked smaller than she'd expected a pit bull to be. She was cute, like a cartoon baby hippo.

"Some are. Most aren't. She's definitely not. Look how docile she is." The dog trotted next to them, her eyes watchful and her tail and ears low, timid. "We'll take her with us to the motel. I know the manager. She'll feed and water her."

They started walking along the shoulder of the highway. "Oh! I just thought of something," Ava exclaimed a couple of minutes later. "How are we going to pay for the motel? I have nothing besides the shirt on my back, and I don't even own that."

"Don't worry. We'll work something out. I promise Lisa won't turn us away. She's not that kind of person." He side-eyed her. "Anyway, I'm pretty sure she'll know who you are, and that you're good for it. I'm also sure the world noticed you were missing."

"How? I was supposed to be alone for the weekend. I mean, my daughters are probably worried because I haven't called them, but no one else was expecting to hear from me till tomorrow."

"The US Geological Survey has radar that monitors landslides. They would've detected the mudslide, and eventually that information would've made it to my boss. She knew you stayed behind after your film crew left. She would've tried to call me to check on the grounds. Since she wouldn't have been able to reach me, it would've triggered a search, particularly for you. They probably started looking for us yesterday by plane."

Ava gasped. "My poor kids. They're going to see pictures of the mudslide and know I'm missing. Oh my God." She covered her face with her hands, guilt coursing through her. "This is all my fault. I shouldn't have stayed for the weekend. Look at what I've caused."

"You didn't cause the mudslide, Ava."

"I know. I know. I just—I shouldn't have—" She shook from the stress flooding her nervous system.

"What? There's no way you could've predicted the mudslide. Everything after, we've been reacting, trying our best to make the right decisions, to get you home as quickly as possible. I'll get a phone signal again soon, and you can call your children and tell them you're OK."

Ava's mind whirred with self-disapproval. She always caused a fuss, putting everyone out with her drama. She always made the wrong decisions. "Do you think we made a mistake hiking down? Maybe we should've stayed and waited for them to find us."

"No. I've second-guessed that a few times myself. But we had no way of knowing whether the campgrounds were safe. The roads and hill-sides weren't stable. There'd already been one mudslide. There could've been more. We don't know. Search and rescue might not have been able to get us for days. Hiking down the mountain was more of a sure thing."

"Yeah, OK. OK." She took a deep breath and forced herself to relax. "I can't wait to call my girls." She looked down at the dog trotting alongside them. "We've been through a lot. But I have a feeling the past two days were worse for her."

"Can you imagine? Dogs have the mental capabilities of a two-year-old child. She didn't know what was happening or why she'd been abandoned by the people who were supposed to love her." His voice took on an angry edge.

Ava looked at the dog again. The dog looked up at her and wagged her tail. "Aww, look at her. Such resilience." She smiled at the pup. "We should name her."

"Why? Do you want to adopt her?"

"No. I wouldn't know how to take care of her. But we can name her anyway, just for fun."

Killian's lips pressed into a line for a fleeting moment. "OK, what do you want to name her?"

"I don't know. What do you name dogs besides Rover and Spot?"

"No one names their dogs Rover and Spot."

"Fido?"

"No."

"Lassie?"

"Does she look like a Lassie to you?"

"Not really, no."

They both studied the dog while they walked down the empty road. They hadn't seen a car since they left the trail, but a couple of semis had passed by with a loud whoosh of air. She wondered whether the truck drivers had even noticed them walking on the hard shoulder.

"How about Babe?" Killian offered.

"Why? Because she kinda looks like a pig?"

"I wasn't thinking that, although now that you mention it... I was thinking of Paul Bunyan's ox, his traveling companion in the wilderness. Also, Babe was a blue ox, and she's a blue pit bull."

Ava thought about it. "I like it. Yes. Her name is Babe." She stopped to crouch before the dog. She tapped Babe lightly on the shoulders and head. "I dub thee Babe." Babe strained to lick Ava's face, but she dodged the big, sloppy tongue. "No face-licking, Babe! Ew."

They reached a mile marker and stopped. Reading it, Killian said, "The good news is we're on the right highway and headed in the right direction. The bad news is that it's another three miles to the motel."

Ava sighed. "I exercise every day, but my legs feel like jelly after all this walking." She squinted at the bright, clear sky as she moved down the road again. "At least it's nice out."

He put his arm around her shoulders. "C'mon, princess, we're on the home stretch."

They ambled down the road at a leisurely pace. "I can't believe we've only been hiking down this mountain for two days. It seems like a lifetime ago when I was filming at the campground." She leaned into him, looping her arm around his waist. "Hey, do you remember our first conversation under the blanket in the rain? I asked you why you became a civil engineer, but you never answered me."

"You really want to know? It's not that exciting."

"Yes, I do. I've told you all these things about me, but you haven't told me that much about you. I mean, I can give you a pass since you're my hero and all. But as we have another hour of walking to do, we should use this time to tie up loose ends."

He chuckled. "All right. Do you want the long version or the short version?"

"Definitely the long version. Spare no detail, no matter how mundane. I want to know your superhero back story."

He grunted his lumberjack grunt, and she got nostalgic over the sound. "When I turned eighteen, I knew they would kick me out of the group home. In anticipation, because I didn't want to be homeless, I figured out how to get into college and have the state pay for it."

"You put yourself through college all on your own?"

"More or less. I got state aid because I was a foster kid."

"Did you go straight into engineering?"

"Yup. I wasted no time. I didn't have the money to explore majors. I picked one and went for it." He pulled his phone from his pocket and checked it absentmindedly. "Still no signal."

"I'm sure we'll get one when we get close to the motel. What made you choose civil engineering?"

He slipped his phone back into his pocket. "I liked bridges as a kid. They always seemed so solid, even in the harshest elements. When I was in— When I was sixteen, I spent a lot of time in the library. I read a book about bridges that fell down, like the Tacoma Narrows Bridge and the Oakland Bay Bridge, and it fascinated me.

"Building bridges that can withstand the strongest winds and the biggest earthquakes wasn't impossible. It was a problem to be solved. Planning, solving problems in tough conditions, gives me a sense of control. I know that control's illusory, but with such an unstable childhood, I crave it." He shrugged. "Plus, you know, I have job security, especially working for the government."

She smiled up at him. "You were wiser than me at eighteen. Engineering is a much more sensible career choice than acting."

He glanced at her again, but she couldn't read his expression. "I don't know about that. You've done well for yourself. Far better than most people. Better than me."

"I would never want my children to do the things I did. I had nowhere to go but up once I got to LA, but it was a greasy, grotesque pole."

"What did you do when you arrived in LA, after leaving the Army?"

"The first thing that I did was get one of those really cheap hotel rooms where I could pay by the week. Talk about a low bar for lodging. That place was gross. It smelled of stale cigarettes and sewage and had cockroaches. And it was in a really dangerous area." She shuddered.

"I immediately threw myself into finding work. I took jobs that put me in proximity to people in the movie industry, no matter how weird or difficult. I didn't know where to start, so I just started. Plus, I needed the money. I had nothing—not even civilian clothes. I'd go anywhere, do anything, so long as it was a job that got me near powerful people and paid my bills.

"After a few weeks, I started a job as a server in the VIP boxes at Dodger Stadium." Her eyes locked straight ahead, far down the road, as she drifted into memory. "I had youth and beauty going for me. So I bought the sexiest work clothes I could get away with. I learned how to fix my hair and makeup, and I glammed it up for the executives I served.

"I was trying to get noticed. And I did." She wrinkled her nose. "But it was a double-edged sword. Those rich old men were *handsy*. They constantly grabbed me, propositioned me, promised me riches if I would sit on their laps. Some tried insincere marriage proposals and brought me lavish gifts." She rolled her lips in disgust. "It didn't bother them that I was eighteen, barely out of childhood, and they were in their fifties and sixties."

She shook off the unpleasant memories of their hands on her person, triggering her shame and fear. "Ironic because I wanted their attention, but I didn't like it when I had it. Although it did get me opportunities, so I persisted.

"To get their attention, and to be bankable on screen, I learned to doll myself up, to make sultry faces, and to flirt and tease. Those were my survival skills. I use them to get what I need—approval, money, opportunities. I guess what I'm saying is, just because I do shallow things, it doesn't mean I'm a shallow person. My image is a tool, but it's fake."

Ava wrestled mightily with a familiar shame. Shame that she was raped because she'd wanted attention. Shame that she doubled down on the male gaze, accepted and exploited it. Shame that her parents were right about her. Shame that she was successful when she was a fraud, a phony.

Her mood plummeting, they walked quietly for several minutes. Then something wet splattered on her head. She stopped dead. Sampling the wet spot in her hair, she looked at her fingers and gasped. "A bird just shat on me! Oh my God! Nature fucking hates me!"

She looked up at the sky. The tension that had been coiling in her chest over the past ten minutes was suddenly too much. She had to scream before she burst. She screamed so loud that it echoed around the countryside.

"Hey." Killian pulled her around until he was hugging her. "It's not that bad. It's supposed to be good luck. Anyway, we'll be at the motel soon, and you'll get to shower."

Tears sprung into her eyes. "I have to walk another two miles with literal shit on my head." The tears spilled over and ran down her cheeks. "I don't know a single person who's had a house fall on them. I'm like the Wicked Witch of the West. Maybe I'm a bad person and I deserve this." She scrubbed the tears away furiously, using her knuckles. "Too much! It's too much."

Killian just hugged her while she choked on her tears. Then she felt something wet and hot on her leg. She looked down to see Babe's soulful eyes while the pup licked her calf. Ava laughed.

"I'm sorry, Babe. I didn't mean to scare you. I'm a crier, OK? I'm sorry." She crouched down to ruffle the dog's ears. "Thank you for the kisses, but you can stop now." She shoved the shame down, deep into that pit in her gut where she kept it locked up and put on a serene mask.

She stood up and saw Killian frowning at her. She gave him a shaky smile. "I'm sorry. I'm exhausted. My emotions are all over the place." She wiped her tear-stained cheeks with the sleeve of his shirt, then grabbed his hand to pull him down the road. "Don't tell anyone how crazy I become when I'm exhausted. It'll ruin the sex symbol mystique."

His frown didn't waver. "I don't think it's healthy to cram your emotions down like that."

"No, no, it's fine. I'm too emotional. Always have been. There's something wrong with me." She picked up the pace. "I can't indulge my tendency for dramatics outside of work. I'm better now. Let's just keep going. We're almost there."

Chapter 12

Half an hour later, Killian was still frowning, and Ava tried to lighten the mood. "Look." She pointed down the road as they crested a hill and turned a corner. "I can see the motel's sign!"

He barely smiled.

She heaved a sigh and stopped walking. "Hey, wait a sec. I had a bad moment when the bird pooped on me. I'm sorry. I didn't mean to bring your mood down. Please, let's be happy now. We made it. Please." She gave him a sweet smile that she hoped her ghastly appearance didn't completely overshadow.

"What? Oh, no, Ava, you're fine. Don't apologize." He smiled, but it barely touched his eyes. "I'm happy we made it." He pulled out his phone. "I have a signal now."

She took his phone when he handed it to her. The wallpaper photo was of a shaggy black dog with semi-floppy ears and a big, lolling tongue. "Is that Lola? I recognize her from your tattoo."

"Yeah." He smiled, more genuinely this time. He stopped walking and turned to check on Babe. "I'll hang back so you can have some privacy while you call your family."

"Thank you." Ava dialed her oldest daughter Audrey's phone number. It rang through and went to voicemail after just two rings. She knew she'd been screened. She opened up the messages app and typed.

Ava [on Killian's phone]: Audrey, it's Mom. I'm borrowing someone's phone. Pick up when I call

She saw three little dots and then the thumbs-up Tapback.

She dialed again. This time Audrey picked up immediately. "Mom! Oh my God, Mom! Is that you?" Audrey's voice was breathless.

"Yes, sweetie, it's me." Ava's smile wavered at the sound of Audrey's voice. When she'd been trapped in her collapsed cabin, she feared she would never hear her daughters' voices again. She feared she wouldn't get to hug them again or see them grow up. She'd pushed those fears away so that she could focus on surviving, but a sudden resurgence ran her over like a freight train.

Audrey screamed and then shouted to someone else in the room with her. "Mom's on the phone!" She returned her attention to Ava. "Mom, Mom, I'm going to put you on speaker."

Ava heard some commotion, and then she recognized her youngest daughter Bette's voice. "Mom! Are you OK?" Bette immediately started crying.

"Bette-bug, don't cry. I'm OK. Everything is OK," she soothed.

Ingrid, her middle daughter, spoke next. "They said your cabin got buried in a mudslide and that you were missing. We couldn't reach you when we called. We were so scared." She started crying too.

Ava felt sick. "I'm so sorry, babies. I didn't mean to scare you. I'm OK. Yes, there was a mudslide. But the park ranger saved me, and we had to walk down the mountain together. We didn't have a signal before now. It's his phone I'm using. I know I was out of touch, but I'm getting to you as fast as I can. I promise you, everything is fine. The worst thing that happened to me was a bird pooping on my head."

"A bird pooped on your head?" Bette sniffed through tears.

"Yes. It was really gross." Ava heard Bette and Ingrid giggle, but no Audrey. "Audrey? Where's Audrey? I need to speak to her."

"She went to get Dad," Ingrid said.

After a few seconds, Ava could hear the excited sound of a dog barking in the background. "Ava?" It was her ex-husband on the line now.

"Jack!" The sound of his voice flooded her with relief. She was going home.

"Where are you? We thought... well, never mind what we thought. We can talk about it later. Are you hurt?"

"I'm fine. I was just telling the girls that the ranger at the camp saved me and we hiked down the mountain. The mudslide washed the roads out. We didn't have a signal before now. We're going to a motel." Before she could stop them, the tears came. Even though she was a crier in general, the past two days had been record-setting for tears. "Jack, take me off speaker."

"OK, Ava, it's just me now." For many years, Jack had been like a light-house in a storm for her. Hearing him, just him, she immediately fell apart.

"The cabin fell down on top of me," she sobbed. "Killian had to use an axe to make a hole and pull me out. It was terrifying!" She had to whisper the last part because her sobs were coming out so harshly that she was barely getting enough air into her lungs. "I thought I was going to die. I thought I was going to miss my babies growing up." Her throat constricted, and she had to force herself to breathe as she was getting lightheaded.

"Oh, Ava," Jack soothed. "Oh, sweetheart. You're safe now. It's OK."

She gulped and recovered her voice. "I lost everything. My purse. My phone. The car. All my clothes. The pendant the girls bought me. We had to leave the camp after the mudslide because it was too dangerous, so we've had no shelter since Friday night. We nearly froze to death in the rain. Then we had to hike down the mountain. I don't know how far it was, but it took two days and I'm so exhausted I can barely stand."

Ava started rambling as the levee holding in all her emotions broke. "I've barely eaten or slept. I fell in the river and hurt my foot and broke my pajamas. I'd be naked if Killian hadn't given me his shirt. There was a snake and bears. Also deer. And a tarantula on my face.

"I had to drink mud through a filter so I didn't get heatstroke. I drank *mud* from a *puddle*, Jack. And I wore mud as sunscreen. I had to pee in the woods and I stepped in poison oak. Then a bird shat on my head. And I had a flashback last night." Her shoulders jerked as she blubbered.

"Ava, sweetheart, it's going to be OK now. Are you hurt? Do you need medical attention?"

"Nothing more than a few scrapes and bruises. I don't need a doctor."

"OK. I'm coming to get you."

"Thank you, Jack. I just want to go home." She sniffed and quieted her tears.

"I know. I'm coming to get you now. But you need to tell me where you're at."

"Oh," she let out a shaky laugh. "Um, I'm not sure. Let me look." She squinted at the motel sign. "The motel's name is The Knotty Pine on Highway 180. But I don't know the address. Maybe there's a mile marker nearby."

"Hold on, Ava, we'll find you." Jack shouted away from the handset. "Audrey, The Knotty Pine on Highway 180. ... uh-huh ... uh-huh ... OK." He returned to the conversation with Ava. "Audrey found it. I'm flying up. You'll be home before you know it. I'm leaving as soon as we're off the phone."

"Thank you." She exhaled audibly and gripped the handset tighter. "Jack, how long have the girls known that I was, er, missing?"

"Since yesterday morning. I got a call from Geoff around dawn that there had been a mudslide and that you and the park's engineer were unaccounted for. The news broke publicly shortly after that. Aerial pictures of the mudslide are on TV and it's the whole spectacle. I had to tell the girls. Their friends started calling. There was no avoiding it."

Her poor children, suffering extra because of her fame. Guilt twisted her stomach again. "I understand," she mumbled.

"We were arranging for search and rescue to begin first thing to-morrow. I was about to head up to help, so I already had the plane ready. The Parks Service said that they couldn't allow a search any sooner because they feared that the ground was unstable. They tried looking for you by air yesterday, but you must've been on your way down already."

She bit her trembling lip. "I feel so bad that the girls were scared. I promise I called the first chance I got. I didn't mean to upset them."

"I know, sweetheart." Jack's voice took on an edge. "Listen, Ava, we all love you. I can't tell you how relieved we are that you're OK. I'm coming to get you right now and bring you home where you'll be safe and then you can put this whole thing behind you. Alright? So just hang tight. I'll get there as fast as I can."

"Mm-hmm," she squeaked, tears threatening her voice again.

"The girls want to celebrate your birthday when you get home. Preparing a birthday party for you kept them occupied and hopeful that you'd be home soon. So they're fine. Esme will be with them. Don't worry about them. You just worry about yourself right now."

She took a deep breath again and relaxed. "OK. I'm OK, Jack. I am. Thanks for coming to get me. I'm going to go see about getting a shower and something to eat. You'll need to pay for the motel for me when you arrive, please. I don't have any money. Also, I need some clothes."

"Sure thing." Jack chuckled a little. "Happy birthday, Ava. You never could do things like a normal person. None of us will ever forget your fortieth."

Ava choked on an unexpected laugh. "Yeah, it has certainly been memorable." She said her goodbyes to Jack and her daughters and then returned the phone to Killian.

"Just as you predicted, the Parks Service was setting up a search and rescue operation for tomorrow. The mudslide made the news. My daughters were scared."

"Are they OK now?"

She nodded. "Yeah. Naturally, there's a media circus."

Killian tapped on his phone. "I better call my boss and call off the calvary."

With a nod, Ava hurried ahead to give him some privacy. She stopped dead when she spied the parking lot. Media vans filled the entire space, spilling out onto the road. Reporters and their crews milled around, broadcasting from in front of the building. This motel was the closest lodging to the campsite, so of course they were all set up there.

Her stomach twisted into knots. She was in no condition—physically or emotionally—to deal with the press. How was she going to get into the motel without them seeing her?

A minute later, Killian and Babe joined her as she gawked at the parking lot below. She turned to face him and wrung her hands. "Look at us." She laughed weakly. "Half naked and filthy from head to toe. I don't want to be photographed like this. It's too much. I'm hanging on by a thread here."

He shrugged off his backpack and unrolled his coat. He handed it to her. "It's still wet from the river, but you can use it to cover your head and face."

"Thank you. You said you know the manager. Do you have her number? Do they have a back door that maybe she could sneak us in if we call her?"

"I don't know. Let me try her." He dialed his phone and put it on speaker.

A moment later, a woman answered. "Killian! Oh my God, Killian! You're alive!"

"Hey, Lisa. There was a mudslide."

"Yes, I know. We thought you didn't make it. Where are you?"

"About four hundred yards from your parking lot, up the hill."

"Did you walk all the way here from camp?"

"We both did. I'm on speaker. Lisa, please meet Ava Blum. Ava, this is Lisa Nguyen. Her parents own the motel, and she manages it."

"Nice to meet you, Lisa," Ava said.

"Oh, wow. Nice to meet you, Ava," Lisa gushed.

"The place is crawling with reporters," Killian continued.

"Tell me about it," Lisa said. "We've booked every single room. Ava's disappearance and the mudslide are all over the news. It's been great for business, even though I'm sure it was terrible for you. They're planning a big search and rescue in the morning." She paused. "But I guess that'll get canceled now."

"Did you say you don't have any rooms?" Ava felt deflated and couldn't keep the distress out of her voice. "The thought of this motel and all the things I was going to do with indoor plumbing and a bed have kept me going for the past two days." She frowned. "I don't suppose I could at least have a cup of coffee and a place to hide until Jack gets here?"

"Jack? As in Jack Bullard?" Lisa's voice lilted in excitement.

Ava wrapped her arms around herself in a self-conscious hug. "Yes. He should be here in a few hours."

"You don't have any rooms at all? Even for a just a couple of hours?" Killian pressed Lisa.

Lisa hummed as she thought. "You know what? I do have one room. It's the ADA room. We have to reserve it for disabled customers until all the other rooms are booked. I so rarely rent it out that I forgot. You can have that one."

Ava nearly squealed for joy. "Oh my God, thank you. I could kiss you," she told Lisa.

Lisa laughed. "I'm happy to help. But it's only got one bed. I'm sorry, but it's all I have left. The bed is enormous, at least."

"It's fine," Ava said. "Thank you."

"I could try to find a cot in storage. But I don't know whether we have any that aren't broken," Lisa offered.

"Lisa, it's fine. Don't go to any trouble," Killian said.

Lisa giggled. "With everyone here, I have to work all night. Otherwise, I'd offer you to come to my place, Kill."

Ava side-eyed Killian.

He sighed. "Don't call me Kill." He looked down at Babe. "There're a couple more things that we need your help with, Lisa."

"Anything."

"We found an abandoned dog on the road. She's sunburnt and needs food and water."

"You can keep her in the room with you. It's no problem. I'll call Dr. Sanderson to come look at her when she gets a chance."

"Thanks."

"Do either of you need a doctor? I'm sure Dr. Ali will make a house call in these circumstances."

"We're fine," Killian said.

"Killian needs stitches on his forearm," Ava said at the same time. "Maybe see if he can do that on a house call."

"OK. I'll make those calls for you. Anything else?"

"Can you sneak us in somehow? To avoid the reporters?" Ava asked.

"Hmm. If you come over along the tree line behind the motel, there's an area by the office where we have the house laundry room and dumpsters. I can meet you over there and bring you to your room. It's a motel and pretty open, so it's not foolproof. But that's your best bet."

"Thank you, Lisa. We'll meet you by the dumpsters in five minutes," Killian said before hanging up.

Ava followed him off the road, down the embankment, and into the trees. "So, is Lisa your girlfriend?" She asked it in a teasing voice, but she felt a brief pang of jealousy in her gut.

"No. We're friends."

"Friends with benefits?"

"Sometimes. I'm not really boyfriend material." He stopped to let Babe do her business in the grass before they crept up to the motel.

Arriving at the rear of the building, the dumpsters in sight, they stopped, staying hidden by the trees. A pretty, petite brunette around twenty-five stood by the large metal containers.

"Ready?" Killian asked, looking at Ava.

"Wait." She bit her lip and made eye contact. "First, I wanted, in case I don't have a chance later..." She took a step toward him, rose onto her tiptoes, cupped his face, and gave him a soft kiss. "I wanted to say thank you for rescuing me, Killian. I really mean it. You saved my life. I will never forget you. I will always be in your debt."

She contemplated kissing him again, harder this time. But thinking better of it—after all, she had literal shit in her hair—she dropped to her heels.

He tipped her chin up with this forefinger and thumb, his eye contact causing her breath to catch. "Ava," he said, but his voice faltered. He searched her eyes for a moment before he dropped his hand. "You don't owe me anything. Let's go inside before someone sees you."

She draped his coat over her head. "OK, I'm ready."

Chapter 13

Lisa spotted them right away and stayed silent, keeping their cover. When they got close, she looked Killian up and down, her eyes resting on the gash in his arm. "Jesus, Kill, you look like you've been to hell and back," she whispered.

She turned to Ava and gave her a huge smile. "Welcome to The Knotty Pine. I'm so glad you made it safely." Her eyes flickered down Ava's body, taking in that she was wearing nothing but Killian's shirt, and that he was shirtless. She raised her eyebrows briefly at Killian with a silent question.

He shook his head curtly in denial. They needed to get a move on. "Where's the room?"

She held up two plastic keycards to Killian. "Follow me. The door to the room is right out front. I'll go first, open the door for you, and then you can rush in before anyone can react."

Ava nodded. "Thank you again, Lisa. We've been through a lot, and the last thing we need right now is to be mobbed."

"Of course. I can't imagine." Lisa led them through the laundry room, halting them in the doorway. "Wait here until I wave you over. It's two doors down that way." She pointed along the front sidewalk adjacent to the parking lot.

A moment later, they rushed down the hallway through the room door, with Killian shielding Ava from view with his body. They made it without drawing attention.

As soon as they were inside and the door closed, Killian pulled Lisa aside while Ava ran straight to the bathroom. "I hate to ask you this, but can we run a tab? We have nothing other than the clothes on our backs and my emergency ditch bag. Besides the room, we need food, water, clothes, and toiletries. I can arrange with my bank to cover it in the morning. Unless you can take my card number saved on my phone."

"A tab is fine, Killian. Of course it is. We can settle up when you check out. Take whatever you want from the shop." Lisa grabbed his hand and inspected his forearm. "If you need anything, I'll be in the front office, calling the vet and the doctor."

He gave her a reassuring smile. "You're the best."

Lisa moved to leave but lingered in the door. "I'm just so happy to see you alive." Her eyes shimmered.

Just as Lisa left, Ava reemerged from the bathroom. She carried an ice bucket filled with water. "For Babe." She set it down on the floor and coaxed the dog over for a drink.

Satisfied that Babe was hydrating, Ava walked to the tiny, tiled entryway and sank to the floor. "I'm too dirty to sit on the furniture," she explained. She pulled her hiking boots off and let out a groan of pleasure so deep that it sounded sexual. "These boots are retired. I'm never wearing them again. I swear to God, I'm going to burn them."

Killian joined her in the entryway. "I'm heading to the shop in the lobby to pick us up some clothes and food. I've worked out a tab with Lisa. You can have first dibs on the shower."

"You probably need your shirt back." She stood up and turned her back to remove it, handing it to him over her shoulder. Without looking at him, her arms across her breasts to maintain a pointless modesty, she jogged to the bathroom. "Thank you, Killian. I've never wanted a shower so badly." He watched her disappear into the room and heard her turn on the water.

Killian slowly buttoned his shirt while he imagined her stepping under the showerhead. He saw enough of her, wet and undressed, that he didn't have to fill in any blanks. The vision in his mind tortured him, but he couldn't help himself.

Ava's emotions weren't the only ones that were all over the place after the past two days. His were, too. Holding her chin behind the motel, looking into her eyes, he truly didn't know what to say to her. All the things he felt were a tempest inside him that eluded clarity of thought. He blamed it on exhaustion.

He hurried to the shop in the lobby of the motel. Once safely inside, he grabbed sweatsuits emblazoned with "The Knotty Pine Motel" and pine trees. Then he picked up a giant bottle of shampoo, toothbrushes, toothpaste, water, sandwiches, and bananas. It was all pretty basic, but it would do. Last minute, he grabbed a Twinkie and some toothpicks from a dispenser on the reception desk. Lisa left him an open bag of dog food on the desk, too.

Once back inside the room, he ditched his boots and filthy shirt, drew the drapes more tightly, and started a pot of coffee. He fed Babe, who tucked in like she hadn't eaten in a week; and perhaps she hadn't—he could see her ribs.

Ava's ruined silk pajamas sat in the garbage can next to the television. He added their bandages and food wrappers that he'd been carrying in his backpack while listening to the patter of the shower and the echo of her singing.

The door to the bathroom was ajar, but he knocked, anyway. "Ava," he called, "I got a large bottle of shampoo. I didn't think those little hotel-sized ones were going to cut it. Do you want it?"

"Yeah," she called back. "Come in."

He stepped inside. The bathroom had a huge open shower made for wheelchairs with a curtain on a ceiling track. The room was wet and steamy.

Ava flung open the curtain. She was completely naked, standing under the stream of water, her skin flushed from the heat.

His mouth went dry. He couldn't move. All he could do was stare.

She stepped toward him, grabbed him by the belt loops of his jeans, and hauled him into the shower with her.

Water poured over his head as he faced her, still clutching the shampoo. He was completely bereft of words.

"Isn't this shower glorious? It wasn't fair that you should have to wait." She gave him a dazzling smile that made her eyes sparkle.

He merely gawked at her like an idiot. His brain had stopped working. Perhaps because all the blood had rushed out of his head and straight to his dick.

She gently pried the bottle of shampoo from his hand. "Here, let me help you." She popped the cap and squeezed the thick white liquid onto her palm. Then, standing on tiptoe, the front of her body mere centimeters from his, she washed his hair.

He stood pliable in his shocked silence. No one had ever washed his hair before. Her fingers felt magical as they massaged, scrubbed, and pulled. Pushing his head back, she rinsed the lather down his back. He closed his eyes and felt her lean into him. Her nipples brushed against his chest, causing him to groan.

Ava stepped back to get more shampoo. She soaped his shoulders and chest. He watched her slide her hands over his body, her eyes locked onto his as she worked. Bubbles streamed down his limbs and onto hers. Everywhere she touched, his skin caught fire. She didn't speak; her eyes did all the talking.

His hazy brain reminded him that he was wearing his jeans in the shower. They were getting uncomfortable, and not just because they were now soaking wet. With clumsy hands, he undid his fly and removed them with his boxers, kicking them out of the way.

As he undressed, he never took his gaze off of her. He had been devouring every inch of her with his eyes for two days. But that hadn't prepared him for how beautiful she looked when unabashedly, intentionally naked.

When her hands slid across his chest, and then down his stomach toward his hips, he couldn't stand it any longer. For two days, she'd been driving him mad with lust. Something inside him snapped. With one swift movement, he lifted her by her ass and slammed her against the wall.

"Oh!" she gasped in surprise before he crushed his mouth onto hers. She dropped the shampoo bottle with a loud thump. Wrapping her legs around his waist and digging her fingers into his hair, she opened her mouth and invited him in.

A deep need growled inside his chest. The sound bubbled out of his throat and into her mouth. His cock throbbed against her. She moaned, making him feral.

He was so hungry for her he felt like he could consume her whole. His tongue sparred with hers. He sucked on her lips and pulled at them with his teeth. He stole her breath like she was his only source of oxygen.

Still pinning her to the wall, he bent down to take one of her breasts into his mouth. He sucked hard on her nipple and she cried out. It was the sexiest sound he'd ever heard. He rotated his hands under her ass and widened her legs. He was going to make her scream.

His brain suddenly came back online and shouted at him to stop. He needed to slow down. He wouldn't fuck her dirty against the wall in the bathroom of a cheap motel, and then never see her again. She deserved better. He needed to control himself.

With a Herculean effort, he tore his mouth away from her breasts—her fucking amazing breasts—and looked at her face. The pupils in her crystal blue eyes dilated, her lips were swollen, and her nostrils flared as she panted.

He grunted. "You are so sexy that I can barely control myself. But I won't do that to you." He set her back on her feet.

"What?" she asked in a daze.

He picked up the bottle of shampoo from the shower floor. Now that he got his senses back, he was going to wash her the way she'd washed him. Using the shampoo, he soaped every part of her body, top to bottom, gently scrubbing away the physical reminders of their journey.

He washed her silvery blonde hair, wrapping its strands around his hand, tugging on it to move her head and expose her neck. Unable to resist her tantalizing skin, he kissed where her throat and shoulder met and watched her pulse leap.

He licked and kissed all over her glistening body: her throat, her clavicle, the inside of her wrist, her breasts, her hipbones, the inside of her thighs, behind her knees, her fingertips. He tasted every inch of her skin before kneeling, hooking her leg over his shoulder.

He hesitated, remembering the things she'd told him. He looked up at her, making sure she was OK. "I can stop. Do you want me to stop?"

"No. Don't stop. I want this, Killian..." She breathed his name and closed her eyes.

He teased the outer rim of her with a finger and lapped lightly at her clit with his tongue, watching her squirm. "Say my name again."

"Yes, Killian," she moaned. "Yes."

He slipped a finger inside her and massaged her interior wall while continuing to torture her clit with his tongue, flicking, pressing, and sucking. "Louder."

"Killian!"

He added a second finger and increased the speed and pressure. She ground her hips. He brought her to the edge, feeling her tighten around his fingers. Then he stopped moving, and she whimpered in frustration.

"Killian, don't stop."

He started stroking and licking her again, slowly at first, and then building momentum. He brought her to the edge once more and then stopped.

"Killian, please," she begged.

"I want you screaming my name," he told her. "You don't get to come until you're screaming my name."

He looked up at her again. Her eyes were hooded and her mouth was in the shape of a silent O. "Let go, princess," he coaxed her. "Let go for me."

Using one hand, he lifted her leg higher, so that she was open wide. He licked the full length of her, from bottom to top and back down again, until he felt her legs trembling in his hands.

Lapping at her slowly, he brought her to the edge once more. Pausing, he listened to her pant his name in frustration. "Killian," she pleaded. "Why are you stopping?" Her fingernails dug into his shoulders.

She was desperate. She was ready. He sucked hard on her clit while pushing his fingers inside of her again. Hot, slick, and tight, her walls clamped down the moment he penetrated her. He stroked her, keeping the pace steady while alternately pressing and sucking on her clit with his tongue.

He felt her tightening and tightening, but he was unrelenting, not stopping this time. And then she finally let go. "Killian! Oh, God, Killian!"

He felt her orgasm rip through her body as she came apart around his fingers. Her knees buckled. He held her weight while she sagged against the wall, her eyes squeezed shut and little whimpers escaping her lips.

He continued to tease her fading orgasm with gentle licks until she pulled on his hair. "Stop, no more," she whimpered. She removed her leg from his shoulder to stand on her own. "Oh my God, that was…" She looked at him, surprised and sleepy.

He gave her a smug look. "I know, princess."

He stood up and washed her all over once more, his hands memorizing her shape as they glided over her skin. He washed himself again too, with her help. Soon he had to snatch her hands away from stroking his cock before he came all over her stomach. They needed to get out of the shower before he lost control. He shut off the water.

Ava pushed the curtain aside and grabbed two towels. She handed him one. "These motel towels are tiny and kind of rough," she lamented. "Do you want another one?"

"No, it's OK." He vigorously dried himself off, dropped the towel on the counter, and went into the main room. He handed her a sweatsuit when she followed. "I'm sorry. This was all they had."

Not taking the clothes, she looked at him with pure, naked lust. "Let's not get dressed yet."

He kissed her on her forehead, pressing the sweatsuit into her arms. "You need to eat something. And I made you coffee."

"Coffee," she squealed, delighted. "OK, I can take a quick break for coffee." She threw her arms around his neck and kissed him passionately, molding her body to his. He got so turned on that he nearly tossed her onto the bed with thoughts of pounding her into the mattress.

Babe saved him by whining and pawing at their legs, reminding him to slow down.

Chapter 14

K illian pulled on a pair of sweatpants but didn't bother with the sweatshirt. He filled a Styrofoam cup with coffee and handed it to Ava. She put on her sweatshirt but left the pants to the side so that her long legs were on display under the shirt's hem. Between the two of them, they could just piece together an entire set of clothes.

"Thank you," she said, taking a large whiff out of her steaming cup. She closed her eyes as she breathed deeply. "The smell of coffee is probably my second-favorite smell."

"What's your favorite?" Killian asked, grabbing his own cup.

She blushed prettily. "Men's soaps, the ones that smell musky and woodsy. Like the kind you use. I could smell it on you that first night in the rain."

He took a sip from his cup. The hot coffee soothed his throat; he was parched. Reaching into the shopping bag, he grabbed two bottles of water and cracked them open, handing one to Ava.

"Definitely better than puddle water," she joked after gulping down half a bottle in one go.

He sat at the little table between two tub chairs under the window. "Come eat."

She pressed her hand on her stomach. "Mmm, I'm starving. What culinary masterpieces did you find us?" She sat down in the chair opposite and drew her legs up to her chest with her arms wrapped around her knees.

His eyes lingered on the lines of her thighs where the hem of the shirt pulled back by her raised legs. But he hadn't changed his mind that she was off-limits. Sure, he'd had a momentary lapse in the shower—more than momentary. He couldn't stop himself from tasting her. But at least he stopped himself from roughly fucking her against a wall.

"Turkey sandwiches and bananas," he answered, tearing his eyes away from the spot where her inner thighs disappeared under the shirt. He handed her a sandwich. "I know it's probably not what you're used to, but it was the best that they had, and it beats emergency ration bars."

She smiled. "A sandwich and a banana are perfect." She split the banana peel open and tortured him by eating it first, mewling her delight around each mouthful. He stared at her mesmerizing lips wrapped around the fruit.

The sandwich, as it turned out, wasn't much better. He noticed how her long fingers delicately held the bread. He noticed how her lush lips pursed as she chewed, and how her tongue darted out to lick up crumbs after each bite. He noticed the gentle movement of her throat when she swallowed.

"What are you thinking about?" she asked. "You're making a funny face."

"Nothing." He clipped his response like an asshole, making him wince. He was far too turned on. Everything she did looked like porn.

After he finished his food, she got up, walked the few steps around the table to him, and dropped into his lap. She held her hand up in the manner of ticking items off a list.

"We've eaten." She held one finger up. "We've had coffee and water." She held a second finger up. "We've had a shower." She held a third finger up, leaving her one remaining finger down. "So the only thing left on the list is going to bed. Come to bed with me."

His resolve vanished. He stood up with her in his arms, about to give in to his selfish desire, when a knock on the door saved him. "It's Lisa with Dr. Ali," Lisa said from the other side.

He set Ava down. "Coming," he replied. Ava hot-footed it to the bathroom, snatching her sweatpants on her way. When the bathroom door clicked shut, he let Lisa and the doctor in.

"Dr. Sanderson said she'd come by to look at the dog tonight on her way home from her clinic," Lisa advised, walking in with Doctor Ali. She hastily shut the door behind them. "The news knows you and Ava are here and the search was called off. They're all creeping around, trying to figure out which room you're in. Some of them saw Dr. Ali arrive, but hopefully they won't figure it out."

Dr. Ali sat down with Killian at the table and examined his cut. "Looks like you've done a pretty good job keeping this clean, given the circumstances, and the cut is neat. It should heal fine. But it's deep enough that we should clean it again and stitch it up. And I want you to take an antibiotic."

Killian grunted and gritted his teeth while the doctor got to work, generous with the iodine and antiseptics, and not too gentle with the scrubbing or the suturing.

Wearing pants for the first time since he'd met her, Ava came out of the bathroom and sat on the bed to watch. No one spoke much until Dr. Ali finished bandaging Killian's arm. "Any other injuries?" the doctor asked him.

He shook his head no.

"I'd still like to see you in the office tomorrow, so we can take some blood tests and give you a basic physical. Just in case." He looked at Ava. "What about you, Ms. Blum? Any injuries? Your foot looks beat up. Is that recent?

"Yeah, that was from this morning, actually. I got caught on a log while crossing a river." She made a face. "And I cut the bottom of my foot yesterday, also in the river. But, other than being accident-prone in rivers, I think I'm OK."

"Let me see." The doctor examined her, cleaned her cuts, and gave her his blessing. "Please get a physical. I know it was only two days, but it was a lot of stress on your body. You're certainly dehydrated, so drink plenty of fluids."

Ava gave him her dazzling movie-star smile. "I will. Thank you for coming, Dr. Ali."

After they gave him their information for billing, he left with Lisa. Although they were alone again, the vigorous scrubbing of his cut with iodine was just the dousing of his ardor that Killian needed.

Ava, however, licked her lips and lowered her lashes. She pulled off her sweatpants. "It's too hot for all these clothes," she purred.

Killian hastily stood up. "Since you didn't get to celebrate your birthday yesterday, I got you a birthday Twinkie for dessert. It was the closest thing I could get to a birthday cake."

She looked taken aback. "Really?"

"Yup." He fetched the Twinkie and the toothpicks from the plastic shop bag. "And a birthday candle. And by birthday candle, I mean I'm going to light a toothpick on fire and hope we don't cause another disaster."

She laughed. "You sure know how to make a lot out of a little, Killian Kelly." Her eyes followed him while he grabbed a lighter from his pack, stuck a toothpick into the Twinkie, and lit it on fire.

"Happy birthday." He placed the Twinkie in front of her. "I'm not going to sing because my singing is considered a human rights violation under international law."

Ava gave him a huge smile. "This may be one of the best birthday cakes I've ever had. But I'll only eat half. You have to eat the other half."

"Deal. That toothpick won't last long. You better make your wish."

She tried to blow out the flame several times, but failed. With a giggle, she snatched the toothpick out of the Twinkie and vigorously shook it until she snuffed the flame. "That's not cheating," she informed him. "That's a demonstration of the wisdom that comes with age."

He laughed. "Did you make a wish first?"

"Yes. But you know I can't tell you." She tore the little cake in half and handed one piece to him. "I don't think I've had a Twinkie in twenty years. I don't normally eat sugar." She took a bite. "Oh, wow, that's sweet."

He watched her eat, once again staring at her mouth as she licked the crumbs and cream off of her fingers and lips. He glanced up at her eyes. She had definitely noticed this time. Her expression was smoldering.

She walked over, picked up his hand, and tugged on it. "Time for bed."

Killian took a deep breath. "Ava, I want to." He pulled his hand from hers and scrubbed it through his hair. "I really want to. But I don't think we should."

Her face twisted in shock and then anger. "What are you talking about? Why?" She took a step back from him.

He opened his mouth to answer her, but she spoke again first. "Are you worried about pregnancy?"

"No, I'm not worried about pregnancy."

"Because I have a prescription for a morning-after pill that I can take when I get home, so it's not a risk."

"I'm not worried about pregnancy."

"At forty, the chances of me getting pregnant aren't that high, anyway, but I'll still take the pill."

"Ava, I'm not worried about pregnancy."

"Maybe they have condoms in the shop if you don't trust me."

She wasn't hearing him. He tried a different tack. "I've had a vasectomy."

She snapped her mouth shut and looked at him, surprise in her eyes. "You have? But you're so young."

"After growing up as an unwanted kid, I didn't think it was responsible to add more to the world. And, having never experienced parents, I'm not well equipped to be one."

Ava sunk on to the end of the bed. "I'm sorry. I didn't mean to pry." She pursed her lips. "So if you're not worried about pregnancy, then what is it?"

He hesitated before answering. "A lot of reasons. Eight, to be exact. I made a list."

Her face fell. "You—you made a list of reasons why you don't want to have sex with me?"

"No, Ava. No. It's not that I don't want to. I definitely want to. I made a list of reasons we shouldn't."

"Oh." She scooted back on the bed, lying on her side with her head propped on her elbow, looking at him, studying him. "You make a lot of lists, don't you? Like for everything."

"Not for everything."

"Mm-hmm. Did you make this list just now, while the doctor was here?"

"No."

"So, how long have you had this list?"

He looked away from her.

"How long, Kill?"

"In my head since Friday."

"Since Friday. Oh, well, that's interesting." Amusement flickered across her features. "Alright then, let's hear all your reasons why we shouldn't both be naked, right now, in this bed, when we both want it."

He squinted at her. "OK. Number one, you've just survived being buried alive by a mudslide."

"Get rid of that one. I've survived it, thanks especially to you. It's in the past." She waved her hand dismissively. "Next reason."

"Number two, we were busy surviving the mountain."

"Survived, done and dusted. Next."

"Number three, given the stress of these events, you're vulnerable. And I'm not a creep who takes advantage of vulnerable women."

Her eyebrows snapped together. "I'm not vulnerable."

"Yes, you are. We've just been through a stressful ordeal—a near-death experience, for you. We feel bonded because of it, but it's not our real lives. The high arousal of the situation means you might not be making the best decisions right now, and I don't want to take advantage of you."

"How do you know I wouldn't want to have sex with you under normal circumstances, like if we met at a grocery store on a Tuesday and hit it off?"

"Because that would never happen. You're a famous movie star, and I'm not. That was actually my reason four. We're completely unsuitable. We'd never have met under normal circumstances. Honestly, you're out of my league."

She shook her head slightly.

He continued, "In an hour or two, you're going to head home, and we're never going to see each other again. You're not the type of woman who does casual, one-night stands. You flat-out told me that. And it's for a good reason. I respect it. But casual—that's all I do. I'm *only* interested in no strings attached. Actually, it's more than that: that's all I'm capable of. You deserve far more than anything I could ever give you."

Ava leaped to her feet, her face screwed up in fury. "Hold on," she said angrily. "You think I can't know my own mind about whether to have casual sex?"

Killian blinked in surprise at her sudden rage. He was trying to be considerate. "Not in the present circumstances, no."

"Then what the fuck just happened in the shower? What would you call that?"

"A momentary lapse in judgment, by both of us." He rubbed his temples and squeezed his eyes shut. How did they go so wrong?

"Look at me," she demanded.

He opened his eyes.

She pulled the sweatshirt off and stood before him, naked. She made a sweeping gesture in front of her body. "This is my body. I decide what to do with it. If I decide I want to have sex, that's my judgment to make. I appreciate you worrying about my well-being, but I don't need you to protect me from myself."

She put her hands on her hips. "Good grief, Killian. I'm a forty-year-old woman. I think I can handle the emotional fallout of a one-night stand. What matters to me is that I feel safe with the man I'm with. That's not easily achievable for me. But I felt, I *feel*, safe with you. It's so rare, I want to take advantage of it. And I don't want to second-guess it. I want this, for once, for myself."

She tilted her chin up and gave him a haughty, challenging look. "I want to have sex with you. That's my choice. It means nothing more than that. But it's now or never. So, what are you gonna do?"

Standing there, confident in her own skin, her eyes flashing with indignation, she was the sexiest, fiercest woman he'd ever seen.

He wanted her. He wanted her so much that it'd been scrambling his brain for two days. His cock was throbbing, desperate to be inside of her. She was right there, naked, inviting him to take what he desired.

He still thought she was off-limits, but he suddenly forgot why, and then he stopped caring.

Chapter 15

Ava stood naked in front of a man demanding that he have sex with her. It was, in a word, uncharacteristic. Fortunately for her self-esteem, the look he gave her was so heated that she was certain she'd catch fire.

When he stood up, she let out the breath she didn't realize she'd been holding, and gave him her sultry smile. With a grunt, he snatched her up and dropped her onto the bed. He followed her, his calloused hands all over her body.

She squirmed, her back arching when he sucked on her breasts. "Take your pants off," she breathlessly demanded.

He rolled off of her and onto his back, stripping the sweatpants off. Taking advantage, she straddled him, leering at his hard body. "Hands off. I want a minute. I want to look at you." Her voice was thick with desire.

The corners of his mouth turned up in a lazy half-smile. Still strad-dling him, she folded over and explored him with her hands and mouth. Her fingers traced his tattoos and the ridges of his muscles. She licked, kissed, and tasted him the way he had her in the shower.

By the time she'd made it down to where his abdominal muscles cut in to his pelvic bones, his hands were fisting the bedspread. She brushed her teeth over the tops of his thighs, watching his cock jerk as she hovered over it.

"Touch me," she commanded, sliding up his body, seeking his mouth with hers. He gripped her ass and shoved her until she could feel his erection pressing against her pussy.

As she kissed him, his broad hands burned circles over her back and up the sides of her breasts. Then he cupped the back of her neck with one hand and grabbed a fistful of her hair with the other. Angling her head, he deepened the kiss.

He was back in charge. Killian's mouth demanded everything from her, and she gave it. Willingly. Without reservation.

Soft moans and whimpers filled her ears, and she realized they were hers. She had to have him. She had to have him inside her. Her core ached and trembled.

She tore her mouth from his and rose above him so that she was straddling his hips and looking down at him, her hair wild around her face and shoulders.

His dark gaze burned her skin. "You're so beautiful," he said, cupping her breasts. He rubbed his thumbs over her sensitive, peaked nipples, sending jolts through her body.

She moaned and arched her back, grinding against him. "Killian."

"I'm not going to do it. You have to do it. You have to choose it. You're on top."

"Yes," she breathed. "I want you so badly."

"Then what are you waiting for, princess?" He pinched a nipple, making her gasp.

"I want you to be desperate for me, the way you made me desperate for you in the shower." Reaching behind her, she found his cock and circled her grip around him.

"I'm already desperate for you, Ava."

She rose higher onto her knees and positioned herself above him. Guiding him with her hand, she teased the tip by smearing her wetness on him, gyrating her hips.

She was driving herself mad. Her pussy throbbed. She needed him to fill her up. Yet she frustrated them both by moving back and forth, back and forth, not letting him in. She bit her bottom lip and watched his face as she prolonged their sweet torture.

Still gripping her breasts, he closed his eyes while she hovered over the crown of his cock. "Ava," he groaned, and she realized he couldn't wait much longer. It emboldened her, knowing she could turn him on as much as he'd turned her on.

"Do you want to be inside me?"

"Yes."

"I want you to say it. Tell me what you want me to do."

"Take me inside of you, Ava." He moved his hands to her hips and gripped her. "I need you. Let me in. All the way."

"Yes." Her blood rushed in her ears. Every inch of her body hummed as she took the head of Killian's cock inside her, just the tip, lowering herself with painful, deliberate slowness. She closed her eyes and rolled her head back.

Pounding.

There was a loud pounding on the motel room door.

Ava barely heard it from within her sex haze. She had only one goal in her mind, only one thought that dominated her entire existence: Killian. Inside. Now.

A dog barked.

Banging.

Banging on the door.

"Ava! Ava, let me in." It was Jack. His voice cut through her brain like a hot knife. She froze, her eyes flying open.

No! She wanted to cry out loud, to throw her head back and scream. She very nearly did.

"Fuck," she groaned softly instead. "I'm coming!" she shouted so that Jack would stop pounding. She climbed off of Killian.

Rolling off the bed, she tossed Killian's sweatpants at him. "It's Jack," she grumbled. She pulled her sweatshirt over her head, frustrated tears burning her eyes. She snuck a glance at Killian, who was grimacing but also getting dressed.

Babe barked and ran excited circles around the room. "Babe, be quiet," she snapped. The dog ignored her and jumped on the bed.

Ava's mind raced. Maybe she could send Jack away somehow. She didn't need long; they could be quick. She searched mentally for excuses to be alone with Killian.

None came to mind that weren't embarrassingly transparent. Maybe she should be direct and tell Jack to go away for an hour so she could bone. But she dismissed the idea even as it popped into her head.

She frantically hopped into her sweatpants, cursing as she stumbled around on her sore foot. She saw Killian, fully dressed now, settle against the headboard. He crossed his legs at the ankles and put a pillow over his lap like a teenage boy. Babe wiggled over and laid down next to him, resting her head on the pillow, giving him convenient cover.

Finally dressed, Ava unchained the door and barely had it open before Jack pushed his way in and slammed it behind him. She glimpsed a throng of reporters gathering on the sidewalk as he rushed in.

They'd found her.

Once safely inside, Jack crushed her in a bear hug. "Ava." He stepped back and inspected her before kissing her forehead and hugging her again. "Never scare us like that again," he said into her hair.

Ava relaxed into his hug. They might not be married any longer, but she would always feel safe with him. After about thirty seconds, she stepped out of his embrace. "How many are there?" She gestured towards the door. "We snuck in, but it looked like a whole three-ring circus in the parking lot."

He nodded. "The place is lousy with reporters. They were milling around when I arrived, watching every door and hallway for some glimpse of you. I couldn't escape notice. It would've been futile to even try. They followed me to the lobby and then to your room."

He made a disgusted face. "Fucking parasites. I already put out a statement from the family saying you're safe and requesting privacy, but you know they never respect that."

Ava heaved a sigh. The noise and demands of the real world came crashing back on her like a tidal wave, suffocating her. Oddly, she was going to miss the quiet simplicity of their time hiking down the mountain. She was going to miss being alone with Killian, working single-mindedly on their shared goal, no one around to demand anything from her.

Killian! She'd rudely forgotten to introduce him, thanks to her whipsawed mental state. "Jack, this is Killian. He saved my life by pulling me out of the collapsed cabin and leading me down the mountain." She tossed Killian an apologetic look she hoped Jack didn't see.

At the reminder that she'd almost lost her life, Jack crushed her into his chest again. "Thank you for bringing her back to us safely," he said to Killian over her head. "Our family is forever in your debt."

"It was nothing," Killian demurred.

"It's not nothing," Jack countered.

"I've already told him that," Ava added, trying to sound casual. She pointed at Babe, who'd been slowly climbing higher onto Killian's lap, making Ava envious. "And the dog is Babe. We found her abandoned on the trail."

Jack let her wiggle out of his embrace. "It sounds like you've had quite the adventure."

"You don't know the half of it." She forced herself to sound light, even as her heart got heavier and heavier with the realization that this was goodbye.

Jack turned back to Killian. "The press knows who you are, and that you've arrived here with Ava. But they might not know that you're in this room. If I were you, I'd lie low until they leave. Otherwise, they're going to bother you for days."

Killian nodded slightly but remained expressionless.

Jack turned back to Ava. "We should go. The longer we stay here, the more of them there'll be. We're already going to have to fight our way through a crowd, and I didn't bring bodyguards. I didn't want to make you wait another two hours while I organized security. I know you're eager to get home." He hugged her again.

"So thoughtful, Jack," she murmured, unfairly and wildly annoyed.

Jack glanced around the room. "You said you've got nothing with you."

Ava nodded.

He tugged lightly on her sweatshirt and gave her a teasing grin. "I'm sure you don't want to being photographed in this. I brought you a change of clothes, like you asked. The girls picked everything out." He handed her a small duffel bag that he'd had slung across his shoulder.

"Thank you. I'll go change." She went into the bathroom. She was relieved to see gray slacks, a soft sweater in plum, panties, a bra, and black flats. Also in the bag was a hairbrush and some makeup. She couldn't wait to kiss her daughters.

After making herself presentable, which took extra time because of how unruly her hair had been, she stepped out of the bathroom to find Jack sitting in a tub chair, scratching Babe's head. He and Killian were deep into a discussion about the reintroduction of wolves in America and its impact on farmers.

She cleared her throat. "I'm ready to go." She saw her hiking boots on the floor by the door. "Just one thing." She walked over, picked them up, and ceremoniously dropped them into the trash can.

Killian laughed. "I thought you were going to burn them."

She smiled. "No time. Hopefully, the waste management company will incinerate them for me." She walked over to Babe and crouched down. "Bye, Babe. I didn't know you long, but you were the best dog I've ever had." She ruffled the dog's ears.

Jack took the duffle, which she'd stuffed with her The Knotty Pine sweats. She'd kept them as a souvenir. "Are you ready, Ava?"

"Almost." She walked over to where Killian sat on the bed. She grabbed his hands and squeezed. The pressure of her grip telegraphed a thousand unspoken words of longing, frustration, and a jumble of deeper emotions that she didn't want to untangle or name.

Killian stood up and pulled her into a brief, sturdy hug. "Take care of yourself, Ava Blum. Stay out of the woods."

Tears burned her eyes, and she blinked rapidly to keep them in. "Goodbye, Killian Kelly." She tugged gently on his beard.

Turning away, she fixed her serene mask over her features and walked to the door, where Jack stood waiting. "Alright," she said, squaring her shoulders, "let's go."

Frowning slightly, Jack wrapped a protective arm around her and opened the door. He pulled her in close to his chest, shielding her as he pushed his way through the throng. They didn't say a word to the shouting reporters as they hurried to his parked rental car. But the message in Jack's glare was clear: "Back off. She's been through enough."

The two of them didn't speak again until the winding highway settled into gently curving foothills. "What was that?" he asked finally.

"What was what?" she replied absentmindedly. She gazed out of the window, watching the trees zipping by like a meditation.

"You and Killian. You were upset when you said goodbye. I saw your face. You can't hide your emotions from me. I know you too well. Did something happen?"

"No. Yes. I mean, you'd be surprised how close you can feel to someone in just two days when you're in a survival situation. And he risked his life to save mine. How do you just walk away from someone forever after that? So, yes, something happened, a lot of things happened, but I don't know how to talk about it yet. It's going to take me some time to process it all."

Jack patted her knee. Reading her mood correctly, he changed topics. "Are you hungry? Should we get some food before flying back?"

All she wanted was to get to her daughters. She was going to hug them and never let them go. "No, I'm not hungry. Killian got me a sandwich and a birthday Twinkie." She smiled softly at the memory of the flaming toothpick.

Jack's eyebrows shot up. "*You* ate a Twinkie?"

"Yes. Well, half of one."

"I'm not sure what I find more difficult to believe: you drinking muddy water from a puddle, or you eating a Twinkie." Jack laughed.

Ava laughed too. "*Half* a Twinkie." She stifled a yawn, feeling bone weary. "Is there a bed on the plane? I'm exhausted."

"Yes." He pulled into the airport. "It's a short flight, but you have enough time for a catnap."

A nap sounded divine, even if it would only be for an hour. But first, she had to scratch a little itch. She let out a small, resigned breath. Imagining having sex with Killian while touching herself wasn't the same thing as actually having sex with him, but it was the closest she was ever going to get.

Chapter 16

After the door clicked shut behind Jack and Ava, Killian listened to the fading shouts of the reporters calling her name. Soon the little room was quiet—too quiet, too empty, even though he and Babe were still in it.

He turned on the news out of a morbid curiosity. The reports quickly disabused him of any notion that his life would soon return to normal.

The live news cameras followed Ava as Jack rushed her through the crowd and she ducked into a dark car. A helicopter circled overhead, giving him an aerial glimpse of the madhouse of reporters in The Knotty Pine's parking lot, with occasional shots of the door to his room. Creepy.

The helicopter followed Jack and Ava's car for miles down the highway while commentators speculated on her health, the ordeal she'd survived, and where she was headed. Then the newscast cut to aerial pictures of the campground.

As he'd surmised, the hillside beneath the parking lot had given way. The lot had partially collapsed, taking his truck and Ava's SUV down the slope with tons of mud and asphalt. The slide had sideswiped her cabin, the force of it shoving the structure off its cinder block foundation.

The bulk of the mudslide directly crashed into her two neighboring cabins, turning them into matchsticks, snapping nearby trees, and mangling their vehicles. The road was impassible with debris. But his own cabin miraculously still stood, undamaged.

Killian took in the images, his mind slowly accepting the destruction. The campground might have to be condemned. It was closed until further notice, although Parks would attempt to clear the road on Monday.

He wondered what his job would look like for the rest of the year, if he even had one. Where was he was going to live? Would he have access to his belongings? How was he going to get around without a truck?

He'd avoided thinking about these things on their hike down, focusing on their survival, and distracted by his comely companion. But now the possibility of losing everything punched him in the gut. He didn't have much, but he hadn't planned to start over from nothing. All the years of careful planning, guarding his belongings, controlling the variables... was it all pointless?

As he was still reeling, unsteady in a way that he hadn't been since childhood, the newscast put his name and face on the screen. They'd received his employee badge photo from Parks, and broadcasted it for the entire world, making him feel exposed. The anchor reported he was confirmed safe, having arrived at The Knotty Pine with Ava Blum.

From there, the newscast went off the rails. "Expert" commentators sat around a table discussing hypotheticals, speculating on his time with Ava, and giving questionable survival advice. Then the panel turned gossipy. They wondered aloud about their relationship, and what they'd done while alone together in the wilderness.

Disturbed, Killian turned the TV off. Babe scratched at the door. She needed a walk, and so he couldn't avoid going out. Sighing, he put on his boots and lassoed Babe with the rope. She hopped excitedly, thrilled to see the world. Somehow, despite having been abandoned, she didn't know that people sucked.

As soon as he opened the door, strangers with cameras pointed them at him. Off-putting as that was, the reporters didn't mob him, at least. They gave him enough space that he could walk with Babe to the lawn. But they tried talking to him, and he didn't like talkative people.

"How are you feeling?"

"Did either of you get injured?"

"Were you and Ava Blum trapped in the mudslide?"

He watched Babe circle in the grass and squat before he acknowledged any of them. Looking at the last person to ask a question, he said, "I wasn't trapped in the mudslide, but Ava was. It's up to her whether she wants to talk about it. It's not my place. I'd prefer it if you'd leave me alone."

He thought that was clear, but several reporters pressed. Babe was still sniffing the grass, forcing him to stand there.

"Did you rescue her?"

"What happened to you?"

"How did you make it down from the campground?"

"We walked," he said flatly. Babe strained on the rope; she had the zoomies and needed to run around. He tugged lightly on her leash so that she'd follow him to the woods behind the motel. "Excuse me."

"Is that your dog?" asked a young woman with enough social savvy to try breaking the ice so that Killian would talk.

It worked, sort of, because he saw an opportunity to help Babe find a home. "Ava found her abandoned on the trail this morning. I expect she'll be up for adoption through the county shelter in a few days."

He kept walking around the building with his uninvited entourage.

The same reporter, having taken an inch, went for the mile. "What's the nature of your relationship with Ava Blum?"

He paused. "There isn't one." Then he walked the dog into the trees so they'd have a little peace.

By the time he returned to his room twenty minutes later, Lisa had arrived with the vet, pizza, and beer. "I got the kind with all the meats," she said, setting the pizza down on the table. She twisted the cap off a bottle before passing it to him. It tasted pretty damn good.

Dr. Sanderson brought vaccines, subcutaneous fluids, flea medicine, and a salve for Babe's burned skin. "Can you foster her?" she asked when she finished taking blood and fecal samples and administering shots. "The county shelter won't take her, and I don't have any space. The waiting period before anyone can adopt her is six days."

"I don't know," Killian demurred. "I don't know yet whether I'm homeless and unemployed. I might not have a place to keep her."

"You can keep her here," Lisa offered. "It's fine. And you can stay as long as you need."

"No Lisa, you've been generous enough," he argued.

"Not that generous," she responded. "Jack Bullard gave me a thousand-dollar tip for the trouble of all the reporters being here, which was no trouble at all because we've made more money this weekend than we'd made all last month. And all this publicity has tripled our bookings for the rest of the summer. Then he put his credit card on file and told me to use it for your entire bill, even if you have to stay for weeks."

Killian grimaced. "I can pay my own bill. I have money, just no wallet."

She handed him a slice of pizza. "Just accept someone doing something nice for you. You've earned it."

"So you'll foster the dog?" Dr. Sanderson cut in as she packed up her supplies.

Killian shrugged. "I guess so."

"Good. I'll report her to the county animal services so they can list her for adoption. Bring her into my office in two days for worm preventatives."

She clapped him on the shoulder. "Thanks, Killian. You're doing a good thing." Then she left.

Lisa handed him another beer. "I know you're tired. I don't have to stay."

"No, stay. Have a beer with me." He wasn't ready for the oppressive emptiness of the hotel room just yet.

They drank a couple of beers together and polished off the pizza before exhaustion hit Killian like a ton of bricks. Lisa noticed and got up to leave without being asked. From the doorway, she gave him a little wave. "I'm glad you didn't die, Killian. I would've missed you. See you later."

Within minutes, he crashed and slept like the dead for twelve hours. He would've slept longer, but Babe had jumped on his chest and licked his face until he let her out the next morning.

That first full day after Ava left, with nothing to occupy him, Killian spent most of the time thinking about her. His boss, Mary, had insisted that he stay in the motel and take a couple of days "to recover from your ordeal." She blew off his protests, but at least she'd assured him he still had a job and they would get him to his cabin later that week.

He tried reading, but couldn't concentrate. He sat on the bed and stared at the wallpaper. Ava had left him frustrated and fixated, and boredom definitely wasn't helping. He wasn't used to inactivity.

He felt like he was in jail, which made him itchy. He couldn't go outside, go for a drive, or watch TV to distract himself. Even Babe wasn't much of a distraction, as she'd become lethargic from the vaccines and was recovering from her sunburn.

Lisa came around in the mid-afternoon and drove him to town to replace his bank card, buy a change of clothes, and get some proper food. They let Babe stick her head out of the window of Lisa's car to taste the wind. Then they went to the pet store, and he bought her a bed, collar, bowls, and a leash.

When they got back to the motel room, he removed the bandage around Babe's leg where she'd had blood drawn, and thought of Ava tending to his arm.

Settling back on the bed with the dog, he saw a spider run across the wall and thought of Ava freaking out at the tarantula.

At the store, he'd bought a fresh flannel shirt, and thought of Ava calling him a lumberjack.

He heard Britney Spears in the grocery store and thought of Ava singing.

He saw toilet paper—toilet paper!—and thought of Ava holding poison oak.

His friend Mac texted him to see how he was holding up. They discussed their upcoming paddling trip. He thought of Ava falling in the river and losing her shirt, and how he'd carried her.

He cleaned the mud out of the Life Straws in the bathroom sink, repacked his emergency bag, and made a list of replacement items and additions. And he thought of Ava the entire time.

He took a shower, and thought of Ava... long and hard.

Later that night, staring at shadows from bed, he had trouble sleeping because he was alone. He'd slept alone every night of his life, except for the two nights he and Ava were on the mountain. Yet, it felt like a regression to sleep without her curled into his side.

He punched his pillow in frustration, drawing an irritated look from Babe. "This is ridiculous," he grumbled to the dog. "I knew her for less than two days. I've known *you* longer now." Perhaps he should try better distractions, like sex with another woman to douse the fire she'd started, because jerking off in the shower wasn't doing it.

On the third day, he'd stared at the wallpaper in his room so long that the pattern annoyed him. Thankfully, Mary called with the news that tomorrow he could go to the campground with a colleague and assess its safety for the public, whether repairs were feasible, and whether he needed to move out of his cabin. His totaled truck belonged to his employer, so they were bringing him a new one. This lifted his mood somewhat.

When Lisa came by later that evening, Killian made a half-hearted attempt at flirting with her. She required little prompting; she already wanted to fool around. But when she sat on his lap, it was Ava he saw. Aggravated, he made a lame excuse about having to get up early for work and herded her to the door.

Lisa paused on the threshold and gave him a searching look. "I don't think you're OK," she said at last. "Want to talk about what happened on the mountain?"

Talking was the last thing he wanted to do. "No."

She gently turned his forearm to inspect his stitches. "Did something happen with Ava?" She made unflinching eye contact, demanding honesty.

"No."

Lisa raised her eyebrows, dropped his arm, and placed a hand on his chest. "OK, Killian. Call me when you're feeling like yourself again." She thumped him lightly and gave him a saucy grin. "I can't guarantee I'll be available, though. I'm a catch."

She'd been a good friend all week, and he felt like a jerk. He looked at her and really saw her for the first time in days. Her olive skin glowed in the low light from the bedside lamps. "You really are a catch. And I'm not worth waiting for."

She rolled her eyes. "Yes, yes, you're a lone wolf, blah blah blah." With a soft chuckle, she gave him another thump and then left.

Killian didn't notice Lisa leaving because his mind filled again with Ava. He saw her standing before him, fiercely declaring that she didn't need him to protect her from herself.

She was right. She didn't need him. And he didn't need her. What he needed was to stop ruminating and go back to work.

Killian was up at first light the next morning. After showering and taking care of Babe, he walked a mile down the road to a local diner. The morning air was crisp, and it felt good to stretch his legs after being cooped up.

The Black Bear Cafe had a life-sized wooden carving of a black bear and cub in the gravel by the front door. He smiled slightly at the memory of Ava telling a real-life black bear she took self-defense classes.

An hour later, his colleague, Randy, showed up with his replacement truck. "Hey, man, it's good to see you. We thought we'd lost you."

Randy waved at the waitress to fill up his coffee mug. "We finished clearing the road yesterday. It held for the bulldozer, so we should be fine in the truck when we drive around to take measurements."

Randy added creamer to his coffee and took a sip. "You won't believe this. The production company wants to come back up for more filming—reshoots, they said—and they want us to make the camp safe. Apparently, their lawyers made some threats to Mary."

He took another leisurely sip of coffee. "Even crazier, they told Mary that they want to come back in a month. She said we need to be quick about assessing things so that she can work it out with them and avoid a lawsuit."

Randy shook his head as he continued to drink his coffee. "Hollywood types have no clue. They think the world revolves around them. I don't know how you could stand being around them for all those weeks."

Killian grunted. "If it's not safe, we'll tell them no. I'm not dragging another movie star down a mountain. This job doesn't pay enough for a repeat of that."

He remembered Ava shouting at the sky after the bird pooped on her head. "Anyway, I can't imagine that Ava will come back. She was pretty traumatized by the time we made it to the motel. How much could they possibly do without their lead actor?"

"I don't know. But we can't let them back if there could be more collapse." Randy drained his mug and dropped a five-dollar bill on the table. "We better get going. We have a long day ahead of us."

After picking up Babe, they drove to the campground. Randy and Killian tried their best to find reasons to condemn it. But ultimately it would be safe for visitors, so long as it didn't rain and the parking lot stayed off-limits.

Killian could also move back into his cabin. So once the debris got removed, the camp would reopen for reshoots, but would stay closed to the general public for the rest of the year. They still needed to stabilize the hillside before the winter rains.

With a sigh and a bit of trepidation, Killian called Mary and told her that they could allow the film crew to return in a month. Mary arranged for tow trucks, bulldozers, and a dumpster on site by the end of the week.

It was already dark by the time Killian drove Randy home. Afterward, he checked out of the motel and returned to his little cabin. He went inside his humble home for the first time in almost a week. It felt much, much longer.

The cabin was eerily quiet. The thud of his boots echoed across the rustic wood floors. He dropped his bags on the table and lit the oven for whatever unsatisfying instant meal he had stored in the freezer. Babe found the couch and made herself comfortable.

Killian remembered why he had Lola all those years. Dogs were good company. He decided it was time to get another one. Coming home to the cabin would be much better with a mutt wagging its tail in greeting.

He switched on the rest of the lights and sank into the couch, pondering the knowledge that the film crew would be back in a month. He wondered whether Ava would be with them. Frankly, it didn't matter. A few weeks and lots of physical exertion should be plenty of time for him to forget about her.

The next morning, when the sun came up, he noticed that the cabin had a layer of grime from years of neglect. He had reports to write for work, but he wasn't ready to sit in front of a computer all day. After days of confinement, he was still restless and needed to move.

He gathered his cleaning supplies and began scrubbing. It took all day, and he was surprisingly tired by the time he was done, but he'd scrubbed from floorboards to ceilings. His shoulders and back burned from hours of repetitive motion. But it was a good exhaustion.

He popped open a beer and surveyed his handiwork in the waning sunlight. The cabin looked a lot more hospitable. Hospitable for whom, he had no idea. For himself, he decided.

Chapter 17

It took Ava two days to remember that Killian's phone number was in Audrey's call history. Between dealing with the production company's insurance and lawyers, recovery from exhaustion, and her daughters needing extra love and reassurance, the days whizzed by.

But then her new phone arrived by FedEx. She watched her text messages load from her cloud backup. She remembered the last phone she'd used to text her daughter, and the man it belonged to.

Pilfering Audrey's phone after her daughter went to bed, Ava discreetly saved his contact. She didn't know why she was being sneaky about it. But when she thought about that motel room, or, more accurately, what they did while in it, she felt uncharacteristically shy.

A week later, she returned to her house in LA after recovering at Jack's place in San Diego. Lying in her enormous, embarrassingly opulent bed, her mind wandered again to Killian, and the incomplete way they'd left things. She picked up her phone and stared at it. She'd still not attempted to call or text him.

Earlier that day, her manager told her that the producers wanted her to go back for reshoots. Since that call, her mind kept returning to the possibility of going back up the mountain. Maybe she could see him. But how would she have the nerve to see him if she didn't even have the nerve to text him?

Feeling lonely, Ava resolved to do it. She would feel better knowing he was alright. She needed to know how he was, and get his opinion on the campground's safety, before she could entertain the idea of heading back for reshoots.

With a nod and a sharp inhale of breath, she typed his name. Then she stared at the keyboard for several minutes because she didn't know what to write. "Ava, you're a grown-ass woman," she reminded herself in disgust. Willing her fingers to move, she typed in a hasty message and hit send before she could second guess it.

Ava: Hey Paul Bunyan

His reply was quick.

Killian: Ava?

Ava: Yes

Killian: Don't call me that

She relaxed and smiled, deciding it might be fun to play with him.

Ava: Should I call you Dudley Do-Right instead?

Killian: Why would you?

Ava: Because you're like a do-gooder Mountie who saved me in the wilderness. At least according to the media. And they're not wrong

There was a certain fairy tale-like familiarity to the story that she was a fair maiden who'd been rescued by the humble woodsman. The press ran with it and the public ate it up.

Killian: Your nickname game is weak, Hollywood

He was right. Dudley Do-Right wasn't a good nickname. She could do better. She tapped her chin.

Ava: What should I call you? I can't call you Survivor Ken. Your coloring is all wrong for that

She scrunched her nose while trying to think of a better nickname, but nothing fit. Well, nothing funny, anyway. She could think of other things to say, though. Dirty, dirty things.

Killian: My name is Killian

She furrowed her brow, trying to think of a clever response. Why was she having so much difficulty with words? He didn't wait for her reply.

Killian: I know you know it. I made you say it a bunch to be sure

Ava blushed, and her core tightened.

Ava: If you want to hear me say your name again, then call me

She'd sent it impulsively, without thinking. Her eyes huge, she threw her hand over her mouth. What on Earth was she doing? She just meant to check in on him to make sure he was OK. It's been over a week since the motel room. How could a mere few minutes of texting ignite so much lust in her that it immediately scrambled her brain?

His name lit up her screen. Butterflies erupted in her stomach.

"Hello?" Her voice sounded cool and comfortable, even though she was anything but. Thankfully, she was a talented actress.

"How could I refuse an invitation like that?" The deep, masculine rumble of his voice made the butterflies in her belly clash and riot, and her inner thigh muscles flex. She drew in a sharp breath and gathered herself.

"Killian," she breathed out his name in a sultry tone. Then she grinned like the Cheshire Cat even though he couldn't see her. "That first time was a freebie. If you want to hear it again, you'll have to inspire me."

He made a low, growly noise. "You left me pretty frustrated, princess."

"Did I?" She feigned innocence. "What did you do about it?"

"You first. Did you make yourself come while you thought of me?"

"Yes."

He groaned in approval. "Good girl."

"More than once. First on the flight home. Then again the next day in the shower. And a few times since."

"Where are you now?"

"I'm in bed. Where are you?"

"Also in bed."

Ava closed her eyes. "My bed is cold. I don't sleep as well without you warming me." She recalled the feel of his hands rubbing her skin, creating friction and fire wherever they went.

"The problem could be your clothes. You wear very little," he teased.

"Could be. Actually, I'm not wearing anything at all." Ava was telling the truth because she'd just pulled her panties down to her ankles and kicked them off.

"You're naked?"

"Mm-hmm. Should I get dressed? Or can you think of something else that will make me hot?"

"Touch yourself."

"I will if you will."

"I already am. The sound of your voice makes me hard. Do you get wet talking to me?"

"Hmm, let me see." She dipped a finger in between her legs. "Oh, my. I'm a mess." She skated her fingers up to her clit and sucked in air between her teeth at the sensation. She was fully primed. "I've been wet for you ever since I left. Nothing seems to satisfy me."

"Mmm. I think about you when I shower. I can still taste you."

"I'm using my fingers to tease myself, just like you did." She pushed a finger inside. A moan escaped her lips. She arched against the mattress. "Oh, I'm so turned on. I'm getting close already."

"No, not yet. Slow down. Wait until I give you permission to come."

She stilled her hand and groaned. "I'm desperate for you," she whimpered. "I've been desperate for days."

"Patience, princess."

"How can you deny me?" she pouted.

"How are you going to convince me to let you come?" His voice was wickedly playful, sinful, delicious.

"I'll say your name," she offered.

"Try it."

"Killian," she moaned his name in her sultriest, sexist, breathiest voice. "Please, Killian, make me come."

"Touch yourself again. Tell me when you're close."

Ava's body thrummed as she circled her clit and listened to his heavy breathing. "Are you stroking your cock for me?" she asked between ragged breaths.

"Yes. I'm thinking about how hot you looked on top of me, how turned on you were."

She smiled, knowing she was the star of his fantasies. "I liked the feel of your cock. It was so thick, it took up my entire hand. I liked teasing you, making your tip wet with my arousal. Do you think about that when you stroke yourself?"

He groaned.

She moved her fingers faster, building the pressure. "Killian, I'm close. Can I come, please?"

"Not yet. Take your hands off your pussy before you lose control. Put them on your breasts. Pinch your nipples. Make your nipples hard for me."

"Yes." Ava sighed loudly as her breasts tingled and her nipples tightened.

"Harder, princess."

She pinched harder and gasped. "That feels good."

"You have the most beautiful breasts I've ever seen. They're fucking gorgeous." His voice sounded gruff with desire. "Again. Pinch them harder for me so I can hear you moan."

Ava twisted her nipples this time, a jolt of pleasure bursting through her body, causing her to jerk against the mattress. "Killian!" she cried in a breathy gasp. Her core spiraled and tightened. "I need..."

Not waiting for permission, she moved her hands off of her breasts and back down to her pussy. She pressed her fingers against her clit, keeping her movements slow and lazy so that she wouldn't come on the spot.

But she couldn't wait any longer. She begged, just like she had in the shower. "Please, I need to come." She was aching and uncomfortable, squirming on her mattress. "Killian, fuck, you turn me on."

"I like the way my name sounds in your mouth." His voice was raspy and she knew he was right there with her. "But I keep imagining something else that I would like in your mouth. That smart, beautiful mouth."

Ava would do anything to orgasm. "Let me come now, and I'll get down on my knees for you." Imagining taking him into her mouth nearly undid her on the spot. "I'll say your name while you choke me with your cock. I'll suck and swallow every drop of your come down. But only if you let me come now. I need it now."

"Fuck, what an image." He groaned again. "Yes, come for me, Ava. Let me hear you come."

She quickened her fingers. A few moments later, her core curled into a tight ball and then exploded like a supernova. "Oh, yeah! Killian, I'm coming for you!"

She heard him groan and knew he'd joined her in release.

They didn't speak for several long seconds as they floated in their receding orgasms.

"I didn't know that phone sex could be so hot," Ava said with a soft laugh.

"Me neither. How did you get so good at dirty talk?" His voice was lighter now, teasing.

"You inspire me." It was true; she'd never talked so dirty before. "Maybe it's all the frustration from not finishing what we started. I think it broke my brain."

The line was quiet for a moment. "Are you coming up with the rest of the film crew for reshoots next month?"

A heavy feeling chased away her afterglow. "I don't know. We just started talking about it today."

"Does the idea of coming back here make you anxious?"

"A little, yeah. I'm not sure how I'm going to feel about seeing the spot where I was buried alive." She also wasn't sure how she was going to feel about seeing him. She didn't want to get her hopes up. "Are you back in your cabin? Are you OK? Is everything OK?"

"Yeah. Everything is fine. I had to wait a few days in the motel before I could come back up. The truck was a total loss. Three cabins too. But my cabin was unscathed. A crew came up a few days ago and cleared the debris."

"I'm glad to hear that it wasn't worse. I haven't heard much about the damage. I'm avoiding the news, and the producers are keeping me in the dark because they're worried about upsetting me before reshoots."

"They underestimate you."

"Yeah, well, I'm used to that." Ava snuggled into the blankets, even though his voice and words made her feel warm.

"I hope to see you if you come back up," Killian said.

Ava smiled. "I'll stop by your cabin on one condition."

"What's that?"

"You offer me coffee."

"I can do that."

"Good." Going back up the mountain seemed less scary now.

"What have you been doing since you got home?" Killian asked.

"I spent an ungodly amount of time dealing with insurance adjusters. I could never be a lawyer. All that paperwork makes me want to shoot myself." She snickered. "Other than that, I've been spending time with my daughters. They were traumatized because they thought I was dead. You won't find *that* in any parenting books. I'm trying to restore their sense of security. I think maybe I should involve a therapist—call in a professional."

"You sound like a wonderful mom. You're home with them, and that's the most important thing. Counseling can't hurt, though."

"Thank you," she said softly. "How'd you know just the right thing to say to make me feel calmer? You have a knack for it."

"I was in a lot of therapy as a kid."

"Oh. Uh... Why?"

"I acted out. Attachment disorder. Pretty common for foster kids. The schools and the state guardians had me in group and individual therapy by the time I was seven, and that continued for ten years."

"Did it help?"

"Yeah, I think it did. I'm not in jail, so I think that was really their goal."

"I wanted to know—I mean, the reason I texted before we got sidetracked is that I was wondering if you're OK."

"I'm OK, Blondie. Doing just fine."

She took a deep breath. "I think I'm still processing our experience with the mudslide and hiking down the mountain. You'd think I'd have some profound epiphany from my near-death experience. I did nothing but stare at trees for two days. But I'm just as confused as before. I'm now forty plus nine days, and I'm no wiser. Maybe something is wrong with me."

"Nothing is wrong with you. I don't think there's some correct way to deal with an experience like surviving a mudslide."

"Well, what about you? How are you dealing with it?"

She heard Killian exhale. "I wasn't the one who was buried by the mudslide, princess," he said gently.

"Yeah, but what about everything that happened after that?"

"Not traumatic. I was mainly concerned about getting a certain city mouse off that mountain. The most traumatizing part for me was being stuck in a motel for days while I got stalked by news crews. Thankfully, everyone has now left me to my solitude."

"You're all alone?" Ava's heart dropped, and she worried anew. What if something happened? Who would be there for him?

"Don't worry. I'll be fine," he reassured her, reading her mind. "I think it might be time for me to get another dog, though."

"What happened to Babe?"

"I'm fostering her. Apparently, the county had a record number of applications for her adoption because she's famous. It's taking some time for them to go through them all."

"Why don't you adopt her? If you're thinking about getting another dog, you've already got one."

"I thought about it. She's already made herself at home here. It's almost like she's always been here. But with all the people applying, someone is bound to get her before me."

"You should ask. Maybe they can give you preference, or something. It doesn't hurt to ask." Ava suppressed a yawn. "I think I have to go to sleep."

"Yeah, me too. Goodnight, Ava."

"Hey, Killian?"

"Yeah."

"Call me tomorrow?" She didn't like him being alone. They could talk instead, and it would be good.

"Sure. Yeah, I'll talk to you tomorrow."

She smiled. "OK. Goodnight, Kill."

"Don't call me that, Blondie."

Ava scoffed. "Why are you better at nicknames than me?"

"I just am. You should give up."

"No way. I will come up with one. It'll be perfect. You'll see."

"Whatever you say, princess. Goodnight."

"Goodnight." She hung up and fell asleep with a smile on her lips and her phone in her hand.

Chapter 18

"I've known you for over twenty years, and I've never seen you blush at the mere mention of a man." Carmen poked at her salad and grinned at Ava.

"Me neither," Mina said, popping a piece of croissant into her mouth. Unlike Ava and Carmen, Mina wasn't an actress, so she had the luxury of eating bread.

Carmen and Mina were Ava's best friends. She met them when all three waitressed at the baseball stadium. Years later, Carmen became a television star, and Mina became a lawyer.

"You're imagining things," Ava argued. "I can't believe you're still boy crazy at for—"

"Don't you dare say it!" Carmen warned, narrowing her eyes.

"—twenty-nine. But you're projecting. You're such a man-eater."

"One of us has to be." Carmen wagged her finger at Ava. "It always falls on me to keep the group entertained. If one of you would have a steamy affair, I could take a well-deserved break from my hot mess love life and be the boring friend for once. I've been carrying you two for far too long."

"As if," Ava snorted. "And why does it have to be me? Mina is way overdue for a steamy affair."

"I've been married for fifteen years," Mina responded dryly.

"That's what I mean. You're overdue. You've done nothing salacious since your wedding day."

"I can't believe you brought that up. You're definitely hiding something." Mina turned to Carmen. "Ava's deflecting. All I asked was whether her park ranger was as dreamy as the news made him out to be, and she turned bright pink. We need to know everything about this."

"Yeah," Carmen agreed. She poked her fork at Ava. "Talk."

Ava sighed. "I don't know what to tell you, or even where to start."

"Have you had sex?" Carmen got right to the juicy stuff.

"Not exactly."

Mina's perceptive brown eyes pierced into Ava's very soul. "What does that mean?"

Ava grimaced. "Well, for the last three weeks, we've been talking on the phone... and, you know... stuff."

"Phone sex?" Carmen supplied.

"Yeah."

"What else have you done?" Mina asked, getting into cross-examination mode.

Ava shrugged innocently and stuck a bite of kale into her mouth. "Nothing."

Carmen looked at Mina. "She lyin'. Lyyyying."

Mina nodded. "Ava, we're going to get the truth of out of you, so you might as well not fight it. I have to be back at work by three, so chop chop."

Ava squinted at her two best friends. "OK, fine. Something did happen at the motel. I pulled him into the shower—"

"You? *You*?" Carmen scoffed. "You pulled him into the shower?"

"Yeah."

"I presume he went willingly," Mina commented.

"He was a little surprised at first. But then he went down on me—"

"In the shower?" Carmen fanned herself with a menu. "Damn, Ava. This is not what I expected to hear at lunch today."

"But you didn't have sex? Other than oral sex?" Mina pressed, taking a sip of her water.

"We were about to. We were in bed and this close"—Ava held up her thumb and her forefinger pinched together—"when Jack interrupted us."

Mina started coughing on her mouthful of water.

Carmen threw back her head and guffawed. "Jack—" She had to catch her breath. "Jack cockblocked you?"

Ava bit her lip and nodded. "Not that funny," she muttered.

Mina recovered her breath. "And now you're doing the phone sex thing?"

"Yeah."

"OK, we're going to need to back up," Mina said. "Start with his vital stats, then give us the summary of what happened and where this is going."

Carmen nodded. "Leave nothing out. I had almost lost hope that the beautiful and talented Ms. Ava Blum would ever take a lover."

Ava rolled her eyes. "His name is Killian, which you probably knew from the news. He's a civil engineer, but he looks like a lumberjack—"

"A lumberjack?" Carmen frowned.

"Mm-hmm. Broad-shouldered, seriously built, lives in the woods, wears flannel, dark beard, literally carries an axe. Which he used to rescue me..." She sighed, a faraway look in her eyes.

"Sounds dreamy." Mina rested her chin on her hand.

"So a hot mountain man saved your life and then gave you oral in the shower. You liked it because you're talking dirty on the phone with him. Why are you with us instead of in his bed?" Carmen asked.

Ava heaved a sigh. "Because it doesn't matter how attractive I find him, it could never work between us."

"Why not?" Mina asked.

"Who cares?" Carmen asked at the same time. "Go get some."

Ava answered Mina first. "For a lot of reasons. I live in this massive city, and he lives in a tiny cabin in the mountains. It's a five-hour drive from here on a good day. He likes peace and solitude. All the attention he's gotten thanks to my fame is his idea of hell. And, let's be honest, I didn't become an actress because I'm an introvert."

Ava took a sip of water to suppress an unwelcome squeeze in her chest; it was an inappropriate feeling for having known the guy a mere month.

"I'm too old for him. I'm forty and a single mom. He's thirty-three and a devoted bachelor. He doesn't want kids, and I have three. He told me he's only capable of casual flings, and he can't give me what I deserve. I should take him at his word."

Ava's voice caught, and she chased away her pesky tears. "I want to get married again while I'm still attractive enough to find a decent man. That'll be harder now that I'm a middle-aged single mom, so I can't waste time."

"How often do you talk to him?" Mina asked.

Ava got control of herself and drank more water. "Often."

"How often is often?"

"Every day. He's all alone up there because the grounds are closed and I don't like it. What if something happens, and no one is there to help him? I get anxious so he calls me every night, and we text."

"How long have you been talking every day?" Mina pressed.

"Just the last three weeks."

Mina arched an eyebrow. "I don't know, Ava. That doesn't sound casual to me. New, yes. Casual, no."

Ava shrugged. "He indulges me so that I won't worry. He knows about my PTSD."

"Casual guys don't care whether their hookups worry because they have an anxiety disorder," Mina said flatly.

"What Mina said." Carmen nodded vigorously. "How'd he find out about your PTSD?"

"The second night we were on the mountain, I had a flashback—one of the really vivid ones that I used to get all the time before Jack started bringing me to therapy. He comforted me, and I felt I owed him an explanation."

"What did you tell him?" Carmen asked.

"Everything."

"Everything? Wow. Now I'm even more confused about why you're *not* having naked time with him."

"Because we're wrong for each other in every conceivable way. Our lives are too different. We're too different. We want different things." Ava's voice was steady, but she hated how her stomach pitched.

"Yeah, but Ava, who cares?" Carmen asked again, this time more gently. "Maybe you should just allow yourself to enjoy a no-strings-attached, sexy fling with a man who knows all your secrets and likes you anyway. You've never done that. Why does it have to be anything else? You deserve to have a passionate, reckless love affair at least once in your life."

Carmen waved her hands excitedly. "I mean, look at you! You're one of the world's most beautiful women. That's objective fact. Men worship you, but you always say no. You never let loose. When are you going to believe you're worth experiencing some happiness?"

"I don't know, Carmen," Ava mumbled, looking down at her salad.

"Do I need to get you drunk and drop you on his doorstep? Because I will fucking do it." Carmen poked her fork at Ava again.

Feeling helpless, Ava looked at Mina for back up.

"Don't look at me. I agree with Carmen. Just go have a fling. You've never really moved on from Jack, and you've been miserable since your divorce. Maybe it's time to explore and enjoy being single for once. Don't worry about relationships or the future or getting married again. I think hot sex with no strings is exactly what you need right now."

Ava sat back in her chair and toyed with the straw in her water. "I don't know, Mina."

"I think you do know. I think that's why you're having phone sex. I think you're just scared. Why are you worried about getting married again? You don't need a man for anything except hot sex," Mina said bluntly.

"OK, yeah, I *am* scared," Ava admitted. She stared down at her hands for a moment, which she clasped tightly in her lap. "When we were in the motel, I thought I would never see him again. We had this intense experience together, and I felt so safe with him. I didn't want to think past the moment. That's different to me going back up there just to have sex with him. That feels like something... something that could get me hurt."

She looked up at her friends and let them see her heart on her sleeve. "I was buried alive. I thought I was going to die in there, all alone, and never see my daughters again. I didn't think I could ever go back to that mountain and relive any of those memories. I mean, I already have PTSD."

She pressed her hand to her eyes briefly. "Then the producers told me they want me to go back for a few days for reshoots, which I think was a really unfair ask. I could refuse. I almost did. Instead, I said I would think about it." She gulped a deep breath.

"And when I thought about it, I knew the only way I'd feel safe enough to go back up there was if I knew he was there too. I know it doesn't make logical sense, but I feel like he wouldn't let anything bad happen to me. So I worked up the courage to text him, and now we're talking. And not only do I feel brave enough to go for reshoots, I *want* to go back because I want to see him. I want to see him badly enough that I can overcome my anxiety."

She was clutching her hands together again, twisting her fingers. "But those aren't casual, one-night stand feelings. Those are deeper feelings."

Mina and Carmen listened to her intently, letting her spill her guts without interrupting or judging. She smiled at them weakly. "He turned me down for sex at first."

Carmen gasped. "What? Why?"

"Because he said I wasn't a one-night stand kind of woman. He said he didn't want to take advantage of me while I was vulnerable after the mudslide."

"Aww, that's kind of sweet," Carmen said.

"Obviously, he changed his mind because you were in bed when Jack interrupted, right?" Mina surmised.

Ava wrinkled her nose. "Because I stood naked in front of him and demanded that we have sex."

Mina's jaw dropped. "Holy crap, Ava! That's so unlike you. What did he say?"

"There wasn't a lot of talking after that. Then, a few minutes later, Jack turned up."

"Oh my God, that must've been so frustrating." Carmen laughed, putting a hand over her mouth.

"You don't even know." Ava groaned. "So I'm also afraid he might reject me again because he knows I'll struggle with it being casual. I already feel addicted to him. I want to talk to him all the time. I want to know how he is. I worry about him. When we talk, it isn't just dirty, you know. He knows so much about me, the real me, already."

"Oh, sweetie." Carmen reached across the table and patted her hand.

"But I've never been so hot for a man. I think about having sex with him, like, all the time. I can't seem to cool off. I might not move on until after I close the deal with him. I might be stuck."

She unclasped her hands and pressed her palms on her thighs to prevent fidgeting. "It's driving me crazy. I feel compelled—absolutely compelled—to go back so that I can finally fucking do it. Maybe if I have a bunch of sex with him, I'll get this insane lust out of my system, and then I can return to normal. Maybe I can have a fling, and it'll be exactly what I need.

"But what if"—her voice hitched, and she had to take a steadying breath—"what if all it does is make me hopelessly attached? I could get really hurt, and I'd have only myself to blame."

Fear wrapped itself around Ava's throat, strangling her. She fell silent and looked at her lap. Her friends didn't speak for a long moment.

"I think you should go," Carmen said finally. "You're already feeling angsty. If you go, the possible upside is a fling, lots of great sex, you get him out of your system, and you feel better. The possible downside is that you still feel angsty, but at least you'd have gotten laid."

Ava choked out a surprised laugh. "Well, when you put it like that..." She glanced at Mina.

"Yeah. Carmen's right. Go get laid," Mina said with a shrug. "You're already in too deep. At least enjoy the upsides of it."

Ava looked at both of her friends and then nodded. "Alright, I'm texting my manager right now and telling him I'll commit to the reshoots."

She sent the message and gave her friends a brave smile. "So I guess I'll be putting an official end to my dry spell. I should probably buy some lingerie, really make an event out of it."

They clinked water glasses, and Ava hoped she wasn't making a huge mistake.

Chapter 19

Mary scheduled the film production to resume tomorrow for one week. Ava told Killian last week that she would complete her reshoots with the rest of the production. She said that she was scheduled for three days of filming, late in the week. She was cagey about it, so he didn't push for details.

He sat at his kitchen table for a mid-morning coffee break. Babe hopped on the couch, sighing in exaggerated patience because they'd been inside all morning while he worked on his laptop. He should take Babe for a short walk. Instead, he texted Ava.

Killian: Good morning, sunshine

Ava: Good morning. What are you doing?

Killian: Coffee break. Care to join me?

Ava: You know coffee is my love language. I just made myself a cappuccino

Killian: Sounds delicious

Ava: I'll have to make you one sometime. I've got it down to a science. I can steam up the milk just right, hot and frothy

Killian: That sounded dirty in my head

Ava: You should see me drink it, nice and slow. So delicious. So creamy

Killian: Naughty girl. Besides making me jealous of foam, what else are you up to?

Ava: I made a list of possible nicknames for you

Killian: You should let it go, Elsa

Ava: How do you know the princess in *Frozen*?

Killian: I live on a mountain in California, not a monastery in Tibet

Ava: You used Google, didn't you?

Killian: Did you use Google to come up with your list?

Ava: Maybe

Killian: Do you think you came up with any good ones?

Ava: Definitely. Prepare to have your mind blown

Killian: OK, I'm curious. Try one

Ava: Grumpy Bear

Killian: No

Ava: What's wrong with it?

Killian: I'm not grumpy

Ava: Like hell you're not

Killian: Only before coffee

Ava: That counts

Killian: It doesn't. You're the only one who has ever seen me before coffee, Goldilocks

Ava: Stop giving me nicknames!

Killian: But it's so easy

Ava: How about Aragorn?

Killian: I'm not a ranger, I'm an engineer. Also, so nerdy

Ava: So picky

Killian: What's wrong with calling me Killian?

Ava: Kraken?

Killian: What?

Ava: It has two Ks in it

Killian: Do better, Hollywood

Ava: Pork Chop

Killian: No

Ava: Hot Sauce

Killian: Lame

Ava: Stud Muffin

Killian: What's with the food? Are you hungry?

Ava: Hungry for you

Killian: Come by my cabin anytime and I'll feed you

Ava: Mr. Clean. Ironic because of how dirty you are

Killian: lol, ready to admit defeat, Blondie?

Ava: Never! I've got a good one

Killian: I have my doubts

Ava: Sexy Beast

Killian: I'll allow it

Their silly conversation made him smile for the rest of the day. He hadn't heard from her since, which was a little unusual. But he figured they would talk later that night, like they had every night for the past month.

He sat on the couch next to Babe in the late afternoon. The mid-summer weather was warm, and the days were long. Killian didn't expect the sun to go down for a few more hours. Everything was ready for the film crew to arrive tomorrow, and he didn't have any other projects to work on for a few days.

He should finish the final paperwork to adopt Babe. He'd worked a few times with the sheriff's deputies who did animal control in the county. When he told them he'd like to keep Babe permanently, they told him she was as good as his. He could skip the application, but he needed to register her and get her tags.

His phone vibrated on the coffee table. It was a text from Ava.

Ava: WYD

Killian: About to start the paperwork to register Babe

Ava: Put on a pot of coffee

Killian: It's a little late for coffee

Ava: Not if you're going to be up all night

Killian: The paperwork isn't that hard, princess

There was a knock on his door. The unexpected sound startled Killian. He might've thought he'd imagined it, but Babe started barking.

His phone vibrated again.

Ava: Aren't you going to let me in? You promised me coffee, and it's been a really long drive

Killian dropped his phone onto the couch and rushed to the door, flinging it open. She stood there, giving him a smirk. "Hey Paul Bunyan, you're looking particularly lumberjack-y today."

She was so beautiful that it took his breath away. But he recovered quickly. He grabbed her hand and jerked her into the cabin, flinging her against his chest. "What, you just show up without warning? I could've had company. I could've been entertaining a lady friend. That would've been awkward."

But even as he joked, his hands snaked their way underneath her shirt and up her spine, pressing her to him. They both ignored Babe leaping in circles around them, still barking.

She tipped her chin up to meet his gaze. Her crystal blue eyes smoldered. "You said I could come by your cabin anytime."

"I did, didn't I?" He was glad he said that.

She wrapped her arms around his neck and gave him her bone-melting, sultry look. "It's nice to see you, Killian." Then she raised herself onto her tiptoes and kissed him, molding her luscious body to his.

It took a mere few seconds for his pent-up lust for her, whipped into a frenzy by a month of dirty talk, to take over him with a maddening fervor. His mind swam with the need to feel her, taste her, and breathe in her scent. She was a hurricane blowing apart all his senses.

Never breaking their kiss, Killian maneuvered Ava to the couch, pulling her onto his lap as he sat. She straddled him and framed his face with her hands as she kissed him deeper. Her tongue aggressively drove into his mouth and invited him into hers.

He didn't know what she was wearing. It hadn't registered. But he knew he wanted it off of her. He tugged her shirt out of the front of her waistband.

Babe hopped onto the sofa and aggressively pushed herself between them, forcing them to break off their kiss.

"Babe!" Ava laughed. "What did I tell you? No licking my face." She leaned back so that she could greet the dog. Glancing over his shoulder at the loft, she asked, "Is it possible to prevent Babe from coming into your bedroom? I want to go to bed, but I don't want her interrupting us."

He nodded and loosened his grip on her waist so that she could get up. He visually took her in as she stood and started toward the stairs. Even though he wasn't used to seeing her in pants, she still looked incredible in her slim-fit jeans.

He blocked the stairs with a kitchen chair and followed Ava. Babe whined grievously before returning to her usual place on the sofa, a look of utter betrayal in her eyes.

Once upstairs, Ava went to unbutton his shirt. "I want to do it," she told him, slapping his hands away when he tried to help. "Be patient."

"I've already been plenty patient," he grumbled.

"Yeah, so what's a few more minutes?"

Agonizing. Those few minutes were agonizing. She slowly undid each button, treating every pop as a new revelation of skin that she could caress and kiss. When his shirt was fully open, she lazily slid it off his shoulders and down his arms, capturing his wrists behind him. She circled around him, lightly kissing, softly touching, sweetly frustrating him.

"With all the times I fantasize about you, I need to make sure I've got all the details right in my memory," she murmured into his ear from behind, giving his lobe a playful nibble.

"Ava," he growled as she tugged the shirt off his wrists and tossed it onto his dresser. "If you get to take my shirt off, I get to take yours off." He really wanted to see her glorious breasts again.

"No. I'm going to undress you. And you're going to watch while I undress myself." Her fingers slid open the button on his jeans and he was at her mercy.

But she didn't keep undressing him. She stepped back and pulled her top over her head. Then she pushed her jeans down and stepped out of them. She laid them both on the dresser with his shirt.

"What are you wearing?" Killian's voice was hoarse. She looked insane in a black lace teddy that cut a deep V down between her breasts and ending at her navel. Sheer material wrapped around her hips, leaving nothing to the imagination. Her nipples peeked through the lace, inviting him to pull on them with his teeth.

"Do you like it?" She gave him a coquettish smile. "I bought it just for you."

He swallowed hard when she stepped back in front of him and sank down to her knees. She ran her fingers under the waistbands of his unbuttoned jeans and boxer briefs before firmly pulling them down his legs.

His cock sprang free, hard and tall, irrefutable proof of just how much he liked her, whatever she was wearing.

Ava instructed him to step out of his pants. She neatly placed them on the dresser with the rest of their clothes before kneeling in front of him again. She ran her hands down the outside of his legs and then up the center of his thighs, causing his cock to jump and his balls to tighten.

"Ava," he groaned again, half plea, half demand. He wrapped her silvery blonde locks around his hand.

"I promised you something the first night you let me come with you on the phone. I'm here to pay my debt." She gazed up at him through her lashes.

He watched her lick her lips and nearly came undone at the sight. "Ava, I want you so badly. Keep looking at me like that, and it's going to be over before we've started."

"We have all night." She took the crown of his cock into her mouth and sucked. "We actually have all week." She flicked the underside of his head with her tongue.

She pulled back and looked up at him again. "The cabin I was staying in last time seems to be unavailable, and the motel is full. So I thought I would just stay with you."

She reached a hand up and gave his balls a gentle tug before circling the base of his cock and stroking him. "In your bed."

Her mouth followed her hand back down, and she took him deep into the back of her throat. He had to concentrate to keep his orgasm at bay.

Pulling her mouth back off him, she slowly but firmly pumped his cock with one hand and massaged his balls with the other. She tilted her face up again and gave him a wicked smile.

"What would you like me to do?" She opened her mouth wide and stuck out her tongue as an invitation for him to push all the way into her throat.

She leaned forward and pulled him more firmly with her fist, ready to take him and urging him to give it to her.

He didn't answer with words, but with deeds. His hand cupping her head, he buried his cock deep within her mouth. She hummed her approval, vibrating around him.

He fucked her slowly at first. But she felt so good, looked so good, that he soon lost himself. He pushed faster, rougher. He could see her gag when he went all the way in. She sucked air through her nose and her eyes watered. But she never stopped looking up at him.

She kept humming and moaning with her face full of his dick. The tips of her lips pulled up, hinting at her alluring smile. Her mouth was warm and inviting and even better than he'd imagined it to be—and he had imagined it *a lot*.

With a tenuous grasp on his control, he pulled out all the way to give her some air. "Don't stop," she gasped. "I like it. I want you to fuck my mouth until you come. I want to swallow it all down." She dug her fingers into the back of his thighs in encouragement.

He groaned and pushed his cock all the way to the back of her throat. Then he pulled all the way out. "Say my name, princess." He thrust fully in and out again. "I want you to say my name while you swallow my cock."

"Killian," she groaned before relaxing her jaw again and taking another thrust. "Mmm, Killian, so good," she moaned when he pulled out again.

"Good girl."

"Yes, give it all to me, Killian," she purred the next time he pulled out, causing him to thrust back in hard and choke her. But she didn't stop. She chanted his name between thrusts until he couldn't hold back anymore and fucked her mouth roughly, barely giving her time to gulp her breaths.

She clawed at his ass and closed her eyes when he came. He watched her swallow it down as he pushed into her one last time. Mesmerized, he wanted to stay buried in the wet heat of her mouth but thought she might need to breathe. Reluctantly, he let her go.

She sat back on her heels, licked some of his cum off the corner of her lips, and gave him a self-satisfied smile. "Now we're even," she declared. "But we're just getting started. Make some coffee and recover because we're not sleeping tonight."

Chapter 20

After he retrieved her suitcase from her SUV, they drank coffee and watched the sun sparkling through the trees from his kitchen table. The open front door let the breeze in. Ava enjoyed the simple pleasure of leaving a door open without fear. Babe settled on the floor next to them.

"I came up early, and I don't have to do any filming for several days. What's your work schedule like?" Ava sipped her coffee in her black teddy, snuggled in Killian's lap. They were alone together, no one for miles, which suited her just fine. Everything was perfect.

"I'm ahead on my work. I have nothing pressing," Killian answered.

"That's good. I was worried that I'd be bothering you."

"You could never bother me, sunshine. Luckily, I can spend the next couple of days with you, unless something comes up with the film crew. I'm still responsible for the campground."

"Even though that was what brought me up here, I hate that all those people are coming tomorrow and we won't be alone."

"Are you worried about everyone seeing that you're staying with me?"

Ava gave him a quizzical look. "No. Are you?"

Killian shrugged. "You just said you'd prefer no one be here. Is that because someone might tell gossip sites you're here with me? Do we have to worry about being bothered by the press?"

"No. I just like being alone with you, without distractions. That's all I meant. I like the quietness of being out of the city, and not being constantly bothered with busyness."

"OK, but I had to avoid reporters for days, so shouldn't we be worried about them?"

She finished her coffee and set the mug on the table, then swiveled on his lap until she was straddling him. "The crew all sign NDAs, and most people honor them. The press has been speculating about us since the first day, and if someone leaks that I'm spending time with you, that will fuel more speculation. But we don't have to pay any attention to it. No one is going to bother us here because the set is closed and we have security."

Killian nodded. She rested her forehead on his. He tucked a strand of her hair behind her ear. Ava gazed into his eyes, and the light touch of his fingers on her cheek made her feel like she was floating.

Ava might have a lot of emotions, but usually she could name them. She knew she was falling for Killian. She knew it from all their phone conversations, actually. But her heart's reaction to being in his arms made it irrefutable. That's why she said the next thing, knowing that it was equally full of lies and truth.

"I came because I've never been so revved up, and I want to finish what we started a month ago. I want to have a little fun with you and work this out of my system. In a few days, we'll part as friends. We don't have to be seen together. It doesn't have to be complicated. Let's not waste time worrying."

She didn't give him a chance to respond. He had something that she needed, and now that she'd finished her coffee, she was growing impatient. Resting her head on his shoulder, tucking her nose into his neck, she inhaled the scent of his skin. "Whatever soap you're using, never stop. It's the best smell in the world."

He explored her body with his hands, stoking her fire. Lifting her head, she played with the hair at the nape of his neck and then traced her fingers along the ridge of his back muscles that connected to his powerful shoulders.

She leaned in, her lips hovering a few centimeters from his. "Everything about you is sexy," she breathed against his mouth. "Everything about you turns me on. I don't think that's normal."

His hands moved into her hair. Instead of kissing him, she slinked off his lap. "Enough recovery. We have a mission. March your sexy ass upstairs right now."

He got up and closed the front door. "After you. I'll block the stairs again, unless you consider chasing the dog out of the room to be foreplay."

"We've had more than enough foreplay." She turned and waggled her finger at Babe, who had hopped to her feet the moment Killian got out of his chair. "Sorry, girl, no dogs allowed." Ava ran up the stairs. "Nothing, and I mean nothing, is going to stop me from having sex with you right now."

Killian laughed. "Don't tempt fate, Blondie." He made it to the top of the landing and reached for her.

She dodged his grip and shoved him toward the bed. "Are we in danger of any natural disasters right now?"

"I don't think so." He sat back on the bed and gave her an appreciative leer. "You look so gorgeous in that; I almost hate to take it off of you."

With a flick of her wrist, she loosened the little ribbon that held the two sides of her teddy together across her breasts. The lace went slack. "You're not expecting anyone to show up and interrupt us, right? No doctors or friends?"

"Nope. And I wouldn't answer the door if anyone knocked, unlike what you did," he teased.

"My ex-husband isn't within several hundred miles of us," she assured him.

He grabbed her around the wrist and gave her a tug, causing her to stumble onto the bed next to him. "That's how I prefer it."

"Same." She straddled his lap. He reached one hand under the lace of her teddy and pinched the nipple of her left breast. Ava drew in a sharp breath as pleasure spiked through her body. "I like that."

With a hand between her shoulder blades, he pushed her forward and sucked on her nipples through the lace until they both ached. Then he skimmed one with his teeth and she cried out, arching her back.

Killian had just returned to the other nipple when his phone rang from where he'd left it downstairs on the couch.

They both froze. They both groaned.

"We have the worst luck," Killian said.

"Don't answer it," she begged. "Keep going."

His phone rang again. "The only calls I get are from you and work. Since you're here, it's probably my boss. It could be an emergency. I have to get it." He shifted her off his lap. "Stay right there."

Ava flopped dramatically onto his pillows but let him go.

A few minutes later, he returned holding his phone. "It was nothing. My boss wanted to make sure the camp was ready for the crew tomorrow. I turned my phone off." He tossed it onto the nightstand.

He lowered himself on top of Ava. "Where were we?" He pushed the lace aside fully exposing her breasts. "You have magnificent breasts. They're perfect." He fondled, pinched, and sucked on her until she writhed beneath him. He pushed the straps of her teddy off her shoulders and peeled it to her waist, moving his teasing touches down her stomach.

She whimpered and squirmed. She might come from his featherlight caresses alone. She trembled. He stopped and gave her a heated look. "Not yet, princess."

"Killian, please," she whispered.

"Please, what?"

"No more teasing. I need you..." Her words turned to moans when he rubbed his hand on her pussy through the sheer mesh of her teddy.

"You need me to what?" His gruff voice betrayed how much he needed her right back. "Tell me what you want. Don't be shy. I know the filthiness that comes out of your mouth daily." He moved lower and pushed her legs apart, gripping her inner thighs, then sucked on the gossamer fabric covering her clit.

"Killian!" She wasn't above begging. Or demanding. Or saying anything he wanted, so long as he *did* what *she* wanted. "I need you inside me. I've never needed something so badly in my life. Fuck me. Right now. I can't wait another minute."

He stretched up over her again and kissed her hard on the mouth. His dark eyes sparkled in amusement at her torture. "OK."

He pushed her teddy over her hips, down her legs, and off of her body. She laid nude on the bed, vibrating with desire so strong that her heart pounded in her chest. She watched him toss the lacy bit of fabric aside and remove his jeans.

She parted her knees. He settled between them. She tilted her hips and closed her eyes. Her stomach muscles tightened. Ready. Anticipating.

Her phone rang.

Ava's eyes flew open. "That's the ringtone for my children," she choked. "It's supposed to be for emergencies only." She pressed her palm on her forehead. "Fuck, I have to get it."

She rolled off the bed and retrieved her phone from her jeans pocket on the dresser. "Bette-bug, what's wrong?" she answered.

"Ollie got scared and ran into a closet, and I can't get him to come out!" Bette burst into tears.

Ava sighed. "Honey, stop crying."

"He's scared and I can't get him to come out, not even for treats. I don't know what to do. Audrey and Ingrid won't help me. Grandma told me to leave him alone and go outside and play. No one will help me."

Ava tamped down her frustration at her daughter. She took a breath and kept her voice soothing. "I understand that you're upset, baby. But that's not an emergency. Remember, this number is just for emergencies. Ollie just needs a little alone time."

"But he hissed at me," Bette sobbed. "Does that mean he doesn't love me anymore?"

Ava sighed. Her youngest had such big feelings.

"No, honey. When a cat hisses, it means they are feeling upset about something. It doesn't mean that Ollie doesn't love you anymore. He just needs to be left alone until he feels calm. It's your job as someone who loves him to give him a little space, OK? Let him have a time out until he feels better."

"Mom, you won't help me, either?"

"You didn't listen to me. I just told you what you need to do. What else do you think I can do from here?" Ava's exasperation bubbled out, but it only caused Bette to cry harder.

"Can you come home?" Bette asked in a small voice.

"What?"

"Can you come home, Mom? I want you to come home."

So there was the real reason Bette had called. "Honey, we talked about this. I'm safe here. Nothing bad is going to happen to me. OK?"

Ava had sat her children down two days ago and told them she was going back up the mountain for a week. They said they were fine with it. But when she'd dropped them off at their father's house yesterday, they clung to her and cried—even her oldest, Audrey—and they wouldn't let her leave right away.

Guilt washed over her. She'd come here for sex, and now her daughters were crying and afraid. Could she be any more selfish? Self-conscious of her nudity, she took her blouse off the dresser and pulled it over her head.

Bette was still crying. "Bug, I'm safe. I am."

"Are you sure?" Bette whispered. "What if something happens?"

"Yes, I'm sure. I promise I'll be home in a few days, safe and sound." She tugged on her jeans and sat on the floor, listening to her daughter's sniffles.

"Mom?"

"Yes, Bette?"

"I had a nightmare last night."

"You did?"

"Mm-hmm. I dreamt that we were riding on a magic carpet over a river. The magic carpet unraveled, and we fell into the water. It was freezing. I swam around looking for you, but I couldn't find you. I couldn't find you ever again."

Ava swallowed hard. "Aww, baby, that sounds scary."

"Yeah. Daddy and Esme let me sleep in bed with them."

"Did that help?"

"Mm-hmm. It made me feel safe."

Ava understood precisely what her daughter was talking about. "Where is your father? You know you can always go talk to him when you feel afraid."

"He went with Aunt Dee to look at a horse. He said I can have a horse because we have a barn at his new house." Suddenly, Bette was no longer crying. "He should be home soon. Oh! Ollie came out. He wants on my lap."

"That's great, Bug. Are you feeling better now?"

"Mm-hmm."

"Good. See, sometimes when you're feeling upset, you just need a little time to calm down and feel better. That goes for cats too."

"Yeah."

"When I get back in a few days, we can go to the pet store and get Ollie and Scruffles some special treats and toys. Does that sound like something we can look forward to?"

"And horse treats." Bette added, her voice brightening.

"And horse treats."

"I love you, Mom."

"I love you too. Bye, Bette-bug."

Ava hung up. She swiveled around on the floor to make her apologies to Killian. He'd followed her lead and redressed. She twisted her mouth. "I'm sorry."

"Is everything OK with your kids?"

"Not entirely. When I dropped them off yesterday, they were really struggling with me coming back here. I underestimated the emotional impact of all this on them. I feel like an asshole. I shouldn't have left them again so soon. But now I'm committed to be here, so I need to call Jack. I'm sorry, but I can't just ignore that they're suffering."

"Don't apologize. I need to take Babe for a walk, anyway. She's used to doing a couple of miles with me after work."

"If you can wait a few minutes for me, I'll change and come with you."

"Sure." He got up from the bed. "We'll wait for you downstairs."

Ava called Jack and explained that their daughters needed extra emotional support that week. Then she changed, put on her new hiking boots, and they went for a walk down a trail that connected to the campground.

"I can see the appeal of living away from the city," Ava told Killian as they strolled past pines and redwoods. "I like the privacy. It's nice to just be able to walk and not be bothered. Until coming up here, I'd forgotten what that was like."

"Every time you tell me what it's like to be famous, it makes me shudder," he replied. "It sounds awful. So why keep doing it? Don't you have enough money?"

He had his arm around her shoulders, and she was tucked into his side with her arm around his waist. Because no one was around, they let Babe off her leash so that she could chase the squirrels.

"There are plenty of downsides to fame, I'll admit." She thought about it for a moment. "But I still enjoy acting, always have. I like the creativity. I'm good at it. I also like that my movies are fun and bring people happiness for a couple of hours. And to be honest, when it's appropriate, I like the attention. I mean, it's not horrible to have people tell you that you're beautiful and special."

He turned to kiss her temple. "You are. But you shouldn't need other people to tell you that. You should know it already."

"Thanks," she said. "I know it sounds weird, but I don't have great self-esteem. I've been to therapy, but I don't get better. I don't know how some people can just feel good about themselves without other people reassuring them constantly. All the adulation is fake, I know, but I don't want to quit it."

"You don't want something more from your career than adulation?"

"Sometimes I think I should use my platform to do something... something meaningful, I guess. When the Me Too movement started, I thought about going public about how I was treated by the Army. But I didn't have the nerve. Wouldn't I just be reliving the trauma and upsetting my daughters and inviting attacks by strangers? I don't know what good it would do. So I didn't."

They walked along in silence for a few minutes before Ava changed the subject. "Tell me something about you. You ask me about me, and I end up doing all the talking while you listen."

He chuckled. "I prefer it that way."

"Yeah, well, I want to hear something about you now."

"I've literally never talked to another person as much as I have you. I think I've told you all the important things already."

"Oh, that can't be true. I'm sure there are plenty of things that you haven't told me yet, and you're just not thinking of them." She pursed her lips. "Oh, I know. Tell me about your first love." Ava imagined him as an awkward teenager crushing on a girl and giggled.

"I've never been in love." He sounded a bit clipped.

Ava blinked. "Really?"

"Really."

"Not with any of your girlfriends?"

"I've never had a girlfriend." He didn't sound like he wanted to discuss it further.

Dumbfounded, she stumbled over a rock and lurched forward. He caught her and kept her upright.

She stopped walking. "You're always catching me when I stumble." She gave him a goofy smile. "I don't think I like regular hiking as much as spicy hiking, so I have to create moments of danger to entertain myself."

"Spicy hiking?" His mouth quirked.

"Yeah, you know, where there's risk of hypothermia, wild animals, injury, dehydration... Extreme hiking, if you will. I think I became an adrenaline junkie. I blame you, really." She grinned at him.

"I wouldn't mind spending time with Survivor Barbie again." He brushed her hair off her forehead and gave her a heated leer. "She hikes naked."

Feeling naughty, Ava lowered her voice. "Maybe she can come out to play." She looked around. "We've seen no one else on the trail, and since the campground is closed, can I assume it'll stay that way?" She pulled her shirt off, revealing her sports bra, and stepped back against a pine.

"I've hiked this trail dozens of times with Lola and with Babe, and I never see anyone." He stepped forward and pinned her to the tree.

"Good," she said. "You know, I've never had sex outside. It's almost always a terrible idea to be naked outdoors when you're famous. But we're alone right now." Bunching his shirt in her fists, she yanked him to her.

She kissed him, demanding and uninhibited. Digging her fingers into his hair, she straddled his thigh and rode his leg. He cupped her breasts and scraped his thumbs over her nipples.

"I want more," she murmured against his mouth. "No foreplay. I want you to fuck me." She hooked a leg around his waist. "We can do it right here. I'm flexible."

"Flexible, huh?" He tore his lips from her mouth and moved them down her neck. He tugged her bra down and pushed her breasts over the top. She moaned so loudly that it echoed in the surrounding trees.

She heard a gasp from the trail. "Oh my God, I'm so sorry!" said a surprised female voice.

Killian straightened, his eyes closed, an irritated look on his face. "Why are we always getting interrupted?" he muttered under his breath.

"Because our god is a cruel god," Ava groaned.

"Babe?" the voice said.

Ava yanked her bra back into place and peeked around Killian as he turned around. Lisa stood patting Babe, looking surprised. She held onto a dog on a leash. Her dog was sniffing Babe's tail-end, ignoring the humans.

"Killian?" Then her face split with silent glee, and she slapped her hands over her mouth. "Ava!"

"Hey, Lisa," Killian sheepishly acknowledged her.

"I knew it!" She laughed out loud. "I mean, I'm so sorry for disturbing your, uh, hike." She narrowed her eyes at him. "You lied to me, K-Pop. You said there was nothing going on with Ava."

Ava pushed out from behind him and approached Lisa. "K-Pop! That's a good one. Mind if I steal it?"

"Go for it," Lisa said in a stage-whisper. "But be warned, he hates it."

"He hates all my nicknames too." She embraced Lisa warmly.

"I think Rusty wants to keep walking," Killian grumbled from behind Ava.

Lisa looked down at her dog. "Yeah, I suppose he does."

Ava smacked him on his upper arm. "Don't be rude, K-Pop."

"Ava. No."

"What?" She batted her eyelashes.

"Come on, Rusty." Lisa gave his leash a tug. "Nice to see you again, Ava. Bye." Lisa gave them a little wave and disappeared around a bend.

"Why does she get to call you K-Pop and I can't call you anything?" Ava pouted.

"Neither of you do." He leaned down to whisper into her ear. "If you need me to remind you what my name is, I'm happy to oblige."

She shivered at his words. "Yup. I think I'm going to need that lesson as soon as we get back to the cabin. Walk fast. I really—and I cannot stress this enough—*really* can't wait any longer."

He laughed. "The universe is conspiring to leave you desperate and unsatisfied."

"I refuse to accept that." She smacked him on the butt. "Hustle up, Kelly. I need you inside me within the next ten minutes before I spontaneously combust."

Chapter 21

As Ava predicted, they didn't sleep that night, but they did spend plenty of time in bed. They also took a lengthy shower and damaged the kitchen table.

Finally satiated, they put on some clothes—sweatpants for him, his flannel shirt for her—and watched the sunrise from the couch. He wrapped Ava in a blanket and started a fire so she wouldn't be cold.

"I feel so much better," she declared, stretching like a kitten. She laid her head on his lap.

He chuckled. "It was touch-and-go there for a bit."

"I know that's a metaphor about planes, but it's also literal in our case."

He stroked her hair. "I'm glad you're here."

Ava traced lazy circles on his thigh with her index finger. "I think I'd like to walk over to where my cabin used to be. Will you come with me?"

He wondered why, but agreed nonetheless. "Of course."

"You haven't heard the catch yet," she pointed out.

"What's the catch?"

"I don't know how I'll react to being there. I'm afraid I might have a panic attack or scream or something." She turned her face into his leg as though to hide embarrassment.

He kept stroking her hair. "I'll still come with you."

"There's another catch," she said, partially muffled by his thigh. "I'd like to go now, this morning, before anyone arrives. I don't want anyone to see me have a meltdown. Hopefully, I won't, but I can't be sure until we get there."

He stifled a yawn. "OK, but after we get back, we're going back to bed. For sleep this time."

She sat up and gave him a sassy look. "Sleep is for the weak, Kelly."

"Those are my terms. Take 'em or leave 'em, Blum."

"You drive a hard bargain." She gave him a quick kiss to seal the deal and got up. "I suppose I should put on some pants."

"Not necessary. You hiked the entire mountain in less than what you're wearing now."

She wrinkled her nose. "Are you ever going to stop teasing me about that?"

"Nah."

"I'm uninviting you."

He smacked her on the butt. "Go get dressed. The sooner we go, the sooner we can get back and go to sleep."

Fifteen minutes later, they arrived at the clearing where her cabin had stood six weeks before. Killian had already been here. He'd watched the bulldozers scoop up the debris of the fallen dwelling and whatever she had owned and lost inside it. He knew that all that they would see now were the concrete blocks that had been the cabin's crude foundation.

When they got to the spot, Ava didn't scream or panic. She just stood there, staring at the empty ground. She shivered. He didn't know whether it was from the crisp morning air or from her memories. He didn't ask. He simply stepped up behind her and wrapped his arms around her.

"It's kind of good that it was so dark when you pulled me out," she said, leaning back into him. "I couldn't see anything, so I don't have an image of what it looked like burned into my brain. I just remember how it looked standing. It's weird that it's gone now. But there's nothing here that reminds me of what it felt like when it collapsed."

She spun in his arms until she faced him. She stood pressed into his chest, back arched, head thrown back to make eye contact. "Do you remember what it looked like that night?"

"Some of it. I had my flashlight. But I also couldn't see that much." He remembered seeing the slicks of mud and the wrecked cabin. She'd looked like a ghost when she crawled out of the hole he'd made. But he didn't share any of that with her. Her face already looked haunted.

"Were you ever scared? At any point during those two days?" Her eyes searched his.

"I was afraid you'd died when I saw the mudslide. I heard the rumble, and I knew some cabins had been swept away. When I got here, you didn't answer me right away when I called your name. After we made it to stable ground, I was never afraid. Well, except when I worried you would get heatstroke because you wouldn't drink."

"I'm still amazed that you came for me. Not everyone would have." Her lower lip quivered. "Why did you? You didn't even know me, and yet you risked your life."

"I did it for the reward money," he deadpanned. "I'm still waiting."

"I rewarded you plenty last night."

"Meh. You were OK."

She thumped him on the chest and stepped out of his arms. "Watch yourself, Paul Bunyan."

"Don't call me that."

She ignored him.

She wandered around the foundations of the old cabin for a few minutes, scuffing at the dirt with her toe. She stooped to pick up something that caught the sunlight and gasped. "Oh my God!" She rushed over to show her find to Killian. "I can't believe it!"

Ava held up a delicate gold necklace with a diamond embellished pendant that said "Mom." After blowing and brushing the dirt off, she opened the clasp and held it up to him. "Will you help me put it on?"

He took the necklace. She turned her back to him and pulled her hair to the side. He clasped it before softly kissing her nape.

Turning back to him, she brought both her hands up and clutched the necklace's pendant to her breastbone. "I can't believe I found this." Her eyes glistened. "I can't believe it survived and was just waiting here for me."

Tears spilled down her cheeks. "When I was trapped inside, I was so afraid that I would never see my daughters again. I thought of all the things I would miss in their lives and how it would hurt them to not have me around. That was worse than anything else I feared the entire time I was on this mountain." She sniffed and scrubbed the tears away with her sleeve. "I'm sorry. I really try hard not to cry so much."

He frowned. "I don't think you should do that."

"What? Cry?"

"No, I don't think you should try to be someone you're not."

Ava blinked at him, wiping away her remaining tears. "I don't understand."

"If you want to cry, cry. I don't think you should hide your emotions because other people don't like them. Other people's comfort isn't your responsibility. Your feelings are valid, and there's nothing wrong with expressing them. Be yourself. You're perfect, just as you are."

"Oh." Ava's face scrunched, and she cried again.

He pulled her into a hug. "Why are you crying, Blondie? Was that the wrong thing for me to say?"

She gurgled out a laugh. "No. The opposite. My whole life, I've been told that my feelings and reactions are wrong. You don't know how badly I needed to hear that they're not."

He held her, keeping silent and stroking her hair, until she finished crying. She pulled out of his hug, took his hand, and gave him a dazzling smile. "Thank you for coming with me. Let's go back. We both need sleep."

They spent the rest of the day and the next night in his cabin. They heard the film crew arrive and set up, but they ignored them. Other than a call that Ava made to her daughters to tell them about the necklace, they silenced their phones for a full twenty-four hours. Babe's exercise needs were neglected, although she didn't care because she got extra snuggles.

The next morning, as dawn filtered through the windows, Killian leaned up on an elbow and looked down at Ava as she slept. Her hair swirled around her face in a tangled cloud. Her cheeks flushed. Her skin glistened with sweat. Beautiful.

He got aroused again. He swallowed a groan and laid back on his pillow to stare at the ceiling. They'd been going at it like teenagers for hours, yet he couldn't get enough of this woman. Scratch that. He hadn't even done this as a teenager. He'd never stayed in bed with a woman for hours before.

He knew this wouldn't last. It couldn't.

It didn't matter. He resolved not to think too hard about it.

He'd just drifted back to sleep when she stirred. She snuggled into his side and placed her cheek on his chest. "Morning."

"Good morning, sunshine."

"We should get out of bed today. Go outside, get some fresh air, see the sun." She twirled her fingers through his chest hair.

He was too sleepy to answer her, so he grunted his agreement and stroked her head instead. They slept cuddled like that until it became too decadent to sleep in any later.

Then they got up together. They took a shower together. They brushed their teeth together. They got dressed together. They went downstairs together.

Killian put on a pot of coffee while Ava poked around his fridge, pulling out and trashing expired items, and making clucking noises. When she was done, she shut the door and sat down at the table. Killian handed her a cup of coffee.

"We need to buy some food. Is there a market nearby?" Ava wrapped both of her hands around her coffee mug. She blew on the steaming black liquid.

"There's one about twenty minutes away. I'll drive."

"No, I can go. That way, you don't have to be seen with me in public. Just tell me what you like."

He shook his head. "We can go together. It's a small mountain town. The people who own the market know me, and we shouldn't be hassled. We just need to avoid the tourists."

"OK." A bright smile graced her face. "I love going grocery shopping. Usually, I have to get things delivered, and it's just not the same."

Half an hour later, they walked into the market. Ava grabbed a cart and headed to the produce section. "What do you eat?" she asked Killian.

They'd been living off hard-boiled eggs, coffee, and a frozen lasagna. He knew it wasn't to Ava's standards, but they'd been too distracted by each other's bodies to care much about food.

"Beef and the occasional pizza."

"You should eat some vegetables and fruits." She picked up a bag of mixed green salad and dropped it in the cart.

"Why?"

"So you don't get scurvy." She held up a tomato for emphasis before placing it in a plastic bag and setting it in the cart.

He chuckled to himself. He usually forgot about any produce he bought and it would go bad in his fridge, so he didn't bother. His diet consisted of eggs, beef, and frozen meals, which bored him, but also didn't require planning beyond assuring that he got adequate protein. He planned enough in his life, and this was where he arbitrarily drew the line.

She filled the cart with enough food to feed a small army. He didn't know what they were going to do with all that food. But she told him to leave it to her. She seemed happy, so he didn't argue. He insisted on paying, though.

Then she asked him to take her to a drugstore. She added wine, a glass jar, refillable water bottles, a water filter for the tap, an apron, and dish gloves to their haul. He didn't know what she needed all that for, but she smiled and seemed happy, so he didn't question it. She insisted on paying that time.

On the way back up the highway, he stopped for some gas. It was just past noon and hot outside, so he grabbed her a cold bottle of water from the mini-mart's fridge. He handed it to her before climbing back into the truck. "I don't want you to get dehydrated."

"Thank you." She twisted the cap open and took a drink. "Your water game has improved significantly since we first met."

"Count yourself lucky. You promised to drink mud any time I asked. Don't think I've forgotten. That's going to bite you on the ass someday."

"That promise expired."

"I don't think so. That wasn't in the fine print."

She fiddled with the radio. "What kind of music do you like?" she asked. "Please don't say death metal because that's a hard no."

"What's wrong with death metal? You sound so closed-minded. That could be my favorite genre. Won't you be embarrassed."

She gave him side-eye. "Do you like death metal?"

"Not really."

"Because I could put some on. Just for you. Show you how open-minded I am."

"I thought you said it was a hard no."

"I'm growing as a person."

"I'm sure." He laughed.

"So what do you listen to, if not death metal?"

"Mostly classic rock from the seventies."

She looked surprised. "You like music that's a decade older than me?"

"Led Zeppelin set the bar for music, and no one has surpassed it."

She snickered. "OK, dad."

"What do you listen to? Besides the Spice Girls and show tunes?"

"I'm not telling you."

"Why?"

"Because you're just going to mock me and tell me how much cooler your musical tastes are than mine."

"I won't, I promise. Have I once teased you about liking the Spice Girls? And that's objectively mock-worthy."

She glanced at him and pursed her lips, but didn't answer. She played "Old Time Rock & Roll" by Bob Seger over the truck's Bluetooth stereo instead.

"Who's mocking whom?" he asked. "This is a good song, but it's not lost on me that you're making fun of me by playing it."

"Not true. I just really like the movie *Risky Business*."

"Is that so?"

"Yup. Me and Tom go way back. I'm a fan of all his movies."

"Do you really know him?"

"Yes, I do. He wanted me to do one of his *Mission: Impossible* movies, but I had to turn it down because I got pregnant with Bette."

When they got back to the cabin a few minutes later, she kept the music going on her phone, cranking it up. She selected a seventies classic rock playlist that featured several Led Zeppelin songs. The music filled the little kitchen while she put away groceries and donned the apron.

He added the water filter to the tap and then sat at the table and watched her complete her tasks. She seemed to have a particular way that she wanted the food stored in the yellowing fridge.

He wasn't sure what she was doing, but she narrated to him as she went along. She filled the glass jar with water, added tea bags, and stuck it in the sun outside the cabin. "For sun tea," she explained. She filled the water bottles, added sliced strawberries, and put them in the fridge. "For a hike later," she said.

Next, she chopped a bunch of vegetables for a salad. "Lunch will be ready in about twenty minutes," she told him, putting a tray of bacon in the oven. She frowned. "I might have made too much bacon."

"There's no such thing as too much bacon," he assured her.

She giggled. "That should be on a T-shirt."

As cute as she was to watch, swaying around the kitchen to the music in her little apron, all her activity made him feel idle. They had used up most of the wood for the cast-iron stove that heated the cabin. So he got up, took off his shirt, grabbed the axe, and went outside to chop some more.

He had nearly finished when he glanced up and caught her watching him through the kitchen window. She was biting her lip. When he made eye contact, she flushed but didn't look away.

He knew that look. He'd seen it often over the past two days.

He walked back into the cabin with the wood about five minutes later. He heard the front door shut behind him. Dropping the bundle on the floor next to the cast-iron stove, he turned and saw her wearing nothing but his unbuttoned flannel shirt, the one he'd taken off when he went outside to chop wood.

She stood with her back pressed against the door. "I didn't think I was into lumberjacks, but I get it now." She crooked her finger, summoning him to her.

He sauntered over and pinned her against the door with his arms over her shoulders. "I'm not a lumberjack."

"Could've fooled me." She ran her hands down from his clavicle to his stomach before latching onto his waistband and jerking him closer. "You're so sweaty." She chewed her lip again.

He dipped down and kissed her neck. "What about lunch?"

"Oh, shit!" She shoved him back and ducked under his arms. "The bacon!" She darted to the oven to turn it off and pull the tray out before it started to smoke. "Well, I hope you like your bacon crispy," she called over her shoulder. "At least it's not black!"

After she set the tray and potholders down, he stalked up behind her and scooped her up by the waist. He carried her to the couch.

She squealed. "What about lunch?" she asked, squirming in his arms.

"Later."

Chapter 22

Ava and Killian quickly fell into a routine during her three days of filming. In the morning, Ava got up and took a shower for her early call time. Killian didn't have to be up for several more hours, but he still got up with her and made her coffee. Even though she intermittent fasted while filming, and wouldn't eat until dinner, she made him breakfast. Then she left for set just as the sun rose.

In the evening, after she showered off all the makeup, they would walk Babe together. Then they would make dinner together, wash the dishes together, and snuggle on the couch together with a glass of wine.

After her last day of filming, she offered to make dinner so that Killian could catch up on some work. He settled at the kitchen table with his laptop and notebooks filled with lists and calculations.

Slipping upstairs, she stripped out of her clothes from their walk. She put on a pair of expensive red panties and covered the rest of herself with the apron. Then she went back downstairs to make dinner, amused at playing sexy housewife.

Focusing on his work, he didn't notice her lack of clothing until she bent over to slide chicken and Brussels sprouts into the oven to roast.

"That looks delicious," Killian said from the table.

"The key to making food delicious is to use herbs and spices. That's why I stocked such a variety," she responded, bent over in front of the oven.

"I wasn't talking about the chicken."

He walked up to her, sneaking in a grope of her butt just as she stood up. She turned around. "Took you long enough to notice," she pouted.

"Do you cook at home like this, too?" He opened a bottle of wine and poured her a glass.

"You mean, in nothing but a pair of panties and an apron?" She took the wineglass from him and winked.

He put some cheese and fruit on a plate. "I assume you wear more than that when your kids are around."

She followed him to the couch. "Most nights, yeah."

"Shouldn't you wear pants all of the time, not just most of the time, when your kids are around?" he teased.

She shrugged, playing along. "We're all girls."

She changed the music she'd had playing on her phone.

After putting the plate on the coffee table, he sat down. "How'd we go from Bob Dylan to—who is this?"

"Kylie Minogue."

"Kylie Minogue?"

"You don't know who Kylie Minogue is? She's only, like, the biggest pop star ever in Australia. I swear, you're such a grumpy old man."

"I'm not grumpy just because I don't listen to Australian pop."

"I beg to differ." She giggled and sipped her wine. "Ooh! I got a nickname for you. Waldorf!"

"What?"

"You know, one of the grumpy old-man Muppets that heckle from a balcony."

"Muppets were before my time," he said, a wicked gleam in his eyes.

She gasped. "So mean." She sat at the end of the couch and nudged him with her foot.

"I'm surprised you cook so much. I assumed you'd have a cook and a maid and a nanny to help you out."

"I had a house manager who did all those things. Jack got her in the divorce, and then she retired." She sighed wistfully. "I miss Myrna. She made the best omelets."

"You didn't hire anyone else?"

"No. Well, I have a part-time nanny who comes when I need extra help. And I have a housekeeper who comes twice per week, so I'm not spending my days slaving away like Cinderella. But I want to cook for my kids. We eat dinner together and do homework, and I get them ready in the mornings and pack their lunches. I enjoy spending time with them. They're so fun. And it's important that they learn real life skills and experience a normal home life."

She felt that pang of guilt again, being up here, indulging herself, instead of being home with her kids. She missed them—she did—but sometimes a little time off from being a mom is... *nice*.

"I'd get rid of the nanny completely if I lived closer to Jack. He'd take them more during the week, but it's a long drive between LA and San Diego." She swirled her wineglass and stared into the deep purple liquid. "Jack hates the girls being in LA—says Hollywood is a warped environment for kids—and he's right. I should just move to San Diego. It would be better for them."

"So why don't you?"

Ava frowned. The truth felt ugly, and she didn't want him to see her that way. She confessed it, anyway. "Because I don't want to be alone. My two best friends are in LA, and they're the only people who know the real me and love me anyway." Her mood sinking, she picked up a slice of apple. "It's selfish, I know."

She shrugged off her uncomfortable feeling and bit into the fruit. "I should just do what's best for the girls. The back and forth between cities messes with their schooling. They have to be tutored when they're at Jack's. I should either move or quit acting so I can stay home."

He rubbed her calf. "I wish I could help you, but I know nothing about parenting."

"It's OK. We can talk about something else." She shivered in the chilly evening air.

Killian squeezed her foot. "You could try putting on clothes."

"Ha ha," she said in a monotone. "I thought you liked me without clothes on."

"I do. But I don't want you to be cold." He got up and fetched her a blanket, tucking it around her.

"Thank you." When he sat back down, she slid closer to him, draped her legs over his lap, and ducked her head under his arm. She breathed in the smell of his soap and smiled.

"I've never had a woman stay over for a night before, and you've been here for six. I think it has something to do with the fact that you hate wearing pants."

"I don't hate wearing pants."

"Could've fooled me." He worked his free hand under the blanket to caress her thighs. "It was bold to invite yourself to stay here for the entire week," he teased. "What would you have done if I'd said no?"

"I brought an arsenal of sexy lingerie... and other things. I was prepared to persuade you, had it been necessary." She drank her wine calmly, letting the words hang in the air.

"There's more?"

She set the blanket aside and toyed with the apron's ties. "There's more."

"I folded too early."

She laughed. "I think you've done alright."

"I have been eating better since you've been here," he admitted.

"Speaking of, I need to pull dinner out of the oven." She stood up. "It'll take a few minutes to cool. What shall we do to kill the time?"

"I'd like to know what else you've got in your suitcase."

"After dinner." She blew him a kiss from the oven, bent over and wiggled her ass. "Take in the view while you can. I'm going to put on some pants. This is not proper dinner attire."

Killian cleared the table and plated their food while she dressed.

"What's your movie about?" he asked, making dinner conversation. "I've just realized that I've never asked what you were working on."

"It's a modern adaptation of *A Midsummer Night's Dream*."

"Shakespeare?"

"Mm-hmm. The original play takes place in a forest, so that's why we're filming here."

"I read the play in college. All I remember is that a fairy turned a guy into an ass, which I claimed in an essay is what relationships do to men. My teacher said I misunderstood the play, and I argued with her. I didn't want to get a C, so I rewrote the paper into whatever she said was correct. I've forgotten what that was now."

Ava stabbed a Brussels sprout with her fork. "Is that why you don't watch rom-coms? Because you think the characters are acting like asses?"

"No. I just don't have any interest."

"How do you know you wouldn't like them if you haven't ever watched one?"

"Do you watch kung fu movies?" he countered.

"No."

"Why not?"

"OK, I get it," she conceded. "I don't watch them because I've never been interested in them."

"You're missing out. Kung fu movies are pretty entertaining."

"I guess I could watch one. I just never have." She looked up at him. "See, that's me being open-minded again."

"You've at least seen *Kill Bill*?"

"No. I don't like Quentin's movies. They're too violent for my tastes."

He looked shocked. "You haven't seen *Kill Bill*?"

"No."

"You've seen *Pulp Fiction*?"

"Yes. But I didn't like it."

"You... what? That movie's a classic."

"*Casablanca* is a classic. *Pulp Fiction* is a movie that makes light of murder and sexual assault."

"I haven't seen *Casablanca*."

"*What?*" It was Ava's turn to be shocked. "I don't think we can be friends anymore."

"We're friends?" he deadpanned.

She took a swallow of wine. "I honestly don't know what we are."

"Let's not worry about it."

She pushed a piece of chicken around her plate. "Actually, I think we should talk"—she swirled her fork in the air between them—"about us."

He gave her a wary look. "Conversations that start with 'we should talk' are usually unpleasant."

"This one doesn't have to be." She took a small bite of chicken. "I think we're usually pretty open and honest with each other. At least, I am with you. I just need some clarity. Are we going to still talk after I leave tomorrow? What would that even look like?"

"Do you want that?" His wary expression hadn't changed.

"I don't know." She swallowed. "I already told you I came here with the intent of, um, finishing what we'd started in the motel. Thing is, we'd been teasing each other for weeks. I didn't think I'd be able to move on until after we, you know, completed. I hoped that, after we had sex, you'd be out of my system."

"Am I?"

"No." She felt the heat rising in her cheeks. "What about you? Have you had enough—of me, I mean?"

"I've already spent more time with you than I have with any other woman."

She cast her eyes downward and nodded, regretting starting this conversation.

"I've enjoyed you being here," he continued.

She braced herself for the rejection, even though she knew, logically, this was a fling. No matter how hard she tried to be good she was never good enough.

"I've never wanted a woman the way I want you. I know it can't last forever. But apparently it can last for longer than a week. So, no, I haven't had enough of you yet."

Ava's heart staggered in her chest. He hadn't rejected her. She blinked rapidly at the wine in her glass. "Oh." She took another bite of chicken and chewed it slowly before swallowing it down around a lump that had lodged itself in her throat. "I think we have a situation, then."

He ate in silence, waiting for her to elaborate.

"I mean, if we look at this logically, this doesn't really make sense as anything other than a fling. Our real lives don't mesh. So what do we do now? It doesn't make sense to keep going, but neither of us wants to stop. How do we deal with that?"

"I don't know."

"Do you remember making a list of reasons why we shouldn't sleep together? You told me about it in the motel room."

"I remember."

She went to the kitchen counter where he'd piled up his notebooks and pencils. She picked up one and turned to a blank page. "I think we should make a list of all the ways we're wrong for each other, so that we will do the right thing when the time comes."

Killian leaned back in his chair, crossing his arms. "My list of reasons we shouldn't have sex didn't stop us, though."

"I know. I think that's because the reasons you told me weren't strong enough. I could refute them." She sat down at the table and wrote "All the Ways We're Wrong" on the top of the page and underlined it.

"What makes you think your list will be better than mine? How do you know that this'll work?"

"Because it has to." She tapped the paper with the pencil and wrote the number one. "I'll start, I guess. I live in LA. I'm a city mouse. Number two. You live in a remote cabin on a mountain, far from any city."

He began washing the dishes. "Keep going, I can help you from here."

"OK. Number three. It's at least a five-hour drive to see each other. We can't just pop over for a quickie."

"And you think that a drive between LA and San Diego is long. That's like an hour and a half."

"Not with traffic. The traffic in LA would blow your mind."

"I grew up in New Jersey, remember. I've seen traffic." He laid the clean baking dish on a kitchen towel to dry. "I hate traffic. I don't want to live in places where I have to deal with all that noise and aggravation."

Ava nodded. "Number four. You like peace, quiet, and solitude. Number five. I'm noisy, famous, and extroverted."

Killian returned to the table with the bottle of wine and refilled Ava's glass. "I will never understand why you'd want to be famous. Getting photographed and pestered by strangers, even for a few days, was awful."

"Number six. The attention that comes with my fame is your idea of hell."

"You're right, Blondie. Your fame would be the main reason I'd avoid visiting you in LA."

Ava studied their list so far. "See, I knew we could do this. Let's keep going. This is good." She took a sip of wine. "Number seven. I'm forty. I'm too old for you."

"Forty isn't old, Ava."

"Debatable. But regardless, it's too old for you. Number eight. You're thirty-three."

"That doesn't matter to me."

"But it matters to me!" Her face scrunched as she fought a rush of emotions. "You don't understand. I'm a middle-aged, divorced mother. I want to get married again and grow old with a partner. How am I ever going to find someone to love me now? It was hard enough when I was in my twenties. My prospects only get worse as I get older. That's just how it is for women."

"I don't think it's that dire, Ava. You don't have to believe the lie that women are valued only for their fecundity."

"Fecundity. Wow, there's a million-dollar word."

"You know what I mean." He sat next to her, resting his hand on her knee under the table.

"I'm not sure I do. Hold on, I'll Google it." She picked up her phone and tapped on the screen for a few seconds. "Fecundity. 'The ability to produce an abundance of offspring.' OK, yeah, that's what I thought it meant. Well,

I've already had three children. That's plenty for me. Babies are great, but I'm done with all that."

She set down her phone and wrote again in the notebook. "Number nine. I have three kids. Number ten. You don't want kids."

He sighed. "Well, you got me there."

"Number eleven. I want to get remarried. Number twelve. You want to stay single." She set the pencil down and looked at him. "I'm not judging you, in case it sounds that way. It's perfectly fine that you don't want a wife and kids. That's an acceptable choice. It's just incompatible with what I want. I know I want to get remarried someday. Now that I'm older, I don't have time to waste on relationships that can't progress."

He took his hand off her knee and leaned forward. "Let me explain."

Ava shook her head and gave him a wan smile. "No. You don't have to explain."

He slipped the pencil from between her fingers and turned the notepad to him to write. "Number thirteen. You're out of my league."

"No, I'm not." Ava added "under protest," in parentheses after his addition to the list. "That's ridiculous. If anything, I'm not good enough."

"The world won't see it that way. And they'd be right, because I was broken the moment my parents decided they didn't want me. I never had a chance."

"What are you talking about? You're not broken. Look how successful and competent and educated you are. You taught me a new word not even five minutes ago."

"I get by because I've been through decades of therapy. I've gone to therapy as an adult, not just as a kid. So I've got decent coping skills, but I'm still broken."

He took her hand. "When I was a kid, a school psychologist diagnosed me with attachment disorder, and that label followed me for the rest of my childhood. I suspect it made it harder for me to get adopted because I was a kid with documented psychological and behavioral issues."

Ava looked at their joined hands. "OK, so what does that mean?"

"When nobody wants you at a young age, you learn you can't trust people, you can't rely on anyone. I write lists and keep my life simple because it helps me have some sense of control. I avoid crowds and people because people are unpredictable.

"It's more comfortable for me to be alone. I prefer animals. I get nature, physics, math. That's why I'm an engineer. Because I didn't have parents, even adopted parents, I never learned what a parent should be like. Because no one ever cared about me and I had no permanent relationships, I never learned how to do those things either."

He squeezed her hand again. "Trust me when I tell you, I'm doing you a favor by not misleading you. You deserve better, and that's why my last point stays on the list."

She stood up and motioned him to hug her. From inside his arms, she said, "I don't know what to say, but it makes me sad."

"These are the facts, though, right? Isn't that the point of the list you just wrote? Acknowledge the cold, hard truth and act accordingly, without emotions leading you wrong?"

"Yeah," she agreed. She sat down and looked over the list again. "Do you think we missed anything?"

He shook his head. "I think we're done with it."

"So now that we have the list, what do we do with it?"

"I don't know. Maybe that's enough for tonight. Let's do something easy, like watch a movie. Anything you want. Your pick."

"Really? What if I pick *Casablanca*?"

"Anything you want," he confirmed.

Ava set the pencil down and scanned the completed list again. She took a picture with her phone. "You're in charge of the original," she said, handing the notebook to Killian.

<u>All the Ways We're Wrong</u>

1. I live in LA
2. You live in a remote cabin in the woods
3. It's a five-hour drive to see each other
4. You like peace and quiet
5. I'm famous and noisy
6. The attention that comes with my fame is your idea of hell
7. I'm 40
8. You're 33
9. I have 3 kids
10. You don't want kids
11. I want to get remarried
12. You want to stay single
13. You're out of my league (under protest)

Chapter 23

The final morning of Ava's stay, Killian woke before dawn. They didn't need to get up so early and he didn't have to work that day. Attempting to return to sleep, he pulled Ava tighter into his side.

"You're awake," she said.

"So are you." He stroked her spine. "We've been getting up early the past few days, so we must be used to it."

"Yeah." She yawned. "I was thinking, I have a long drive ahead of me, but I don't have to be home at any particular time. Jack's got the girls till tomorrow. Maybe I don't need to leave until later in the afternoon."

"OK."

He held her close for another hour before getting up to make them their morning coffee, and she made them breakfast. They ate together in silence, watching the sunrise. After breakfast, they took Babe on a six-mile hike.

"On our first day walking down the mountain, I asked you to tell me about your childhood. You didn't tell me much. Maybe you can tell me now," Ava panted. They'd kept a vigorous pace, and she was slightly out of breath.

"You don't want to know. I was a bad kid."

"You were a kid. How bad could you have been?"

"Bad. I got into fights, bullied other kids, broke things, stole things. I'm not talking childish hijinks. I was a petty criminal with a chip on my shoulder by the time I was five. No one could control me.

"If the teachers put me on timeout, I would leave school. When I was seven, I ran away and hid in a Chuck E. Cheese for two days, living off pizza I stole from people's tables when they weren't looking. After that, they put me in therapy, probably because I was too young to jail."

Ava stopped walking to drink fruit-infused water from the bottles she'd made them. She peered at him while she drank, processing what he'd just told her. He didn't know why he was so honest with her just now, or the day before. She had a way of getting past his usual boundaries.

"So you were the bad boy, and I was the good girl," she said, screwing the lid back onto her bottle. "It would be a cliché, except you're not bad now."

He shrugged. "I wish I could go back and apologize to the kids I tormented. I was always bigger than everyone, so I never lost a fight. I used to fat-shame this one kid in fifth grade. I couldn't stand that he had parents who got him the best toys, and he never had to worry where his next meal came from. It's embarrassing to remember the things I called him in front of the rest of the class."

Pain crossed her face. "When I was a kid, I tried to be the best at everything, because I was never high-achieving enough for my parents. I've always been extra, and I got bullied for it. I never thought about what my bullies were going through that made them act out like that." She started hiking again, slowing their pace. "When did you stop acting out?"

"High school. I was growing fast and was down to a single set of clothes that fit. Another kid made fun of me for wearing the same thing every day, so I broke his jaw. They sent me to juvie for a year." He glanced at her, and saw her stricken expression. "I don't know why I'm telling you this, princess. Let's talk about something else."

"What happened to you at juvie?" she asked, her voice barely louder than a whisper.

"Nothing. The kids in there were messed up—worse than the kids in the group home. I didn't want to be like them. So I made different choices. I figured that college was my ticket out of poverty, so I focused on doing better in school, and spent a lot of time in the library. I went to therapy, kept to myself, didn't socialize. I didn't have any friends or girlfriends, but that's how I stayed out of trouble. After a year of being locked in, I hate being cooped up, and that's a big reason why I like to be outdoors so much."

Emotions flitted across her face. Her eyes grew wide and glassy until they overflowed with tears. She kept walking, letting them run down her cheeks.

"You don't need to cry for me, Ava."

"Somebody has to." She let her tears silently fall for several minutes, her lip quivering and her cheeks red. Eventually, she stopped, and they walked the rest of the way back without talking.

The air between them had been heavy since the night before. But Killian still didn't want her to leave, and he still wasn't sure what would happen after she did. She'd casually suggested that they go cold turkey after today, but they hadn't reached a consensus on that yet.

Instead, they went about the day's mundane activities, ignoring the elephants in the room. She offered to make lunch while he showered after their hike. They ate, and then she went upstairs to shower. He sat at the table, lazily responding to email, patting Babe, and repeatedly trying to banish the heavy weight that sat on his chest.

When she came downstairs again, he nearly choked on his own tongue. Ava wore a leather corset cinched so tightly that her breasts barely stayed contained within it. She also wore lacy black panties, garters, fishnet stockings, and the highest, spikiest heels he'd ever seen a woman successfully walk in.

"Something else you had hidden in your suitcase?" he sputtered.

"Mm-hmm." She glided over and nudged his chair leg with her toe. "Scoot back." When he did, she straddled his lap and sank down, giving him an eyeful of her heaving bosom. "My eyes are up here," she teased.

Dragging his gaze away from her luscious breasts popping above the leather panels, he was equally captivated by her bright blue irises contrasted against a cloud of black eyeshadow. Rendered speechless, he watched her, waiting to see what she would do next.

"So I think I figured it out," she said in preamble. "The reason we can't seem to get enough of each other, I mean." She widened her thighs and settled lower on him, igniting familiar sparks of desire in his core.

"OK. What is it?" He played along, but he knew why he couldn't get enough of her: she was the hottest woman he'd ever seen or touched. In this moment, she'd raised the bar to a dizzying height. His insatiable dick strained against his jeans.

She twirled her fingers through the hair on his nape. "We both realized that we could never be more, as we confirmed with our list. We both knew it all along. That gives our coming together"—she smirked—"pun intended, a forbidden-fruit energy. We're opposites, wrong for each other, making us want each other all the more. Because wrong is hot." She smoldered, lowering her lids, and tilting her head back.

Cupping her chin, he rubbed his thumb across her lower lip, smudging her perfectly drawn crimson lipstick. He wanted to suck on that lip. He wanted to smear her lipstick everywhere. "That's a pretty good theory."

"I've thought of a way we can test it."

"Is that so?" He toyed with the laces at her back.

"I bet that if we talked through all the little ways we're opposites, the subtle ways we're wrong, rather than getting turned off, we'll get more turned on."

He barely heard a word she said because she'd started grinding into his hips. He started planning all the ways he would make their last time together one for the record books—an afternoon of debauchery that they would both never forget. Last night, he'd learned that she'd brought toys.

Gripping her ass—bare because she was in a thong—he stood up from the chair and carried her with him. She wrapped her legs around his waist. He brought her to the couch and sat down. He was going to take his time peeling that leather corset off of her.

She settled on him again, thighs flanking his and her breasts inches from his hungry mouth. She leaned back, moving them just out of his reach. "Let's begin," she said. "What is your favorite movie?"

"Why?"

"Just answer my question."

"*Helveti.*"

"Your favorite movie is about ancient warring Germanic tribes starring my ex-husband?"

"Yeah. It's a good movie."

"See, that's weird. You're a fan of my ex-husband. We're weird together."

"What's your point?"

"My point is that my favorite movie is *Moulin Rouge*. I bet you've never seen it."

"You're right. I haven't."

"See, we're opposites. Incompatible in our movie tastes."

"I don't think it matters."

"It wouldn't if it were only this one thing. But it's just an example." She swiveled her hips, grinding into him again, and he had to swallow a groan.

"I can feel how turned on you are, by the way. So far, our incompatible tastes have done nothing to cool either of us off. Your turn."

He couldn't think of anything because she had replaced his blood with fire. "I don't know. Let me help you out of that corset."

"No. Try harder." She began undoing his shirt buttons. "Give me a way we're opposite, or I'll stop, go upstairs, and change into a turtle-neck."

"Did you pack a turtleneck? In August?" he asked dryly.

"Do you want to find out? Or would you rather I stay dressed like this?"

He chuckled. "OK, Blondie, you win." He thought a moment. "You like Britney Spears."

She leaned forward and nibbled on his neck. "Mm-hmm."

"I'm not listening to that."

"You listened to it the other day. And you still fucked me immediately afterwards." She sat back and slid open more of his shirt buttons.

His hands were still holding her ass. Sliding a finger under the strap of her thong, he snapped it. Then he stooped his head and bit the tops of her breasts.

She threw her head back. "I'm a good girl. And, especially right now, you're being a very bad boy."

"You are a good girl," he agreed, pushing his finger under her thong and into her wet pussy. He pulled his soaked finger back out and pressed it to her lips. "You taste good too. Open your mouth."

While she licked and sucked on his finger, she slid a hand inside his open shirt and scraped her fingernails down his pecs. "It's your turn," she said when he removed his finger from her mouth with a pop.

He wracked his brain. "You like to sing, and I really can't. That's no exaggeration." He reached for the back of her corset and pulled on a lace.

"You won't let me give you a nickname, but you call me all kinds of nicknames." She slipped her fingers into his waistband and unbuttoned his pants.

"That's because I prefer to make you say my real name." He pulled on another lace. "My turn. You insist on giving me a nickname."

"No, that's cheating. Do another one." She yanked his shirt over his shoulders and down his arms, popping a button that she'd forgotten to undo.

"You know nothing about the outdoors." He pulled on another lace and the corset slackened. "I fear for you."

"You can't cook." She scraped her fingernails across his shoulders. "I mean, seriously, you have the diet of a teenage boy."

Not dignifying that with a response, he gave her corset a yank downwards. Her breasts spilled out over the top. He grabbed them with a sense of accomplishment, immediately steering one to his mouth. He grazed a nipple with his teeth.

She arched her back, giving him full access to her breasts. "Oh, Killian," she moaned.

"That's right, princess, you know what to say." He smiled against her ample flesh as he sucked on her.

"It's your turn, but as your mouth is busy, I'll go ahead. You're grumpy."

"I'm not grumpy," he muttered from within her cleavage.

She snaked her hand inside his pants, searching for his cock. She found it and rubbed along his length.

"Yeah? You probably hate Christmas. I love Christmas, so it's stands to reason you don't. Do you like Christmas?"

He sat back. "No."

"I knew it."

He snapped her thong again. "Stand up and take your panties off."

She complied. "We're probably never going to see each other again. That means all bets are off. We can be as filthy as we want to be."

"That's one way we're compatible." He pulled his throbbing cock out of his pants and stroked it, watching her watch him. "Get back on my lap. I want you to ride me."

She climbed on top of him and widened her knees. Using her hand to guide him, she took him fully inside. She rocked back and forth and rode him, eyes shut, head back, mouth slack.

"I want more," she panted. "I want you harder."

Obliging, he grabbed her hips, lifted her until she was poised on the tip of him, and then slammed her back down.

"Yes," she cried. "Like that."

He moved her up and down him in long strokes, over and over, until he felt her pussy tightening around him. But before she could come, he stopped her, holding her still, hovering on the tip of him.

She opened her eyes and gave him an angry look. "Killian, no. I want you to fuck me. Stop edging me."

"Such a demanding little princess." Slowly, deliberately, cruelly even, he lowered her again. He paused, then pulled out of her completely, laughing outright at the frustrated face she made.

She groaned. "I told you I wanted you to fuck me. Here's another way we aren't compatible. We're both too dominant." She kissed him hard and bit his lower lip for emphasis.

"I don't think so." He lifted her off of his lap and set her on the couch next to him. "On your hands and knees."

She did as he asked. "What does that mean, 'I don't think so'? Are you kidding? I'm very demanding."

"You are demanding," he agreed. "And insatiable. But I think that if I got a little rough, you'd take it like a good girl, and you'd like it." He kneeled behind her and pushed her corset up so that he could grip her waist with one hand. He dragged a finger through her slick pussy until he pressed on her clit.

She gasped. "What makes you think that?" She pushed back into his hand, demanding more.

Moving his hand from her waist to her hair, he dug in and gently yanked until her back arched. "That." He took his hand off her clit and gave her bare ass a smack, just hard enough to leave a red mark. She shuddered and whimpered. "And that."

"Did you just spank me?" Her husky voice registered surprise.

"Yes. And you liked it." With one smooth thrust, he pushed inside her, pulling on her hair to keep her in place as she took the length of him. With no other people around for miles, she didn't censor her passionate, throaty scream.

He pulled back out and gave her ass another slap before pushing back in hard. Her thighs shook. He thrust over and over, gripping and slapping her ass, until she protested that her legs were about to give.

He flipped her over and brought her knees to her chest, angling to fuck her deep and slow. As he did, her face swam in his vision. It was as if the two of them were the only people who existed in the universe.

She gripped his cheeks and kissed him. "Let go," she said against his mouth. "Come with me. I want us to come together."

He moved faster, fucking her in time with her demanding tongue in his mouth. And when they both came, he squeezed his eyes shut and everything turned black. They'd destroyed the universe and left it shattered into a billion pieces, with nothing remaining but their ragged breaths and thundering hearts.

"See," she panted, pulling him onto her chest and wrapping her legs around his waist. "We're so wrong, it feels right."

Chapter 24

Ava left late afternoon. They made no agreements. They made no plans. They made no promises, except for her to text him when she made it home so that he would know she was safe.

He kissed her goodbye against her car door. Then he watched her drive off. He watched the road for a long time after she disappeared. The film crew had left early that morning, while they'd been out hiking. Once again, he was alone.

Restless and having nothing better to do, he went to bed at eight with a book. He couldn't concentrate, so he stared at the ceiling. About an hour later, she texted him.

Ava: Hey Special K. I made it home

Killian: Are you comparing me to ketamine or corn flakes?

Ava: The drug cuz you're so addictive ;)

Killian: Did it take you the entire drive to think of that?

Ava: No. Maybe. Shut up

Killian: How was the drive?

Ava: Long. I'm exhausted. I'm going straight to bed

Killian: Get some sleep, princess

Ava: You too. Goodnight

Killian: Goodnight

He struggled to sleep.

For almost a month, Killian didn't call or text Ava, leaving things up to her. She didn't call or text him either. He had the list; they both knew what this was. After the first week passed with no contact, he didn't expect to see or hear from her again.

He spent his days working and surveying the mountain with Babe. Every night, Babe jumped onto the bed, even though he told her no. When he worked in the cabin, she curled up at his feet or guarded the front door. She was the perfect companion, the perfect relationship for him.

With the campground closed to the public, he rarely saw other people. He thought about calling Lisa just to see another human being. Not yet, though.

He knew in time he would be content again. The restlessness would fade. Eventually, he would stop thinking about Ava. Until then, he kept his own company.

He stayed busy—so busy, in fact, that he'd completed two months' worth of work in one. He put in long hours and worked weekends. Mary suggested, and then insisted, that he use his vacation days.

Early one morning, the Thursday before Labor Day weekend, Babe whined and scratched at the floor next to the bed. She'd dropped a toy between the mattress and the nightstand and couldn't reach it. Killian moved the nightstand out of the way and saw Ava's "Mom" pendant necklace on the floor.

He stared at it for a long time.

Then he packed a few items into a bag, texted Mary that he was taking off through the long weekend, loaded Babe into his truck, and drove down the mountain.

He got to LA by early afternoon. He stopped for gas and sent Ava a message.

Killian: I found your necklace

While waiting for her response, he pumped gas and made plans to take Babe to the beach. If she didn't respond, he would get a motel room for the night, and then drive back to his cabin tomorrow. While he mapped out a route to the nearest dog-friendly beach, a text came through.

Ava: OMG! I thought I lost it again. I was beside myself. Can you send it to me?

She sent him her address.

Ava: Or I could come get it

Killian: I'm in LA. I could just drive it over

She took an agonizingly long time to respond. But in reality, it was only about thirty seconds.

Ava: Can I call you?

Rather than respond by text, Killian punched her name on the phone's display to call her.

"Hello?" Ava answered.

"Hey, princess." He didn't like that he suddenly felt nervous.

"Hey, Paul Bunyan. You're in LA?"

"Yeah."

"Why?"

"My boss said I had to use some of my vacation time, so I thought I would drive to the city and see how your kind live. I thought it might be good for Babe to see the ocean."

She snickered. "You drove to LA so that Babe could go swimming? Yeah, I'm calling bullshit."

He pulled at the back of his neck in embarrassment. "That obvious?"

"Mm-hmm." Her voice lowered. "It's OK. I want to see you. The only thing is, my daughters will be home in less than an hour."

Ironic that he'd forgotten about her kids, since he was delivering a necklace with the word "Mom" on it. "I'm sorry, Ava. I didn't think. I don't want to impose. I can drop it off before they get home. It'll take five minutes. That's really all I came here to do."

"No. Killian, please. Have dinner with us. My girls will go bananas over Babe."

He didn't answer her immediately.

"Please," she begged. "I really want to see you for more than five minutes. You came all this way."

The idea of meeting her kids warred with his desire to see her. But he'd been driving for half a day, and her voice was doing things to his guts. "OK. Is the address you sent your home?"

"Yes. It's a gated community. I'll let the guard know you're coming so that they'll let you in."

LA traffic was as terrible as Ava had said. It took him more than an hour to get to her place. As soon as he pulled into her driveway, she came skipping down her front steps to greet him, wearing khaki shorts and a white T-shirt. Even in such a simple outfit, her extraordinary beauty was striking.

When he got out of his truck, she ran up to him and practically jumped into his arms, giving him a tight hug. "I've missed you," she breathed into his ear, before pressing a quick kiss on his mouth and stepping back.

Killian opened the rear door to the truck and gave Babe the command to hop out. Babe jumped on Ava, knocking her back, before zooming circles around the lawn. Killian grabbed Ava's arm and kept her upright. "I'm sorry. She's been cooped up for too long."

Ava looped an arm around his waist. "It's OK. Let's get her inside and introduce her to the kids. They'll entertain her for a while." She led him up the steps and through the front door. Her house was palatial. He'd never been inside a house this large. He was pretty sure his entire cabin would fit inside her living room.

They found her daughters sitting around the table in her enormous dining room, their homework spread across the top. Babe ran straight to them, resulting in surprised girlish peals.

"Girls, meet my friend Killian and his dog Babe," Ava told them as they walked into the room. "Killian, the oldest one is Audrey, the middle one is Ingrid, and the youngest is Bette."

Three blonde mini-Avas waved and murmured hellos as they were introduced. But their attention never faltered from Babe. Bette jumped off her seat and kneeled next to the dog, hugging Babe's neck and getting licked all over her face.

"Girls, you can take Babe out back and play fetch with her. She has lots of energy to burn after a long drive. You can use some of our tennis balls." They all ran outside without a backwards glance.

Ava stepped close to him and snaked her arms around his neck. "Now that we're alone, you can give me a proper kiss," she murmured against his mouth, darting her tongue against his lips.

He tried to keep control, but within seconds he was breathing her in like a suffocating man sucking oxygen. And she was doing it right back.

Ava finally tore her mouth from his, although she stayed in the circle of his arms. She arched her back to look up at him. Her eyes were dark with desire.

"How long are you here for?" she asked, her voice husky.

Killian lifted his shoulders in a half shrug. "I don't have any firm plans. I'm off work till Tuesday."

"The girls go to school early tomorrow and then will head straight to their father's for the long weekend. I want you to stay. Please stay for the weekend." Her eyes made a lusty promise that he couldn't refuse.

"OK," he agreed. "I'll find a motel tonight for me and Babe and come back tomorrow after your girls leave."

"I'm not sure I can wait until morning," she pouted. "But I appreciate you being so considerate."

They made dinner and easy conversation about their lives over the past month. But the ease he felt disappeared when he sat down at the table with Ava's offspring.

Three sets of curious eyes openly stared at him. Ava asked them about their schoolwork, but they gave her perfunctory answers and continued to study him instead.

Finally, Ingrid braved a question. "Are you my mom's boyfriend?"

Killian's eyebrows shot up. Before the denial could leave his lips, however, Audrey cut in. "You're the one who saved Mom from the mudslide, aren't you?" she asked quietly. "I saw your name on my phone, and Babe is the dog you and mom found on the trail."

He nodded. "That's right."

Bette jumped out of her chair, ran around the table, and threw her arms around him in a hug. He gave Ava a panicked look, but she merely shrugged and smiled softly.

Bette looked up at him with doe eyes the color of olives. "Thank you," she said. "You're Mom's hero, and you're my hero too." She offered him a trembling, tearful smile that reminded him of Ava.

"You're welcome," he responded, charmed and a little embarrassed at being called her hero.

Bette let go of him and bounced on her toes. "I like your dog. Does she chase cats?" Bette skipped back to her seat.

"I don't know. We haven't met any cats yet."

"We have a cat at my dad's house," Bette explained. "His name is Ollie. Our dog Scruffles chases him when Ollie gets too close to Scruffles's food bowl. Ollie doesn't learn, though."

Killian laughed. "Cats are stubborn."

"What's your dog's name again?" Ingrid asked.

"Babe."

"Babe." Ingrid seemed to taste the name in her mouth the same way that Ava did his name the first night after he pulled her from the collapsed cabin. "Why'd you name her that?"

"She's named after Paul Bunyan's blue ox," Killian explained.

"Oh." Ingrid nodded seriously. "But she doesn't look like an ox."

"Your mom kept trying to give me nicknames while we were hiking down the mountain and they were all terrible. Isn't that right, Blondie?"

Ava gave him a dirty look.

"One nickname she tried was Paul Bunyan. So when we found Babe, she got named following the same theme."

Ingrid glanced at her mother, her brow furrowed. "Mom, why'd you nickname him Paul Bunyan?"

"Because he looks like a lumberjack," Ava answered.

Ingrid looked back at him again, studying him. After a moment, she nodded. "I can see it."

Ava laughed. "Ha! See!" She turned to Ingrid. "He had an axe and everything."

Killian changed the topic. "Did your mom tell you about how she drank mud?"

Audrey gave him a dubious look. "She drank *mud*?"

Killian recounted how they didn't have water, how they had to drink from a mud puddle using a special straw, and how he had to throw mud at Ava to get her to cooperate. All three of the girls paid rapt attention. They pealed with laughter at the thought of their mother getting all muddy.

The girls peppered the conversation with commentary about what Ava must have looked like, and how she might've reacted to being pelted with mud. They weren't wholly wrong in their assessments.

Then he told them about how she screamed at the tarantula.

"I would scream if I woke up to a tarantula on my face too," Audrey said.

"Me too," Bette agreed.

"Yeah," said Ingrid.

"*Thank* you," Ava exclaimed, triumphantly. "That's a perfectly normal reaction to a spider."

"Yeah, but you didn't hear how loud she screamed," Killian defended.

Ingrid shook her head. "We've heard her scream before. Remember the coyote?" she asked, turning to her sisters.

Bette giggled. "She was so loud, it woke me up."

"It was in the front yard chasing Mrs. Peterson's cat. It surprised me when I walked out. I didn't expect a wild animal in the middle of our neighborhood," Ava explained.

"Coyotes are all around us, even in cities," Audrey said. "I Googled it."

"To be fair, your mom saw a bear and its cub on the mountain, and she didn't scream." Killian told them how she'd stood her ground with him, letting the mama bear take her cub and leave.

"I want to go camping," Audrey said. "But I'm afraid of bears."

"You don't need to be afraid of bears." Killian taught them all about black bears, much like he did their mother on the mountain. "Camping is fun. You shouldn't avoid it because of bears," he summed up.

"I didn't know you wanted to go camping," Ava said to Audrey, looking surprised. "Since when?"

"We all want to go. We've talked about it," Ingrid advised.

"Yeah," added Bette. "We want to go camping because Dad told us you were safe because you were camping, and people camp all the time. Aunt Dee said she went camping with Dad when they were our age. We asked him to take us, but Esme said that she didn't understand why people would sleep on the ground when they have beds."

Ava laughed. "Sleeping on the ground *is* cold and uncomfortable. But maybe we could try camping, anyway. Maybe the kind where you don't have to sleep on the ground?" She looked at Killian. "That's a thing, right?"

He nodded.

"I want to do the kind of camping where you don't have to pee in the woods because there are no toilets," Ingrid added.

"I had to do that," Ava remarked. "It was gross. I definitely would prefer camping somewhere that has facilities." She looked at Killian again. "Also a thing?"

He nodded again.

"What did you use for toilet paper?" Audrey asked around a mouthful of vegetables.

"Don't talk with your mouth full," Ava corrected before going into more detail about roughing it. "Killian told me I had to watch out for a poison plant—what's it called again?"

"Poison oak."

"Yeah, poison oak. I'm glad you were around to make sure I didn't accidentally use poison oak as toilet paper. You're pretty handy to have around in the woods, Kill."

"Don't call me that."

"What's poison oak?" Ingrid asked Killian. He gave more life lessons about the outdoors.

After dinner, he helped clear the table. Then Ava sent the girls into the kitchen to wash the dishes. She returned to the table with two cups of coffee—fancy cappuccinos topped with a cloud of foamed milk.

"This is really good," he said, after taking his first drink.

"I told you," she said. "I have an awesome machine. It makes all the difference." She sat next to him, across the corner of the table. "You know," she said in a low voice, "I had been working up the nerve to text you for an hour when you texted me this morning. I was trying to figure out how to invite myself over for the long weekend."

She grasped his hand between both of hers. "I'm sorry I didn't call. I was trying..."

"I know."

"I had to re-read the list at least ten times a day to keep my resolve. But I couldn't do it."

"I was leaving it up to you," he replied. "Obviously, that went out the window this morning when I found your necklace." He took another drink of coffee.

Her hand went up to her throat and clutched the pendant. "Thank you for bringing it back to me." She blinked away tears that shimmered in her eyes.

"You're welcome."

"You've got foam on your mustache." She half-stood and leaned across the table, using her thumb to swipe his upper lip. Then she leaned in further and gave him a featherlight kiss, lingering for several seconds.

Giggling sounded from the doorway to the kitchen. With a sigh, Ava sat back down. "Girls, if you're done with the dishes, go upstairs and get your things packed for the weekend."

After they shuffled off, Killian stood. "Babe and I should go."

Ava stood, too. "I wish you didn't have to."

"I'll see you in the morning."

She frowned, then nodded. "I'll walk you out."

After he loaded Babe into the backseat, Ava kissed him goodbye against his truck's door. In his rearview, he saw her watching as he drove away.

Chapter 25

"Time for bed," Ava announced around nine, shooing her daughters upstairs. Normally, Ava didn't force a strict bedtime or rush them. But tonight, she felt scattered and needed stillness.

Audrey stayed behind. She sat down on the living room sofa next to Ava and snuggled into her side. "Mom? Do you want to talk about it?"

"You're my kid. I don't think I should." Ava squeezed her shoulders.

Audrey looked offended. "I'm fourteen now. You can tell me things."

Ava smiled at how grown up her daughter thought she was. "OK, go get your hairbrush. I'll braid your hair for bed, and we can girl talk."

While she waited for Audrey to return, she thought about how impatient she was to get Killian into her bed. The problem that vexed her, though, was that she wanted more than the gratification of sex. She wanted her pillows and sheets to smell of him when she went to sleep.

The list they made wasn't working. She'd read it so many times, she could recite it by rote. Yet, for the past month, it took everything she had to not contact him, to not get into her car and drive up the mountain.

Audrey settled on the floor in front of Ava and passed the hairbrush over her shoulder. "You've been different since the mudslide."

"Different? How so?"

"I don't know. It's hard to explain. I guess you're thinking about stuff all the time. Not sad like you were after you and Dad got divorced. But not happy either."

She ran the brush through Audrey's long, silvery blonde hair. "Hmm. Yes, I've been thinking about a lot of things."

"Like what? Killian?"

"Yes. And other things too. There are some things about myself I wish I could change, but I don't know how."

"What things?"

Ava split Audrey's hair into three sections. "For one, I'm not very good about asking for what I want in relationships, because I don't want to make the other person upset and have them reject me. That's what happened with your father. If I hadn't been so afraid, we'd probably still be married. The ironic thing is, in trying to avoid my fears, I made them come true. I don't want to do that next time, if there ever is a next time."

Audrey stayed still while Ava braided her hair. "Why wouldn't there be a next time? Dad got remarried. Why wouldn't you?"

Ava tied off Audrey's braid with an elastic, then kissed the top of her head. "Because, sweetie, your dad's easy to love. It's not the same for me. I never feel like I'm good enough, and I don't know how to fix that."

"That's the most ridiculous thing I've ever heard you say, Mom. You're easy to love too." Audrey turned to face her, giving her a sassy look. "A while ago, Aunt Dee was helping me with my science homework, and I got frustrated and told her I was stupid. She told me not to talk about myself that way."

"She's right. You shouldn't call yourself stupid because you're not."

Audrey nodded. "Aunt Dee gave me a trick. Whenever I want to say something mean about myself, she told me to pretend like I was saying it about someone I love, like Ingrid, or you. If I would get angry at someone for talking like that about you, then I shouldn't talk like that about myself."

"Have you tried that? Does it work?"

"Yeah. The other day, I didn't get invited to Amber's slumber party. I told Ingrid it's because I'm too boring to have friends. Ingrid asked me how I would respond if someone said she was too boring to have friends. And I said that I'd say they were stupid because Ingrid is the funnest girl I know. Ingrid said I'm the funnest girl she knows. Then I realized I shouldn't call myself boring. I was just being mean to myself because I felt rejected."

Ava stroked her baby's cheeks. "Oh, sweetie. You're not boring. Ingrid's right. And Aunt Dee's right too. That was very mature of you to recognize that you were feeling rejected, and that rejection can make you draw the wrong conclusions about yourself."

"Yeah, so now you try it. If someone told you I wasn't good enough to love, what would you say?"

"I'd say they're crazy. You're perfect." Ava pinched Audrey's nose between two knuckles.

Audrey ducked out of her mom's grasp and rolled her eyes. "That's not true. I asked Fernando to the Sadie Hawkins dance, and he said I was too tall. I'm only like an inch taller than him."

"That's Fernando's loss. You can't stop people from making dumb decisions."

"That's what Ingrid said."

Ava stood, pulling Audrey into a hug. "I'm glad you have sisters. You'll always have someone in your corner, no matter what. I wish I'd had sisters."

Audrey cuddled into her. "You have Carmen and Mina. They're like your sisters."

"Yes, and right now, they're driving me crazy. They think I should give it a shot with Killian. They're giving me a hard time about it."

"I don't understand. We saw you kissing him. He's not your boyfriend?"

"No." She let go of Audrey and sat back on the sofa with a sigh. "It's complicated."

"What's complicated about it?" Audrey plopped down onto the sofa next to Ava.

"We're all wrong for each other. It'll never work out. The only problem is, I can't seem to stop thinking about him." She'd been so obsessed that Carmen and Mina teased her, telling her to go have more hot lumberjack sex in the woods and stop mooning. "I tried not talking to him anymore. That obviously failed."

"Because that's not what you want. You just said that you have a hard time asking for what you want. Maybe try it. What's the worst that could happen? You don't talk to him anymore? Seems dumb to not try."

Ava frowned at her daughter. "When did you become fourteen going on forty?"

Audrey got up. "I'm going to bed. I love you, Mom."

"I love you too, sweetie."

Killian and Ava didn't leave the house for the entire weekend, in part because they wanted to avoid paparazzi, and in part because they kept getting naked.

On Sunday, Ava spent the afternoon teasing him by modeling another set of lingerie she'd brought to his cabin but hadn't shown him. Then, when he reached for her, she skirted out of his grasp, and changed back into her yoga pants.

Truth be told, he liked her in yoga pants too. He reached for her again, and she slapped him away, telling him she wanted to get her routine in before she lost flexibility. Then she snuck glances of him gawking at her while she posed.

At dinner, she put the lingerie back on, but made sure she gave him peeks of it from under her dress. She kept dinner conversation dirty, telling him which things he did to her in bed that were her favorites. It was quite a long list.

"Did you like the leather corset from the back?" she asked, feigning innocent sincerity. "Like when you had me bent over on the couch, so you could spank me? Do you think you'd like what I'm wearing now better? It has these conveniently placed holes in the back. I'll show you later, so you can compare."

He set down his fork. "You'll show me now."

She giggled, despite her best efforts to stay sexy. "But you've barely touched your dinner."

He scooted his chair back. "Get over here, Blondie."

She twisted her mouth, holding back more giggles. Then she darted from the table, running to her bedroom. "If you want me, come and get me."

He caught up to her just as she reached her bedroom door, snatching her around the waist. They crashed together, all limbs and tongues and teeth. They stumbled toward her bed.

In one smooth movement, he spun her around and pulled the zipper of her dress down her back. The dress fell to the floor. She kicked it out of their way, and he bent her over the mattress.

Slapping at her inner thighs until she stood on her toes and widened her legs, he said, "I can't take it easy on you after all that teasing."

"I don't want you to." She hiked one of her knees up onto the side of the mattress to give him better access. "Give me everything I deserve."

He smacked her sharply on her ass, the sting of it reverberating straight through her core. "You're right. These holes are very convenient." He ran his hands over her body, then spanked her again.

Then his hands stilled.

"Why'd you stop?"

"Babe."

She'd forgotten about the dog. "What about her?" She lifted her head and saw the dog lying on the bed opposite to her. Babe's chin rested on the mattress a mere two inches from Ava's face, staring at her with big, frightened eyes. "Oh. That's a little creepy."

Babe licked Ava on the mouth. "Oh! Yuck! No face licks!" Ava jumped up, blowing raspberries and scrubbing at her lips. "Gross!"

"I think it scared her when I spanked you. We were a little too rough. So she had to check to make sure you're OK."

"Aww, Babe, I'm fine," Ava said, patting the dog's head. "That's so cute. But never interrupt sex."

Ava turned towards Killian, who was scowling at the dog. He was still dressed—mostly—with his shirt half-unbuttoned and askew, and his pants shoved down around his knees. She giggled. "Get undressed and onto the bed. I'll put Babe out in the hall."

When Ava returned, she crawled onto her bed next to him, lying back into a cloud of pillows. She reveled in the heat of Killian's body as he climbed on top of her and hovered above her. Her hands twitched in their need to touch him.

Suddenly and painfully aware that this might be their last night together, she tried to memorize every line of his torso with her fingertips and palms.

She drew her legs up, rubbing her calves along his flanks. "Killian," she breathed into his ear.

In marked contrast to their frantic movements from a few minutes before, when he entered her, he took her with long, languid strokes. While he buried himself inside her, he kissed her. "You're so beautiful," he murmured.

As he took her, she felt lost and found all at once. Ava breathed his scent and mewled encouragements.

She felt them climbing to their peak. He pushed harder and her eyes closed. Her core turned to liquid.

Faster. They climbed and climbed until they reached the edge.

She whispered his name.

And then they went over together. Down, down, down. It felt like forever.

She tilted her hips, wrapped her legs around his waist, and clutched his back. All she could do was hold on to him. She held on for dear life. She held on because he was the only way she could survive. She held on because he was her life preserver in the disorienting, tumultuous rapids of her orgasm.

He stilled on top of her, breathing hard.

Tears sprung into her eyes. She didn't know why—probably from the intensity of the myriad sensations running through her body. She blinked them away. Slowly, her muscles relaxed and her limbs slackened around him.

After a few delicious moments, Killian rolled off of her. He stared up at the ceiling and threw his forearm across his forehead. "Jesus, Ava." He took a deep breath and reached for her hand.

She could've stayed lying there, holding his hand, all night long. But the urge to say what she needed to say became overwhelming. Ava took a deep breath. "I don't think this is a fling."

She held her breath as soon as the words came out, afraid of rejection. After all, if this wasn't a fling, then it was a relationship. And he didn't do those. And it was all wrong, anyway, and destined to end in disaster.

"No," he said quietly.

Ava exhaled. "I tried," she said. "I tried so hard. Not talking to you for a month was miserable. I hated it."

"I know," he said.

"And I don't want to stop. I don't want this to be our last night."

"I know."

"So what should we do?" she asked.

"I don't know."

She rolled onto her side so that she was facing him. There was a shadow over his dark features. She wasn't sure whether it was the low lighting or the conversation.

She twined her legs with his and laid her arm across his chest, placing her hand on his cheek. She rubbed his beard with her palm. "I think maybe we should just go with it."

He was listening, so she pressed on. "We don't have to define it. It doesn't have to be serious or hard. We can talk and see each other when we have time, like on the weekends. I can go up there. You can come down here. It doesn't have to be every weekend, just whenever we feel like it. No pressure."

He pressed his lips together in a line. She could see that he was thinking about it. "What about the list?" he finally asked.

"It's not working for me." She wanted to persuade him that continuing was harmless, and possibly inevitable. "We both know that this isn't forever, for all the reasons we listed. But we're both adults. We can have fun, be casual. Neither of us is ready to stop. So why are we fighting it? It's easier to let it run its natural course."

After a moment, he nodded.

Ava gave him a dazzling smile. She felt like her heart was going to explode in her chest from happiness. She had asked for what she wanted, and she got it.

She leaned up and brushed a kiss across his mouth. "I want you," she whispered, having not intended to say it out loud.

He quirked an eyebrow at her. "I'm going to need a minute to recover, you insatiable minx."

She giggled and rolled out of bed. "I'm going to take a quick shower. Women can't just go to sleep after sex without cleaning up. It's one of our many curses." She crooked a finger at him. "Come join me. I promise to keep it clean."

After they showered, they went back to bed, having forgotten completely about dinner on the table. It was dark by the time she curled into his side. He held her tightly. She closed her eyes and listened to his breathing, feeling content.

After a few minutes, she heard Babe whining. "The dog," she said sleepily. "I forgot about her."

She opened the bedroom door. "I'm sorry I forgot to let you in, Babe," Ava cooed to the dog. "I promise I won't do that again." Babe ignored her, chewing on something. "What's she eating?" Ava flipped on the light and gasped. "She's eating our chicken!"

Killian laughed. "Well, we weren't eating it."

Ava wagged her finger at the dog. "I'm letting you get away with this, just this once, as a payment for forgetting to let you back in. But dogs don't belong on the dining room table. Consider this your only warning."

Babe finished eating and then jumped onto the bed. "Cheeky," Ava chided. Even though Ava always kicked her off the bed at night, she found Babe at their feet every morning. She didn't think this was a battle she would ever win. So she let her stay.

Ava yawned and switched off the light before cuddling back into Killian's side. He was half asleep already. "If she's going to sleep in the bed with us, I want to get her groomed. Are you OK with that?"

He grunted. "I'm fine with it, but I'm not sure how Babe will feel." As though she knew what they were talking about, Babe snorted before settling on her back, paws in the air.

Relaxing in Killian's arms, Ava soon drifted into a contented slumber. She stayed curled in his arms for most of the night. It was the best, most restorative sleep she'd had in a month.

Chapter 26

L isa stopped by Killian's cabin on a crisp afternoon in early November. Killian was going to dog-sit Rusty for a few days while she took a trip to San Francisco. Rusty played well with Babe, plus Killian owed her one.

When she arrived, he invited Lisa in for a beer. Rusty and Babe ran circles and then flopped onto the floor by the table. Lisa hadn't been to Killian's cabin in months—since before the mudslide.

"Holy crap," she said, looking around as she sat down at the table.

"What?" Killian glanced around but saw nothing amiss.

She gave him a teasing grin. "Man, you got it bad."

"What?" He didn't know what she was talking about.

Lisa swept her arm around her, gesturing widely. "Ava is everywhere."

Ava came to his cabin almost every weekend. On the weekends when she wasn't visiting him, he took the Friday off and drove down to see her. In the two months since they started this arrangement, they hadn't missed a single weekend.

With Ava came *things*. She kept the fridge stocked with fresh food, and the freezer was full of meals she made for him. They always had iced tea and fruit-infused water and quality wine. Babe had a pink rhinestone collar, matching leash, and weekly baths.

Objects appeared: Ava's shoes and clothes, lingerie and sex toys, her toothbrush, feminine soaps and lotions, candles. She upgraded the bedding and added throw pillows to the couch. A shiny copper pot sat on the stove. Her apron and matching oven mitts were hung next to the window. The cabin always smelled like baked goods.

To help with her anxiety, he made an emergency ditch bag for Ava and set it next to his by the wood-burning stove. The next weekend, she put hooks on the wall, and their packs were moved off of the floor. He also bought her a decent outdoor coat. He hung that on a hook next to the door. Her new hiking boots sat on the floor nearby.

Lisa smiled at him again. "She's good for you. I'm happy to see you in a genuine relationship. Humans aren't meant to be alone all the time."

"I'm not alone. I have Babe. And before that, I had Lola." He handed her a beer.

"And now you have Ava." She took the bottle and drank. "Don't be defensive, K-Pop. Having a girlfriend who takes care of you and leaves stuff at your place is normal. It's healthy."

"I've told you not to call me that."

"And I never agreed." She blew him a kiss.

He rolled his eyes. "She's not my girlfriend. She visits a lot, so it's just easier for her to leave things here for the next time." He sat down at the small table and drank his beer.

Lisa looked at him like he was stupid. "No, man, she's definitely your girlfriend."

He shook his head. "She's not."

"What is she then?"

"We don't call it anything."

Lisa leaned forward and rested her chin on her bridged hands. "How often do you see her? Every weekend?"

Since people in the nearby mountain town saw them together when they went to the market, he didn't bother to deny it. They'd even bumped into his boss once at the Black Bear Café when they forgot to buy coffee. "Yup."

"How often do you call or text her?"

"Every day."

"More than once?"

"Yeah."

"Are you seeing anyone else?"

"No."

"I assume you're not platonic, based on what I saw on the trail a few months ago."

Killian drank his beer and refused to dignify that with a response.

Lisa counted on her fingers. "This has been going on since June, and now it's November. That's five months. Have you seen anyone else during the past five months?"

"No."

Lisa threw her hands up and laughed. "She's your girlfriend!"

Killian frowned but stayed silent.

"Why don't you want to call her what she is?" Lisa sat back in her chair and tilted her head. "I mean, I'd ask that in any situation. But your girlfriend is Ava fucking Blum. She's so hot, I'd change teams if I thought I had a chance with her."

He studied his beer, tugging on a loose corner of the label. "Ava and I decided we weren't going to define it. We're just going with the flow. It's easier."

"Easier for whom?" Lisa challenged.

"For both of us."

"Are you sure it's not actually just easier for you, and that she's merely going along with it?"

"Why are we talking about this?" he countered. "Everything is fine with Ava. There's no problem that needs solving."

"Because we're friends, and friends talk about each other's lives." She gave him an annoyed look.

"OK, then tell me about your life. Why are you going to San Francisco?"

"For a boy," she answered, a broad smile lighting up her face. "It's still new." She clinked her beer bottle to his. "Look at the two of us, doing grown up dating. Oh, how the mighty have fallen!"

"Does he like kung fu movies? If he doesn't, I don't see how he could keep your interest," Killian teased. Lisa was a Bruce Lee fangirl.

She nodded. "And sci-fi! He's perfect." She pretended to swoon.

"Lucky. I can't get Ava to watch anything half decent. All she likes are rom-coms and musicals."

"Well, she is the Rom-com Queen." Lisa quirked an eyebrow at him. "OK, I have to ask, since you're the only person I know who's dating a movie star. Is it weird seeing your girlfriend in movies?"

"She's not—"

"Save it." Lisa interrupted his denial by holding up a hand. "Just answer the question."

"I've never seen any of her movies."

Lisa sputtered, barely swallowing her beer down without making a mess. "What the fuck, Killian?" She coughed and regained her composure. "Aren't you curious? Is she OK with that?"

Killian frowned. "I stay out of that side of her life as much as possible. She's fine with it. We like our privacy."

Lisa studied him for a moment. "You should watch her movies. I'm serious. Just take a little advice from me, OK? You should take an interest in her career because it's an important part of her life. That's what a good boyfriend would do."

"I'm not—"

"Stop! Jesus, Killian. If you're not, then what are you doing? Just fucking? I wouldn't believe you if you told me that's all it is." She swept her arm around again, gesturing at Ava's influence throughout the cabin.

"We're not just fucking," he admitted.

"No, you're not." Lisa wagged a finger at him for emphasis. "It doesn't matter what you call it, you're in a relationship. You better learn what that means so you don't fuck it up."

Killian peeled the label off of his beer, his brow furrowed. Lisa was right. He was in a relationship. Weirdly, he was fine being exclusive with Ava. She could be the only woman in his life for the rest of his life, and it wouldn't bother him. The problem was, he didn't know how to be in a relationship, and didn't know how to not fuck it up.

Lisa stayed another ten minutes. They chatted about the best dim sum restaurants in San Francisco, and Rusty's separation anxiety. When she finished her beer, she stood up and gave him a friendly embrace. "Thank you for watching my doggo. Think about what I said. I'll see you in a couple of days." She brushed a quick kiss on his cheek and left.

Killian spent the rest of the afternoon finishing his final report about the mountain's erosion and his recommendations. He emailed it to Mary around four, and she called him fifteen minutes later.

"I got your report. You got it done two months earlier than expected."

"Yeah. I figured you needed to get started on the work or the campground would be closed for another full year, if not two."

"Thank you. With the closures and the snow coming, I don't think you should stay there. Have you thought about where you want to go next?"

He sighed. "Yeah, but I haven't made any decisions. I know I need to start looking. I just wanted to get the report done first."

"Your position was budgeted through the end of the year. You'll get paid your full salary, even if you leave early. Lord knows you've earned it." The landline crackled while she paused. "It concerns me that you're there alone, and there's no reason for it. I'm strongly encouraging you to leave early. You could go to LA and spend time with your girlfriend, or travel ahead of a new position. I'll give you any help you need securing a transfer."

Killian drummed his fingers on the table, absorbing her words. He hadn't planned to move early, but Mary made sense. "Thank you. I'll make a plan. Ava is here this weekend. I'll talk to her. I'll let you know next week when I can be out of here. You're right, it's an unnecessary risk for me to stay here during rain and snow."

"Good. You know, there are plenty of jobs in Angeles National Forest in LA County and Cleveland National Forest in Orange and San Diego Counties. They have a lot of roads and infrastructure projects. You might want to start your job search there."

"Thanks again, Mary." They hung up.

Not five minutes later, Ava arrived. He opened the door to find her juggling several large paper grocery bags on her hips.

Two boisterous dogs mobbed her, and she almost dropped the food. "Whoa! Babe, get down! You too, Rusty! Get off me!"

He took the bags from her and set them on the counter. Unpacking them, he found lamb chops in butcher paper, fresh rosemary, new potatoes, and a green vegetable he couldn't identify. He held it up. "What's this?"

"Broccolini." She set down her overnight bag and gave him a kiss on the cheek. "It's a hybrid cross between broccoli and asparagus. You'll like it."

"Fancy," he replied.

She reached into the bag and produced two biscuits for the dogs. "The girls and I made peanut butter biscuits for Babe and Scruffles. I brought some for Rusty, too." She made the dogs sit before handing them both their treats.

He unpacked several bottles of Bordeaux from the vineyard she owned with Jack in France. "What's the occasion?" He popped the cork on one and poured them both glasses.

"I wanted to celebrate you getting your report done. You said this morning that you would have it turned in today. Since you always get things done early, I figured it was a safe bet that congratulations were in order. So, did you?"

"I did. And that means I'm done with my position here." He followed her to the couch and handed her a wineglass. "Speaking of, we need to talk about something."

Ava paled and set down her glass. "If you're going to break up with me, do it before I drink anything so that I can drive home. Mountain roads are scary enough in the dark without me drunk and crying."

That surprised him. He sat down next to her. Looking at her stricken face, he stroked a thumb across her cheek. "No, sunshine, that's not what I was going to say. Why would you think that?"

"Because we're going with the flow. And I know that the flow ends with you breaking up with me. I just don't know when." She picked up her wineglass and took a deep swallow of the purple liquid.

"So Lisa was right." He pulled Ava onto his lap to calm her down.

"Right about what?"

"When she dropped Rusty off earlier, she insisted that you're my girlfriend. When I told her we'd agreed to not define things, she told me that was for my comfort, and not yours."

"Oh." Ava drank more wine, looking withdrawn.

"So, are you?" he asked.

"Am I what?"

"Are you my girlfriend?"

She looked at him. "Do you want me to be?"

"I want you to stay. Even though I don't have the first clue on how to be in a relationship, the fact of the matter is, we're in one. If that makes you my girlfriend, then you're my girlfriend." He stroked her cheek again. "I have to warn you, I'll probably fuck it up. But hopefully not today."

"OK, yes, I'm your girlfriend." She scooted off his lap and settled on the end of the couch, her calves resting on his thighs. "So, what *did* you want to talk about?"

"Well, now I want to talk about why you're so certain that I'd ever be crazy enough to break up with you." He rubbed her calves. "Is it the list? I think it was a mistake to make that. We should rip it up, or better yet, burn it."

He got up and walked over to the kitchen drawer where he kept his notebooks. He pulled out the list. "In fact, we're going to go through it right now, and if it's not valid, we're going to toss it in the fire."

He sat down next to her and they studied it, their heads close together.

All the Ways We're Wrong

1. I live in LA

2. You live in a remote cabin in the woods

3. It's a five-hour drive to see each other

4. You like peace and quiet

5. I'm famous and noisy

6. The attention that comes with my fame is your idea of hell

7. I'm 40

8. You're 33

9. I have 3 kids

10. You don't want kids

11. I want to get remarried

12. You want to stay single

13. You're out of my league (under protest)

"Right, I'm striking the first three." Using a pencil, Killian crossed out the first three reasons. "We've been making things work just fine, despite the distance, and now I'm moving."

"Wait, what? When are you moving?"

"I don't know. That's what I wanted to talk to you about. But first, we're going through this list."

He crossed out four, five, and six. "I'll never understand why you choose to be famous. But as long as you don't make me do it, I don't see an issue. Lots of famous people have non-famous partners. We've not had any problems maintaining our privacy so far."

"Those reasons don't just talk about my fame, though. I'm *extra*. Always have been."

"I don't even know what that means, princess. I like you just as you are. I don't understand why you think you're so flawed and unpleasant when you're anything but."

She scrunched her nose. "You don't think I'm too loud?"

"Nope. You're the right amount of loud. I'll never fear sneaking up on a bear again."

She jostled him with her elbow.

Next, he crossed out numbers seven and eight. "I already told you, I don't think our ages matter."

"And I already told you, it matters to me." She crossed her arms stubbornly. "I'm too old to waste time on relationships that can't go anywhere."

"I hate to break it to you, but we're already in a relationship. We established that five minutes ago. So unless *you're* planning to break up with *me*, then our ages are moot."

Her mouth twisted wryly. "How do you know I'm not planning to break up with you? You're awfully cocksure over there."

He set the notebook and his wine on the coffee table. Then he leaned over her, pinning her to the couch. "Are you?"

She bit her lip. "No."

"Good." He kissed her.

She squirmed. "Hey, get off of me. I have to make dinner."

He sat up. "We have to finish this list first." He crossed off numbers nine and ten. "You're done having kids, and I don't want any. Seems we agree about babies."

"But number nine—I have three kids. Doesn't that bother you?"

"If it did, we wouldn't be here. I know nothing about kids and parenting. But, luckily for your daughters, they have a father, so you don't need to rely on me for that."

"Yeah, but..." She took a deep breath. "The thing is, the longer we're together..." She wrung her hands. "What about numbers eleven and twelve? I want to... I mean, I need... I'm already forty..." She froze, her mouth working.

"What are you trying to say, Ava?"

She stood. "Can I see that?" She took the notebook out of his hand and paced in front of the couch. "Why do I care? I'm fine. I can't believe..." She stopped pacing, her brow furrowed, as she glared at the paper in her hand. "Audrey doesn't need to be married to prove that she's worth loving."

Killian frowned. He couldn't piece together her thought process. She wasn't talking to him, anyway; she was having an argument with herself.

With an angry snort, she tore the page with the list out of the book and crumpled it in her fist. "This isn't the problem. Everything I wrote is nonsense." Stalking over to the wood-burning stove, she threw the paper into the fire. "It's more useful as kindling."

He waited to see if she would explain.

"I can't believe I've gotten to forty and I'm still stuck on the same things," she said at last. "I never feel like I'm good enough. I just realized why I feel like such a failure being divorced. It's because I believe that if I'm not married, that's more proof that I'm not good enough to love."

"Good enough for who?" Killian asked.

"For anyone. For my parents." She came to stand in front of him. "One of the reasons why my parents wouldn't pay for me to go to college was that I was going to get married and have children, so a college education didn't make economic sense."

She perched on the edge of the couch and rubbed her hands over her knees. "It's like they raised me to be a fifties housewife. I was taught to please. And that's—that's what I do. That's why I got raped." Her lower lip trembled.

Horrified, he scooted to her and wrapped his arms around her trembling shoulders. "Ava, it's not your fault that you were raped."

"Logically, I know that. At the same time, I was vulnerable. I was so desperate for attention, for validation, that I let him in. Because I wanted to please, I didn't say no loudly or clearly enough. Then I couldn't protect myself. That's why I want my daughters in self-defense; I don't want them to experience what I experienced, or to feel what I feel."

She leaned forward and set the empty notebook back on the coffee table. "When I have my PTSD attacks, my brain spirals to the darkest, worst feelings. Even when I'm not having an attack, they're always there. I think I deserved it, that I invited it, that I did something wrong. I feel ashamed.

I feel like all I'm good for is enticing men to have sex. And that makes me feel worthless."

Killian pulled her into his lap again. "Ava, you didn't deserve it. You didn't do anything wrong. You're not to blame." As she shook in his arms, he wished he could take her pain away, to fix everything for her, and he felt helpless.

She sniffed and burrowed into his chest. "Sometimes I regret my choice in career. I tried to take these feelings and make them my strength. I thought if I controlled my sexual desirability, and was successful and made money because of it, I wouldn't feel so worthless. But all I've done is remind myself that I'm not good for anything else."

Her tears dampened his shirt. "It doesn't help that my parents and the Army both blamed me. I internalized that too much." She took a deep, shuddering breath, and he felt her back stiffen. "No. You're right. I didn't do anything wrong," she whispered.

Killian rubbed his hand up and down her strong spine. "Say that again, but mean it this time."

She looked up at him, her face turning resolute. "I didn't do anything wrong."

"Louder. Say it louder."

She slid off his lap and ran to the front door. She threw it open and screamed into the night air, "I didn't do anything wrong!"

Chapter 27

After slamming the door shut with a dramatic flourish of her arm, Ava returned to the couch and straddled his lap. She cupped his face between her hands and smiled. "Thank you. I feel much better."

"I didn't do anything. That was all you."

"Yes, you did." She rested her forehead on his. "You do a lot for me. You rescued me from this mountain, for starters."

"You walked down the mountain on your own two feet, Blondie."

"Yes, but you showed me the way." She pecked him on the mouth. "We're supposed to be celebrating turning in your report. I'm going to make dinner. You just relax, and keep me company, big man." After kissing him again, she hopped off of his lap and moved to the kitchen.

He followed her and settled at the table. "Now that I've turned my report in, my job is done. There's no reason for me to stay here. And with the winter coming, and rain and snow, it's an unnecessary risk. I also need to find another job for the new year, and I can go to another national park or forest."

Ava's back was turned to him as she tied her apron and prepared seasoning for the lamb. He couldn't see her face, but she kept her tone light. "So, where are you thinking?"

"Mary suggested I take a job in LA or San Diego County. I thought that sounded like a good idea. I told her I would talk to you about it this weekend, and then let her know next week if I want her recommendation for one of those jobs."

"That would certainly save us some gas."

Killian laughed. "That wasn't my first thought, but that's true."

He watched her sear the lamb. After she placed the meat in the oven, she turned to look at him. "How does this work? Will you get transferred right away? Do you stay here until you get another job?"

"The government doesn't work that fast. Even if I applied for several positions on Monday, it would probably be a couple of months before I got one. It'll be even slower over the holidays. I'll have some time to kill. Normally, I would travel."

She turned her back again to prepare the vegetables. "Travel, huh? Where would you go?"

He got up and stood next to her at the counter. "To the dangerous, traffic-infested urban jungle called Los Angeles. Babe loves the beach."

She turned to him, wiping her hands on the front of her apron. "You'd come to the city? But you hate it."

"It's only for a couple of months. I'll get an Airbnb or something. That way, I can see you more."

She flung her arms around his neck. "I love that idea. But you're not staying in an Airbnb. You'll stay with me."

He grimaced. "I don't know. Do you really want me around constantly for a couple of months? What about your daughters?"

"It's only temporary. The girls will be fine with it. They know you're my boyfriend already."

"How? I only realized that six hours ago."

"They're smarter than you." She snickered. "Anyway, I have ten bedrooms. You could stay in the pool house for weeks and no one would know."

"I don't know, Ava. I haven't lived with other people since I left the group home at eighteen."

She rolled her eyes. "You're not living with me. You're *visiting* till you get another job. It'll be fun! And it'll be the holidays soon. Christmas is my favorite time of year. Ooh, there's so many things we could do!"

"Now I'm even more convinced I shouldn't."

"Oh, c'mon. Don't be a grump. We'll have fun together, I promise." She made that sultry face that she usually reserved for magazine covers. "Think of the possibilities. I'll put on that black leather corset on day—well, night—one."

"Hmm. Tempting." He slid his hands from her waist to her butt and gave it a squeeze. "Tell me more about what you plan to do once you're in that corset. I need details before I can agree."

Ava rose onto her tiptoes and whispered promises with such colorful bawdiness that it would've made a sailor blush.

"Well, that's certainly a creative use of Babe's leash, a grapefruit, and a spatula." He moved his hands up her sides, brushing her breasts. "I don't think that's an offer I can refuse."

"That's the last of it." Killian closed the rear gate on Ava's SUV. Together, they moved him out of the cabin the following week, taking advantage of the Veterans' Day holiday.

He had approximately four times as much stuff now that he was dating Ava than what he'd moved in with. Normally, he kept a list of all his possessions. But when he tried to take an inventory, grumbling about how long the spreadsheet was going to be, Ava mocked him mercilessly. He gave up on the idea, figuring most of the stuff was hers anyway.

Ava hopped into the driver's seat. "You did all the heavy lifting, so I'll drive." He'd already returned his work truck to his boss. He planned to buy a new truck once they were in LA because he needed adult self-sufficiency.

After she pulled out of the campsite, Ava fiddled with the stereo. She selected Christmas music.

Killian groaned. "What the hell, Ava? It's November."

"It's Veterans' Day. That's the start of the holiday season. Actually, I'd argue that it's Halloween, but some people might find that extreme."

"Christmas music on November eleventh is extreme. And torturous. If this is what my next two months look like, I might get that Airbnb after all."

She patted his knee. "Don't be grumpy. I don't understand how you couldn't like Christmas. It's fun."

He side-eyed her. "Seriously? I was a kid without a family, who never got Christmas presents except for what a charity might toss my way. Why would I like Christmas?"

"Oh." She frowned, but she switched the music to the Eagles. "Hotel California" came on. "Better?"

"Much." Although he wondered about the song selection.

Six hours later, he unpacked while she made dinner. He brought their clothes and Babe's things to her bedroom, piled the boxes of housewares in a corner in her garage, and stored their emergency bags in her SUV. While unpacking a few items in the bathroom, he noticed that she'd stocked an entire case of his soap.

The girls returned on Sunday evening. Bette hugged Babe as soon as she walked into the house. "She's shivering." Bette frowned and led Babe by the collar to the sofa. "Come here, Babe. I'll warm you up. You're wet from the rain." She pulled Babe onto her lap and gave her a full body hug.

"No wet dogs on the sofa," Ava scolded.

"But she's cold!" Bette looked distressed.

"Oh, well, we can't have that. I've got something for her. Warm her on the floor, though, not the sofa. I'll be right back." When Ava returned to the room a few minutes later, she was holding a Christmas sweater... for dogs. "It was supposed to be for her to wear on Christmas, but she can wear it all holiday season instead."

Raising his eyebrows, Killian sat on the sofa, watching Bette put clothes on his dog. The besweatering of Babe brought unceasing joy to all the females in the house, Babe included. She wagged and wiggled and ran circles around the living room.

"She looks so cute," Bette enthused, admiring her handiwork. "Can she have a camping sweater too? She can't ruin this one before Christmas."

"Are Killian and Babe going camping with us too?" Ingrid asked.

Ava blushed a light pink. "I haven't asked him yet."

"Mom said she would take us camping over Thanksgiving," Ingrid told him. "You should come."

"I might have to." He smiled wryly. "Your mom isn't supposed to be unsupervised in the woods."

"Hush," Ava said.

"She won't be unsupervised. Dad and Esme will be there. And Aunt Dee and Uncle Ricky. And Grandma," Ingrid explained.

"And Scruffles and Aunt Dee's dog Wilbur. Wilbur is also a pit bull rescue. Babe could play with him, but he's kinda lazy," Bette added.

"I see," Killian replied, hiding his surprise that Ava hadn't told him about a trip she'd planned to take before inviting him to her house.

Before he could get an explanation, Ava shooed her daughters out of the room. "Girls, go upstairs and get your things ready for school tomorrow."

When she returned, she gave him an apologetic smile. "I'm sorry. I didn't mean to drop it on you like that. I didn't know how you'd feel about going on a holiday trip with me, my daughters, and my ex-husband's entire family." She cringed.

"A little uncomfortable," he admitted.

She sat on her knees on the sofa next to him. "Please come," she pleaded. "It's camping. You like camping."

"Not with a group of strangers."

"I know. It's a lot of people. They're good people, though, and if you need some space, we can go for hikes, just the two of us." She batted her eyelashes.

He already felt his resistance softening. "Why late November? It's going to be cold and wet, unless you're going to the desert."

"Actually, I wanted your advice on that. We were thinking about the redwoods. There isn't another break in everyone's schedules till next summer, and it's important that all the adults go. The girls' therapist said it would help if they experienced camping as something safe and fun—exposure therapy—and having everyone around will ensure that. They're still having nightmares about me, and I want to get in front of it before it permanently alters the neural pathways in their developing brains."

He sighed, knowing he was going to agree.

"Please, Killian. I would also feel safer if you were there. I still have my own anxiety about it."

"When have I ever said no to you, Blondie?"

"You say no to me all the time."

"Let me rephrase. When have I ever said no to you and stuck with it?"

"So you'll come?"

"I'll come."

She squealed girlishly and threw her arms around him. "Thank you. You're the best!"

Over the next week, Ava planned their trip, asking Killian a thousand questions. She had him approve of their campsite. He helped her make lists. She dragged him shopping, which got them photographed together, much to his annoyance. At her insistence, he taught her how to pack, even though they wouldn't be hiking their gear into camp.

He almost backed out when she added him to a group chat that included all the adults in Jack's family. He grumbled. She distracted him with a satin negligee.

The group decided on the coastal redwoods. He'd suggested Joshua Tree, as it was high season in the desert, but the girls said that real camping involved trees, and Joshua trees didn't count. They wanted pine trees.

Having completed preparations for their trip, they spent the Monday and Tuesday before Thanksgiving baking fifty pies for a homeless shelter. He'd never baked a pie before, but Ava taught him how to make the dough and press it into the tin for the crust. The girls came in and out of the kitchen, helping Ava mix fillings and getting rewarded with spoons to lick.

Ava played Christmas music the entire time they baked. She twirled around the kitchen, making messes, singing along. Her daughters sang too. Their infectious joy made the music tolerable—ish. He only grumbled a few times. She only called him Grumpy McGrumper-Scrooge once.

By the time the shelter's volunteers had picked up all the pies on Tuesday evening, they were both exhausted. They were driving north on Wednesday, so everyone retired to their rooms early.

Killian stood by the end of the bed, unbuttoning his shirt, when Ava wandered out of the bathroom. A frown pulled on her face as she stared at her phone. "Goddammit."

"What?"

"You know how tomorrow morning I'm scheduled to go to the studio to re-record some of my lines before we drive up?"

"Yeah."

"Jack texted that Esme has an emergency hearing in the morning, and they're going to be late picking up the girls. I texted the babysitter, but she can't come last minute because she's already traveling for the holidays. So now I don't have anyone to watch the girls while I'm in the studio, and I really can't reschedule." She tossed her phone on the bed with a dramatic flourish. "I'd let Audrey babysit, but her school has a policy of reporting it any time children are left without an adult, and Bette might accidentally blab."

"I'm here. It's fine."

Her eyes snapped to his face. "You'd watch the girls?"

"Yeah, why wouldn't I? It's only for a couple of hours."

"I just thought... Are you sure?"

"Ava, it's no big deal. Stop stressing."

She flew to him, crashing into his chest, surprising him. She threw her arms around his waist and squeezed. "Oh, Killian, thank you. You're the best. I never have to worry when you're around. I love you so much."

He stood rigid, arms at his side, shocked.

She looked up at him. "Oops. I didn't mean to say that out loud."

"You were being effusive, right? In your gratitude? It's really unnecessary. All I'm doing is making sure no one commits any crimes or sets the house on fire while you're out. I'm confident the girls won't do any of those things."

"No." She stepped back. "I mean, yes, I was being effusive. But also no. I've been telling you in my head that I love you for weeks."

Her words felt like a hot knife slicing through him, from his navel to his heart, spilling his guts onto the floor. He swallowed a lump in his throat. "You love me?"

"I do. I love you."

"I don't know how to respond to that."

Her face crumpled for a moment before she smoothed it over. "Normally, people say 'I love you too.'"

"What if I don't?"

"Don't you? You act like you do."

"I don't know. Nobody's ever told me they loved me before. I've never said it to anyone either."

She paled. "Nobody? Never? Even when you were a kid?"

He shook his head. "I don't have any family. I've never had a girlfriend before. Who would've said it to me? I've never learned what love is, and I don't know that I'm capable of it." He sat on the edge of the bed.

"Oh, oh, Killian..." Silent tears welled in her eyes. Taking a step forward, she sunk to her knees before him and laid her head on his lap.

He patted her hair, feeling bad about upsetting her. "You don't need to cry for me, Ava."

"Somebody has to." She looked up at him, her face blotchy and her eyes shimmering. "I'm not just crying for you. I'm crying for every child that was never loved. It's not fair. It's not right. It makes my heart hurt."

"You're so soft," he said, wiping her tears with his thumb. "I'm sorry that I don't know how to love. I told you I'd fuck this up. I'm trying my best, but you deserve so much more than what I can give you."

"Oh, Killian." She laid her head on his lap again. "You don't see. You *do* know how to love. Love isn't just a word that you learn to say at the right times. It's not a one-time feeling that strikes you like a lightning bolt, leaving you thunderstruck. Love is more like a practice, a habit, a way of existing with another."

She sought his hand with hers. "It's like with Babe. She needed a home, so you adjusted your life to give her one, without resentment or demanding anything in return. You rescued her. That's love."

She took a deep breath. "Every time you made room for me in your life, you told me without words that you loved me. Every time you did something that made you uncomfortable because it made me happy, that's love. Every time you listened to me, comforted me, and made me feel safe and validated, every time you picked me up when I stumbled, that's love. Every time you trusted me with vulnerable sides of yourself, that's love. When I hurt, you hurt too, because you love me."

She peered at him intensely. "Even though you didn't know me from Adam, you put yourself in danger to save my life. You never left me on that mountain. You made sure I didn't die. Those are acts of love for a fellow human. Not only do you know how to love, you love very well. Better than most people, in fact."

She stood up, lifting his hand in hers. "And you're able to do all that—you're everything that you are—a competent, successful, thoughtful, brave, beautiful man—despite having nothing since before you could even walk. It's me who doesn't deserve you, honestly."

Killian met her eyes but shook his head again. "I don't know how to respond to any of that."

"Then don't. Just trust what I'm telling you." She lifted his knuckles to her lips and brushed them with a kiss. "You don't have to tell me you love me back. I won't pressure you. I won't expect it, or demand it. But please, let me tell you every day that I love you."

She climbed onto his lap and snaked her arms around his neck. "I can never make things even after all you've done for me, but please accept this one thing. Let me tell you how much I love you until you feel it in your bones. I want you to know, with certainty you feel to your very core, that you are wanted, and that you, Killian Kelly, are loved."

Chapter 28

"Let's go through everyone again." Ava patted Killian's knee. He drove her SUV up the mountain to their campground on Thursday morning. The back was stuffed with gear she'd bought to make the trip a perfect and therapeutic learning experience for her daughters.

Since there wasn't enough room for Babe, the gear, and the girls, Jack drove the girls up on Wednesday afternoon. Having gotten a late start, Ava and Killian stopped on Wednesday night at a motel—and re-enacted a few things—before leaving early Thursday morning to meet the rest of the group at the campground.

Her anxiety made him anxious. "No need. I got it. Just relax. Remember, camping is supposed to be fun."

"I know. I'm sorry. Just humor me." She drummed her fingers on the center console until he flattened her hand with his.

"Alright. Obviously, the girls, and Jack. Esme is his wife, and she's a judge. I met her yesterday when they picked up the girls. Meg is Jack's mom, and she's a retired farmer from Kansas. His sister Dee is a veterinarian, and her husband Ricky is retired from the Army's special forces."

"Yep. And Dee has a six-month-old baby named Ginny. The dogs are Scruffles—he looks like Tramp from *Lady and the Tramp*—and Wilbur, who looks like a pig."

"Yep, I got it." He really did. His presence wasn't that necessary, and probably no one would notice if he forgot their names, anyway. "Why are you so stressed, sunshine?"

Ava blew out a breath. "I just want everything to be perfect for the girls. It's the first holiday that I've spent with Jack and his family since he and Esme got married. The holidays last year were a little, let's say, *dramatic*. Meg chewed me out good on Christmas, and has pretended like it didn't happen every time I've seen her since. Oh, goddammit!"

"What?" Killian pulled into the campsite. As expected, since they'd reserved the entire place for privacy reasons, it was empty except for two RVs. Between the two RVs was a large tent with tables and chairs. The seating area under the tent sparkled with fairy lights. "It looks like everyone is here."

"Yeah. But Jack's gone over the top. I should've expected this from him. He thinks he's being practical, making sure everyone's comfortable. But the point of this trip was for the girls to experience normal camping and to feel safe in the woods. That's why we brought tents. He's spoiling them with such a lavish setup."

Having been cooped up in the car too long, Babe launched out of the SUV the moment Ava opened her door, making a beeline to the other dogs. Soon, all three dogs were sprinting around the campground, barking and kicking up dust in their wake.

Jack and Esme walked over to greet them. Jack shook Killian's hand. "Nice to see you, Killian."

"Yes, likewise."

Killian shook Esme's hand. "Hello, again, Esme."

Esme turned to Ava and gave her a hug. "Ava, you're looking well." Esme was petite with black hair, the polar opposite to Barbie doll Ava.

Ava gave Esme a smile, but then rounded on Jack with a glare. "What's with the fancy RV and the massive tent? The girls said they wanted to go camping like a normal family. Only rich people can afford a setup like that."

"We *are* rich," Jack replied smoothly. "I hate to break it to you, but the girls are already aware of that fact."

Killian could see Ava's temper rising with the color on her cheeks. He put an arm around her shoulders, feeling her relax into his side.

"You could've discussed it with me," Ava said to Jack.

Jack laughed. "You would've just gotten mad sooner."

Esme batted at Jack's arm. "Don't be an ass."

"The whole point of this is to make sure they have a positive experience in the woods. If they're in the lap of luxury the whole time, they won't get the experience they need," Ava said. "And they specifically requested that we have a 'normal' trip, and not act like movie stars. You know they're always going on about being a normal family."

"I know," Jack replied. "They'll still get to experience the woods. You've got them sleeping in a tent, and Dee and I have some plans for them for the next couple of days, OK? Bette is already chattering nonstop about forest animals to Dee."

Ava looked unconvinced. "That RV is too fancy, though. They won't want to sleep in tents when their father brought a five-star hotel. I know there's enough space in that thing for them, and they're going to know it too."

"You know Esme has health issues," Jack countered. "I won't have her be in pain all weekend. And, anyway, we've been down this road before. The girls beg us to take them some place, we get there, and half an hour into it the whining starts. Remember the trip to Aspen? We made it down the bunny slope one time before they were too cold, too hungry, too uncomfortable. You didn't ski once all week because you were attending to their every need."

"That's every mom on every vacation with small kids," Ava responded. "They're older now. I got them everything they need for this trip."

Jack shook his head. "You always try so hard, and you just end up miserable, Ava. Let go a little. The RV will solve all of their complaints once they decide they've had enough tent camping. Why should we suffer all weekend when I know where this is going and can head off problems?"

Ava sighed. "Jack, they need to learn to make do with a little discomfort. If we don't teach them resilience now, when we can control the circumstances, then they won't know what to do when they have hardships as adults. We won't always be there to solve all their problems for them. They're already struggling with nightmares at the mere thought of me having had to survive in the woods for two days."

Jack opened his mouth, but Esme shot him a look and he shut it again.

"That's a valid point," Esme said to Ava. "Jack was thinking of you and me, which I'm sure you can appreciate. I'm sorry we didn't talk to you about it first. We didn't consider things fully. We can do better in the future."

"Thank you," Ava said to Esme. "Well, it is what it is. Let's have fun this weekend. The girls were really looking forward to this trip." She looked around. "Where are they, anyway? I need them to help unload the gear and set up their tent."

"They're in the RV playing video games with Meg," Esme said. "That Harry Potter LEGO one they like. She made them waffles for breakfast."

Killian laughed. "I don't think they're going to last thirty minutes in the tent, Blondie."

Ava pressed her lips in a flat line. "They're at least pitching it and trying it for one night. After all that effort we went through, they're going to do that much." She marched over to the RVs, calling their names.

Jack turned back to Killian. "On a scale of one to ten, how stressed is she? She usually gets pretty worked up trying to make everything perfect for everyone."

"I'd say a solid eight."

"I can make her a martini. That usually works."

"It's a little early for hard liquor. Let's see how she does with setting up the tents first."

"Fair enough. Let me introduce you to the rest of my family." The girls and an older woman, tall and slim with long gray hair in a braid, emerged from one of the RVs. Killian surmised that was Jack's mother, Meg, and Jack introduced them.

"How did you get Ava to accept a dog in her house?" Meg asked him once the introductions were done. "I really need to know. The girls and I worked on her for years, and she wouldn't budge."

Killian shrugged. "I'm pretty sure I just showed up at her house with the dog, and that was that."

"Mmm." Meg squeezed his bicep. "You're a hunky one. I bet that's the reason she let the dog in."

A woman with honey-blonde hair and a familial resemblance to Jack joined them. "Mom! Stop groping Killian. I swear to Christ I'm going to put you on Silver Singles. You need an outlet." She smiled at him and held her hand out. "Hi, I'm Dee." She pointed at a man heading toward them, holding a baby. "That's my husband Ricky and our daughter Ginny."

A moment later, Ava rushed up, looking agitated. "I think we've got half an hour of their attention, tops, before they return to that video game. So we better get the tents up."

Forty-five minutes later, they had pitched two tents—one for the girls and one for Ava and Killian—and set up five cots with sleeping bags. They didn't bother with any other gear. Ava conceded it'd be easier to use Jack's setup for cooking and seating.

"You're an excellent teacher," Ava murmured, slipping her arms around Killian from behind while the girls set up their cots and sleeping bags.

"The girls are enthusiastic students. Makes it easy." He laid his arms on top of hers, enjoying her presence. Six months ago, if you'd told him that he'd enjoy spending Thanksgiving with a woman and her kids, teaching them things about the outdoors, he'd have immediately denied it.

She laid her head on his shoulder blade. "I think it's going to be pretty cold all day. Do you think a fire's a good idea? I saw a pit and we could drag chairs around it."

"I can make you a fire, princess, but you have to help me gather wood."

"OK. The girls can help too. You can show us how. I'm embarrassed that at forty I've never learned how to make a fire. It seems like such a basic life skill."

After Killian explained how to find and harvest dry wood and kindling, he tasked Bette with gathering the tinder. It took the five of them another hard and sweaty hour to gather enough fuel to last the day. Then Killian showed them how to arrange it in the fire pit.

The girls huddled around him while he showed them emergency fire starters and explained how to use them. "What's the best way to start a fire?" Ingrid asked.

"This way." He reached into his pocket and pulled out a lighter. Ava snickered. Killian lit some bark and, when he had a solid flame going, lit the tinder at the center of the campfire.

"Did you build a fire while you and Mom were on the mountain?" Audrey asked.

"Yup. The second night. I used long matches to start that one. The tinder was a little damp because it'd been raining, and sometimes matches are easier to use when you need to hold the flame longer to light it. Then I had to blow on it a lot to make sure the kindling caught fire." The girls nodded, and he showed them how to tend the flames until the wood glowed.

Bette crouched next to him and he helped her poke at the burning kindling with a stick. "Playing with fire is fun," she observed. "I know I'm not supposed to play with fire, but I think it's OK as long as you're with me." She threw the stick into the flames and hugged him.

Killian chuckled. "I have to admit, playing with the fire is my favorite part of camping. It's important to be safe when building fires, and you should never be in the woods alone. Always camp and hike with a friend."

While Killian and the girls were blowing and poking at the campfire, Ava dragged chairs over and circled them around the pit. When the flames burned strong and hot, they all sat in a circle, making idle conversation and waving smoke out of their faces from the shifting winds.

Eventually, the girls fidgeted and asked to go inside. "Alright, you can go play your game. You've earned it," Ava said, getting up from her chair. The girls ran off. She squatted down next to Killian. "I'm going to check on the others to see if they need help with dinner. Enjoy a little alone time. You've earned it too." She kissed him on the cheek.

He leaned back in his chair, gazed into the fire, and got lost in his thoughts. Mentally, he ran over lists and reviewed his conversation with Ava last Tuesday night, when she first told him she loved him. She'd since told him several more times. He'd yet to say it back, but she kept her word and hadn't pressured him.

His solitude was short-lived. Esme appeared and took a chair next to him, handing him a beer. "Jack knew something was going on between you and Ava from the first time he saw you together at the motel," she said without preamble.

She held her beer bottle out to him in cheers. He knocked his bottleneck into hers with a dip of his chin.

Esme took a drink from her beer. "There was a lot of media interest in you two right after the mudslide, yet you've avoided the paparazzi all this time. How? They got me on my first date with Jack and haven't left us alone since."

"We've spent most of our time together in the woods, away from other people. The first time we've been out in public in the city was last week when we shopped for this trip. And we were immediately photographed. I'm pretty sure the cat's out of the bag now." He took a swig of his beer. "You must be exhausted. How early did you get up to get everything together before we arrived?"

Esme chuckled. "We didn't set it up. Jack's assistant rented the RV, and it was delivered and set up for us before we arrived last night."

Killian raised his eyebrows. "I should've realized when you weren't driving that big rig yesterday to pick up the girls. I've never had anyone to do things for me, so it never crossed my mind."

"I know what you mean." Esme nodded. "It's weird dating someone with so much wealth and fame. Jack never worries about money. He'll spend it for our convenience without thinking twice." She took a long drink of her beer. "I'll admit, it's not terrible. He grew up poor, so he's not ostentatious about it, which makes me more comfortable with it. It still took getting used to, even though I do alright for myself. Wealth and fame like his are like being in an entirely different reality."

Killian considered Esme. "Money doesn't come up much with me and Ava. We're simple. It's just us most of the time, entertaining ourselves with walking and talking. I think that works for us."

"She seems different with you," Esme observed. "I wouldn't have described Ava as simple or predicted she'd be this enthusiastic about camping."

Jack walked up behind Esme. "Ava's not different. She's just letting her true self out more." He sat down in a chair next to Esme. "Ava was never shallow. For her own reasons—I presume you know some of them—she kept her image in place like an armor. But for the past several months, she's been less guarded. At first, I thought it was the near-death experience. Now I think maybe it's you. You've already seen her vulnerable, so she doesn't have to try so hard."

Killian didn't know how to respond to that, so he drank his beer, finishing it.

A moment later, Dee and Ricky turned up with a twelve-pack. "You've got a good fire going," Ricky said, tearing open the box and passing more beers around.

"Thanks." Killian took another beer from him. "Did you do a lot of camping in the Army?"

Ricky handed a beer to Dee. "Not like this. Camping in an RV with the wife is a thousand times better. I've got a bed with a mattress, for starters."

Killian chuckled. "Sleeping on the ground became less appealing after I turned thirty. I've never tried an RV, though."

"Dee and I plan to travel once Ginny is a little older. An RV is a convenient way to do that with the kid and the dog," Ricky said.

"Where's the baby?" Jack asked. "I was worried you two were going to be stuck in the RV all weekend. Dee said she's not been sleeping well lately."

"She hasn't been," Dee moaned. "Pediatrician said sleep regression is common at six months. Mom's feeding her. Thank God for grandparents."

"No, thank God for Mom. Ava's parents are the devil." Jack addressed Killian. "Be forewarned. They're coming for Christmas. They're difficult, and they stress Ava out. Have you met them yet?"

"No." Killian shook his head. "But she told me a story about her pet rabbit once that gave me pause."

"What happened to her pet rabbit?" Dee asked.

Jack shook his head. "That's not a Dee-appropriate story. You won't like it."

"What? Now you have to tell me!" She threw her bottle cap at Jack.

"Hey, DeeDee, no violence." Jack laughed. "Ricky, control your wife."

Ricky snorted. "Control Dee? That might be the dumbest thing you've said to me in the more than forty years I've known you. It'll save us all a lot of time if you just tell her."

"I have to admit, I'm curious too," Esme added.

"Alright," Jack said, relenting. "When Ava was a kid, she got a pet rabbit. She hid it from her parents because they didn't approve of pets. When they caught her, they served her rabbit for dinner and told her it was her pet. It wasn't, but it freaked her out so much that she gave her rabbit away and hasn't had a pet since."

Dee jumped from her seat. "What? Why would anybody tell their kid that they're *eating* their pet? That's fucking terrible! There's a reason we keep livestock separate from pets on the farm."

"I said you wouldn't like it," Jack said. "Why don't you ever listen?"

"I listen to you all the time, even when I shouldn't." Dee glared at him.

Ava walked up. "Listen to him about what? Is he giving you parenting advice again? I'd like to point out that he's the one who showed up with the Taj Mahal on wheels when we are supposed to be 'normal' camping."

Dee ran over to Ava and hugged her. "I'm so sorry about your rabbit. I'm sorry my mom was giving you hassle about getting a dog. She didn't know. But you should still have pets. You'd do well with a cat as a first pet. Don't you agree, Esme?" Dee let go of Ava.

"Cats make great pets. There are plenty who need homes at the shelter I bring the girls to for volunteering," Esme said.

"We've got Babe already," Ava replied absently, her eyes taking in the group. She looked at Killian. "Why are you all talking about Edelweiss?" She raised her eyebrows.

"Why are you looking at me? I'm just sitting here, drinking a beer." Killian's mouth quirked.

"Because, Paul Bunyan, you're the one most likely to tell me the truth," Ava responded.

"Paul Bunyan?" Esme murmured. "Yeah, I can definitely see that."

"See!" Ava pointed gleefully at Killian.

"Is that why the dog is named Babe?" Esme asked.

Ava tapped her nose with her finger, her eyes never wavering from Killian's. "You haven't answered my question, K-Pop."

He winced. "Seriously, Ava, do not call me that."

"Then answer the question," she shot back.

He shrugged. "Ask Jack. He's the one who told Dee the story."

"Wow, man. Way to throw me under the bus," Jack complained.

"What?" Killian shrugged. "I'd rather she be mad at you than me. She already divorced you."

Ricky laughed. "You can't fault the man on his logic."

"Jack?" Ava crossed her arms. "Why were you telling them that story? Were you making fun of me?"

Jack's tone softened. "Ava, of course not."

She looked unconvinced. "Then why?"

"Meg was so impressed at how you've taken to Babe. She told us all about it earlier," Esme interjected smoothly, sparing Ava the embarrassment of hearing that they were discussing her parents. "Jack was telling us why you've been resistant to having pets before Babe."

Ava looked at Esme, then back at Jack.

"What Esme said," Jack confirmed.

Ava narrowed her eyes, then dropped her arms, satisfied with the explanation. "Was that so hard, sugar plum? Honestly."

Killian laughed. "Sugar plum? So the bad nicknames are a lifelong problem."

Jack sighed. "Unfortunately."

Esme stood up and put an arm around Ava. "Come have a beer, sister. So much has happened to us in the past year. We have so much to be thankful for today. You're still here, for one." Esme swayed Ava affectionately.

Ava smiled at the petite woman. "I'm glad you're still here too, Esmerelda."

Esme jostled Ava with her elbow. "Yup. We both survived. And now we're here in the forest, far from the paparazzi, and this is my first-ever Thanksgiving. So cheers." She handed Ava a beer. "I have something else to tell you, Ava—well, everyone, really." Esme glanced at Jack, who merely raised his eyebrows.

Ava tilted her head curiously. "What?"

"Jack and I are having a baby. Actually, we're having twins. We just found out." Esme beamed. "Your daughters are going to have new siblings."

Ava snatched the beer from Esme's hand, horror on her face. "What? How? I thought you had a hysterectomy when you had cancer."

Dee clapped. "That's great news! Congratulations!"

Esme carefully pried her beer from Ava's shocked fingers. "We're using a surrogate. Madison."

"Oh." Ava let go of Esme's beer. "Madison?" Her mouth twisted wryly. "I guess that was the only way that she was going to have Jack's baby."

Esme cackled. "That's what I said."

Ava's wry smile widened into a grin. "So you knew. Not surprising. That girl has mooned over Jack for at least a year. She wasn't subtle about it, either."

"I did. Jack didn't—until I told him. He's clueless."

"Jack's always been clueless about stuff like that," Dee said. "I think it's because women have always fallen all over themselves for him. He thinks that's normal behavior."

"Can confirm." Ava nodded.

"Why are all the women ganging up on me?" Jack said to no one in particular.

The women ignored him. "Congratulations on the pregnancy," Ava said. "Do the girls know?"

"Not yet," Esme replied. "We want to surprise them. We haven't decided how to tell them, and we may decide to wait till after the first trimester. So mum's the word."

Ava nodded. "I'm glad you get to have your baby—babies—Esme." She giggled. "In some ways, a surrogate would be so much better. Pregnancy sucks, right, Dee?"

Dee laughed. "Right. If I'm never pregnant again, it'll be too soon."

"You told me just last night to put a baby in you," Ricky observed dryly.

"Ricky! Don't tell them that," Dee hissed.

Ava laughed. "Enough pregnancy talk. You're going to scare Killian off. Before I added him to the group chat, you all swore to be on your best behavior."

Killian reached for Ava's hand. "If adding me to a group chat didn't scare me off, I'd say we're on solid ground, Blondie."

Chapter 29

After an enormous Thanksgiving meal, everyone decided on an early night. As expected, Ava insisted the girls sleep in their tent. Babe, in her turkey-induced lethargy, chose to sleep with the girls. It was cold, so Bette dressed Babe in her new sweater.

As they were only a few feet away, Ava and Killian could hear everything that the girls were doing in their tent. Which meant, conversely, the girls could hear everything they were doing. Keeping things G-rated, they grabbed an empty cardboard box and turned it into a table between their cots so they could play rummy by lantern light.

"I used to play rummy all the time when I was in high school," Ava told him. "It's been so long. But I'm sure I'll remember it after a hand or two." She shuffled the cards.

"Don't expect me to take it easy on you, princess. You picked the game."

"Only if you don't expect me to take it easy on you." She blew him a kiss.

She dealt the cards, and he immediately laid down a book of three jacks. "Wow, lucky start," she grumbled. She laid down a run of low face-value spades.

The night air was chilly. Ava put on a wool hat and wrapped her sleeping bag around her so that only her hands and face were sticking out. "I'm surprised that the girls are still in their tent," she whispered. "It's freezing." She looked cute with her pink nose and cheeks.

"They're tougher than they look," he said. "Like their mom."

She blew him another kiss. They played for half an hour in virtual silence, occasionally goading each other, listening to the girls telling childish ghost stories.

"This is going to end badly," Ava whispered, jerking her thumb over her shoulder. Ingrid had launched into a tale about a ghostly serial killer in the woods with a hook for a hand.

"Should we stop them?" Killian whispered back.

She shook her head no. "Let them have their fun."

As they listened to the ridiculous and gory tale, Ava got a mischievous gleam in her eye. She set down her cards and rose from her cot.

"What are you doing?" Killian mouthed. He gave Ava a suspicious look.

She put her finger over her lips in a hushing gesture and slipped out of the tent. Killian followed, poking his head out to watch with morbid curiosity.

Ava crept over to the girls' tent, picked up a stick, and crouched down. She waited until the ghost story reach a crescendo. Then, using the stick, she poked and scraped at the nylon wall of the tent.

The girls erupted into terrified screaming. Babe barked loudly.

"We know Krav Maga!" Audrey yelled.

"Babe! Attack!" Bette screeched.

"Fuck off!" Ingrid shouted.

"Ingrid! Language!" Ava stood up.

Inside the RVs, the other two dogs barked raucously. The lights came on.

Killian stepped out of the tent and crossed his arms. This was going to end badly, indeed.

By the time the girls unzipped their tent, the other two dogs arrived and crashed into them, barking, jumping, and tails wagging. The tent collapsed around their wiggling bodies, with Audrey and Ingrid still inside. They started screaming again.

"What the hell is going on?" Jack shouted. The remaining adults gathered outside their respective RVs, looking expectantly at Ava. Ava looked like a kid who had just been caught stealing from the cookie jar. Bette, who had freed herself from the tent before the dogs invaded, sprinted to Jack. She launched herself at her father's waist.

"The girls were telling a ghost story, and I thought I'd give them a little scare," Ava explained.

Jack gave her a murderous look. He unwrapped Bette from his waist. "Seriously, Ava? You're going to wake the baby."

"The baby's fine," Dee said. She laughed. "Looks like you got them good, Ava."

Killian helped Ava lift the tent, freeing the dogs and girls. A moment later, all three dogs rushed out and sprinted around the campground. Audrey and Ingrid climbed free of the wilted nylon. They were disheveled but giggling.

"Good one, Mom!" Ingrid high-fived Ava.

Audrey took the stick from Ava's hand and inspected it. Holding it up, she laughed so hard that she doubled over. "Did you see the dogs? They were running around like crazy! They destroyed our tent. Now we can't sleep it in." She rubbed mirthful tears from her eyes.

Bette laughed too. "Can you believe I told Babe to attack?"

"That was pretty funny, Bette," Ingrid said, snickering. "Did you hear what I said?"

"Don't repeat it," Ava warned.

Jack picked Bette up. "Bug, you're getting so big. You can sleep in the RV tonight. We'll fix the tent in the morning. C'mon, girls. Time for bed." He turned and carried Bette inside. The other two girls and the dogs followed.

The doors slammed, and the night fell silent again. Killian glanced at Ava. She was standing next to the collapsed tent with her mouth twisted. Her eyes were bright.

"I thought you didn't want them to sleep in the RV," Killian remarked.

"Unintended consequences," she choked. Then she covered her mouth with both hands, doubled over, and laughed hard. After a minute, she took a deep breath. "Oops."

"Are you ready for bed, princess?"

She leveled her naughty gaze at him. "Mmm. That sounds more appealing now that we're alone. Maybe I don't mind them sleeping in the RV after all."

They ducked back into their tent. "I don't think sex is a good idea because you're so loud," he teased. "You'll wake them all up again."

"Is that so?"

"Mm-hmm."

Her mouth twitched. "I won't be loud if you put something in my mouth to keep me quiet, especially if it's something big that gags me." She pressed against him, walking her fingers up his chest. "Survivor Barbie wants to play."

"Survivor Barbie, huh?" He put his arms around her.

She nibbled his earlobe. "C'mon, play with me."

"OK, but not here. We're too close to the others. They'll hear us." He picked up his coat. "Put this on. Keep your shoes. Take everything else off. You said you always wanted to try sex outside, so we're going to, over in the trees."

"Yay, outdoor sex," she whispered excitedly, wrapping her naked body up in his coat. "Walk fast, though. It's cold, and I need you to warm me."

Using a flashlight, they stalked to a copse of trees about a hundred yards away from their tent. He pushed her against the trunk of a pine and slid his hands inside the coat, caressing her bare skin.

He lifted her leg up and hooked her knee over his elbow so that she was balancing on one leg between him and the tree. He slid a hand lower. "All that yoga pays off."

"Flexibility is important." She giggled before grabbing his chin and kissing him ferociously. After a few minutes, she pulled back to take a breath and reach for his pants.

He saw her eyes flicker over his shoulder an instant before she shoved him hard, causing him to drop her leg and stumble backward. Before he could regain his balance, she hurled whatever objects she could get her hands on—rocks, pinecones, sticks—at something just over his left shoulder.

As he turned to look at her target, he heard the telltale scream of a mountain lion. It crouched on a branch about five feet from the trunk of the tree where they'd been leaning. The mountain lion ran off, but Ava continued throwing things at the branch where it once stood.

Killian heard a savage noise. He realized it wasn't the mountain lion, it was Ava. She was half-screaming, half-growling, while tears ran down her face.

He went to her. Pulling her from the tree, he hugged her and wrapped her tightly in his coat. "Ava, it's OK. It's gone. We're safe." She shook violently, her eyes unfocused. He kissed her forehead and cupped her face. "You did exactly the right thing, Boudicca."

That got her focus. "Boudicca?"

"She was a fierce warrior queen." He held his hand out to lead her back to their campsite.

"Oh," Ava said, taking his hand. "I like that one."

Once back at the tent, he guided her inside. "Get dressed." He gathered her clothes, handing them to her, piece by piece. He helped her hook her bra, and then held her shirt so that she could slide into the sleeves. "We're always getting interrupted," he joked, steadying her as she pulled her pants on. "It's incredibly annoying."

She giggled. "We have rotten luck."

He wiped her tear-stained cheeks. "No more crying, OK?"

She took a deep breath. "I won't be able to sleep knowing there's a mountain lion nearby."

"What do you want to do?"

"I want to sleep in the RV."

"OK. What do you want to tell the girls about why we aren't sleeping in the tent?"

She chewed her lip. "I don't want them to know about the mountain lion. That's a good point. I'll just tell them that if everyone else is sleeping in a bed, why shouldn't we?"

A few minutes later, they knocked on Jack's RV door, setting off the dogs. Jack answered, looking irritated. His expression softened when Ava explained in a hushed whisper about a nearby mountain lion that she'd scared away by throwing things.

"I don't want the girls to know, because I don't want to frighten them," she said. "But can we sleep inside?"

He nodded. "I'll bring Bette over to sleep with Mom in Dee and Ricky's RV. Audrey and Ingrid can share a bed, and you can have the sofa."

A little while later, Killian and Ava climbed into the sofa bed after getting the girls and Babe situated. Ava rolled onto her side and propped herself on her elbow. She looked pale in the low lamplight.

"You didn't see, but it was going to jump on you. I'm certain of it." She shuddered. "I was so scared. I was really afraid it was going to hurt you. I would have fought it. I would have fought a mountain lion to save you."

He ran a thumb over her trembling lip. "I think that makes us even."

"For what?"

"For saves."

"Oh." She smiled wanly. "Hopefully, that's the last time."

"Hopefully." He settled into the pillow. "Hey, I wanted to tell you something, and this seems like as good a time as any."

"OK. What's that?"

"I've watched all of your movies."

She blinked in surprise. "All of them? I've made over fifty."

He chuckled. "Then not all of them. Maybe twenty of them. The ones that seem to be the most popular."

"When did you do that?"

"Here and there, ever since Lisa told me that's what a good boyfriend would do."

Ava pressed a kiss on his mouth. "Aww, that's sweet. You didn't have to. I know you don't like rom-coms."

"I wanted to. I wanted to see what you spend your time doing."

"Why? You already know what I do."

"Because you drove me to madness."

She made a face.

He tweaked her nose. "I was just kidding. I watched them because they're an important part of your life, and you're an important part of mine."

A small smile flickered across her lips. "I can't believe you watched my movies. Did you like any of them?"

"I did. Some of them were funny. You're very funny. Not just in your movies, but in real life too."

"Thanks."

"The plots were usually a little silly."

She rolled her eyes. "Like the plots of kung fu movies are so solid."

"Fair." But his expression became serious. "The problem is that they're unrealistic and teach people to have false expectations on how to deal with interpersonal conflict. You can't have major conflict and then expect it to resolve because one person chases the other through a crowd. That's magical thinking. Most of the characters needed therapy if they were going to be in a healthy relationship."

Ava laughed. "Calm down there, Rotten Tomatoes. No one wants to watch a movie about fucked-up people going to therapy. We want our medicine with a spoonful of sugar."

"What does that mean?"

"People want happy endings. It gives them hope things will turn out when they struggle for real. A story, whether it's a movie or a novel or a song, can touch on difficult topics more easily when it's sugar-coated with humor or sex or a guaranteed happy ending. Because that's what we all want, right? Hope that it'll all turn out in the end, and a little fun along the way."

"Is that what you want? A happy ending?"

"Among other things, yeah. I want to look back at my life and feel like it was more good than bad, that I loved, and was loved in return."

He stroked her cheeks with his thumbs. "Besides watching your movies, I've also been going to therapy."

Ava's mouth fell open. "You have?"

He nodded.

"Why? When?"

"After I realized we were in a relationship, I didn't want to fuck it up. So I signed up for therapy over videoconferencing. Therapy worked for me when I was younger, and I thought it could help me now. I function OK, but it's not like I'm past all my issues. And this is new for me."

"Why didn't you tell me?"

"I wasn't ready. I didn't know what I was doing—still don't, honestly. Then you told me you loved me, and I froze. I know that's not healthy. So while you were gone on Wednesday morning, I emailed my therapist. She emailed back and suggested I make a list. I did, and I want to show it to you."

Killian reached over her to the back of the sofa where he'd laid his coat. He dug the list out of his pocket and handed it to her. Ava sat up and took the paper from his hand. He watched her unfold it and read it silently.

Why I Love Ava Blum:

1. She survived a mudslide and a hike down a mountain, because she's a badass

2. She survived a violent sexual assault, because she's a badass

3. She made herself successful in a male-dominated, sexist industry, with no help, because she's a badass

4. She cries because she's brave

5. She's friendly and kind, even to strangers

6. She's authentic and open

7. She loves me, even though she's a famous movie star and I'm a broken kid from New Jersey

8. She respects herself enough to know her intimacy boundaries and gives herself space to manage her PTSD

9. She's complicated because she's not shallow

10. She's talented

11. She's smart

12. She likes my dog

13. She's a good mom

14. She's funny

15. She's supportive

16. She's generous

17. She's sweet and compassionate

18. She's patient

19. She's a good cook, and she takes care of me

20. She's the sexiest woman on the planet, and she's all mine

He watched her eyes widen and her cheeks flush. When she was done reading, she looked back at him but said nothing.

"I've got a problem, though," he began with careful nonchalance. "I was pretty happy about it being a nice, even twenty reasons. Now I have to add, 'She saved me from a mountain lion, because she's a badass,' and that's going to ruin the numbering. Which one should I take off?" He gave her a cheeky grin.

Making a strangled noise, she dropped the paper and shoved him in the chest with both hands.

"What the hell?"

But she couldn't answer because she collapsed into a mess of soul-wrenching sobs. He pulled her into his lap and rocked her for several minutes. "What's wrong, sunshine? Tell me."

Finally, she sucked in enough air to form a sentence. "I'm sorry. I didn't mean to shove you. It was some kind of reflex." She rubbed her eyes. "All those things you wrote...they were all the things I've ever wanted someone to think about me. I—I didn't think they could be real. Did you mean them?"

"Every word."

She gulped air and leaned back to look into his eyes. "Let me try again." She grabbed his face with both hands and kissed him with wild abandon. "I love you too."

Chapter 30

Ava floated through her days for the next month. It was Christmas, and she was in love. Everything felt like pure magic.

She had never made a Hallmark holiday movie, but she felt like she was in one. Killian helped her decorate the house with a tree, lights, and stockings hung on the mantel. She got stockings made for him and Babe, and she dressed them both in ugly sweaters.

He helped her bake cookies that she gave to shelters and hospitals. She dragged him along with a group of neighbors to go caroling. He steadfastly refused to sing, but he walked with his arm slung over her shoulders, making her laugh at his snarky commentary about Christmas song lyrics.

He agreed to go caroling on the condition that he didn't have to go to any industry holiday parties with her. He had no desire to be photographed on red carpets or trapped in a room for hours making small talk with strangers. Ava thought that was fair. Keeping things simple and private worked for them.

Her days and nights sparkled. But they did one thing you'd never see in a Hallmark movie: they had sex on every surface of her house when the girls weren't home—which was a lot of surfaces in her very big house.

Two days before Christmas, Ava's parents arrived from Florida. She'd told them about Killian after Thanksgiving. They responded by reminding her how stupid she was for divorcing Jack.

The gate guard called to tell Ava that her parents' car was approaching. She pulled Killian to the front steps to greet them. Standing next to him, she fidgeted. As soon as her parents were out of the car, she gave them stiff hugs and made the introductions. "Mutter, Vater, this is my boyfriend, Killian Kelly. Killian, these are my parents, Stefan and Ada Blum."

Like her, Ava's parents were tall, slim blonds, although her father had very little hair left and had grown a slight belly. Ada was elegant and looked somewhat younger than her seventy years, having always been meticulous about her appearance. Ava had been told her entire life that she was Ada's spitting image.

Her parents gave Killian brisk handshakes and then moved into the house without making small talk. For the rest of the day, they said very few words to either her or Killian, preferring the company of their grand-daughters. At six sharp, they all sat down for dinner.

"I made salmon Niçoise just like my chef in France taught me," Ava said to her mother, trying to break the ice. "It was one of your favorite dishes when you visited our vineyard."

"Oh, the one Jack bought you in Bordeaux? That was such a nice prop-erty." Ada shook her head, poking at her salad. "I'll never understand why you got divorced. You'll never again find a man who can afford to buy you a French winery."

Ava winced. "Mutter..."

"I've told you since you were a little girl, you can fall in love rich as easily as you can fall in love poor. Now look what you've done. I thought you'd got it right the first time and we could retire, knowing you'd be taken care of after we die. But then you threw it away, waiting till you were forty, no less. Not to mention, divorce is a sin. I worry about you, Schatzilein. Your antics are a lot of strain on my aging heart."

Ava glanced at Killian at the backhanded insult. But if he caught it, he didn't show any outward reaction. "You don't need to worry about me, Mutter. I'm fine. I can buy myself a winery if I want one."

"Is that the example you want to give our granddaughters?" Stefan chimed in. "That instead of focusing on their family and keeping a good husband happy, they should strip to their unmentionables on camera in front of millions of people? Feminism ruined you, but it's not too late for meine Kuschelhasen."

Bette and Ingrid giggled at being referred to as cuddle bunnies. Ava seethed. She'd accepted that her parents would never approve of her career, but it was harder for her to tolerate their criticism of her parenting.

Audrey, who was old enough to pick up on her mood, came to her rescue. "Oma, Opa, did Mom tell you? Killian was the one who saved her from the mudslide."

"Yeah," Bette added. "And he taught us survival skills. He's my hero." Bette popped a cherry tomato into her mouth while grinning at Killian.

"Yes, your mother told us how they met," Ada said dismissively. "What were you filming, Ava? Another fluffy romance? How much longer can you get cast in those?"

"It was an adaptation of *A Midsummer Night's Dream*."

"Shakespeare? Oh, well, that's excellent. I'm glad to see you are doing something cultured and more age-appropriate." Ada chewed a small forkful of salmon. "How'd you cook this salmon, dear?"

"I broiled it."

"Next time, broil it with the skin-side up for a couple of minutes first, before flipping it. That will make the skin crispier. Soggy salmon skin is a travesty." She wrinkled her nose, poking at the remains of her salad.

"Oh, good idea. I'll try that," Ava murmured.

With incredible ill timing, Ingrid snuck a piece of salmon skin under the table to Babe. Her sneaking skills were terrible, and everyone saw her.

Stefan dropped his fork in disgust. "Ingrid! That's unsanitary. Do you know how much bacteria is in a dog's mouth? Go wash your hands."

He turned to Ava. "Animals do not belong in the house, Ava. Your filthy habits are going to make everyone sick. What has gotten into you?" His eyes flickered to Killian, so it was clear to Ava that his question was rhetorical. Her father knew exactly what—or who—had gotten into her.

Ava glanced at Killian again, who was now outwardly frowning. "Ingrid," she said. "Put Babe outside and then go wash your hands before returning to the table."

"Yes, Mom." Ingrid ran off, dragging Babe by the collar.

Everyone ate in silence until Ingrid returned. Ada attempted conversation again. "Ava, I saw a picture of you in the paper the other day. Some kind of red-carpet thing. You were wearing a silver gown. Where was that taken?"

Ava relaxed and smiled. "It was a holiday fundraiser ball for the children's hospital. I'm on the board. I just started doing that this year at Mina's request. She does some legal work for them."

"Oh. You went alone? Your boyfriend wasn't in any of the pictures." Ava noticed that they never referred to him by his name.

"I went alone. It's easier for us to maintain our privacy if he doesn't join me at red carpet events."

Ada nodded. "Oh. That makes sense, Schatzilein. I didn't think of that. It must be so different for you now, having to do these things alone. Jack's so famous, you didn't have to exclude him."

"Mm-hmm." Ava shoved a large piece of endive in her mouth so she wouldn't have to talk.

"Anyway," Ada continued, "you looked lovely. It was nice to see you in a dress that wasn't so revealing for once. I guess that's because the nature of the event? But I do wish you'd stop wearing red lipstick. It really doesn't suit. It makes you look like a prostitute."

Killian stood abruptly. "That's enough insulting Ava in her own house. If you can't control yourselves, you can leave." He picked up their plates. "Ava, we're finishing our meals in the kitchen."

He led her into the other room. They stood at the island, but she'd lost her appetite and was too restless to sit on the stool. She started cleaning up instead. Killian helped by washing the dishes.

"I'm sorry," she said. "I know that was uncomfortable."

"Jack warned me. I tried at first to not interfere, because they're your parents, but it became intolerable."

She came up behind him and put her arms around his waist. She laid her head on his back. "I'm sorry they were so insulting to you."

He stopped washing dishes for a moment. "I couldn't give two shits what they think about me. It was how they talk to you that I found intolerable."

"They mean well. They just want what's best for me."

He grunted. "I noticed how silent you are when your parents are around. You don't talk, or laugh, or sing. It's like they installed a mute switch on you, and they activated it the moment they walked into the house."

She stepped away from him and returned to putting away leftovers. "I was just focused on my hostessing duties. I wanted to make sure the food and the house were perfect. So much to do. I'll be better tomorrow at Jack's."

He grunted again but dropped the subject.

The next morning, they headed to Jack's house for Christmas Eve. Killian drove her and Babe in his truck, and her parents drove the girls in her

SUV. It took them four hours to drive ninety miles. Traffic was terrible, fouling everyone's moods.

As soon as Ava opened her door, a pent-up Babe scrabbled over her and leaped out of the truck. The dog ran to the SUV where her kids and parents were getting out. She barked, jumped, and ran circles around the vehicles, full of unbridled joy and explosive energy.

Babe jumped at Ava's father just as he closed the driver's side door. "Damn dog!" Stefan kicked, connecting with a thud and catching Babe by surprise. Babe yelped and cowered.

"Hey! Don't do that!" Ava ran over to protect Babe, crouching to inspect her and confirm she wasn't injured.

Stefan grabbed Ava by the upper arm and hauled her upright. "That dog is ill-trained and a menace. It's going to hurt someone." He kicked in Babe's direction again, eliciting a growl and bared teeth. "See, it's violent. It's going to bite someone, like your kids. It's irresponsible to keep it around."

For a moment, Ava's courage rallied in defense of her dog. "What the fuck is wrong with you? She's not violent. You're scaring her. She's just an innocent animal, and you're being aggressive." Babe cowered between Ava's legs. "Back off, Vater!"

But Stefan didn't budge. His hand tightened and pinched her skin. Ava heard a door slam, and a moment later, Killian was at her side.

"Let go of her." His expression was as dark as his eyes.

Stefan glared at him. "She's *my daughter*."

"So? She doesn't belong to you."

"She doesn't belong to *you*," Stefan snapped.

"I know. She's a human being, not a possession. And you're assaulting her." Killian was as immovable as a brick wall, and Ava noticed how much larger and stronger and younger he was compared to her father. Her fear returned, crashing over her like a tidal wave.

"Vater, please let go," she whispered.

Stefan ignored her and held fast.

"Remove your hand, or I will remove it for you," Killian growled in a low voice. "And that will add hospitals and police to our day, almost certainly ruining Christmas for the girls."

Time slowed. Ava's legs shook so hard that she was surprised she could stand. The thought of Killian going to jail to protect her made her nauseous.

Ava was about to ask Killian to leave and let her handle it when Ada appeared at Stefan's side. "Stefan, let go. We will deal with this later. People are watching," she said under her breath.

Ava looked around and saw that Jack and Esme had appeared on the porch to greet them. Her daughters were pressed into Esme's sides with fearful looks on their faces.

Stefan dropped his hand from her arm. "I'm sorry, Ava. I didn't mean to lose my temper. I just don't want that dog to hurt anyone." He shot a dirty look in Killian's direction. "It's a pit bull. A *stray*."

Stefan stepped back and walked up the stairs with her mother to greet their hosts. Ava watched him for a moment, sagging against Killian because her weakened legs couldn't hold her.

Her father had never apologized to her before, and it took her a moment to process the words. But she knew he wasn't sorry; he said it because other people were present, while simultaneously insulting Killian.

Killian inspected her reddened arm and then crouched to check Babe. Already better, Babe licked him and then sprinted off to join Scruffles and Wilber playing in the yard. "He's been physical with you before."

"It's been a long time. Last time was before I got married. He never would've done that in front of Jack. I'm surprised he did it in front of you. I think he just forgot himself." She shrugged.

Killian brushed her hair out of her eyes. "Are you OK? You're shaking."

"I'm OK. It brought back memories. Sometimes he was violent, but not all the time. It wasn't like I was *abused*-abused. There were consequences to misbehavior. So I stayed out of the way because I didn't want to get punished. My father had a temper, and my mother hung a leather strap on a hook in the kitchen."

Killian closed his eyes briefly. "Even I didn't get beaten, Ava, and I was an actual hooligan. Why do you make excuses for them?"

"Because it was a different time. Some schools I went to still spanked. You didn't have that because you're a youngin'." She poked him in the arm to lighten his mood, but he was unmoved.

She sighed. "My parents thought that being strict was right. Don't spare the rod and spoil the child. I grew up afraid of them, but it did work. I was well-behaved." She shrugged. "It was a long time ago. I've chosen to parent differently. That's all that matters."

"Ava, you're not trembling like a leaf because you're unscathed. They've hurt you. Being around them opens old wounds. It isn't good for you."

"But—"

Ava's retort was interrupted by Dee, who'd called from the front door. "Ava, Jack's making chocolate martinis. They're special for Christmas with a bit of peppermint. You want one?"

"Oh, hell yeah!" It was a lot of sugar, but Ava decided she could have one. Just one. It would help her take the edge off. And she wasn't in charge of dinner or the household, so she could sit and relax. She eagerly pulled Killian into the house in search of her sweet, alcoholic salvation.

Four—or was it five?—martinis later, Ava was wasted. She sat pressed into Killian's side, silently drinking for the entire afternoon. Every time her glass emptied, Jack or Dee refilled her before she could stop them.

Wrapped in the scent of Killian's soap and the protective shield of his arm, she listened to the others talk and watched her daughters play.

And she thought.

She thought about how it felt to have someone protect her. She didn't know she needed that. She worked hard at being well paid, and she'd made herself successful. She worked at Krav Maga. She worked at her therapy and avoided her triggers so she could feel safe. Until she met Killian, she didn't know that she needed to feel protected too. He'd risked his life for her from the first moment they met. Today, he showed he'd go to jail for her.

She stared at Killian adoringly. She loved him so much.

The room swam a little.

She thought about how hard she worked at being perfect. She tried to be perfect growing up. She tried to be perfect now. To please every-body. To never put herself above others. To titillate, and amuse, and appear flawless.

Why wasn't that good enough? Why wasn't she good enough? She wasn't ever good enough for her parents, or for anyone.

Except Killian. He thought she was good enough. He even made a list of all the ways she was good enough. She'd read it so many times that she'd memorized it. Her eyes misted. He loved her and told her she didn't do anything wrong.

"What?" He noticed that she'd been looking at him like a cartoon puppy with heart eyes for the past five minutes.

She smiled brightly. "Nothing. I just love you."

He pressed a kiss on her temple. "I love you too."

The conversation among the other adults soon lagged. Dee turned to Ava, attempting to get her to talk for the first time since they'd arrived. "Ava, do you have any interesting projects coming up?"

Sobering her expression, Ava turned her attention to Dee. "Well, I have one thing. I'm pretty nervous about it. I'm recording an interview with Jacqueline Ross-Caruthers in January. I'm going public about being raped while I was in the Army. It's been in the works since November."

Killian knew, of course, that Ava had decided to speak out. He supported her decision and reminded her she had nothing to feel ashamed about. Talking about it was a big step in combating the symptoms of her trauma. And she hoped it would help other victims, too, if she came forward.

Her unplanned announcement shocked the room, however. The only other people who knew she'd been raped were her parents and Jack. Everyone stared at her in silence.

"You were what?" Audrey asked after a long pause. Her voice trembled.

Ava winced. In her alcohol haze, she'd forgotten to censor the news for her girls. "Oh, honey, yeah. You heard right. I'll tell you and your sisters about it later. It happened when I was eighteen."

Audrey ran across the living room and flung herself into her mother's arms. "Mom," she sniffled into Ava's shoulder.

"Ava, look, you've upset Audrey," Ada admonished her. "And on Christmas Eve. Was that really necessary?"

Ava smoothed her daughter's hair while she held her. "She needs to know, Mutter. It's time."

"Do you really think an interview is the best idea?" Ada pressed. "Why would you want to talk about that publicly? Are you that desperate for attention?"

"Oma!" Audrey shouted in horror, jumping to her feet.

"Take your sisters into the other room, Audrey. Let the grown-ups talk. Your mother's had too much to drink. You'll see in the morning that she's just being dramatic." Ada waved her granddaughter off.

Audrey, Ava, and Jack all spoke at once.

"Oma, you're being mean!" Audrey cried.

"My daughters can stay," Ava said. "You're not their parent, and it's not for you to decide what they can hear."

"Don't call her dramatic," Jack snapped.

Stefan stood calmly, exuding the confidence of a man who was used to being listened to. "That's enough." He leveled Ava with a look. The room went silent again except for her three daughters' sniffles, as they were all now crying. "Girls, go to other room and play. It's Christmas tomorrow, and you should be excited, not crying." He sat back down and looked at them sternly.

Audrey looked at her mother and then at her father. Jack nodded. Her other two daughters joined Audrey in standing before Ava. Ava leaned forward and wiped all their tears away.

She smiled at them. "It's OK, babies. I *am* a little drunk. I didn't mean to tell you about this on Christmas Eve. It happened a long, long time ago. You don't need to be sad. Go play your video game. I'll come up before dinner and answer all your questions." She stood and kissed them on each of their foreheads. She sat once more and snuggled into Killian's side, needing his strength, and watched her girls file out of the room.

After they'd gone, Stefan turned in his chair to face her. "Ava, you've always been dramatic, ever since you were a girl. It's why you went into acting. And thank goodness that worked out because I don't know where you'd be otherwise."

He took a sip of his water, his stare unflinching. "I'm sorry, but you're too old to be rolling out this charade again. We all know you invited that boy to your room. We all know how you dress and behave, both back then and now." He flourished his hand at her, even though she wasn't wearing anything skimpy, or sporting her practiced sultry expression.

Stefan continued, "Don't you think accusing someone of rape, twenty-two years later, is unfair? The Army already cleared him of any charges. You're going to embarrass him, the Army, and yourself. You're going to embarrass your family. Think about someone beside yourself for once."

A white-hot fury rose in Ava. She made a low, strangled noise. "He wasn't a boy, and I accused him of rape the day it happened. Because that's what it was. He, and the Army, *should* be embarrassed." Killian squeezed her tighter in comfort.

"He didn't rape you, Ava. You didn't want to be in the Army, so you pulled a stunt, knowing it was fraternization. And because you look like you do, the poor sap fell for it, and barely hung onto his career." Stefan took another calm sip of his water. "Tell the truth."

Jack stood. "Get out of my house," he said with barely controlled rage. "You are no longer welcome here."

Even though she was furious and hurt at her father's words, Ava shook her head, tears springing into her eyes. "Jack, no. It's Christmas. Think of the girls."

"Ava, I *am* thinking of the girls. I don't want them around our daughters. They'll warp them just like they did you."

"But our daughters need their grandparents." Ava couldn't stop the tears from falling, even though she knew her parents would consider them proof of her hysterical nature. Grief and fear supplanted her anger, flooding her.

"I'll be all the grandparents they need," Meg offered.

Ava's head swiveled in surprise. She thought Meg was still mad at her. Her mouth formed a surprised "oh," but she couldn't speak because she was struggling under the weight of her pain.

Meg gave her a soft smile. "Ava, I've watched them shit on you for years. If I've seen it, your children have seen it. It's not good for them to witness their mother getting mistreated, and it's not good for you, either."

"I'll call a car," Jack said.

Ava looked at her parents through her tear-hazy vision. They seemed frozen, unable to decipher whether they should stay or go. She looked down at her hands, wrestling with her own indecision. "No," she said. "Jack, please. They're still my parents."

"And that's why I've put up with them for as long as I have."

Ava looked at Jack and could see he'd decided. He rarely got stubborn; but when he did, she knew there was no arguing it.

She looked at her hands again and saw a tear land on her thumb. She contemplated leaving the girls and going back to LA with her parents. It was her fault for causing this. She ruined Christmas by getting drunk and blurting her news about the interview.

"I'm sorry," she murmured to everyone, and to no one in particular.

"Ava." Killian lifted her chin until she rotated and faced him. "Why are you sorry? You didn't do anything wrong."

"I didn't?"

"No. Ava, sunshine, I think you've tolerated this long enough. Look how upset you are. And you're blaming yourself? They've done a number on you."

He looked at Stefan and Ada, fury on his face. "All she ever does is think about other people. You don't know your own daughter."

"We've known her forty years longer than you," Ada sniped. "She's always used tears and dramatics to manipulate people and get what she wants. It's obvious she's got you wrapped around her finger." She stood and pointed at her daughter. "Ava, get control of yourself. You're making everyone uncomf—"

"Not another word," Killian snapped, silencing Ada. "In the past two days, all I've heard you and your husband do is criticize, shame, and gaslight Ava. I've seen you assault and abuse her. I've watched you dim her light. And that's just in *two days*. She's got an entire lifetime of pain from you. It's amazing she does as well as she does. Everything she is, it's in spite of you."

Ada flushed. "How dare you? You don't know what you're talking about. Everything we've ever done was for her. We've sacrificed our entire lives for her. Even when she disappoints us, she's our daughter, and we love her."

Killian shook his head, disgusted. "I grew up knowing my parents didn't love me. But you're worse, Ada, because you lie about loving your daughter. You say you love her, but you don't treat her like it. Love isn't just a word, it's how you behave. Ava taught me that, in fact."

Cupping her face, Killian gently wiped Ava's tears. "Stop trying to earn their love. They're never going to give it to you. Don't waste time on people who don't want you."

He stood up and looked at Ava's parents. "She cries because you hurt her. But I'm not letting you do that anymore." He held out his hand. "Ava, you don't deserve abuse. You don't owe them anything. Choose yourself."

Ava stared at Killian's hand for a long moment and remembered the first time she saw him holding his hand out to her. Then she took it. Together, with him pulling and her rising, they freed her from her prison.

She followed him from the room, out into the yard, and half a mile up the rolling hills of Jack's sprawling property. Finally, they reached a ridge and stopped to watch the sunset.

He wrapped her in his arms from behind, keeping her warm in the cool December evening. "You saved me again," Ava said, tipping her head back to look at him.

"No, princess. You walked out of there on your own two feet. I just showed you the way."

One year to the day after Killian pulled Ava from the mudslide, they returned to the campground for her forty-first birthday. This time, they were joined by Ava's daughters, Jack, and his entire family. The group decided on a summer reprise of their Thanksgiving camping adventure, with a dose of exposure therapy for Ava and the girls.

Killian arranged with Mary for exclusive use of the campground for the week. The National Parks Service had completed the stabilization work and scheduled the campground to re-open to the public in July.

The ground where Ava's cabin once collapsed on top of her remained bare, marked only by the foundation's cinder blocks that resembled weathered headstones. Ava and Killian arrived early in the morning, after an overnight at The Knotty Pine, to give Ava a moment in solitude to react.

"I'm OK," Ava said, staring at the blank ground. "I'm really OK." She leaned back into Killian. "I'm OK because you're here." She smiled up at him. "I always feel safe with you around."

"You say that like your promise to drink from a mud puddle on command isn't hanging over your head like the Sword of Damocles."

She turned in his arms, facing him, and tugged on his beard. "I trust you not to abuse my faith and utter devotion to you." She batted her eyelashes.

"A misplaced trust, I'm sure." He fingered the "Mom" pendant hanging around her neck.

"No. I put my trust in you on day one, and it's never been misplaced." She rose on tiptoe to brush a kiss across his lips.

When she dropped back on her heels, he said, "I wanted to talk to you about something, and this seems like as good a time as any."

"OK, what?" She felt no fear about what he might say next. She knew, in the depths of her soul, that he loved her.

"Is it still important to you to be married?"

Her eyebrows came together. "What?"

"I wasn't sure how you felt about that now. It doesn't matter to me at all. But if it's important to you, I'm not opposed. Ava, you're the only family I've ever had. You're the only family I'll ever need. But I do need you. I've been wondering whether I should lock you down." He pecked her on the nose.

She laughed softly. "Oh, honey child, I'm already locked down. The day I burned the list, I decided marriage wasn't a deal-breaker. I plan to grow old with you and tell you daily that I love you, no matter what. But, yeah, I want that official union. If given the choice, I want to be your wife."

"OK, then."

"OK."

She kissed him again, more passionately this time. But they were soon interrupted by Babe, who jumped and pawed at their legs, trying to get between them. "Ugh, Babe is so naughty," Ava said, stepping back from Killian.

The rest of their group arrived and settled in by lunchtime. Since the spot where her cabin once stood was a convenient clearing, the group dragged stones over and marked off a fire pit. They set up chairs, gathered wood, and Killian and her daughters built a roaring campfire.

"Sit. You've earned a break, birthday girl," Killian said, leading Ava to a chair by the fire. Within moments, the rest of the group—all except Killian—settled into chairs with her and passed around beers.

"I hate you all," Dee moaned, sipping from her water bottle. "I miss beer so much. I swear on all that is holy, this is the absolute last time I get pregnant."

"Remember, it'll all be worth it," Ricky said, patting her belly. Dee was about five months along.

"Shut up, Lucifer. This is all your fault." Dee's grumpy words were belied by her playful grin.

"Nope. I'm not taking all the blame. It takes two, Dee. I would've assumed they'd taught you that in vet school."

She rolled her eyes. "You're not funny. Where's Ginny? Mom just walked up, so who's watching our little troublemaker?"

"In the cabin," Meg answered, sitting down in the chair opposite Dee. "I put her down for a nap, and Audrey said she'd watch her."

"Thank God for nieces." Dee took Ricky's hand and closed her eyes, tilting her face to the sun.

"Are you ready for the twins?" Ava asked Esme when she sat down. "How's Madison doing? Last I saw her, she was as big as a house."

"Madison's complaining even more than Dee," Esme answered. "I think she's ready to be done. More ready than I am. Your birthday party last weekend is probably the last time we'll see other adults for a while."

Ava had invited Mina and Carmen to camp with them for her birthday. Both women declined, telling her that God invented luxury homes in Bel Air for a reason. So before heading up to the mountains, she had a proper Hollywood soiree for her "twenty-ninth" birthday in her palatial house. All the stars came, which, of course, included Jack and his wife.

"Having babies in the house is a strange time. I both miss it and am glad it's over." Ava patted Esme's hand.

"I can scarcely conceive how our lives are going to change with two newborns, and I'm terrified." Esme wrinkled her nose. "I know it's what I wanted, but I'm worried that I'll miss being child-free."

"You'll be fine, dear," Meg piped in. "It goes by quickly. Before you know it, your kids will be in their forties, and you'll wonder where the time has gone." She patted Wilbur on the head after the dog curled on her feet to nap. "The next few years will be exhausting but fun."

Esme changed the topic. "I saw your speech to the VA on Military Sexual Trauma on C-SPAN," she said to Ava. "It was very moving. There wasn't a dry eye in the place by the time you were done."

"Thanks." Ava played with the label on her beer bottle. "You know, I'm used to having fans. I'm used to strangers gushing about my movies or how much they love me. But nothing, absolutely nothing, could have prepared me for the experience of other survivors approaching me since my interview. In just the past six months, so many people—women, and men too—have come up to me, some in tears, telling me how much my story helped them. So many have told me I gave them the courage to come forward and seek help. It's the best thing I've ever done. I wish I hadn't waited twenty-two years to speak out."

"Aw, sister, that's beautiful." Esme beamed at her. "Trauma has a way of isolating you, making you think you shouldn't talk about it. You should be proud of yourself. Tackling it head on is a testament to your strength."

"That's very kind," Ava murmured. "I don't feel strong all that often. I have to work at it every day."

"Understandable. Have you spoken to your parents since Christmas?"

"No. I've been zero contact."

"Good riddance," Jack said from the other side of Esme.

Ava gave him a wan smile. "I know you see things more clearly than me, Jack, because you're on the outside. But you have to understand, it feels like they suddenly died. It's been really hard. I grieve both the people I know, and the parents I never had, but wished for. If it weren't for therapy, the girls, and Killian, I would've begged their forgiveness already."

Meg got out of her chair and squatted next to Ava, taking her hand. "I owe you an apology, Ava. I've been hard on you over the years. Even though I'd seen how your parents treated you, I didn't put it together. I wrongly assumed you were preoccupied with Hollywood, and I didn't give you your due."

Tears sprang into Ava's eyes. "You don't have to apologize, Meg. We're good."

Meg patted her hand. "Even though you divorced my son, which I obviously think was the dumbest thing you've ever done, you'll always be my daughter, and I love you." She kissed Ava's cheek and returned to her seat.

"Well, it's a good thing you feel that way," Ava said to Meg, wiping her eyes. "Because now that I'm moving to San Diego with the girls, you all are the only people I know. I'm probably going to wear out my welcome."

Ava and the girls were moving from LA during the last week of June. She had waited until the school year ended, but it had been hard. Killian had taken a job in San Diego in January as part of their plan, which meant they'd been back on weekends-only for the past six months. Ava hated it.

"You and the girls being closer is going to make everyone's schedules so much easier to manage," Esme said. "Now that you're doing all this speaking and activism, we'll have more flexibility to take the girls without disrupting their education. It'll be good."

"Have you told Esme about your planned trip to DC in the fall?" Jack asked.

"Oh, no. I forgot." She turned to Esme again. "I'm going to speak to Congress along with the Secretary of the Army, both at official hearings and at some private meetings. The Army has reopened a bunch of old assault cases, so more victims are going to see justice. And they're disciplining officers who swept reports of sexual assault under the rug at their commands."

"Making a difference!" Esme clinked her beer bottle to Ava in salute.

"One upside of my celebrity is that the Army is paying attention. For once, I can use the paparazzi's rabid attention for good instead of evil."

"I was friends with a female medic in my unit around the time you were in the Army," Ricky said. "She complained of a sexual assault and was shuffled out of the command. I never saw her after that. I think everything you said in your interview happened a lot. I'm glad to see the Army finally doing something about it, even if it's two decades overdue."

"I'm sorry about your friend. Maybe she'll be someone who gets justice, even if it's delayed," Ava said.

"Hope so." Ricky nodded. "For a lot of reasons, I don't want my daughter to follow in my footsteps."

"Speaking of, are you and Dee coming back to San Diego? You got to travel for what, three, four months, before Dee got pregnant again?" Ava asked. She waved her beer bottle in front of Dee, teasing her.

"You know, Ava, you were my favorite sister-in-law, but that just knocked you down a peg. Esme's number one again," Dee said.

"Shouldn't Esme always be number one, since Ava divorced me?" Jack asked.

"I love Esme to bits, but only Ava will karaoke with me." Dee's eyes sparkled with humor.

"I do love karaoke," Ava confirmed.

"And I don't," Esme added. "Those are facts. No hard feelings, Dee." She winked at her sister-in-law.

"But—" Jack started.

"You're still my favorite brother, so why are you complaining?" Dee asked.

"I'm your only brother," Jack retorted.

"Take the win, Jack, or you might get demoted too. I have two brothers-in-law, remember?"

"You're so mean when you're pregnant," Jack grumbled. "Hey, Ricky, do us all a favor and stop knocking up my sister."

Ricky shook his head. "I would if I could. She won't leave me alone. Woman's insatiable."

Dee threw a small rock at Ricky. "Don't tell them that."

Esme started laughing. "What did I marry into? Ava, you could've warned me."

"If anyone can keep up with the Bullards, it's you, Esme." Ava looked around. "Have any of you seen Killian? He's been gone for a while."

Meg jerked her thumb over her shoulder. "He's on his way back now."

Ava watched him march down the hill to the group, his long legs eating up the ground, and smiled. "Where've you been?" she asked as he approached carrying a grocery bag.

"I had to run to the market." He unpacked a Twinkie and two large candles with the numbers 4 and 1. Then he passed around the paper bag and instructed everyone to take a Twinkie.

"Last year, on her fortieth birthday, the only thing I could find for her birthday cake was a Twinkie in the motel gift shop. It's also the only cake I've ever seen Ava eat. By default, it's now her birthday tradition," Killian explained to the group. He pushed the two candles into her Twinkie, lit them with his lighter, and handed it to her.

"These candles are bigger than the Twinkie," Ava complained.

"I thought this year you'd own your age, as you've successfully turned over a new leaf." Killian grinned at her. "Blowing these out should be easier than the toothpick, but you better do it before you melt your Twinkie."

She pursed her lips. "Alright, if I'm going to publicly celebrate being forty-one"—she mock-shuddered—"then you have to sing 'Happy Birthday' to me. Actually sing, Killian. I mean it. That's my birthday wish."

He shook his head. "Fine. But you're going to regret it. Don't say I didn't warn you."

"Just do it." She poised to blow out the candles, waiting expectantly for the group to sing.

They sang to Ava, Killian included, and she blew out the candles with a quick whoosh of air. After she finished her Twinkie—a whole one this time—she gave Killian a kiss. "Thank you for the birthday Twinkie. But, yeah, you were right. Never sing again. Your voice could torture terrorists."

"I told you."

She clapped suddenly. "Oh my God, I got it!"

"What?"

"The perfect nickname!"

"Oh, no..."

"Sinatra!" She beamed at him.

"Wow. That's just mean."

"No, it's perfect. He's from New Jersey. And he was married to Ava Gardner, who I was named after."

Killian looked surprised. "You were?"

"No, but I like to tell people that. Anyway, Sinatra is the perfect nickname for you."

"No. No more nicknames."

Her eyes twinkled naughtily. "Whatever you say, Ol' Blue Eyes."

"You can't have a nickname for my nickname. And my eyes aren't blue."

"Who says? You? Because you're Chairman of the Board?"

His dark eyes blazed, and he leaned in, lowering his voice. "Do I need to teach you my name again?"

She blushed, glancing around to see if the rest of the group heard him. "Killian…"

He sat back, a smug look on his face. "That's better."

.

Bonus Scene: Found Family

With fame comes family.

Now that Ava and Killian are engaged, his kin have come a-knockin'.

Click or scan here to read the bonus scene now.

Always Rate or Review to Support Independent Authors

4.8

Independent authors may be on Amazon, but that doesn't mean we have big publishing companies behind us. In fact, **most of us are creating and publishing completely by ourselves.** (Where you see the "Publisher" information in my book, I list my company instead of my legal name for privacy reasons.)

Independent authors make a dollar or two for every one of our books that you read on Kindle or purchase in paperback. We aren't getting rich doing this. **We do it because we love writing and sharing stories with you, our readers.**

To pay for our publishing costs, such as editors and cover design, we need to sell some books. This is not very easy to do. We have to compete against the big PR machines of major publishing houses, including Amazon's publishing companies, who get better visibility and website placement than the rest of us.

The primary way we can climb the ranks on Amazon's lists, increasing our visibility so that new readers can find us, is with a lot of five-star reviews.

If you love what I write and **want to see more from me**—or any independent author—**please rate or review my work.** It takes only a few seconds to click five stars, but it can make all the difference in the world.

Without readers rating me 4.4 stars or above, I can't sell my books. And if I can't sell my books, I can't write them.

If you're reading this electronically, click here or on the stars image above for the Amazon Review Form for *All the Ways We're Wrong*. You can also go through your Amazon account, your Kindle app, or your e-reader.

Without you, I wouldn't be here. Your positive feedback means the world to me.

AUTHOR

Note From the Author

When I wrote scenes from Ava's perspective, I could literally hear "Spice Up Your Life" in my head. Ava is loud, sensitive, silly, and sweet. She says she's "extra," and she certainly talks a lot more than Killian. Even though Killian has an extra chapter, more total words are devoted to Ava (yes, I keep track!).

I had to be careful, because she's a scene-stealer and she almost runs aways with the whole book.

But it wouldn't have done Killian's character justice to make him louder to compete with her, just for the sake of equal words. He wouldn't want that much attention, and he's a man of few words. He's quiet and grounded. And, at first blush, seems like the polar opposite of Ava.

Looks can be deceiving. Ava and Killian are not opposites. They are two sides of the same coin. That's what makes them suitable helpmates. They have the same trauma—a childhood without parental love—and that gives them a deep understanding of one another as their story progresses. Their differences are in their learned coping mechanisms.

Killian's trauma is plain on its face. He's known all along what his problem is, and has been working on it since adolescence. He might've been an angry kid, but he's a stable adult because he faces that anger and makes deliberate choices about his life. When Ava's presence in his life forces him to stretch and grow, he's able to face his issues because he's got self-awareness and some established tools.

In contrast, Ava's not able to quite see or accept the true depth of her trauma. This is because she's been gaslit her whole life. When you learn how deeply Ava's sense of self-worth is harmed, her triggers around not being good enough to be chosen and loved, and her inability to trust her own perceptions, her behavior across two novels (she's an important character in *Conduct Unbecoming a Judge* as Jack's ex-wife and sometimes antagonist) is much easier to understand.

Ava just wants to be loved, and she spends all her energy striving to be perfect and pleasing to get it, only to fail every time because it's illusory. It's supposed to be a jarring contrast between how Ava sees herself, and how the world describes her (i.e. as an extraordinary beauty).

Jack tried to help her, and there are mentions of that throughout both books. But he had a stable childhood with parents who loved and supported him, so he wasn't able to fully understand or connect. Ava needs the example of Killian—as someone whose accomplishments and character she admires despite not him having parents—to know that she can survive her childhood wounds, too, and become the person she chooses for herself.

Ava needs Killian to guide her and keep her steady, which he does from the very first pages of this novel. In turn, Killian experiences a sweet and unconditional love from Ava. She takes care of him—literally warming and feeding him, washing and healing him, hugging him, and crying for him.

Parts of this book were difficult for me to write. That's because the trauma of an abusive childhood with pervasive gaslighting is something I've experienced. I'm nothing like Ava personality-wise, but I understand Ava, and struggled with similar wounds well into my forties. My husband has helped me a lot, but it's not something that you can heal instantly. It's pervasive in how you related to the world and yourself. Ava will struggle for a while, even if she is finally in a place of healing.

At the inception of this novel, I thought I was writing an adventure tale. The mountain turned into a metaphor and I somehow ended up writing my sweetest story to date. For the readers who recognize any of the traumatic experiences of these two characters, whether firsthand or as an observer of another, this book is a tearjerker, even with Ava singing and skipping her way through the pages.

Acknowledgements

F oremost, I want to acknowledge my husband, who has gone through the process of three published novels with me at this point. My "mountain book" has always had a special place in his heart, and he's contributed ideas, criticism, jokes, and his enthusiastic campfire knowledge. He's getting a little sick of me reading my drafts out loud to him, but he endures it anyway, because he's utterly certain that someday he will see my novels at the airport bookshop.

Thank you to my editor, Sarah Pesce at Lopt and Cropt. We're now three in, and you haven't fired me, so I think that's a good sign. We're gelling and I agree with 99.99% of your edits and suggestions now. But there's always one that makes me question *everything*. This time, it was the "granny knot" comment.

Thank you to my friends, family, and author colleagues, who read my drafts, or who commiserated, or who gave me advice and encouragement. You all gave me the confidence to persevere in the face of my author anxiety, which I still suffer from like crazy.

Thank you to my readers. Some aspects of this book were hard to write, but I do it for you, as much as for myself.

Thank you also to my amazing friends, sister, husband, and mother-in-law for helping me as I went through a similar journey to Ava in recent months. I don't wish it on others, but I'm glad to have had the source material for this book at my fingertips.

About the Author

Amelia Elliot works as a trial lawyer, copywriter, and author. She publishes on topics of law, business, and politics. 'Amelia Elliot' is the pen name for the author's works in women's literary fiction and romance. She lives with her husband and their three big dogs on a sailboat.

Amelia is disabled with chronic illness. She reads romances because they help her stay optimistic through pain and exhaustion. As a novelist, she writes stories that are funny, tragic, sexy, and real. Her novels have mature themes that contemplate human experiences, purpose, and trauma. She hopes that her books help struggling readers find solace. They will always have a happily ever after.

Linktree: linktr.ee/ameliaelliot
Website: ameliaelliot.com

Facebook: authorameliaelliot
Instagram: authorameliaelliot
TikTok: authorameliaelliot
Twitter: authorameliae

Thunderstruck Book One: Both Sides of the Fence

That's the thing about soulmates—you have to be brave enough to stay with them.

Dee Bullard acted responsibly her whole life. She worked hard, went to college, and became a veterinarian. Now in her late thirties, she's stuck in the one place she always vowed to leave: her childhood home on a farm in Kansas. Then the boy next door breezes back into town, and past heartache catches up with them both.

After years in the Army's special forces, there are some things that Ricky Lee never talks about. One of those things is the real reason he hasn't come home in eight years: Dee. She's a troublemaker who's left him bearing the consequences one too many times. When Ricky's father suddenly dies, he's forced to return to care for his sick mother. Back in Dee's orbit, Ricky can't deny her. But he doesn't think he can survive her either.

With nothing but a low cattle fence and a lifetime of memories standing between them, Ricky and Dee face a reckoning that will either break them forever or unite them for good.

Both Sides of the Fence is an epic love story about the choices you make when you're young and how they impact you as you age. Spanning thirty-five years, it's also a story about the struggles of millennials growing up in rural poverty and how they grapple with disillusionment with their American dreams and two decades of war as they strive for their HEA.

Available Now

https://mybook.to/MAx6

Thunderstruck Book Two: Conduct Unbecoming a Judge

Rich or poor, sick or healthy, everyone needs love.

For Esme Fernandes, life ended at thirty. First, she lost her ability to have children, and then she lost her husband. Certain she's fated to die young like the rest of her family, Esme married her career instead. And it paid off: now thirty-eight, she's a federal judge, and determined to be worthy of her job.

Jack Bullard, twice *People's Sexiest Man Alive*, is at a crossroads. Two years after a bewildering and brutal divorce, he misses his kids and is unfulfilled by his Hollywood stardom. But he's made a career out of being irreplaceable, and too many people depend on him now.

When Jack and Esme collide—literally—sparks fly. But they also attract attention from the moment they meet, and not the good kind. Between scandalous pictures and Esme's growing political conflict with a senator, things take a dangerous turn.

Just as Jack can see the future forming, the increasing scrutiny awakens Esme's demons—and Jack has to decide whether fighting for her is selfish, or what they both need.

Conduct Unbecoming a Judge is a steamy contemporary romance with a strong female lead struggling with chronic illness, and a protective, cinnamon roll hero.

Available Now
https://mybook.to/CUAJ